About the

Sharon Kendrick started stor[...] and has never stopped. She likes to write fast-paced, feel-good romances with heroes who are so sexy they'll make your toes curl! She lives in the beautiful city of Winchester – where she can see the cathedral from her window (when standing on tip-toe!). She has two children, Celia and Patrick, and her passions include music, books, cooking, and eating – and drifting into daydreams while working out new plots.

Kate Hewitt has worked a variety of different jobs, from drama teacher to editorial assistant to youth worker, but writing romance is the best one yet. She also writes women's fiction, and all her stories celebrate the healing and redemptive power of love. Kate lives in a tiny village in the English Cotswolds with her husband, five children, and an overly affectionate Golden Retriever.

Carol Marinelli recently filled in a form asking for her job title. Thrilled to be able to put down her answer, she put writer. Then it asked what Carol did for relaxation and she put down the truth – writing. The third question asked for her hobbies. Well, not wanting to look obsessed, she crossed the fingers on her hand and answered swimming but, given that the chlorine in the pool does terrible things to her highlights – I'm sure you can guess the real answer.

The Italian's Christmas Passion

SHARON KENDRICK

KATE HEWITT

CAROL MARINELLI

MILLS & BOON

First Published in Great Britain 2023
By Mills & Boon, an imprint of HarperCollins*Publishers* Ltd,
1 London Bridge Street, London, SE1 9GF

www.harpercollins.co.uk

HarperCollins*Publishers*
Macken House, 39/40 Mayor Street Upper,
Dublin 1, D01 C9W8, Ireland

The Italian's Christmas Passion © 2023 Harlequin Enterprises ULC.

The Italian's Christmas Housekeeper © 2018 Sharon Kendrick
The Italian's Unexpected Baby © 2019 Kate Hewitt
Unwrapping Her Italian Doc © 2014 Carol Marinelli

ISBN: 978-0-263-32111-1

This book is produced from independently certified FSC™ paper
to ensure responsible forest management.

For more information visit: www.harpercollins.co.uk/green

Printed and Bound in the UK using 100% Renewable Electricity
at CPI Group (UK) Ltd, Croydon, CR0 4YY

THE ITALIAN'S
CHRISTMAS
HOUSEKEEPER

SHARON KENDRICK

To Maura Sabatino, who is funny and beautiful and whose help for this book was invaluable.

Mille grazie for bringing Naples alive with your words – and for helping me to create a Neapolitan Christmas!

CHAPTER ONE

SALVIO DE GENNARO stared at the lights as he rounded the headland. Flickering lights from the tall candles which gleamed in the window of the big old house. They made him think of Christmas and he didn't want to think about it—not with still six weeks left to go. Yet here in England the shops were already full with trees and tinsel and the kind of gifts surely no sane person would want for themselves.

His mouth hardened as the dark waters of the Atlantic crashed dangerously on the rocks beneath him.

Christmas. The *least* wonderful time of the year in his opinion. No contest.

He slowed his pace to a steady jog as dusk fell around him like a misty grey curtain. The rain was heavier now and large drops of water had started to lash against his body but he was oblivious to them, even though his bare legs were spattered with mud and his muscles were hot with the strain of exertion. He ran because he had to. Because he'd been taught to. Tough, physical exercise woven into the fabric of his day, no matter where in the world he was. A discipline which was as much a part of him as breathing and which made him hard and strong. He barely noticed that his wet singlet was now clinging to his torso or that his shorts were plastered to his rocky thighs.

He thought about the evening ahead and, not for the first time, wondered why he had bothered coming. He was here because he wanted to buy a prime piece of land from his aristocratic host and was convinced the deal could be concluded more quickly in an informal setting. The man he was dealing with was notoriously difficult to pin down—a fact which Salvio's assistant had remarked on, when she'd enquired whether she should accept the surprise invitation for dinner and an overnight stay.

Salvio gave a grim smile. Perhaps he should have been grateful to have been granted access to Lord Avery's magnificent Cornish house, which stood overlooking the fierce midwinter lash of the ocean. But gratitude was a quality which didn't come easily to him, despite his huge wealth and all the luxury it afforded him. He wasn't particularly looking forward to dinner tonight. Not with a hostess who'd been eying him up from the moment he'd arrived—her eyes lit with a predatory hunger which was by no means unusual, although it was an attitude he inevitably found tedious. Married women intent on seduction could be curiously unattractive, he thought disdainfully.

Inhaling a lungful of sea air, he grew closer to the house, reminding himself to instruct his assistant to add a couple of names to the guest list for his annual Christmas party in the Cotswolds, the count-down to which had already begun. He sighed. His yearly holiday celebration—which always took place in his honeystone manor house—was one of the most lusted-after invitations on the social calendar, though he would have happily avoided it, given the opportunity. But he owed plenty of people hospitality and you couldn't avoid Christmas, no matter how much the idea appealed.

He'd learnt to tolerate the festival and conceal his aversion behind a lavish display of generosity. He bought expensive gifts for his family and staff and injected yet more cash into the charitable arm of his vast property empire. He took a trip to his native Naples to visit his family, because that was what every good Neapolitan boy did, no matter how old or successful he was. He went back to the city which he avoided as much as possible because it was the home of his shattered dreams—and who liked to be reminded of those? For him, home would always be the place where he had been broken—and the man who had emerged from the debris of that time had been a different man. A man whose heart had been wiped clean of emotion. A man who was thankfully no longer at the mercy of his feelings.

He increased his pace to a last-minute sprint as he thought about Naples and the inevitable litany of questions about why he hadn't brought home a nice girl to marry, nor produced a clutch of bonny, black-haired babies for his mother to make a fuss of. He would be forced to meet the wistful question in her eyes and bite back the disclosure that he never intended to marry. *Never.* Why disillusion her?

He slowed his pace as he reached the huge house,

glad he had declined his hostess's invitation to accompany her and her husband to the local village that afternoon, where a performance of Cinderella was taking place. Salvio's lips curved into a cynical smile. Amateur dramatics in the company of a married woman with the hots for him? Not in this lifetime. Instead, he intending making the most of the unexpected respite by trying to relax. He would grab a glass of water and go to his room. Listen to the soothing soundtrack of the ocean lashing hard against the rocks and maybe read a book. More likely still, he would chase up that elusive site in New Mexico which he was itching to develop.

But first he needed to dry off.

Sinking her teeth into a large and very moist slice of chocolate cake, Molly gave a small moan of pleasure as she got her first hit from the sugary treat. She was starving. Absolutely starving. She hadn't eaten a thing since that bowl of porridge she'd grabbed on the run first thing. Unfortunately the porridge had been lumpy and disappointing, mainly because the unpredictable oven had started playing up halfway through making it. Not for the first time, she wondered why her bosses couldn't just have the kind of oven you simply switched on, instead of a great beast of a thing which lurked in the corner like a brooding animal and was always going wrong. She'd been working like crazy all morning, cleaning the house with even more vigour than usual because Lady Avery had been in such a state about their overnight guest.

'He's Italian,' her employer had bit out. 'And you know how fussy they are about cleanliness.'

Molly didn't know, actually. But more worrying still was Lady Avery's inference that she wasn't working hard enough. Which was why Molly dusted the chandeliers with extra care and fastidiously vacuumed behind the heavy pieces of antique furniture. At one point she even got down on her hands and knees to scrub the back door porch—even if she did manage to make her hands red raw in the process. She'd put a big copper vase of scented eucalyptus and dark roses in the guest bedroom and had been baking biscuits and cakes all morning, so that the house smelt all homely and fragrant.

The Averys rarely used their Cornish house—which was one of the reasons why Molly considered being their resident housekeeper the perfect job. It meant she could live on a limited budget and use the lion's share of her wages to pay off her brother's debt and the frightening amount of interest it seemed to accrue. It was the reason she endured the isolated location and demanding attitude of her employer, instead of spreading her wings and finding somewhere more lively.

But the winter had made her isolation all the more noticeable and it was funny how the approach of Christmas always reminded you of the things you didn't have. This year she was really missing her brother and trying not to worry about what he was doing in Australia. But deep down she knew she had to let go. She *had* to. For both their sakes. Robbie was probably having the time of his life on that great big sunny continent—and maybe she should count her blessings.

She took another bite of chocolate cake and did exactly that, reminding herself that most people would revel in the fact that when the Averys *were* around, they entertained all kinds of amazing people. Guests Molly actually got to meet—even if it was only in the context of turning down their beds at night or offering them a home-made scone. Politicians who worked with Lord Avery in the Palace of Westminster, and famous actors who spouted Shakespearean sonnets from the stages of London's theatres. There were business people, too—and sometimes even members of the royal family, whose bodyguards lurked around the kitchen and kept asking for cups of tea.

But Molly had never heard Lady Avery make such a fuss about anyone as she'd done about the impending arrival of Salvio De Gennaro, who was apparently some hotshot property developer who lived mostly in London. Earlier that day she had been summoned into her boss's office, where the walls were decked with misty photos of Lady Avery wearing pearls and a dreamy expression, in those far-off days before she'd decided to have a load of extensive work done on her face. A bad idea, in Molly's opinion—though of course she would never have said so. Lady Avery's plump lips had been coated in a startling shade of pink and her expression had been unnaturally smooth as she'd gazed at Molly. Only the hectic flicker in her pale eyes had hinted how excited she was by the impending visit of the Italian tycoon.

'Everything is prepared for our guest's arrival?' The words were clipped out like tiny beads of crystal.

'Yes, Lady Avery.'

'Make sure that Signor De Gennaro's bed linen is scented with lavender, will you?' continued her boss. 'And be sure to use the monogrammed sheets.'

'Yes, Lady Avery.'

'In fact...' A thoughtful pause had followed. 'Perhaps you'd better go into town and buy a new duvet.'

'What, *now*, Your Ladyship?'

'Yes. Right now.' A varnished scarlet fingernail began tracing a circle on the sheet of blotting paper on the desk and an odd, trembling note had crept into her employer's aristocratic voice. 'We don't want Signor De Gennaro complaining about the cold, do we?'

'We certainly don't, Lady Avery.'

The last-minute purchase of the new duvet had been the reason why Molly hadn't been on hand to greet the Italian tycoon when he'd arrived. And when she'd returned from her shopping expedition—gasping under the bulky dimensions of a high-tog goose-down duvet— there had been no sign of him. Only his open suitcase and a few clothes strewn around his room indicated he was somewhere in the vicinity, although he was nowhere to be seen in the house. Which at least meant Molly had been able to make up his bed in peace— though her heart had started racing when she'd spotted the faded denims slung carelessly over a stool. And when she'd picked up the dark sweater which lay crumpled beside it, she had been startled by the softness of the cashmere as she'd automatically started to fold it. Briefly, her fingertips had caressed the fine wool before she had taken herself downstairs for tea and some restorative cake and she was just on her third mouthful when the kitchen door opened then slammed shut with a rush of icy air and Molly looked up to see a man framed in the doorway who could only be the Italian billionaire.

Her heart crashed against her ribcage.

The most perfect man she could have imagined.

Her mouth opened slightly but she clamped it shut and the chocolate fudge cake she'd been eating suddenly tasted like glue against the roof of her mouth.

Mud-spattered and windswept, he was standing perfectly still—his singlet and shorts surely the craziest choice of clothes he could have selected for the bitter winter day, although a fleecy top was knotted around his narrow hips. His olive skin was silky-smooth and his body was… Molly tried not to shake her head in disbelief but it took some doing, because his body was sensational—and she was certainly not the kind of woman who spent her time analysing men's bodies. In fact, her interest had never really been sparked by anyone.

Until now.

She swallowed, the cake she was holding suddenly forgotten. It took a lot for Molly to disregard the sugar craving which had always been the bane of her life, but she forgot it now. Because she'd never seen a man like this. Not someone with a rocky torso against which his wet top clung to every sinew, as if it had been painted on with a fine-tipped brush. Nor such narrow hips and sculpted thighs whose glorious flesh was exposed by the shorts he seemed to wear so comfortably. Her eyes moved up to his face. To eyes as black as one of those moonless nights when you couldn't ever imagine seeing daylight again. And his lips. Molly swallowed again.

Oh, those lips. Sensual and full, they were hard and un-smiling as they looked at her with something it took a moment for her to recognise. Was it…*disdain*? Her heart pounded uncomfortably. Yes, of course it was. Men with whiplike bodies which didn't carry an ounce of extra weight would be unlikely to approve of an overabundant female who was bulging out of her ugly uniform and stuffing a great big fix of carbohydrate into her mouth.

Flushing to the roots of her hair, she put down the half-eaten cake and rose to her feet, wondering why the ground beneath them suddenly felt as if it were shifting, the way she'd always imagined standing on quicksand might feel. 'I'm…' She blinked at him before trying again. 'I'm so sorry. I wasn't expecting anyone…'

His voice was sardonic as his gaze met hers for one heart-stopping moment, before dropping briefly to the crumb-laden plate. 'Clearly not.'

'You must be…' *A dark angel who has suddenly fallen into my kitchen? The most gorgeous man I've ever seen?* Her chest felt tight. 'You must be Signor De Gennaro?'

'Indeed I am. Forgive me.' Jet eyebrows were raised as he unknotted the warm top from his hips and pulled it over his head before shaking out his damp, dark curls. 'I seem to have disturbed your snack.'

Her *snack*? Although his English was faultless, his richly accented voice was nearly as distracting as his body and Molly opened her mouth to say it was actu-ally a late lunch because she'd been rushing around all morning preparing for *his* arrival, but something stopped her. As if someone like Salvio De Gennaro would be interested in her defence! As if he would believe her making out she was a stranger to cake when her curvy body told an entirely different story. Smoothing her uniform down over her generous hips, she tried to adopt an expression of professional interest, rather than the shame of being caught out doing something she shouldn't. And he was still staring at her. Making her aware of every pulsing atom of her body in a way which was making her feel extremely self-conscious... but strangely enough, in a *good* way.

'Can I get you anything, Signor De Gennaro?' she questioned politely. 'I'm afraid Lord and Lady Avery have gone to the village pantomime and won't be back until later.'

'I know,' he said coolly. 'Perhaps some water. And a coffee, if you have one.'

'Of course. How do you take your coffee?'

He flickered her a smile. 'Black, short, no sugar. *Grazie.*'

Of course not, thought Molly. No sugar for someone like him. He looked as if he'd never been near anything sweet in his life. She wished he'd go. Before he noticed that her brow had grown clammy, or that her nipples had started to push distractingly against the unflattering navy-blue uniform Lady Avery insisted she wore. 'I'll do that right away,' she said briskly. 'And bring them up to your room.'

'No need for that. I'll wait here,' he said.

She wanted to tell him he was making her feel awkward by standing there, like some kind of brooding, dark statue—just *staring* at her. As if he had read her thoughts, he strolled over towards the window and she became aware of an almost imperceptible limp in his right leg. Had he injured himself when out running and should she ask him whether he needed a bandage or something? Perhaps not. Someone with his confidence would be bound to ask for one.

She could feel a stray strand of hair tickling the back of her neck and wished she'd had time to fix it. Or had been sitting reading some novel which might have made her look interesting, instead of scoffing cake and emphasising the fact that she was heavy and ungainly.

'I'll try to be as quick as I can,' she said, reaching up into one of the cupboards for a clean glass.

'I'm in no hurry,' he said lazily.

Because that much was true. Salvio had decided that he was enjoying himself though he wasn't quite sure why. Maybe it was the novelty factor of being with the kind of woman he didn't come across very often—at least, not any more. Not since he'd left behind the back-streets of Naples, along with those women whose curves defined fecundity and into whose generous flesh a man could sink after a long, hard day. Women like this one, who blushed alluringly if they caught you looking at them.

He had waited for a moment to see if she would recognise him. If she knew who he was—or, rather, who he *had* been. But no. He was familiar with recognition in all its forms—from greedy delight right through to feigned ignorance—but there had been no trace of any of those on her face. And why should there be? She was much younger than him and from a different country.

How would she have known that in his native Italy he had once been famous?

He watched her busying herself, her curvy silhouette reminding him of the bottles of Verdicchio which used to line the shelves of the city bar he'd swept as a boy, before the talent scouts had discovered him and ended his childhood. She turned to switch on the coffee maker and a sudden dryness turned his throat to dust because...her breasts. He swallowed. *Madonna mia*—what breasts! He was glad when she turned away to open the fridge door because his erection was pressing uncomfortably against his shorts, though, when she did, he then became mesmerised by her shapely bottom. He was just fantasising about what her shiny brown hair would look like loose when she turned around and surveyed him with eyes as grey as the Santissima Annunziata Maggiore—that beautiful church in Naples, which had once been an orphanage.

Their gazes clashed and mingled and something unspoken fizzled in the air as Salvio felt a leap of something he couldn't define. The hardness in his groin was familiar but the sudden clench of his heart was not. Was it lust? His mouth twisted. Of course it was lust—for what else could it be? It just happened to be more powerful than usual because it had taken him by surprise.

Yet there was no answering hunger in her quiet, grey gaze—something which perplexed him, for when *didn't* a woman look at him with desire in her eyes? She was wary, he found himself thinking, with a flicker of amusement. Almost as if she were silently reproaching him for his insolent appraisal—and maybe that sentiment was richly deserved. What *was* he doing survey-ing her curvy body, like a boy from a single-sex school who was meeting a beautiful woman for the first time?

'You're the cook?' he questioned, trying to redeem himself with a safe, if rather banal question.

She nodded. 'Sort of. Officially, I'm the housekeeper but I do a bit of everything. Answer the door to guests and make sure their rooms are serviced, that sort of thing.' She pushed the coffee towards him. 'Will there be anything else, Signor De Gennaro?'

He smiled. 'Salvio. And you are?'

She looked taken aback, as if people didn't ask her name very often. 'It's Molly,' she answered shyly, in a voice so soft it felt like silk lingerie brushing against his skin. 'Molly Miller.'

Molly Miller. He found himself wanting to repeat it, but the conversation—such as it was—was terminated by the sudden sweep of car headlights arcing powerfully across the room. As he heard the sound of a large car swishing over gravel, Salvio saw the way she flinched and automatically tugged at her drab dress so that it hung more uniformly over her wide hips.

'That's the Averys.'

'I thought it must be.'

'You'd better… You'd better go,' she said, unable to keep the waver of urgency from her voice. 'I'm sup-posed to be preparing dinner and Lady Avery won't like finding a guest in the kitchen.'

Salvio was tempted to tell her that he didn't give a damn what Lady Avery would or wouldn't like but he could see the fear which had darkened her soft grey eyes. With a flicker of irritation he picked up his espresso and water and headed for the door. *'Grazie mille,'* he said, leaving the warm and steamy kitchen and walking rapidly towards the staircase, reluctant to be around when the Averys burst into the hallway.

But once back in his own room, he was irritated to discover that the low burn of desire was refusing to leave him. So that instead of the hot shower he'd promised himself, Salvio found himself standing beneath jets of punishingly cold water as he tried to push the curves of the sweet little housekeeper from the forefront of his mind and to quell the exquisite hardness which throbbed at his groin.

CHAPTER TWO

'MOLLY, THESE POTATOES are frightful. We can't possibly ask Signor De Gennaro to eat them. Have they even *seen* an oven? They're like rocks!'

Molly could feel herself flushing to the roots of her hair as she met Lady Avery's accusing stare. Were they? She blinked. Surely she'd blasted them for the required time, carefully basting them with goose fat to make them all golden and crispy? But no. Now she stopped to look at them properly—they were definitely on the anaemic side.

She could feel her cheeks growing even pinker as she reached towards the table to pick up the dish. 'I'm so sorry, Lady Avery. I'll pop them back in the—'

'Don't bother!' snapped her employer. 'It will be midnight before they're fit to eat and I don't intend going to bed on a full stomach. And I'm sure Salvio won't want to either.'

Was it Molly's imagination, or did Lady Avery shoot the Italian a complicit smile from the other side of the table? The way she said his name sounded unmistakably predatory and the look she was giving him was enough to make Molly's stomach turn. Surely the aristocrat wasn't hinting that she intended ending up in bed with him, not with her husband sitting only a few feet away?

Yet it had struck her as odd when Sarah Avery had come down for dinner wearing the tightest and lowest-cut dress imaginable, so that the priceless blaze of the Avery diamonds dazzled like stars against her aging skin. She'd been flirting outrageously with the Italian businessman ever since Molly had served pre-dinner drinks and showed no sign of stopping. And meanwhile, her husband—two decades older and already a quarter of the way through his second bottle of burgundy—seemed oblivious to the undercurrents which had been swirling around the dinner table ever since they'd sat down.

The meal had been a disaster from the moment she'd put the starters on the table and Molly couldn't understand why. She was a good cook. She knew that. Hadn't she spent years cooking for her mother and little brother, trying to produce tasty food on a shoestring budget? And hadn't part of her job interview for Lady Avery consisted of producing a full afternoon tea—including a rich and rather heavy fruit cake—within the space of just two hours…a feat she had managed with ease? A simple meal for just three people should have been a breeze, but Molly hadn't factored in Salvio De Gennaro, or the effect his brooding presence would have on her employer. Or, if she was being honest, on her.

After he'd swept out of the kitchen earlier that afternoon, it had taken ages for her heart to stop thumping and to be able to concentrate on what she was supposed to be doing. She'd felt all giddy and stupidly... *excited*. She remembered the way he had looked into her eyes with that dark and piercing gaze and wondered if she'd imagined the pulsing crackle of electricity between them before telling herself that, yes, of course she had. Unless she really thought a man who could have his pick of any woman on the planet would have the slightest interest in a naïve country girl who was carrying far too much weight around her hips.

In her dreams!

But there was no doubt that Salvio's unexpected trip to the kitchen had rocked Molly's equilibrium and after he'd gone, all the light had seemed to disappear from the room. She'd sat down at the table feeling flat, which was unusual for her because she'd always tried to be an optimist, no matter what life threw at her. She was what was known as a glass-half-full type of person rather than one who regarded the glass as half empty. So why had she spent the rest of the afternoon mooching around the kitchen in a way which was completely out of character?

'Molly? Are you listening to a word I'm saying?'

Molly stiffened as she saw the fury in Lady Avery's eyes—but not before she'd noticed Salvio De Gennaro's face darken with an expression she couldn't work out. Was he wondering why on earth the wife of a famous peer bothered employing such a hapless housekeeper?

'I'm so sorry,' said Molly quickly. 'I was a bit distracted.'

'You seem to have been distracted all afternoon!' snapped Lady Avery. 'The meat is overcooked and the hors d'oeuvres were fridge-cold!'

'Come on, Sarah. It's no big deal,' said Salvio softly. 'Give the girl a break.'

Molly's head jerked up and as she met the understanding gleam of Salvio De Gennaro's ebony eyes, she felt something warm and comforting wash over her. It was like sitting beside a fire when snow was falling outside. Like being wrapped in a soft, cashmere blanket. She saw Lady Avery appear momentarily disconcerted and she wondered if Salvio De Gennaro's silky intervention had made her decide that giving her housekeeper a public dressing-down wouldn't reflect very well on *her*. Was that why she flashed her a rather terrifying smile?

'Of course. You're quite right, Salvio. It's no big deal. After all, it's not as if we're short of food, is it? Molly always makes sure we're very well fed, but—as you can tell—she's very fond of her food!' She gave a bright, high laugh and nodded her head towards the snoring form of her husband, who had now worked his way through the entire bottle of wine and whose head was slumped on his chest as he snored softly. 'Molly, I'm going to wake Lord Avery and guide him to bed and then Signor De Gennaro and I will go and sit by the fire in the library. Perhaps you'd like to bring us something on a tray to take the place of dinner. Nothing too fussy. Finger food will do.' She flashed another toothy smile. 'And bring us another bottle of the Château Lafite, will you?'

'Yes, Lady Avery.'

Salvio's knuckles tightened as he watched Molly scuttle from the room, though he made no further comment as his hostess moved round the table to rouse her sleeping husband and then rather impatiently ushered him from the room. But he couldn't shake off the feeling of injustice he had experienced when he'd seen how the aristocrat treated the blushing housekeeper. Or the powerful feeling of identification which had gripped him as he'd witnessed it. Was it because he'd known exactly how she would be feeling? His mouth hardened. Because he'd been where she had been. He knew what it was like to be at the bottom of the food chain. To have people treat you as if you were a machine, rather than a person.

He splayed his fingers over the rigid tautness of his thighs. He would wait until his hostess returned. Force himself to have a quick drink since she'd asked for one of the world's most expensive wines to be opened, then retire to his room. He glanced at his watch. It was too late to go back to London tonight but he would leave at first light, before the house was awake. All in all it had been a wasted journey, with Lord Avery too inebriated to talk business before dinner. He hadn't even been able to work because the damned Internet kept going down and because his thoughts kept straying to the forbidden... And the forbidden had proved shockingly difficult to erase from his mind. He sighed. How crazy was it that the wholesome housekeeper had inexplicably set his senses on fire, so that he could think of little but her?

He'd walked into the orangery before dinner to see her standing with a tray of champagne in her hands. She had changed into a simple black dress which hugged her body and emphasised every voluptuous curve. With her shiny brown hair caught back at the nape of her neck, his attention had been caught by those grey eyes, half concealed by lashes like dark feathers, which were modestly lowered as she offered him a drink. Even that was a turn-on. Or maybe especially that. He wasn't used to modesty. To women reluctant to meet his gaze, whose cheeks turned the colour of summer roses. He'd found himself wanting to stand there studying her and it had taken a monumental effort to tear his eyes away. To try to make conversation with a host who seemed to be having a love affair with the bottle, and his disenchanted wife who was almost spilling out of a dress much too young for a woman her age.

'Salvio!' Sarah Avery was back, a look of determination on her face as she picked her way across the Persian rug on her spiky black heels. 'Sorry about that. I'm afraid that sometimes Philip simply can't hold his drink. Some men can't, you know—with predictable effects, I'm afraid.' She flashed him a megawatt smile. 'Let's go to the library for a drink, shall we?'

There had been many reasons why Salvio had left Naples to make his life in England and he had absorbed the attitudes of his adopted country with the tenacity he applied to every new challenge which came his way. These days he considered himself urbane and sophisticated—but in reality the traditional values of his Neapolitan upbringing were never far from the surface. And in his world, a woman never criticised her husband to another person. Particularly a stranger.

'Just one drink,' he said, disapproval making his words harsher than he intended. 'I have a busy schedule tomorrow and I'll be leaving first thing.'

'But you've only just arrived!'

'And I have back-to-back meetings in London, from midday onwards,' he countered smoothly.

'Oh! Can't you cancel them?' she wheedled. 'I mean, I've heard that you're a complete workaholic, but surely even powerhouses like you are allowed to slow down a little. And this is a beautiful part of the world. You haven't really seen any of it.'

With an effort, Salvio forced a smile because he found her attitude intensely intrusive, as well as irritating. 'I like to honour my commitments,' he observed coolly as he followed her into the firelit library, where Molly was putting cheese and wine on a table, the stiff set of her shoulders showing her tension. He wasn't surprised. Imagine being stuck out here, working for someone as rude and demanding as Sarah Avery. He sank into one of the armchairs, and watched as his hostess went to stand by the mantelpiece in a pose he suspected was intended to make him appreciate her carefully preserved body. She ran one slow finger over the gleaming curve of an ancient-looking vase, and smiled.

'Are you looking forward to Christmas, Salvio?' she questioned.

He was immediately wary—recoiling from the thought that some unwanted invitation might soon be heading his way. 'I am away for most of it—in Naples,' he said, accepting a glass of wine from Molly—ridiculously pleased to capture her blushing gaze before she quickly turned away. 'I'm always glad to see my family but, to be honest, I'm equally glad when the holiday is over. The world shuts down and business suffers as a result.'

'Oh, you men!' Sarah Avery slunk back across the room to perch on a nearby chair, her bony knees clamped tightly together. 'You're all the same!'

Salvio managed not to wince, trying to steer the conversation onto a more neutral footing as he sipped his wine, though all he could think about was Molly hovering nervously in the background, the black dress clinging to her curvaceous figure and a stray strand of glossy brown hair dangling alluringly against her pink cheek. He cleared his throat. 'How are you and your husband planning to spend Christmas?' he questioned politely.

This was obviously the opportunity Sarah Avery had been waiting for and she let him have the answer in full, telling him how much Philip's adult children hated her and blamed her for ending their parents' marriage. 'I mean, I certainly didn't set out to get him, but I was his secretary and these things happen.' She gave a helpless shrug. 'Philip told me he couldn't help falling in love with me. That no power on earth could have stopped it. How was I supposed to know his wife was pregnant at the time?' She sipped a mouthful of wine, leaving a thin red stain above the line of her lip gloss. 'I mean, I really don't care if his wretched kids won't see me—it's Philip I'm concerned about—and I really think they need to be mindful of their inheritance. He'll cut them off if they're not careful!'

Salvio forced himself to endure several minutes more of her malicious chatter, his old-fashioned sensibilities outraged by her total lack of shame. But eventually he could stand no more and rose to his feet and, despite all her cajoling, she finally seemed to get the message that he was going to bed. Alone. Like a child, she pouted, but he paid her sulky expression no heed. He felt like someone who'd just been released from the cage of a prowling she-cat by the time he escaped to the quietness of the guest corridor and closed the door of his room behind him.

A sigh of relief left his lips as he looked around. A fire had been lit and red and golden lights from the flames were dancing across the walls. He'd been in these grand houses before and often found them unbearably cold, but this high-ceilinged room was deliciously warm. Over by the window was a polished antique cabinet on which stood an array of glittering crystal decanters, filled with liquor which glinted in the moonlight. He studied the walls, which were studded with paintings, including some beautiful landscapes by well-known artists. Salvio's mouth twisted. It was ironic really. This house contained pictures which would have been given pride of place in a national gallery—yet a trip to the bathroom required a walk along an icy corridor, because the idea of en-suite was still an alien concept to some members of the aristocracy.

He yawned but didn't go straight to bed, preferring to half pack his small suitcase so he was ready to leave first thing. Outside he could see dark clouds scudding across the sky and partially obscuring the moon, turning the churning ocean silver and black. It was stark and it was beautiful but he was unable to appreciate it because he was restless and didn't know why.

Loosening his tie and undoing the top button of his shirt, Salvio braved the chilly corridor to the bathroom and was on his way back when he heard a sound from the floor above. A sound which at first he didn't recognise. He stilled as he listened and there it was again. His eyes narrowed as he realised what it was. A faint gasp for breath, followed by a snuffle.

Someone was crying?

He told himself it was none of his business. He was leaving first thing and it made sense to go straight to bed. But something tugged at his... He frowned. His conscience? Because he knew that the person crying must be the little housekeeper? He didn't question what made him start walking towards the sound and soon found himself mounting a narrow staircase at the far end of the corridor.

The sound grew louder. Definitely tears. His foot creaked on a step and an anxious voice called out.

'Who's there?'

'It's me. Salvio.'

He heard footsteps scurrying across the room and as the door was pulled open, there stood Molly. She was still wearing her black uniform although she had taken down her hair and removed her sturdy shoes. It spilled over her shoulders in a glorious tumble which fell almost to her waist and Salvio was reminded of a painting he'd once seen of a woman sitting in a boat, with fear written all over her features. He could see fear now, in soft grey eyes which were rimmed with red. And suddenly all the lust he'd felt from the moment he'd set eyes on her was replaced by a powerful sense of compassion.

'What's happened?' he demanded. 'Are you hurt?'

'Nothing's happened and, no, I'm not hurt.' Quickly, she blotted her cheeks with her fingertips. 'Did you want something?' she asked, a familiar note of duty creeping into her voice. 'I hope… I mean, is everything in your room to your satisfaction, Signor De Gennaro?'

'Everything in my room is fine and I thought I told you to call me Salvio,' he said impatiently. 'I want to know why you were crying.'

She shook her head. 'I wasn't crying.'

'Yes, you were. You know damned well you were.'

An unexpected streak of defiance made her tilt her chin upwards. 'Surely I'm allowed to cry in the privacy of my own room.'

'And surely I'm allowed to ask why, if it's keeping me awake.'

Her grey eyes widened. 'Was it?'

He allowed himself the flicker of a smile. 'Well, no—now you come to mention it. Not really. I hadn't actually gone to bed but it's not a sound anyone particularly wants to hear.'

'That's because nobody was supposed to. Look, I'm really sorry to have disturbed you, but I'm fine now. See.' This time she gritted her teeth into a parody of a smile. 'It won't happen again.'

But Salvio's interest was piqued and the fact that she was trying to get rid of him intrigued him. He glanced over her shoulder at her room, which was small. He hadn't seen a bedroom that small for a long time. A narrow, unfriendly bed and thin drapes at the window, but very little else. Suddenly he became aware of the icy temperature—an observation which was reinforced by the almost imperceptible shiver she gave, despite the thickness of her black dress. He thought about the fire in his own bedroom with the blazing applewood logs which she must have lit herself.

'You're cold,' he observed.

'Only a bit. I'm used to it. You know what these old houses are like. The heating is terrible up here.'

'You don't say?' He narrowed his eyes speculatively. 'Look, why don't you come and sit by my fire for a while? Have a nightcap, perhaps.'

She narrowed her eyes. 'A nightcap?'

He slanted her a mocking smile. 'You know. The drink traditionally supposed to warm people up.'

He saw her hesitate before shaking her head.

'Look, it's very kind of you to offer, but I can't possibly accept.'

'Why not?'

'Because…' She shrugged. 'You know why not.'

'Not unless you tell me, I don't.'

'Because Lady Avery would hit the roof if she caught me socialising with one of the guests.'

'And how's she going to find out?' he questioned with soft complicity. 'I won't tell if you won't. Come on, Molly. You're shivering. What harm will it do?'

Molly hesitated because she *was* tempted—more tempted than she should have been. Maybe it was because she was feeling so cold—both inside and out. A coldness she'd been unable to shift after the telling off she'd just been given by Lady Avery, who had arrived in the kitchen in an evil temper, shaking with rage as she'd shouted at Molly. She'd told her she was clumsy and incompetent. That she'd never been so ashamed in her life and no wonder Signor De Gennaro had cut short the evening so unexpectedly.

Yet now that same man was standing in the doorway of her humble room, asking her to have a drink with him. He had removed his tie and undone the top button of his shirt, giving him a curiously relaxed and accessible air. It was easy to see why Lady Avery had made a fool of herself over him during dinner. Who wouldn't fall for his olive-dark skin and gleaming ebony eyes?

Yet despite his sexy appearance, he had looked at her understandingly when she'd messed up during dinner. He'd come to her rescue—and there was that same sense of concern on his face now. He had an unexpected streak of kindness, she thought, and kindness was hard to resist. Especially when you weren't expecting it. An icy blast of wind rushed in through the gap in the window frame and once again Molly shivered. The days ahead didn't exactly fill her with joy and her worries about Robbie were never far from the surface. Couldn't she loosen up for once in her life? Break out of the lonely mould she'd created for herself by having a drink with the Italian tycoon?

She gave a tentative shrug. 'Okay, then. I will. Just

a quick one, mind. And thank you,' she added, as she slipped her feet back into the sensible brogues she'd just kicked off. 'Thank you very much.'

He gave a brief nod, as if her agreement was something he'd expected all along, and Molly tried to tell herself that this meant nothing special—at least, not to him. But as he turned his back and began to walk she realised her heart was racing and Molly was filled with an unfamiliar kind of excitement as she followed Salvio De Gennaro along the narrow corridor towards his grand bedroom on the floor below.

CHAPTER THREE

'HERE.'

'Thanks.' Molly took the brandy Salvio was offering her, wondering if she'd been crazy to accept his invitation to have a drink with him, because now she was in his room she felt hopelessly embarrassed and out of place. She noticed his half-packed open suitcase lying on the far side of the room and, for some stupid reason, her heart sank. He obviously couldn't wait to get away from here. Awkwardly, she shifted from one foot to the other.

'Why don't you sit down over there, beside the fire?' he suggested.

Lowering herself into the chair he'd indicated, Molly thought how weird it was to find herself in the role of visitor to a room she had cleaned so many times. Just this morning she'd been in here, fluffing up the new duvet and making sure the monogrammed pillowcases were all neatly facing in the right direction. Over there were the neat stack of freshly ironed newspapers Lady Avery had insisted on, and the jug of water with the little lace cover on top. Yet it was funny how quickly you could get used to the dramatic change from servant to guest. The soft leather of the armchair felt deliciously soft as it sank beneath her weight and the warmth of the fire licked her skin. She took a tentative sip from her glass, recoiling a little as the powerful fumes wafted upwards.

'Not much of a drinker?' observed Salvio wryly, as he poured his own drink.

'Not really.' But even that minuscule amount of liquor had started to dissolve the tight knot of tension in the pit of her stomach, sending a warm glow flooding through her body. Molly stared out of the windows where clouds were racing across the silvery face of the moon. Outside the temperature had plummeted but in here it felt cosy—in fact, she might even go so far as to say she was starting to feel relaxed. Yet here she was in a strange man's bedroom in her black uniform and heavy-duty shoes as if she had every right to be there. What on earth would Lady Avery say if she happened to walk in? Anxiety rippled through her as she glanced at Salvio, who was replacing the heavy stopper in the bottle. 'I really shouldn't be here,' she fretted.

'So you said,' he drawled, his tinge of boredom implying that he found repetition tedious. 'But you are here. And you still haven't told me why you were crying.'

'I...' She took another sip of brandy before putting the glass down on a nearby table. 'No reason really.'

'Now, why don't I believe you, Molly Miller?' he challenged softly. 'What happened? Did you get into more trouble about dinner?'

Her startled expression told Salvio his guess was correct. 'I deserved it,' she said flatly as she met his gaze. 'The meal was rubbish.'

Briefly he acknowledged her loyalty. She would have been perfectly justified in moaning about her employer but she hadn't. She was a curious creature, he thought, his gaze flickering over her dispassionately. Totally without artifice, she didn't seem to care that the way she was sitting wasn't the most flattering angle she could have chosen. Yet her abundant hair glowed like copper in the firelight and as she crossed one ankle over the other he was surprised by how unexpectedly erotic that simple movement seemed. But he hadn't brought her here to seduce her, he reminded himself sternly. Tonight he had cast himself in the role of the good Samaritan, that was all. 'And that's the only reason for your tears?'

Molly gave an awkward wriggle of her shoulders. 'Maybe I was feeling sorry for myself,' she admitted, shifting beneath his probing gaze. Because no way was she going to tell him the real reason. He wouldn't be interested in her wayward brother or his habit of accumulating debt, but more than that—she was afraid of saying the words out loud. As if saying them would make them even more real. She didn't want to wonder why Robbie had rung up just an hour ago, asking her if she had any spare cash for a 'temporary' loan, despite his promises to find himself some sort of job. Why hadn't he got any money of his own? Why was he asking her for more, after all his tearful promises that from now on he was going to live his life independently and free of debt? She swallowed. She couldn't bear to think that he'd got himself into that terrible spiral yet again—of playing poker and losing. Of owing money to hard-faced men who wouldn't think twice about scarring his pretty young face...

'Call it a touch of self-pity,' she said, meeting the black fire in his eyes and realising he was still waiting for an answer. 'Not something I imagine you have much experience of.'

Salvio gave a mirthless smile. How touching her faith in him! Did she think that because he was wealthy and successful, he had never known pain or despair, when he had been on intimate terms with both those things? His mouth hardened. When his life had imploded and he'd lost everything, he remembered the darkness which had descended on him, sending him hurtling into a deep and never-ending hole. And even though he'd dragged himself out of the quagmire and forced himself to start over—you never forgot an experience like that. It marked you. Changed you. Turned you into someone different. A stranger to yourself as well as to those around you. It was why he had left Naples—because he couldn't bear to be reminded of his own failure. 'Why do you stay here?' he questioned quietly.

'It's a very well-paid job.'

'Even though you get spoken to like that?'

She shook her head, her long hair swaying like a glossy curtain. 'It's not usually as bad as it was tonight.'

'Your loyalty is touching, *signorina*.'

'I'm paid to be loyal,' she said doggedly.

'I'm sure you are. But even taking all that into account, this place is very *isolato*...isolated.' He gave a flicker of a smile, as if begging her to forgive his sudden lapse into his native tongue. 'I can't imagine many people your age living nearby.'

'Maybe that's one of the reasons I like it.'

He raised his eyebrows. 'You don't like to socialise?'

Molly hesitated. Should she tell him that she always felt out of place around people her own age? That she didn't really do the relaxed stuff, or the fun stuff, or the wild stuff. She'd spent too many years caring for her mother and then trying to keep her brother from going off the rails—and that kind of sensible role could become so much a part of you that it was difficult to relinquish it. And wouldn't that kind of admission bring reality crashing into the room? Wouldn't it puncture the slightly unreal atmosphere which had descended on her ever since she'd walked in here and settled down by the fireside, allowing herself to forget for a short while that she was Molly the housekeeper—so that for once she'd felt like a person in her own right?

'I can take people or leave them,' she said. 'Anyway, socialising is expensive and I'm saving up. I'm intending to put my brother through college and it isn't cheap. He's in Australia at the moment,' she explained, in answer to the fractional rise of his dark brows. 'Doing a kind of…gap year.'

He frowned. 'So you're here—working hard—while he has fun in the sun? That's a very admirable sacrifice for a sister to make.'

'Anyone would do it.'

'Not anyone, no. He's lucky to have you.'

Molly picked up her glass again and took another sip of brandy. Would Salvio De Gennaro be shocked if he knew the truth? That Robbie hadn't actually got a place at college yet, because he was still 'thinking about it', in spite of all her entreaties to get himself a proper education and not end up like her. She licked her lips, which tasted of brandy. She didn't want to think about Robbie. Surely she could have a night off for once? A night when she could feel young and carefree and revel in the fact that she was alone with a gorgeous man like Salvio—even if he had only invited her here because he felt sorry for her.

Putting her glass down, she stared at him and her heart gave a sudden lurch of yearning. He hadn't moved from his spot by the window and his powerful body was starkly outlined by the moonlight.

'What about you?' she questioned suddenly. 'What brought you here?'

He shrugged. 'I was supposed to be discussing a deal with Philip Avery.' He twisted his lips into a wry smile. 'But that doesn't look like it's going to happen.'

'He'll be much more receptive in the morning,' said Molly diplomatically.

'It'll be too late by then,' he said. 'I'm leaving as soon as it's light.'

Molly was aware of a crushing sense of disappointment. She'd wanted... She stared very hard at her brandy glass as if the dark amber liquid would provide the answer. What had she wanted? To see him at breakfast—their eyes meeting in a moment of shared complicity as they remembered this illicit, night-time drink?

'Oh, that's a shame,' she said, sounding genuinely disappointed.

He smiled, as if her earnestness had amused him. 'You know, you're far too sweet to be hiding yourself away somewhere like this, Molly.'

Sweet. Molly knew it was a compliment yet for some reason it offended her. It made her sound like the cake he'd caught her eating. Because sweet wasn't sexy, was it? Just as *she* wasn't sexy. 'Am I?' she questioned tonelessly.

He nodded, walking over to the desk and writing something on the back of a business card before crossing the room and handing it to her. 'Here. Take this. It will get you straight through to my assistant. If ever you decide you want a change, then give her a ring. She knows plenty of people, and domestic staff are always in short supply.' He met her eyes. 'You could always find something better than this, you know.'

'Despite dinner being such a disaster?' She tried to sound jokey even if she didn't feel it, because she realised she was being dismissed. Getting up from the comfort of her fireside seat, Molly took the card and slid it into the hip pocket of her dress.

'Despite that,' he agreed, his words suddenly trailing away as his gaze followed the movement of her hand.

Molly became aware of a subtle alteration in the atmosphere as Salvio lifted his eyes to her face. She'd wondered if the attraction which had sizzled between them earlier had been wishful thinking, but maybe it hadn't. Maybe it had been real. As real as the sudden thrust of her nipples against the soft fabric of her dress and the distracting heat between her thighs. She held her breath, waiting, instinct telling her that he was going to touch her. Despite him being who he was and her being just Molly. And he did. Lifting his hand, he ran the tips of his fingers experimentally over her hair.

'E capelli tuoi so comme a seta,' he said, and when she looked at him in confusion, he translated. 'Your hair is like silk.'

It was the most beautiful thing anyone had ever said to her and when she heard it in Italian it made her want to melt. Was that why he did it, knowing it would push her a little further beneath his powerful spell? Molly told herself to move away. She should thank him for the drink, for his kindness and for giving her his card and then hurry back to her little room to mull over her memories and hug them to her like a hot-water bottle. But she didn't move. She just carried on gazing up into the rugged perfection of his looks, praying he would kiss her and make the fairy tale complete—even if that was all she was ever going to have to remember him by. 'Is—is it?' she questioned.

Salvio smiled, letting his thumb drift from the fire-warmed strands, to hover over the unmistakable tremble of her lips. He felt a tightness in his throat as he realised what he was about to do. He had invited her here because he sensed she was lonely and unhappy—not because he intended to seduce her. Because there were rules and usually he followed them. He no longer took physical comfort just because it was available—because it was pretty much always available to a man like him. Just as he no longer used sex to blot out his pain, or his anger.

But the little housekeeper had touched a part of him

he'd thought had died a long time ago. She had stirred a compassion in his soul and now she was stirring his body in a way which was all too obvious, if only to him. He could feel the aching hardness at his groin, but the urge to kiss her was even more overwhelming than the need to bury himself deep inside her body. He told himself he should resist—gently shoo her out of the door and send her on her way. And maybe he would have done—had she not chosen that moment to expel a shaky breath of air, the warmth of it shuddering softly against his thumb.

How could something as insignificant as a breath be so potent? he marvelled as he stared down into her wide grey eyes. 'I want to kiss you,' he said softly. 'But if that happens I will want to make love to you and I'm not sure that's such a good idea. Do you understand what I'm saying, Molly?'

Wordlessly, she nodded.

'And the only thing which will stop me, is you,' he continued, his voice a deep silken purr. 'So stop me, Molly. Turn away and walk out right now and do us both a favour, because something tells me this is a bad idea.'

He was giving her the opportunity to leave but Molly knew she wasn't going to take it—because when did things like this ever happen to people like her? She wasn't like most women her age. She'd never had sex. Never come even close, despite her few forays onto a dating website, which had all ended in disaster. Yet now a man she barely knew was proposing seduction and suddenly she was up for it, and she didn't care if it was *bad*. Hadn't she spent her whole life trying to be good? And where had it got her?

Her heart was crashing against her ribcage as she stared up into his rugged features and greedily drank them in. 'I don't care if it's a bad idea,' she whispered. 'Maybe I want it as much as you do.'

Her response made him tense. She saw his eyes narrow and heard him utter something which sounded more like despair than joy before pulling her almost roughly into his arms. He smoothed the hair away from her cheeks and lowered his head and the moment their lips met, she knew there would be no turning back.

At first his kiss was slow. As if he was exploring her mouth by touch alone. And just when she was starting to get used to the sheer dreaminess of it, it became hard. Urgent. It fuelled the hunger which was building inside her. He levered her up against him, so that her breasts were thrusting eagerly against his torso and she could feel the rock-hard cradle of his pelvis. She should have been daunted by the unmistakable bulk of his erection but she wasn't, because her hungry senses were controlling her now and she didn't feel like good, rule-following Molly any more. She felt like wanton Molly—a victim of her own desire.

And it felt good.

More than good.

His laugh was unsteady as he splayed his fingers over one of her breasts, the nipple instantly hardening against his palm. 'You are very passionate,' he murmured.

Molly gave a small gurgle of pleasure as he found the side zip of her dress because suddenly she *felt* passionate. As if she had been waiting all her life to feel this way. 'Am I?'

'I don't think you need any reassurance on that score, *bedda mia*.'

He was wrong, of course—but he wasn't to know that and Molly certainly wasn't going to tell him. She felt breathless as he peeled the plain black dress away from her body and let it fall to the ground before stepping back to survey her. And wasn't it funny how a look of admiration in a man's eyes could be powerful enough to dispel all a woman's instinctive insecurities? Because for once Molly wasn't thinking that her tummy was too plump or her breasts unfashionably massive. Or even that her bra didn't match her rather functional pants. Instead she was revelling in the look of naked hunger which made his eyes resemble black fire as they blazed over her.

And then he picked her up. Picked her up! She could hardly believe it. He was carrying chunky Molly Miller towards the bed as if she weighed no more than a balloon at a child's birthday party, before whipping back the brand-new duvet she'd purchased that very morning and depositing her beneath it. It was the most delicious sensation in the world, sinking into the mattress and lying beneath the warmth of the bedding, her body sizzling with a growing excitement—while Salvio De Gennaro began to undress. She swallowed, completely hypnotised as she watched him. The shoes and socks were first to go and then he unbuttoned his shirt, baring his magnificent chest before turning his attention to the zip of his trousers. But when he hooked his thumb inside the waistband of his boxers, Molly squeezed her eyes tightly closed.

'No. Not like that. Open your eyes. Look at me,' he instructed softly and she was too much in thrall to disobey him.

Molly swallowed. She couldn't deny that it was slightly daunting to see just how aroused he was and as she bit her lip, he smiled.

'Me fai asci pazzo,' he said, as if that explained everything.

'Wh-what does that mean?'

'It means you make me crazy.'

'I love it when you talk Italian to me,' she said shyly.

'Not Italian,' he said sternly as he slipped into bed beside her. 'Neapolitan.'

She blinked. 'It's different?'

'It's dialect,' he said and she noticed he was placing several foil packets on the antique chest of drawers beside the bed. 'And yes, it's very different.'

The appearance of condoms somehow punctured some of the romance, but by then he was naked beside her and Molly was discovering that the sensation of skin touching skin was like nothing she'd ever known. It was *heaven*. Better than chocolate cake. Better than... well, anything really.

'Salvio,' she breathed, trying out his name for the first time.

'Sì, bedda mia? Want me to kiss you again?'

'Yes, please,' she said fervently, and he laughed.

His kisses were deep. It felt as if he were drugging her with them, making her body receptive to the caress of his fingers. And, oh, those fingers—what magic they worked as he tiptoed them over her shivering flesh. He massaged her peaking nipples until she was writhing with pleasure, and when he slid his hand between her thighs and discovered how wet she was, he had to silence her instinctive gasp with another kiss.

And because she didn't want to be passive, Molly stroked him back. At first she was cautious—concentrating on his chest and ribcage, before daring to explore a belly which was far flatter than her own. But when she plucked up the courage to touch the unfamiliar hardness which kept brushing against her quivering thigh, he stopped her with a stern look. 'No.'

She didn't ask him why. She didn't dare. She was afraid of doing anything which would shatter the mood or show how inexperienced she really was. Which might make Salvio De Gennaro bolt upright in bed and incredulously question what the hell he was doing, being intimate with a humble housekeeper. But he didn't. In fact, he seemed just as in tune with her body as she was with his. Like greedy animals, they rolled uninhibitedly around on the bed, biting and nipping and stroking and moaning and there was only the briefest hiatus when Salvio reached for one of the foil packets.

'Want to put this on for me?' he questioned provocatively. 'Since my hands are shaking so much I'm beginning to wonder if I can manage to do it myself.'

Some of Molly's composure left her. Should she say something?

Salvio, I've only ever seen a condom in a biology class at school. I've never actually used one for real.

Mightn't learning that send him hurtling out of bed in horror? Yes, he might be as aroused as she imagined any man *could* be, but even so…mightn't it be a bit heavy if she burdened him with a piece of knowledge which wasn't really relevant? After all, it wasn't as if she was expecting this…interlude to actually go anywhere.

And maybe he read her thoughts because he brought his face up close to hers and surveyed her with smoky eyes. 'You know that I—'

'Yes, I know. You're leaving in the morning,' she said. 'And that's okay.'

'You're sure?'

'Quite sure. I just want…'

'What do you want, Molly?' he questioned, almost gently.

'I just want tonight,' she breathed. 'That's all.'

Salvio frowned as he stroked on a condom. Was she for real, or just too good to be true? He kissed her again, wanting to explode with hunger but forcing himself to move as slowly as possible as he pushed inside her molten heat, because he was big. He'd been told that often enough in the past but he had never felt bigger than he did tonight.

But size had nothing to do with her next reaction. The tensing of her body and her brief grimace of pain told their own unbelievable story. Confusion swirled his thoughts and made him momentarily still. With an almighty effort he prepared to withdraw, but somehow her tight muscles clamped themselves around him in a way which was shockingly new and exciting, making him dangerously close to coming straight away.

He sucked in a raw breath, trying desperately to claw back control. Trying to concentrate on not giving in to his orgasm, rather than on the unbelievable fact that the housekeeper was a virgin. Or rather, she *had* been.

But stopping himself from coming was the hardest sexual test he'd ever set himself. Maybe it was her tightness which felt so delicious. Or the uninhibited way she was responding to him. She was a stranger to all the games usually played in the bedroom, he realised—and her naivety made her an unmatchable lover, because she was a natural. She hadn't learnt any tricks or manoeuvres. The things she was doing she hadn't done with any other man before and somehow that turned him on. He revelled in the way she squirmed those fleshy hips as he drove into her. The way she thrust her breast towards his lips, so that he could tease the pointing nipple with first his tongue and then his teeth. He sensed the change in her—the moment when her orgasm became inevitable—and he watched her closely, seeing her dark eyelashes flutter to a close. Triumph washed over him as she made that first disbelieving choke of pleasure and a rosy flush began to blossom over her breasts. And only when the last of her violent spasms had died away did he give in to his own need, unprepared for the power of what was happening to him. It felt like the first time, he thought dazedly. Or maybe the only time.

And then he fell asleep.

CHAPTER FOUR

IT WAS STILL dark when Salvio awoke next morning—the illuminated dial of his wristwatch informing him it was just past six. He waited a moment until his eyes became adjusted to the shadows in the bedroom. In the heat of that frantic sexual encounter which had taken him almost by surprise last night, he hadn't bothered to close the drapes and outside it was still dark—but then, sunrise came late to this part of the world in the depths of an English winter.

He glanced across at the sleeping woman beside him, sucking in a slow lungful of air as he tried to get his head around what had happened. Trying to justify the fact that he'd had sex with the innocent housekeeper, when deep down he knew there could be no justification. Yet she had wanted it, he reminded himself grimly. She had wanted it as much as him.

They had been intimate again during the night—several times, as it happened. His stretching leg had encountered the voluptuous softness of her warm flesh, making him instantly aroused. There had been a stack of questions he'd been meaning to ask, but somehow her touch had wiped them from his mind. The second time had been amazing—and so had the third. She was so easy to please. So grateful for the pleasure he gave her. He'd expected her to start bringing up tricky topics after orgasm number five, but his expectations hadn't materialised. She hadn't demanded to know if he had changed his mind about seeing her again, which was fortunate really, because he hadn't. His eyes narrowed. He couldn't. She was too sweet. Too naïve. She wouldn't last a minute in his world and his own cynical nature would destroy all that naïve enthusiasm of hers in an instant.

Leaning over, he shook her bare shoulder—resisting the desire to slip his hand beneath the duvet and begin massaging one of those magnificent breasts.

'Molly,' he murmured. 'Wake up. It's morning.'

It was a shock for Molly to open her eyes and realise she was staring up at the magnificent chandelier which hung from the ceiling of the guest bedroom. In this faint light it twinkled like the fading stars outside the window and she forced herself to remember that in several hours' time she would be attacking it with her feather duster, not lying beneath the priceless shards of crystal, with the warm body of a naked man beside her.

A shiver ran through her as she turned her head to look at Salvio, her heart punching out a violent beat as she realised what she'd done. She swallowed. What *hadn't* she done? She had let him undress her and explore every inch of her body, with his tongue and his fingers and a whole lot more beside. When he'd been deep inside her body, she had choked out his name over and over again as he had awoken an appetite she hadn't realised she possessed. Somehow he had waved a magic wand and turned her into someone she didn't really recognise and she had gone from being inexperienced Molly Miller, to an eager woman who couldn't get enough of him. Briefly she closed her eyes.

And she wasn't going to regret a single second of it. Because you couldn't turn the clock back—and even if you could, who would want to?

She yawned, stretching her arms above her head and registering the unfamiliar aching of her body. How many times had he made love to her? she wondered dazedly, as she recalled his seemingly insatiable appetite and her own eager response.

She forced herself to ask the question she didn't really want to ask. 'What time is it?'

'Just after six.' There was a pause. His eyes became hooded. 'Molly—'

'Well, you'd better get going, hadn't you?' Her breezy interjection forestalled him because she'd guessed what he was about to say—the heaviness of his tone warning her that this was the Big Goodbye. And he didn't need to. He had to go and she was okay with that. Why ruin everything by demanding more than he'd ever intended to give? She pinned an efficient smile to her lips. 'You did say you wanted to get away early.'

He frowned, as if her response wasn't what he'd been expecting, but Molly knew there was only one way to deal with a situation like this, and that was by being sensible, the way she'd been all her life. She had to face facts, not mould them to suit her fantasies. She knew there could be no future between her and the billionaire tycoon because their lives were too different. Last night the boundaries had become blurred—but one night of bliss didn't change the fundamentals, did it? She was employed as a housekeeper—and lying in an honoured guest's bed was the very last place she should be.

'You're sure you're okay?' he growled.

She wondered where the rogue thought came from. The one which made her want to say, *Not really, no. I wish you could take me with you wherever you're going and make love to me the way you did last night.*

But fortunately, the practical side of her character was the dominant one. As if Salvio De Gennaro would want to take her away with him! She tried to imagine cramming herself into that low-slung sports car—why, her weight would probably disable the suspension! 'Why wouldn't I be okay?' she questioned breezily. 'It was great. At least, I think it was.' For the first time, a trace of insecurity crept into her voice as she looked at him with a question in her eyes.

'Oh, it was more than "great",' he affirmed, reaching out to trace the tip of his finger over the quiver of her bottom lip. 'In fact, it was so good that I want to do it all over again.'

Once again Molly felt her stomach clench with desire and a rush of heat tugged deep inside her. 'But...' she whispered as he moved closer.

'But what, *mia bedda*?'

'There isn't...' She swallowed. 'There isn't time.'

'Says who?'

He slipped his hand between her legs. Molly wondered what had happened to the sensible part of her now. Forgotten, that was what. Banished by the first lazy stroke of his finger over her slick heat. 'Salvio,' she moaned, as his dark head moved down and his tongue found her nipple.

He lifted his head from her breast, dark eyes gleaming in the half-light. 'You want me to stop?'

'You know I don't,' she gasped.

'So why don't you show me what you *would* like?'

Maybe it was the knowledge that this was the last time which made her so adventurous, because Molly suddenly found her hand drifting over his taut belly to capture the rocky erection which was pressing so insistently against her thigh. 'This,' she said shakily. 'This is what I want.'

'And where do you want it?'

'In me,' she breathed boldly. 'Inside me.'

'Me, too,' he purred, reaching out to grab a condom from the sadly diminished pile on the bedside cabinet.

Molly was aware of being warm and sticky as he moved over her. Of her hair all mussed and her teeth unbrushed—but somehow none of that seemed to matter because Salvio was touching her as if she were some kind of goddess. His fingers were sure and seeking and goosebumps rippled over her skin in response as he smoothed his hand over her belly. She felt as if she were *soaring* as she wrapped her thighs around his hips and gave herself up to the exquisite sensation of that first sweet thrust and then the deepening movements which followed.

She loved the way they moved in time. The way she

felt as if she were on a fast shuttle to paradise when another orgasm took her over the top. And she loved his almost helpless expression as his face darkened and he pumped his seed inside her. The way his tousled head collapsed onto her shoulder afterwards as he uttered something intently in what she presumed was more Neapolitan dialect. His breathing was warm and even against her neck and, terrified he would fall asleep and delay his departure, she shook him. 'Salvio,' she whispered. 'Don't go to sleep. You'd better go. Before anyone wakes up.'

'Then you'd better get out of here, too,' he instructed, pushing aside the rumpled duvet. 'Right now. Before anyone sees you.'

For some reason his remark dispirited her and brought her crashing back to earth, allowing reality to puncture her little bubble of happiness. But despite the insecurities which were bubbling up inside her, Molly managed to retain her cheery smile, enjoying the sight of Salvio pulling on his jeans and sweater and quietly opening the door as he headed for the bathroom.

Once he'd gone she got out of bed and pulled on her discarded underclothes—pulling a face as she smoothed her crumpled work dress over her hips and rolled her black tights into a little ball, which she gripped in her hand. She'd be able to do something with her appearance once Salvio had left, she reasoned—glancing up as the door opened as he came back into the bedroom, his dark hair glittering with tiny drops of water from the shower.

In silence he dressed before snapping his overnight

case closed, his expression very serious as he walked towards her. For a moment he just stood in front of her, his gaze sweeping over her like a dark spotlight, as if he were seeing her for the first time.

'So why?' he questioned simply. 'Why me?

Molly expelled a shuddered breath, because in a way she'd been waiting for this question. He hadn't asked her last night and she'd been glad, because she hadn't wanted the mundane to spoil what had been the most fantastic night of her life. In a way, she would have preferred it if he hadn't brought it up now—but he had, and she needed to answer in a way designed to keep it light. Because she didn't want a single thing to tarnish the memory of how glorious it had been. She shrugged. She even managed a smile. 'I don't meet many men in this line of work,' she said. 'And certainly none like you. And you're…you're a very attractive man, Salvio—as I expect you've been told on many occasions.'

He frowned, as if her honesty troubled him. 'I want you to know that I didn't invite you in here in order to seduce you,' he said slowly. 'I'm not saying the thought hadn't crossed my mind earlier, but that wasn't my intention.'

She nodded. 'I know it wasn't. You were being kind, that's all. Maybe that's why I agreed to have a drink with you.'

He gave an odd kind of laugh. 'You had a very profound effect on me, Molly.'

There was an expression in his dark eyes which Molly couldn't work out but maybe it was best that way. She didn't want him telling her it had been an inexplicable thing he'd done. She wanted to hang onto what had happened between them—to treat it as you would one of those precious baubles you hung on the tree at Christmas. She didn't want to let the memory slip from her fingers and see it shatter into a million pieces.

'I'm glad,' she said, holding onto her composure only by a thread, her heart pounding frantically beneath her breast. 'But time's getting on. You'd better go.'

He nodded, as if being encouraged to leave a bedroom was a novel experience for him, but suddenly he turned and walked towards the bedroom door without another word, and Molly's heart twisted painfully as he closed it quietly behind him. She stood there framed in the window, watching as he emerged from the house, his dark figure silhouetted against the crashing ocean, and for a second he looked up, his black gaze capturing hers. She waited for him to smile, or wave, or something—and she told herself it was best he didn't, for who knew who else might be watching?

Throwing his bag inside, he slipped into the driver's seat, the closing door blotting out her last sight of him. His powerful car started up in a small cloud of gravel before sweeping down towards the coastal road and she watched until it was just a faint black dot in the distance. As sunrise touched the dark clouds with the first hint of red, Molly wondered if Salvio's life was a series of exits, with women gazing longingly out of windows as they watched him go.

Her cheeks were hot as she whipped the bottom sheet from the bed and removed the duvet cover. She would come back later to collect the linen and clean the room from top to bottom. But first she needed a hot shower. The Averys had plenty of events coming up and Molly had a long list of things to do today. Perhaps it was good that the weeks ahead were busy during the run-up to Christmas. It would certainly stop her from dwelling on the fact she would never see Salvio again. Never feel his lips on hers or his powerful arms holding her tight. Because this was what happened in the grown-up world, she told herself fiercely. People had fun with each other. Fun without expectations, or commitment. They had sex and then they just walked away.

Quietly, she closed the guest-room door behind her and was creeping along the corridor with the exaggerated care of a cartoon thief, when she became aware of someone watching her. Her heart lurched with fear. A shadowed figure was standing perfectly still at the far end of the guest corridor.

Not just anyone.

Lady Avery.

Molly's footsteps slowed, her heart crashing frantically against her ribcage as she met the accusing look in her boss's pale eyes.

'So, Molly,' Lady Avery said, in a voice she'd never heard her use before. 'Did you sleep well?'

There was a terrible pause and Molly's throat constricted, because what could she say? It would be adding insult to injury if she made some lame excuse about why she was creeping out of Salvio's room at this time in the morning, carrying a balled-up pair of tights. And now she would be sacked. She'd be jobless and homeless at the worst possible time of year. She swallowed. There was only one thing she *could* say. 'I'm sorry, Lady Avery.'

Her aristocratic employer shook her head in disbelief. 'I can't believe it!' she said. 'Why someone like him could have been interested in someone like you, when he could have had…'

Her words trailed away and Molly didn't dare fill the awkward silence which followed. Because how could Lady Avery possibly finish her own sentence without losing face or dignity? How could she possibly admit that *she* had been hoping to end up in Salvio's bed, when she was a married woman and her husband was in the house?

Molly's cheeks grew hot as she acknowledged the shameful progression of her thoughts. Behaving as if the Neapolitan tycoon were some kind of prize they'd both been competing over! Had the loneliness of her job made her completely indiscriminate, so that she had been prepared to leap into bed with the first man who had ever shown her any real affection? 'I can only apologise,' she repeated woodenly.

Once again, Lady Avery shook her head. 'Just get back to work, will you?' she ordered sharply.

'Work?' echoed Molly cautiously.

'Well, what else did you think you'd be doing? We have ten people coming for dinner tonight, in case you'd forgotten. And since this time I'm assuming you won't be obsessing about one of the guests, at least the meat won't arrive at the table cremated.' She gave Molly an arch look. 'Unless no man is now safe from your clutches. I must say you're the most unlikely candidate to be a *femme fatale*. Just get back to work, will you, Molly, before I change my mind?'

'Y-yes, Lady Avery.'

Unable to believe she hadn't been fired on the spot, Molly spent the next few weeks working harder than she'd ever worked before. She went above and beyond the call of duty as Christmas approached and she tried to make amends for her unprofessional behaviour. She attempted ambitious culinary experiments, which thankfully all turned out brilliantly. She baked, prodded, steamed and whipped—to the fervent admiration of the stream of guests which passed through the mistletoe-festooned hallway of the house. And if Lady Avery made a few sarcastic digs about Molly hanging around hopefully beneath the sprigs of white berries, Molly was mature enough not to respond. Maybe her boss's anger was justified, she reasoned. Maybe she would have said the same if the situation had been reversed.

And it didn't matter how busy she was—it was never enough to stop her thoughts from spinning in an unwanted direction. She found herself thinking about Salvio and that was the last thing she needed. She didn't want to remember all the things he'd done to her. The way he'd stroked her face and lips and body, before pushing open her thighs to enter her. Just as she didn't want to think about the way he'd whispered *'bedda mia'* and *'nicuzza'* in that haunting dialect when they'd both woken in the middle of the night. Because remembering that stuff was dangerous. It made it all too easy to imagine that it mattered. And it didn't. Not to him. He'd been able to walk away without a second glance and Molly had told him she was able to do the same.

So do it.

Stop yearning.

Stop wishing for the impossible.

It was four days before Christmas when two bomb-shells fell in rapid succession. Molly had just been about to drive to the village, when she came across Lady Avery standing in the hallway—a full-length fur coat swamping her fine-boned frame. Her face looked cold. As cold as the wintry wind which was whistling outside the big house and bringing with it the first few flakes of snow.

'Molly, don't bother going to the shops right now,' she said, without preamble.

Molly blinked. She'd made the pudding and cake and mince pies, but she still had to pick up the turkey and the vegetables. And hadn't they run out of satsumas? She looked at her boss helpfully. 'Is there something else you would rather I was doing?'

'Indeed there is. You can go upstairs and pack your things.'

Molly stared at her boss in confusion. 'Pack my things?' she echoed stupidly. 'I don't understand.'

'Don't you? It's really quite simple. Surely there's no need for me to spell it out for you. We no longer require your services.'

'But…'

'But what, Molly?' Lady Avery took a step closer and

now Molly could see that all the rage she'd been bottling up since Salvio's departure was about to come spilling out. 'I hope you aren't going to ask me why I haven't given you more notice, because I really don't think the normal rules apply when you've abused your position as outrageously as you have done. I really don't think that *sleeping with the guests* ever made it into your job description, do you?'

'But it's just before Christmas!' Molly burst out, unable to stop herself. 'And this...this is my home.'

Lady Avery gave a shrill laugh. 'I don't think so. Why don't you go running to your boyfriend and ask if he wants you over the holiday period? *Because it's not going to happen, that's why.* Salvio will have moved on to the kind of women he's more usually associated with by now.' Her pale eyes drilled into Molly. 'Do you know, they say there isn't a supermodel on the planet he hasn't dated?'

'But why...why wait until now?' questioned Molly in a low voice. 'Why didn't you just fire me straight away?'

'With wall-to-wall engagements planned and Christmas just over the horizon?' Lady Avery looked at her incredulously. 'I was hardly going to dispense with your services and leave myself without a housekeeper at such a busy time, now, was I? That's what's known as cutting off your nose to spite your face.' There was a pause. 'You'll find you've been paid up to the end of the month, which is more generous than you deserve. Philip and I have decided to fly to Barbados tomorrow for a last-minute holiday and we're going out for the rest of the day. Just make sure you're gone by the time we return, will you, Molly?'

'But…but where will I go tonight?'

'You really think I care? There's a cheap B&B in the village. You can go there—*if* they'll take you.' Lady Avery's mouth had curved into a cruel smile. 'Just make sure you leave your car and house keys on the hall table before you go.'

And that was that. Molly could hardly believe it was happening. Except that she could. Her heart clenched as her old friend Fear re-entered her life without fanfare and suddenly she was back in that familiar situation of being in a fix. Only this time she couldn't blame her brother, or the vagaries of fate which had made her mother so ill throughout her childhood. This time it was all down to her.

Biting her lip, she thought desperately about where she could go and what she could do, but no instant solution sprang to mind. She had no relatives. No local friends who could provide her with a roof over her head until she found herself another live-in job. Her mind buzzed frantically as some of Lady Avery's words came flooding into her mind. How would Salvio react if she called him up and told him she'd been fired as a result of their crazy liaison? Would he do the decent thing and offer her a place to stay? Yet, despite recoiling at the thought of throwing herself on the mercy of a man who'd made it clear he wanted nothing but a one-night stand, it was growing increasingly clear that she might *have* to. Because the second bombshell was hovering overhead ready to explode, no matter how hard she tried to block it from her mind.

Telling herself it was stress which had made her period so late, she pushed the thought away as she remembered the card Salvio had given her—the one with a direct line to his assistant. What had he said? That his assistant knew plenty of people and could help her find a domestic role if ever she needed one. Molly licked her lips. She didn't want to do it but what choice did she have? Where would she even *start* looking for a new job and a home at this time of year?

Quickly, she packed her clothes, trying not to give in to the tears which were pricking at the backs of her eyes. Carefully she wedged in the framed photo of her mother and the one of Robbie in his school uniform, the cute image giving no hint of the gimlet-eyed teenager he would become. And only when she was standing in her threadbare winter coat, with a hand-knitted scarf knotted tightly around her neck, did she dial the number on the card with a shaking finger.

Salvio's assistant was called Gina and she didn't just sound friendly—she sounded *relieved* when Molly gave her name and explained why she was ringing.

'I can't believe it,' she said fervently. '*You* are the answer to my prayers, Molly Miller.'

'Me?' said Molly doubtfully.

'Yes, you.' Gina's voice softened. 'Are you free now? I mean, as of right now?'

'I am,' answered Molly cautiously. 'Why?'

'Because Salvio is having his annual pre-Christmas party in the Cotswolds tomorrow, just before he flies to Naples—and the housekeeper we'd hired has called to say her mother has fallen downstairs and broken her wrist, and she's had to cancel. If you can step in and take over at the last minute I can make it very worth your while.'

Molly pushed out the words from between suddenly frozen lips. 'That's very bad news—about the broken wrist, I mean, but I don't think I—'

But the tycoon's assistant was breezing on as if she hadn't spoken.

'Salvio must rate you very highly to have given you my number,' Gina continued. 'Why, it's almost like fate. I won't even have to bother telling him about the change. He doesn't like to be bogged down with domestic trivia and he's always so busy.'

Molly bit her lip so hard it hurt. This was fast becoming a nightmare, but what else could she do? How could she possibly turn down this opportunity just because she'd had sex with the man who would now unwittingly be employing her? She would just blend into the background and pray that the Neapolitan tycoon would be too busying partying to pay her any attention. And if the worst came to the worst and he discovered her identity—then she would shrug her shoulders and tell him it was no big deal.

Realistically, what could go wrong?

But being rumbled by Salvio wasn't the worst thing which could happen, was it? Not by a long way. The fear which had been nagging at her for days came flooding into her mind and this time would not be silenced, because all her excuses about stress and anxiety were rapidly fading. Because she wasn't sure if anxiety was capable of making your breasts ache and feel much bigger than usual. Or whether it could sap your normally voracious appetite.

She stared at her pale reflection in the hall mirror and saw the terror written in her own eyes. Because what if she was pregnant with Salvio De Gennaro's baby?

CHAPTER FIVE

VISIBILITY WAS POOR—in fact, it was almost non-existent. Salvio's fingers tightened around the soft leather of the steering wheel. Eyes narrowed, he stared straight ahead but all he could see was an all-enveloping whiteness swirling in front of the car windscreen. Every couple of seconds, the wipers dispelled the thick layer of snow which had settled, only to be rapidly replaced by another.

Frustrated, he glanced at the gold watch at his wrist, cursing the unpredictability of the weather. His journey from central London to the Cotswold countryside had been excruciatingly slow and in an ideal world he would have cancelled his annual party. But you couldn't really cancel something this close to Christmas, no matter how preoccupied you were feeling. And he *was* feeling preoccupied, no doubt about it—even though the reason for that was disconcertingly bizarre. An impatient sigh escaped his lungs as he watched another flurry of snow. Because he couldn't stop thinking about the curvy little housekeeper with the big grey eyes, with those luscious breasts, whose tips had fitted perfectly into his hungry mouth. Most of all, he couldn't stop remembering her purity. Her innocence.

Which he had taken. Without thought. Without knowledge. But certainly not without feeling.

Memories of how it had felt to penetrate her beautiful tightness flooded his mind and Salvio swallowed as he touched his foot against the brake pedal. Would he have bedded her so willingly if he'd known she was a virgin? Of course he wouldn't. His desire for the housekeeper had been completely out of character and he still couldn't quite fathom it. He usually enjoyed women who were, if not quite his equal, then certainly closer on the social scale than Molly Miller would ever be.

He thought about Beatriz—the Brazilian beauty with whom he'd been enjoying a long-distance flirtation for the past few months. He had been attracted to her because she'd played hard to get and he'd convinced himself that a woman who wouldn't tumble straight into his arms was exactly what he needed. But as her attitude towards him had thawed, so had his interest waned—and the memory of Molly had completely wiped her from his mind. And although Beatriz had made it clear she would be happy to share his bed after his Christmas party, the idea had left him cold, despite the fact that most men lusted after her statuesque beauty. He had been wondering about the most tactful way to convey his sudden change of heart, when she'd rung last night to say her plane had been delayed in Honolulu and she didn't think she was going to make his party. And hadn't he been struck by an overwhelming feeling of *relief*?

'*No importa*. Don't worry about it,' he had responded quickly—probably too quickly.

A pause. 'But I'm hoping we can see each other some other time, Salvio.'

'I'm hoping so too, but I'm flying out to Naples for Christmas and I'm not sure when I'll be back.' His response had been smooth and seasoned. And distinctly dismissive. 'I'll call you.'

He could tell from her sharp intake of breath that she understood the underlying message and her goodbye had been clipped and cold. She hadn't even wished him a happy Christmas and he supposed he couldn't blame her.

But his mind had soon moved on to other things and, infuriatingly, he kept recalling the sweet sensation of a naked Molly in his arms. He swallowed. The way her soft lips had pressed into his neck and her fleshy thighs had opened so accommodatingly. There were a million reasons why he shouldn't be thinking about her but she was proving a distractingly difficult image to shift. Was that because she hadn't put any demands on him? Because she'd been okay about him walking out of her life? Most women hung on in there, but Molly Miller was not among their number. And hadn't that intrigued him? Made him wonder what it might be like to see her in a more normal setting. Perhaps even take her out to dinner to see how long it would take for her allure to fade.

He'd thought a few times about contacting her—but what could he say, without falsely raising her hopes? No. He was doing her a favour by leaving her alone—

that was what he needed to remember. Breaking hearts was his default mechanism—and no way would he wish that kind of pain on the passionate little housekeeper.

It was the most beautiful house Molly had ever seen. Pressing her nose against the icy-cold glass, she peered out through the taxi window at the sprawling manor house, whose gardens were a clever combination of wild and formal and seemed to go on for ever. Although the sky was pewter-grey, the light was bright with snow and everything was covered in white. Fat flakes tumbled like giant feathers from the sky, so that the scene in front of her looked like one of those old-fashioned Christmas cards you couldn't seem to buy any more.

But Molly's emotions were in turmoil as the cab inched its way up the snowy drive. She had underestimated the impact of leaving Cornwall because even though the job had left a lot to be desired, it had still been her home and her security for the last two years. More than that, her departure had been forced upon her in the most dramatic and shameful of ways. Suddenly she felt rudderless—like a leaf caught up by a gust of wind being swirled towards an unknown destination.

But even worse than her near-homelessness was the confirmation of her worst fears. That it hadn't been stress or anxiety which had made her period so late. That the weird tugs of mood and emotion—like wanting to burst into tears or go to sleep at the most inopportune times—hadn't been down to the *worry* of getting pregnant. She couldn't even blame the sudden shock of losing her live-in job, or the corresponding jolt to her confidence. No, the reason had been made perfectly clear when she'd done not one, but two pregnancy tests in the overcrowded bathroom of the little boarding house she'd stayed in last night. With growing horror and a kind of numb disbelief she had sat back on her heels and stared at the unmistakable blue line, shaking with the shock of realising that she was pregnant with Salvio's baby.

And wondering what the hell she was going to do about it.

But she couldn't afford to think about that right now. The only thing she needed to concentrate on was doing her job—and as good a job as possible. She was going to have to tell him, yes, but not yet. Not right before his party and the arrival of his presumably high-powered guests.

She paid the driver and stepped out of the cab onto a soft blanket of snow. There were no other tyre marks on the drive and the only sign of life was a little robin hopping around as she made her way to the ancient oak front door, which looked like something out of a fairy tale. She knocked loudly, just in case—but there was no answer and so she let herself in with the keys she'd picked up from Salvio's assistant, along with a great big wodge of cash for expenses.

Inside, everything was silent except for the loud ticking of a grandfather clock, which echoed through the spacious hallway, and the interior was even more beautiful than the outside had suggested. It spoke of elegance and money and taste. Gleaming panelled walls carved with acorns and unicorns. Huge marble fireplaces and dark floorboards scattered with silk rugs were illuminated by the sharp blue light which filtered in through the windows. Yet the beauty and the splendour were wasted on Molly. She felt like an outsider. Like the spectre who had arrived at the feast bearing a terrible secret nobody would want to hear. She felt like curling up in a ball and howling, but what was the point of that? Instead she forced herself to walk around the house to get her bearings, just as she would with any new job.

A quick tour reassured her that the cupboards and fridge were well stocked with everything she could possibly need, the beds all made up with fresh linen and the fires laid. She lit the fires, washed her hands and started working her way through the to-do list. Barring bad weather cancellations, twenty-five guests would be arriving at seven. Gina had informed her that there were plenty of bedrooms if bad weather prevented some of the city guests getting back to London, but Salvio would prefer it if they left.

'He's a man who likes his own company,' she'd said.

'Does he?' Molly had questioned nervously, as an image shot into her head of a crying baby. How would he ever be able to deal with *that*?

Maybe he wouldn't want to.

Maybe he would tell her that he had no desire for an unplanned baby in his life. Had she thought about *that*?

A local catering company were providing a hot-buffet supper at around nine and wine waiters would take care of the drinks. All Molly had to do was make sure everything ran smoothly and supervise the local waitresses who were being ferried in from the nearby village. How difficult could it be? Her gaze scanned down to the bottom of the list.

And please don't forget to decorate the Christmas tree!

Molly had seen the tree the moment she'd walked in—a giant beast of a conifer whose tip almost touched the tall ceiling, beside which were stacked piles of cardboard boxes. Opening one, she discovered neat rows of glittering baubles—brand-new and obviously very expensive. And suddenly she found herself thinking about Christmases past. About the little pine tree she and Robbie used to drag in from the garden every year, and the hand-made decorations which their mother had knitted before the cruel illness robbed her of the ability to do even that. It had been hard for all of them to watch her fading away but especially tough for her little brother, who had refused to believe his beloved mother was going to die. And Molly hadn't been able to do anything to stop it, had she? It had been her first lesson in powerlessness. Of realising that sometimes you had to sit back and watch awful things happen—and that for once she couldn't protect the little boy she'd spent her life protecting.

Didn't she feel that same sense of powerlessness now as she thought of the cells multiplying in her womb? Knowing that outwardly she looked exactly the same as before, while inside she was carrying the Neapolitan's baby.

Her fingers were trembling as she draped the tree with fairy lights and hung the first bauble—watching it spin in the fractured light from the mullioned window. And then it happened—right out of nowhere, although if she'd thought about it she should have been expecting it. If she hadn't been singing 'In The Bleak Midwinter' at the top of her voice she might have heard the front door slam, or registered the momentary pause which followed. But she wasn't aware of anything until something alerted her to the fact that someone else was in the room. Slowly she turned her head to see Salvio standing there.

Her heart clenched tightly and then began to pound. He was wearing a dark cashmere overcoat over faded jeans and snowflakes were melting in the luxuriant blackness of his hair. She thought how tall and how powerful he looked. How his muscular physique dominated the space around him. All these thoughts registered in the back of her mind but the one which was at the forefront was the expression of disbelief darkening his olive-skinned features.

'You,' he said, staring at her from between narrowed eyes.

Molly wondered if the shock of seeing her had made him forget her name, or whether he had forgotten it anyway. In either case, he needed reminding—or this situation could prove even more embarrassing than it was already threatening to be. 'Yes, me,' she echoed, her throat dry with nerves. 'Molly. Molly Miller.'

'I know your name!' he snapped, in a way which made her wonder if perhaps he was protesting too much. 'What I want to know is what the hell you're doing here.'

His face had hardened with suspicion. It certainly wasn't the ecstatic greeting Molly might have hoped for—if she'd dared to hope for anything. But hope was a waste of time—she'd learnt that a long time ago. And at least a life spent working as a servant and having to keep her emotions hidden meant she was able to present a face which was perfectly calm. The only outward sign of her embarrassment was the hot colour which came rushing into her cheeks, making her think how unattractive she must look with her apron digging into her waist and her hair spilling untidily out of its ponytail. 'I'm just decorating the Christmas tree—'

'I can see that for myself,' he interrupted impatiently. 'I want to know *why*. What are you doing here, Molly?'

The accusation which had made his mouth twist with anger was unmistakable and Molly stiffened. Did he think she was stalking him, like one of those crazed ex-lovers who sometimes featured in the tabloids? Women who had, against all the odds, come into contact with a wealthy man and then been reluctant to let him—or the lifestyle—go.

'You gave me your assistant's card, remember?' she reminded him. 'And told me to ring her if I needed to find work.'

'But you already have a job,' he pointed out. 'You work for the Averys.'

Molly shook her head and found herself wishing she didn't have to say this. Because wasn't it a humiliating thing to have to admit—that she had been kicked out of her job just before Christmas? 'Not any more, I don't,' she said. She met the question which was glittering from his black eyes. 'Lady Avery caught me leaving your bedroom.'

His eyes narrowed. 'And she *sacked* you because of that?'

Molly's colour increased. 'I'm afraid so.'

Beneath his breath, Salvio uttered some of the words he'd learnt in the backstreets of Naples during his poverty-stricken childhood. Words he hadn't spoken in a long time but which seemed appropriate now as remorse clawed at his gut. It was his fault. Of course it was. Was that why she was looking at him with those big grey eyes, like some wounded animal you discovered hiding in the woods? Because she blamed him and held him responsible for what had happened? And it never *should* have happened, he told himself bitterly. He should never have invited her into his room for a drink, despite the fact that she'd been crying. He'd tried very hard to justify his actions. He'd told himself he'd been motivated by compassion rather than lust, but perhaps he had been deluding himself. Because ultimately he was a man and she was a woman and the chemistry between them had been as powerful as anything he'd ever experienced. Surely he wasn't going to deny *that*.

His eyes narrowed as he studied her. Despite her initial innocence, had she subsequently recognised the sexual power she had wielded over him? It wasn't inconceivable that her sacking had come about as a result of her own ego. She might easily have made a big show of leaving his room, with that dreamy look of sexual satisfaction which made a woman look more beautiful than fancy clothes ever could. And mightn't that have provoked Sarah Avery, whose advances he had most definitely rejected?

Suddenly he felt as if he was back on familiar territory, as he recalled the behaviour of women during his playing days, and one woman in particular. He remembered the dollar signs which had lit up in their eyes when they'd realised how much his contract had been worth. These days he might no longer be one of Italy's best-paid sportsmen, but in reality he was even wealthier. Was that why Molly Miller was here—prettily decorating his tree—just waiting to hit him with some kind of clumsy demand for recompense?

'So why exactly did Gina offer you this job?' he questioned.

She bit her lip. 'Because the woman who was supposed to be doing it had to suddenly go and look after her mother. And I didn't let on that I…' Her words faltered. 'That I *knew* you, if that's what you're worried about. Gina doesn't have a clue about what went on between us. There was a slot to fill, that's all—and I just happened to be in the right place at the right time.'

Or the wrong place at the wrong time. Just like the last time they'd met.

The thoughts rushed into Salvio's head before he could stop them and he felt his body tense as he worked out how best to handle this. Because now he found himself in a difficult situation. He frowned. The amazing night he'd shared with her had haunted him ever since, but nobody was going to deny that it had been a foolhardy action on so many levels. Did she think it was going to happen again? he wondered. Was she expecting to resume her position in his bed? That once all his guests had left, he would be introducing her to another night of bliss?

He raked his gaze over her, unable to suppress the hunger which instantly fired up his blood but resenting it all the same. He shouldn't feel this way about her. He shouldn't still want her. That night had been a mistake and one which definitely shouldn't be repeated. Yet desire was spiralling up inside him with an intensity which took him by surprise and despite his best efforts he was failing to dampen it. With her fleshy curves accentuated by the waistband of an apron, she looked the antithesis of the glamour he'd always regarded as a prerequisite for his lovers. She looked *wholesome* and plain and yet somehow incredibly sexy.

Suddenly he felt a powerful urge to take her in his arms and lie her down beside the Christmas tree. To pull down her mismatched panties and kiss between those generous thighs, before losing his tongue and then his body in all that tight, molten heat. He wondered how she would react if he did. With the same breathtaking eagerness she had shown before—or would she push him away this time? His mouth hardened and so uncomfortably did his groin and, although he was unbearably tempted to test out the idea, he drew himself up, wondering if he'd taken leave of his senses.

He was her boss, for heaven's sake!

Shaking his head, he walked over to the window and

stared out at the thick white layer which was coating the lawns and bare branches of the trees. The light was fading from the sky, intensifying the monochrome colours of the garden so that all he noticed was the diamond-bright glitter of the ice-encrusted snow.

His mouth hardened. He'd thought tonight would just be another evening to get through, before flying out to Naples for a family Christmas. Slowly, he turned around. But suddenly everything had changed—and all because of this pink-faced woman who was standing in front of him, nervously chewing her lip.

'How long are you supposed to be working here?' he demanded.

'Just for tonight. And tomorrow I have to supervise the clean-up after the party.'

'And after that?' he probed. 'What then?'

She rubbed the tip of her ugly shoe over the Persian rug as if she were polishing it. 'I don't know yet. I'll just have to find something else.'

'Including accommodation, I suppose?'

She moved her shoulders awkwardly, as if he had reminded her of something she would prefer to forget, and when she looked up, her grey eyes were almost defiant. 'Well, yes. The jobs I take are always live-in.'

His eyes narrowed. 'And how easy will that be?'

Her attempt to look nonchalant failed and for the first time Salvio saw a trace of vulnerability on her face.

'Not very easy at this time of the year, I imagine.'

Salvio felt the flicker of a heavy pulse at his temple as another unwanted streak of conscience hit him and he recognised he couldn't just abandon her to the wolves.

He had bedded her and she had lost her job as a result of that—so it stood to reason he must take some of the responsibility. He nodded. 'Very well. Tomorrow, I'll have a word with Gina. See if we can't find you something more permanent.' He saw her face brighten and wondered if he had falsely raised her hopes. 'Not with me, of course,' he continued hastily. 'That isn't going to happen. The night we shared was many things, Molly, but it certainly didn't lay down a suitable foundation for any kind of working relationship between us.'

Molly flinched. She had thought him kind and that his behaviour towards her in the past had been thoughtful. But he wasn't kind, not really. He'd made it clear she couldn't ever work for him, not now she had been his lover—so, in effect, wasn't he patronising her just as much as Lady Avery had done? Before she thought she'd seen consideration in his face but that had been replaced by a flinty kind of calculation. Because Salvio De Gennaro could be utterly ruthless, she recognised— her heart sinking as she tried to imagine how he was going to react to her unwelcome news.

'Do you understand what I'm saying, Molly?' he continued remorselessly.

'Of course I do,' she said. 'I wasn't expecting to get a job with you. So please don't worry about it, Salv— Signor De Gennaro,' she amended, unable to hide her sudden flash of sarcasm. 'I won't bother you. You won't even know I'm here.'

The look on his face told her he didn't believe her and, despite her inexperience, Molly could understand why. Because how could they remain indifferent to each other when the atmosphere around them was still charged with that potent chemistry which had led to her downfall before? And wasn't she longing for him to touch her again? To trace his fingertip along the edges of her trembling lips, before replacing them with his mouth and kissing her until she capitulated to his every need.

Well, that would be insane.

Molly swallowed as she picked another bauble from its soft nest of tissue paper and the Neapolitan turned away.

'I need to get showered and changed before the party,' he said roughly. 'Just get on with your work, will you, Molly?'

CHAPTER SIX

SHE WISHED HE would stop staring at her.

Liar. Molly shivered as she picked up an empty wine glass and put it on her tray. *Admit it. You like it when he stares at you. Even though his face looks all dark and savage, as if he hates himself for doing it.*

And how much more savage will he look when he discovers the truth? she wondered.

It was the end of a long evening and only a few die-hard guests remained. Contrary to predictions the snow had stopped falling, allowing the chauffeur-driven cars to take the giggling London guests safely back to the capital. Vintage champagne had flowed, delicious food had been eaten and there hadn't been a single crisis in the kitchen, much to Molly's relief. A group of local singers had trudged through the snow and treated the partygoers to an emotional medley of Christmas carols, before being given mulled wine and hot mince pies and sent on their way with a huge donation to rebuild the roof of the village hall. And now Salvio was standing talking to a dark-suited man in the far corner of the huge drawing room—someone had whispered that he was a sheikh—but every time she looked up, Molly could see the hooded black eyes of the Neapolitan trained on her.

She hurried down to the kitchen where at least she was safe from that devastating gaze and the ongoing concern of how exactly she was going to break her momentous news. At least when you were helping stack clean plates and showing the hired help where to put all the silver cutlery, it was easy to forget your own problems, if only for a while. But at twenty past midnight the last of the staff departed and only the sheikh who had dominated Salvio's company for much of the evening was left, the two men deep in conversation as they sat by the fireside.

Molly was in the basement kitchen drying the final crystal glass when she heard a deafening chatter outside and peered out to see a helicopter alighting on the snowy lawn. Moments later the sheikh, now swathed in a dark overcoat, his black head bent against the flattening wind, began to run towards it. She could see the glint of a royal crest on the side of the craft as the door closed and it began its swaying ascent into the sky. Her hands were shaking as she suddenly realised she was alone in the house with Salvio and she wondered what she should do. She put the glass down. She should behave as she normally would in these circumstances— even if this felt anything like normal.

Taking off her damp apron and smoothing down her black dress, she went upstairs to find Salvio still sitting beside the fire, his stance fixed and unmoving as he gazed into the flickering flames. His long legs were stretched out before him and the rugged perfection of his profile looked coppery in the firelight. Never had he seemed more devastating or more remote and never had she felt so humble and disconnected. How crazy was it that this man had briefly been her lover and would soon be the father of her child?

Molly cleared her throat. 'Excuse me.'

He looked up then, his eyes narrowing as if he couldn't quite remember who she was, or why she was here.

'*Sì*, what is it?' he questioned abruptly.

'I didn't mean to disturb you, but I wondered if there was anything else you'd like?'

Salvio felt his heart slam hard against his chest. If it had been any other former lover asking that question, it would have been coated in innuendo. But Molly's words weren't delivered suggestively, or provocatively. Her big grey eyes weren't slanting out an unspoken invitation. She simply looked anxious to please, which only reinforced the differences between them. Once again he cursed his hot-headedness in taking the curvy housekeeper to his bed.

Even though he could understand exactly why he'd done it.

He'd spent this evening watching her, despite his best intentions. He'd told himself she was strictly off-limits and he should concentrate on his guests, but it had been Molly's wide-hipped sway which had captured his gaze and Molly's determined face as she had scurried around with trays of drinks and food which had captivated his imagination. He had seen the natural sparkle of her grey eyes and had remembered the healthy glow of her cheeks when she had romped enthusiastically in his arms. But her face was pale now, he noted. Deathly pale—as if all the colour had been leeched from it.

'No, I don't think there is,' he said slowly, forcing himself to treat her as he would any other member of staff. 'Thank you for all your hard work tonight, Molly. The party went very well. Even the Sheikh of Razrastan stayed far longer than he intended.'

'You're very welcome,' she said.

'I'm sure we can think about a generous bonus for you.'

'There's no need for that,' she said stiffly.

'I think I'll be the judge of that.' He gave her a benign smile. 'And I haven't forgotten my promise to try to find you some work. Or, rather, to ask Gina to help.' His words were tantamount to dismissal but she didn't move. Salvio saw the faint criss-crossing of a frown over the smooth expanse of her brow and something—he never knew what it was—compelled him to ask a question he usually avoided like the plague. 'Is everything okay?'

Her hands began twisting at the plain fabric of her work dress and he could see the indecision which made her frown deepen.

'Y-yes.'

'You don't sound very sure.'

'I wasn't going to tell you until tomorrow,' she said, her knuckles whitening.

Instinct made Salvio sit upright, his body tensing. 'Tell me *what*?' he questioned dangerously.

Molly licked her lips. She'd thought that a good night's

sleep and the addition of daylight might take some of the emotional sting out of her disclosure. But now she could see that any idea of sleep was a non-starter, especially with the thought of Salvio in bed nearby and the heavy realisation that he'd only ever wanted her that one time. But more than that, the news was bubbling inside her, wanting to get out. She needed to tell someone—and who else was she going to confide in?

'I'm pregnant,' she said bluntly.

There was a moment of silence—a weird and intense kind of silence. It was as if every sound in the room had been amplified to an almost deafening level. The crackle and spit of the fire. The loud thunder of her heart. The sudden intake of her own shuddered breath. And now there was shadow too, as Salvio rose from his chair—tall and intimidating—his powerful frame blocking out the firelight and seeming to fill the room with darkness.

'You can't be,' he said flatly. 'That is, if you're trying to tell me it's mine?'

She met the unyielding expression which had hardened his face and Molly's heart contracted with pain. Did he really think she'd lost her virginity to him and then rushed out to find herself another lover—as if trying to make up for lost time? Or was he just trying to run from his own responsibility? She stared at him reproachfully. 'You know it is.'

'I used contraception,' he bit out. 'You know I did.'

She felt blood rush into her cheeks. 'Maybe you weren't—'

'Careful?' He cut across her words with a bitter

laugh. 'I think that's a given, don't you? Reckless might be closer to the mark. On all counts.'

'Don't,' she said quickly.

His eyebrows shot up imperiously, as if he couldn't quite believe she was telling him what to do. *'What?'*

'Please don't,' she whispered. 'Don't make it any worse than it already is by saying things which will be difficult to forget afterwards.'

His eyes narrowed but he nodded, as if acknowledging the sense of her words. 'Are you sure?' he demanded. 'Or is it just a fear?'

She shook her head. 'I'm certain. I did a test.'

Another silence. 'I see.'

Molly's lips were dry and her heart was racing. 'I just want to make it clear that I'm only telling you because I feel duty-bound to tell you.'

'And not because you're after a slice of my fortune?'

Hurt now, she stared at him. 'You think that's what this is all about?'

His lips curved. 'Is it such a bizarre conclusion? Think about it, *mia bedda*. I'm rich and you're poor. What is it they say in the States?' He flicked the fingers of both hands, miming the sudden spill of money from a cash register. 'Ker-*ching*!'

Molly made to move away but his reflexes were lightning-fast and quicker than hers. He reached out to curl his fingers around her arm before pulling her towards him, like an expert angler reeling in their catch of the day. The movement made her breathless but it also made her hungry for him in a way she didn't want to be. Just one touch and her senses had started jangling, as she felt that now familiar desire washing over her. Meeting the gleam of his black eyes, she prayed she would find the strength to pull away from him and resist him. 'What do you think you're doing?' she demanded.

'I'm doing about the only thing which could possibly make me feel good right now,' he grated and brought his mouth down hard on hers.

Molly willed herself not to respond. She didn't have to do this—especially not after those insults he'd just hurled her way, making out she was some kind of gold-digger. But the trouble was that she *wanted* to kiss him. She wanted that more than anything else in the world right then. It was as if the beauty of his touch was making her realise how she'd got herself into this predicament in the first place. His kiss had been the first step to seduction and even now she found it irresistible. Closing her eyes, she let him plunder her lips until there was no oxygen left in her lungs and she had to draw back to suck in a breath of air. She shook her head distractedly. 'Salvio,' she whispered, but he shook his head.

'Don't say anything,' he warned, before scooping her up in his arms and carrying her out of the room.

Molly blinked in confusion because his hands were underneath her bottom and they were caressing it in a way which was making her want to squirm. As if in some kind of unbelievable dream he was carrying her up that sweeping staircase as if she were Scarlett O'Hara and he were Rhett Butler. And she was letting him.

So stop him. Make him put you down.

But she couldn't. Because *this* was powerlessness,

she realised—this feeling of breathy expectation bubbling up inside her as he kicked open the door of the master bedroom. The heavy oak door swung open as if it had been made of matchsticks as he carried her effortlessly across silken Persian rugs before depositing her on the huge bed.

And even though Molly could see no real affection on his proud Neapolitan features—nothing but sexual hunger glittering from his dark eyes—that didn't stop her from reciprocating. Was it the delicious memory of his lovemaking which made her open her arms to him and close them around him tightly? Or was it more basic than that? As he peeled her dress, shoes and underclothes from her body before impatiently removing his own clothes she began to wonder if there was some deep-rooted need to connect physically with the man whose seed was multiplying inside her.

Or at least, that was her excuse for what was about to happen.

'Salvio,' she gasped as his finger stroked a slow circle around the exquisitely aroused peak of her now bare nipple. *'Oh!'*

His naked body was warm against hers. 'Shh…'

It was more of a command than an entreaty but Molly heeded it all the same, terrified that words might break the spell and let reality flood in and destroy what she was feeling. His eyes were hooded as they surveyed her body, seeming to drink in every centimetre. Was she imagining his gaze lingering longest on her belly? With her notorious curves, she probably looked pregnant already. But now he was kissing her neck and her eyelids were fluttering to a close so that it became all about sensation rather than thought and that was so much better.

Encouraged by the hand now sliding from breast to thigh, Molly flickered her fingertips over the taut dip of his belly, her touch as delicate as if she were making pastry. And didn't his groan thrill her and fill her with a sense of pride that *she*—inexperienced Molly Miller—could make a man like Salvio react this way? Emboldened by his response, she drifted her hand over his rocky thighs, feeling the hair-roughened flesh turn instantly to goosebumps, and something about that galvanised him into action, because suddenly he was on top of her. He was kissing her with a hunger which was almost *ferocious* and, oh, it felt good. Better than anything had a right to feel. She could feel the graze of his jaw and his lips felt hard on hers, though his tongue was sinuous as it slipped inside her mouth.

She gave a little cry as she twisted restlessly beneath him and he gave a low laugh which was tinged with mockery.

'How quickly my little innocent becomes greedy,' he murmured. 'How quickly she has learnt what it is she wants.'

His words sounded more like insults than observations but by then he was stroking her wet and urgent heat and Molly was writhing beneath his fingers. She moaned as the sensation built and built and she realised what was about to happen. He was going to make her have an orgasm with his...*finger*.

'Salvio,' she cried out in disbelief, but just as she went tumbling over the top he thrust deep inside her.

She gasped as he filled her completely—even bigger than she remembered—and he gave a loud moan in response. And so did she. It felt as if her world were imploding. As if a jet-black sky had suddenly been punctured by a million stars. As if the two of them were locked and mingled for all time. Molly clung to him as she felt him momentarily stiffen before thrusting out his own shuddering pleasure.

He stayed inside her for countless minutes and Molly revelled in that sticky closeness because, in a funny sort of way, it felt as intimate as the act of sex had done. Maybe even more so, because now neither of them were chasing the satisfaction which had somehow left her feeling empty and satisfied, all at the same time.

But eventually he withdrew from her and rolled to the other side of the bed. Molly was careful to hide her disappointment as he threw the duvet over them both, quickly covering her up, as if the sight of her naked body offended him. She licked her lips as she waited for him to speak, planning to take her lead from him. It was the habit of a lifetime—of allowing her employer to dictate the conversation—because, technically, Salvio was still her employer, wasn't he? And it seemed vital that she stay quiet for long enough to hear his thoughts. Because what was said between them now was going to determine the rest of her baby's life, wasn't it? His attitude towards her unplanned pregnancy was of vital importance if they wanted to have any kind of amicable future. Not that she was expecting much from him. Not now. She'd thought she could rely on kindness until she'd realised she didn't really know him at all. And now her heart began to pound with anxiety as she wondered whether she should have given herself so easily to him. Could she really hope for respect in the circumstances?

She found herself studying him from between her lashes as she met the hard glitter of his eyes.

'So now what?' he questioned slowly.

She took him literally, because wasn't it simpler all round if she remained practical and continued to do her job? 'I ought to go down and turn off all the lights—especially the tree lights.'

His face was incredulous. 'Excuse me?'

She pushed her hair away from her face and wriggled into a sitting-up position, though she was careful to keep the top of the duvet modestly covering her breasts. 'I haven't switched off the lights on the Christmas tree—and there's also the fire, which we've left unguarded,' she said. 'I can't possibly go to sleep until all that is in place.'

'The fireguard?' he echoed disbelievingly, looking momentarily bemused before nodding. 'Wait here,' he said, and climbed out of bed.

Quite honestly, Molly didn't feel as if she had the strength or inclination to go anywhere—especially not when an unclothed Salvio was walking towards the door, seemingly unaware of the fact that it was the middle of winter and the snow was thick on the ground outside. She gazed at him as if hypnotised—her eyes drinking in the pale globes of his buttocks, which contrasted so vividly with the burnished olive of his thighs. And then he turned round, frowning with faint concern as he surveyed her, as if he had suddenly remembered that she'd just announced her pregnancy and wasn't quite sure how to deal with her any more.

'Can I get you anything?'

She guessed he was being literal too and that it would have been pointless to have asked for a crystal ball to re-assure her about her baby's future. And pointless to have asked for some affirmation that he wasn't planning on deserting his unplanned child, even if he wanted noth-ing more to do with her. But unlike her brother, Molly had never been a fantasist. She cleared her throat and nodded. 'A drink of water would be nice.'

She waited for him to say something like, *I'll bring it to your room*, but he didn't. Which presumably meant it was okay to stay here.

Of *course* it was okay to stay here—they'd just had sex, hadn't they?

But it wasn't easy to shrug off a lifetime of being deferential and Molly even felt slightly guilty about rushing into the luxurious en-suite bathroom and avail-ing herself of the upmarket facilities. She splashed her face with water and smoothed down her mussed hair before returning to the bed and burrowing down be-neath the duvet.

And then he was back and Molly quickly averted her eyes because the front view of the naked Neapoli-tan was much more daunting than the back had been—particularly as he seemed to be getting aroused again.

Did he read something in her expression? Was that why he gave a savage kind of laugh as he handed her the glass of water? 'Don't worry,' he grated. 'I'll endeavour to keep my appetite in check while we discuss how we're going to handle this.'

The large gulp of water she'd been taking nearly choked her and Molly put the glass down on the bedside table with a hand which was trembling. 'There's nothing to handle,' she said shakily. 'I'm having this baby, no matter what you say.'

'You think I would want anything other than that?' he demanded savagely.

'I wasn't... I wasn't sure.'

Salvio climbed into bed, disappointed yet strangely relieved that her magnificent breasts weren't on show, meaning he'd be able to concentrate on what he needed to say and not on how much he would like to lose himself in her sweet tightness again. He pulled the cover over the inconvenient hardening of his groin. Was she really as innocent as she seemed? Physically, yes—he had discovered that for himself. But was she really so unschooled in the ways of the world that she didn't realise that she was now in possession of what so many women strived for?

A billionaire father for her baby.

A meal ticket for life.

And there wasn't a damned thing he could do about it. Fate had thrown him a curveball and he was just going to have to deal with it.

'Tell me about yourself,' he said suddenly.

She blinked. 'Me?'

The sigh he gave wasn't exaggerated. 'Look, Molly— I think you're in danger of overplaying the wide-eyed innocent, don't you? We've had sex on a number of occasions and you've just informed me you're pregnant. Ordinarily I wouldn't be interested in hearing about your past, but you'll probably agree that this is no ordinary situation.'

Molly's heart clenched as his cruel words rained down on her. Wouldn't another man at least have *pretended* to be interested in what had made her the person she was today? Gone through some kind of polite ritual of getting to know her. Maybe she should be grateful that he hadn't. He might be cruel, but at least he wasn't a hypocrite. He wasn't pretending to feel stuff about her and building up her hopes to smash them down again. At least she knew where she stood.

'I was born in a little cottage—'

'Please. Spare me the violins. Let's just cut to the chase, shall we?' he interrupted coolly. 'Parents?'

Molly shrugged. 'My father left my mother when she was diagnosed with multiple sclerosis,' she said flatly.

She saw a flare of something she didn't recognise in his black eyes.

'That must have been hard,' he said softly.

'It was,' she conceded. 'Less so for me than for my little brother, Robbie. He…well, he adored our mother. So did I, obviously—but I was busy keeping on top of everything so that social services were happy to let me run the home.'

'And then?' he prompted, when her words died away.

Molly swallowed. 'Mum died when Robbie was twelve, but they let us carry on living together. Just me and him. I fought like crazy not to have him taken into care and I succeeded.'

His dark brows knitted together. 'And what was that like?'

She thought she detected a note of sympathy in his voice, or was that simply wishful thinking? Of course it was. He was cruel and ruthless, she reminded herself. He was only asking her these questions because he felt he *needed* to—not because he *wanted* to. For a moment Molly was tempted to gloss over the facts. To tell him that Robbie had turned out fine. But what if he found out the truth and then accused her of lying? Wouldn't that make this already difficult situation even worse than it already was?

'Robbie went off the rails a bit,' she admitted. 'He did what a lot of troubled teenagers do. Got in with the wrong crowd. Got into trouble with the police. And then he started…'

Her voice tailed off again, knowing this was something she couldn't just consign to the past. Because the counsellor had told her that addictions never really went away. They just sat there, brooding and waiting for someone to feed them. And wasn't she scared stiff that they were being fed right now—that someone was busy dealing cards across a light-washed table in the centre of a darkened room somewhere in the Outback?

'What did he start, Molly?' prompted Salvio softly.

'Gambling.' She stared down at her short, sensible fingernails before glancing up again to meet the ebony gleam of his eyes. 'It started off with fruit machines and then he met someone in the arcade who said a bright boy like him would probably be good at cards. That he could win enough money to buy the kind of things he'd never had. And that's when it all started.'

'It?'

Molly shrugged. 'I think Robbie was still missing Mum. I know he'd been frustrated and unhappy that we'd been so poor while she was alive. Whatever it was, he started playing poker and he was good at it. At first. He started winning money but he spent it just as quickly. More quickly than it was coming in. And the trouble with cards is that the more you want to win—the worse you become. They say that your opponent can smell desperation and Robbie was as desperate as hell. He started getting into debt. Big debt. But the banks didn't want to know and so he borrowed from some pay-day lenders and they...they...'

'They came after him?' Salvio finished grimly.

Molly nodded. 'I managed to use most of my savings to pay them off, though there's still an outstanding debt which never seems to go down because the interest rates they charge are astronomical. I wanted Robbie to have a fresh start. To get away from all the bad influences in his life. So he went to Australia to get the whole gambling bug out of his system and promised to attend Gamblers Anonymous. That's why I was working for the Averys. They were hardly ever in the house so I got to live there rent-free. Plus they paid me a lot of money to look after all their valuable artefacts. They said their insurance was lower if they had someone living permanently on the premises.'

'And then I came along,' he mused softly.

Molly's head jerked back as something in his tone alerted her to danger. 'I'm sorry?'

His bare shoulders gleamed like gold in the soft light from the lamp. 'A young attractive woman like you must have found it incredibly limiting to be shut away in that huge house in the middle of nowhere working for people who only appeared intermittently,' he observed. 'It must have seemed like a gilded prison.'

'I was grateful for a roof over my head and the chance to save,' she said.

'And the opportunity to meet a rich man who might make a useful lover?'

Molly's mouth fell open. 'Are you out of your mind?'

'I don't think so, *mia bedda*,' he contradicted silkily. 'I base my opinions on experience. It's one of the drawbacks of being wealthy and single—that women come at you from all angles. You must have acknowledged that I was attracted to you, and I can't help wondering whether you saw me as an easy way out of your dilemma. Were the bitter tears you cried real, or manufactured, I wonder? Did you intend those sobs to stir my conscience?'

Molly sat up in bed, her skin icy with goosebumps, despite the duvet which covered most of her naked body. 'You think I *pretended to cry*? That I deliberately got myself pregnant to get you to pay off my brother's debts? That I would cold-bloodedly use my baby as a bargaining tool?'

'No, I'm not saying that. But I do think that fate has played right into your hardworking little hands,' he said slowly. 'Don't you?'

Her voice was shaking as she shook her head. 'No. No, I don't.' Pushing the duvet away, she swung her legs over the side of the bed, acutely conscious of her wobbly bottom as she bent down and started pulling on her discarded clothes with fingers which were trembling, telling herself she would manage. Somehow. Because she had always managed before, hadn't she? Fully dressed now, Molly turned round, steeling herself not to react to his muscular olive body outlined so starkly against the snowy white bedding. 'There's nothing more to be said, is there?'

He gave a bitter laugh. 'Oh, I think there's plenty which needs to be said, but not tonight, not when emotions are running high. I need to think first before I come to any decision.'

Molly was tempted to tell him that maybe he should have done that before he had taken her to bed and then come out with a stream of unreasonable accusations, but what was the point in inflaming an already inflamed situation? And she couldn't really blame him for the sex, could she? Not when she had been complicit every step of the way. Not when she had desperately wanted him to touch her.

And the awful thing was that she still did.

Tilting her chin upwards and adopting the most dignified stance possible—which wasn't easy in the circumstances—she walked out of Salvio's bedroom without another word.

CHAPTER SEVEN

A COLD BLUE light filtered into the tiny bedroom, startling Molly from the bewildering landscape of unsettled sleep—one haunted by Salvio and the memory of his hard, thrusting body. Disorientated, she sat up in bed, wondering if she'd dreamt it all. Until the delicious aching at her breasts and soft throb between her legs reminded her that it had happened. Her heart began to race. It had actually happened. At the end of an evening's service she had informed her employer she was pregnant with his baby.

And had then been carried up the staircase and willingly had sex with him, despite all the things he'd accused her of.

Did he really believe it was his wealth which had attracted her to him, when she would have found him irresistible if he'd been covered in mud and sweat from working the fields?

Slowly, she got out of bed. She didn't know what Salvio wanted. All she knew was what *she* wanted. Her hand crept down to cover the soft flesh of her belly. She wanted this baby.

And nothing Salvio did or said was going to change her mind.

She showered and washed her hair—pulling on clean jeans and a jumper the colour of a winter sky before going downstairs, to be greeted by the aroma of coffee. In the kitchen she found Salvio pouring himself an inky cupful, and although he looked up as she walked in, his face registered no emotion. He merely gestured to the pot.

'Want some?'

She shook her head. 'No, thanks. I'll make myself some tea.' She was certain herbal tea was better for babies than super-strong coffee, but mainly she welcomed the opportunity of being able to busy herself with the kettle. Anything rather than having to confront the distracting vision of Salvio in faded jeans and a sweater as black as his hair. She could feel him watching her and she had to try very hard not to appear clumsy—no mean feat when that piercing gaze was trained on her like a bird of prey. But when she couldn't dunk her peppermint teabag a moment longer, she was forced to turn around and face him, glad he was now silhouetted against the window and his features were mostly in shadow.

'So,' he said, without preamble. 'We need to work out what we're going to do about the astonishing piece of news you dropped into my lap last night. Any ideas, Molly?'

Molly had thought about this a lot during those long hours when sleep had eluded her. *Be practical*, she urged herself. *Take the emotion out of it and think facts.*

She cleared her throat. 'Obviously finding a job is paramount,' she said cautiously. 'A live-in job, of course.'

'A live-in job,' he repeated slowly. 'And when the baby is born, what then?'

Molly hoped her shrug conveyed more confidence than she actually felt. 'Lots of people don't mind their staff having a baby around the place. Well, maybe not lots of people,' she amended when she heard his faintly incredulous snort and acknowledged that he might have a point. 'But houses which already have children tend to be more accommodating. Who knows? I might even switch my role from housekeeper to nanny.'

'And that's what you want, is it?'

Molly suppressed the frustration which had flared up inside her. Of course it wasn't. But she couldn't really tell him that none of this was what she *wanted*—not without betraying the child she carried. She hadn't planned to get pregnant, but she would make the best of it. Just as she hadn't planned for the father of her child to be a cold-hearted billionaire who right now felt so distant that he might as well have been on another planet, rather than standing on the other side of the kitchen. She wanted what most women wanted when they found themselves in this situation—a stable life and a man who adored them. 'Life is all about adaptation,' she said stolidly when, to her surprise, he nodded, walking away from the window and putting his coffee cup down on the table before pulling out a chair.

'I agree,' he said. 'Here. Sit down. We need to talk about this properly.'

She shook her head. 'I can't sit down.'

'Why not?'

'Because I still have to clear up the house, after the party.'

'Leave it.'

'I can't leave it, it's what you're paying me—'

'I said leave it, Molly,' he snapped. 'I can easily get people in to do that for me later. Just sit down, will you?'

Molly opened her mouth to refuse. To tell him that the walls felt as if they were closing in on her and his presence was making her jittery. But what else could she do? Flounce out into the snow, two days before Christmas Day—with nowhere to go and a child in her belly? Ignoring the chair he was holding out for her, she chose one at the opposite end of the table and sank down onto it, her mouth unsmiling as she looked at him questioningly.

'I've given a lot of thought to what's happened,' he said, without preamble.

Join the club. 'And did you come to any conclusions?'

Salvio's eyes narrowed as she stared at him suspiciously. She wasn't behaving as he had expected her to behave. Although what did he know? He'd never had to face something like this before and never with someone like her. After her departure last night, he'd thought she might try to creep back into his bed—maybe even whisper how sorry she was for flouncing out like that—before turning her lips to his for another hungry kiss. He was used to the inconsistency of women—and in truth he would have welcomed a reconnection with those amazing curves. Another bout of amazing sex might have given him a brief and welcome respite from his concerns about the future.

She hadn't done that, of course, and so he had braced himself for sulks or tears or reproachful looks when he bumped into her this morning. But no. Not that either. Sitting there in a soft sweater which matched her grey eyes, with her hair loose and shining around her shoulders, she looked the picture of health—despite the shadows beneath her eyes, which suggested her night had been as troubled as his.

And the crazy thing was that this morning he hadn't woken up feeling all the things he was expecting to feel. There had been residual shock, yes, but the thought of a baby hadn't filled him with horror. He might even have acknowledged the faint flicker of warmth in his heart as a tenuous glimmer of pleasure, if he hadn't been such a confirmed cynic.

'Every problem has a solution if you come at it from enough angles,' he said carefully. 'And I have a proposition to put to you.'

She creased her brow. 'You do?'

There was a pause. 'I don't want you finding a job as a housekeeper, or looking after someone else's children.'

'Why not?'

Salvio tensed, sensing the beginning of a negotiation. Was she testing out how much money he was prepared to give her? 'Isn't it obvious? Because you're pregnant with my baby.' His voice deepened. 'And although this is a child I never intended to have, I'm prepared to accept the consequences of my actions.'

'How…how cold-blooded you make it sound,' she breathed.

'Do you want me to candy-coat it for you, Molly?' he demanded. 'To tell you that this was what I always secretly dreamed would happen to me? Or would you prefer the truth?'

'I'm a realist, Salvio,' she answered. 'I've only ever wanted the truth.'

'Then here it is, in all its unvarnished glory. Tomorrow, I'm flying home to Naples for the holidays.'

'I know. Your assistant told me when she hired me.'

'I return every year,' he continued slowly. 'To two loving parents who wonder where they went so wrong with their only child.'

She blinked at him in confusion. 'I don't…understand.'

'Who wonder why their successful, handsome son who has achieved so much,' he continued, as if she hadn't spoken, 'has failed to bring home a woman who will one day provide them with the grandchildren they yearn for.' He gave a sudden bitter laugh. 'When, hey, what do you know? Suddenly I have found such a woman and already she is with child! What a gift it will be for them to meet you, Molly.'

She stared at him, confusion darkening her grey eyes. '*Meet* them? You're not suggesting—'

'Like I said last night—it's time to lose all that wide-eyed innocence. I think you know exactly what I'm suggesting,' he drawled. 'We buy you a big diamond ring and I take you home to Naples as my fiancée.'

'You mean...' She blinked. 'You mean you want to marry me?'

'Let's put it another way. I don't particularly want to marry anyone, the difference is that I'm *prepared* to marry you,' he amended.

'Because of the baby?'

'Because of the baby,' he agreed. 'But not just that. Most women are demanding and manipulative but, interestingly enough, you are none of those things. Not only are you extremely beddable—I find you exceptionally...*agreeable*.' His lips curved into a reflective smile. 'And at least you know your place.'

Molly stared at him, wanting to tell him to stop making her sound like the UK representative for the international society of doormats. Until she realised that once again Salvio was speaking the truth. She *did* know her place. She always had done. When you worked as a servant in other people's houses, that was what tended to happen.

'So what's in it for me?' she asked, thinking she ought to say *something*.

He looked at her in surprise. 'It isn't very difficult to work out. You get financial security and I get a ready-made family. I can pay off your brother's debt in one swoop, on the understanding that this is the only time I bankroll him. And if I were you, I would wipe the horror from your face, Molly. It really isn't a good look for a woman who's on the brink of getting engaged.' His voice dipped into one of silky admonishment. 'And it isn't as if you have a lot of choices, do you?'

Molly felt the sudden shiver of vulnerability rippling

down her spine. He didn't have to put it quite so brutally, did he? She swallowed. Or maybe he did. It was yet another cruel observation but it was true. She *didn't* have a lot of choices. She knew there was nothing romantic about having to struggle. She'd done all that making-the-best-of-a-bad-situation stuff—seeing how many meals you could get out of a bag of black-eyed beans and buying her clothes in thrift stores. She knew how hard poverty could be.

And this was her baby.

Her defenceless little *baby*.

She was aware of her hand touching her belly and aware of Salvio's gaze following the movement before he lifted his black eyes to hers. She searched their dark gleam in vain for some kind of emotion, and tried to ignore the painful stab in her heart when she met nothing but a cold, unblinking acceptance in their ebony depths. Of course he wasn't going to feel the same way as she did about their child. Why *wouldn't* he look sombre? Having his life inextricably linked to that of a humble little housekeeper was surely nothing for the Neapolitan billionaire to celebrate.

'Very well. Since—as you have already pointed out—I have very little alternative… I agree,' she said, and then, because subservience was as much a part of her life as breathing and because deep down she *was* grateful to him for his grudging generosity, she added a small smile. 'Thank you.'

Salvio felt his gut clench, knowing he didn't deserve her thanks. Or that shy look which made him want to cradle her in his arms. He knew he could have asked her to marry him in a more romantic way. He could have dropped onto one knee and told her he couldn't imagine life without her. But why get her used to an attitude he could never sustain and raise expectations which could never be met? The only way he could make this work was if he was straight with her, and that meant not making emotional promises he could never fulfil.

But he knew one sure way to please her—the universal way to every woman's heart. 'Go and get your stuff together, *nicuzza*,' he said softly. 'We're going shopping.'

Molly stepped out onto the icy Bond Street pavement feeling dazed but warm. Definitely warm. Who would have ever thought a coat could *be* so warm? Wonderingly she brushed her fingertips over the camel cashmere, which teamed so well with the knee-length boots and the matching brown leather gloves which were as soft as a second skin. She caught sight of her reflection in one of the huge windows of the upmarket department store and stared at it, startled—wondering if that glossy confection of a woman was really her.

'*Sì*, you look good,' Salvio murmured from beside her.

She looked up into his ruggedly handsome face. 'Do I?'

'Good enough to eat,' he affirmed, his black eyes glittering out an unspoken message and Molly could do nothing about the shiver which rippled down her spine and had nothing to do with the icy temperature.

After a slow drive through the snow to London, he

had brought her to one of the capital's most famous streets, studded with the kind of shops which were guarded by burly security men with inscrutable expressions. But the faces of the assistants inside were far more open and Molly knew she hadn't imagined the faint incredulity which greeted her appearance, as women fluttered around Salvio like wasps on a spill of jam.

He asked for—and got—a terrifyingly sleek stylist, who was assigned the daunting task of dressing her. Endless piles of clothing and lingerie were produced—some of which were instantly dismissed by an impatient wave of Salvio's hand and some of which were met with a slow smile of anticipation.

'It seems a silly amount of money to spend since whatever I buy isn't going to fit me for very long,' she hissed in a fierce undertone after nearly fainting when she caught sight of one of the price tags.

He seemed amused by her attempt to make economies. 'Then we'll just have to buy you some more, won't we? Don't worry about the cost, Molly. You will soon be the wife of a very wealthy man.'

It was hard to imagine, thought Molly as a featherlight chiffon dress floated down over her head, covering an embroidered bra whose matching panties were nothing more than a flimsy scrap of silk. As she appeared from behind the velvet curtain of the changing room to meet Salvio's assessing gaze, she began to wonder if he'd done this whole transformation thing before. And she wondered whether she should show a little pride and refuse all the gifts he was offering.

But then she thought about the reality. Salvio probably came from an extremely wealthy family who might not take kindly to someone from her kind of background. Wouldn't she feel even more out of place if she turned up looking like a poor relation in her cheap clothes and worn boots? Which was why she submitted to the purchase of sweaters and jeans, jackets and day dresses—and the most beautiful shoes she had ever seen. Gorgeous patent stilettos in three different colours, which somehow had the ability to add precious inches to her height and make her walk in a different and more feminine way.

And when they were all done and the glossy bags had been placed in the limousine which had been slowly tailing them, Salvio guided her past yet another security guard and into a jewellery shop where inside it was all light and dazzle. Locked glass cases contained the biggest diamonds Molly had ever seen—some the colour of straw, some which resembled pink champagne, and some even finer than Lady Avery's vast collection of family jewels.

'So what's your ideal ring? What did you used to dream about when you were a little girl?' asked Salvio softly, his fingers caressing the small of her back as an elegant saleswoman approached them. 'Whatever takes your fancy, it's yours.'

Did he have to put it quite like that? Molly wondered, moving away to avoid the distraction of his touch. The only thing she used to dream about when she was a little girl was making sure there was a hot meal on the table, and wondering if she'd managed to get all Mum's pills from the pharmacy. Yet Salvio was making her sound like someone whose gaze was bound to be riveted by the biggest and brightest ring in the shop.

She could feel her cheeks growing hot, because suddenly this felt like the charade it really was. As if they were going through all the motions of getting engaged, but with none of the joy or happiness which most couples would have experienced at such a time. And while Salvio's handsome face was undeniably sensual, his jet-dark eyes were as cold as any of the jewels on display. Molly lifted her gaze from the display cabinet as a quiet air of certainty ran through her. 'I don't want anything which looks like an engagement ring,' she said.

Hiding her surprise, the assistant produced a ring to just that specification—a stunning design of three thin platinum bands, each containing three asymmetrically placed diamonds which glittered and sparkled in the sharp December sunlight. 'The diamonds are supposed to resemble raindrops,' the young woman said gently.

Or tears, thought Molly suddenly. They looked exactly like tears.

From Bond Street they were whisked to Salvio's home in a fashionable area of London. Molly had heard of Clerkenwell but had never actually been there—just as she'd never been in such a gleaming, modern penthouse apartment before. She wandered from room to room. Everything was shiny and clean, but it was stark—as if nobody really lived there. It was as if some designer had been allowed to keep all décor to a minimum, but its sleek emptiness wasn't her main worry—which was that it was no place for a baby.

What was left of the day rushed past in a whirl of organisation but for once it wasn't Molly doing the organising, since Salvio seemed to have fleets of people at his disposal. People to organise cars and planes. To book hotels and arrange the last-minute purchase of gifts. They ate an early supper, which was delivered and served by staff from a nearby award-winning restaurant who even provided candles and a fragrant floral centrepiece.

'You don't have a chef, or a housekeeper?' Molly asked, as she sat down at the glass dining table and tried not to think about how dangerous a piece of furniture like this might be for a young child.

'I prefer to keep resident staff to a minimum. It optimises my privacy,' Salvio explained coolly, as two delicate soufflés were placed in front of them. 'I hope you're hungry?'

'Very,' she said, shaking out her napkin and trying not to dwell on what he'd just said about privacy—because he was about to have it shattered in the most spectacular way. 'Have you lived here for very long?' she questioned.

'I've had the apartment for about five years.'

'And you're here a lot?'

'No, not really. I have other homes all round the world. This is just my base whenever I'm in London.' He gazed at her thoughtfully. 'Why do you ask?'

She shrugged. 'It's very tidy.'

He laughed. 'I thought, given your occupation, that tidiness might meet with your approval.'

And oddly enough, that hurt. It was yet another reminder of just how far out of her comfort zone she was. A reminder of how he really saw her. She would never be his equal, she thought, as a powerful wave of fatigue washed over her.

'Actually, I'm pretty tired,' she said. 'It's a been a long day and the baby...'

The baby.

Salvio pushed away his wine glass. They hadn't mentioned it all afternoon but the word no longer hit him like a shock. He was slowly getting used to the idea that she was pregnant, even if he wasn't exactly jumping for joy about it. And Molly Miller was proving easier company than he had expected. Undemanding and optimistic. There was something about her quiet presence which made him feel almost *peaceful*. He stared at her washed-out face and felt an unexpected wave of remorse wash over him. Why hadn't he noticed how tired she might be?

'You need to go to bed,' he said resolutely, pushing back his chair.

He saw her throat constrict.

'Where...where am I sleeping?'

'We're supposed to be an engaged couple, Molly,' he said, almost gently. 'Where do you think you'll be sleeping?'

'I wasn't...sure.'

He'd assumed she would be sharing his bed, because why wouldn't he? But something about her pallor and trepidation made him reconsider—for his own sake as well as for hers. Wouldn't a night apart re-establish his habitual detachment—especially since it was obvious neither of them had slept well last night?

He rose to his feet. 'There's no need to sound so fearful, Molly,' he said. 'I'll show you the spare room. You'll have plenty of peace in there.'

He saw the sudden look of uncertainty which crossed her features and then she nodded her head, the way he'd seen her do before.

'That sounds like a good idea,' she said, with what sounded like obedience, and once again he was reminded of the fact that she was, essentially, a servant.

CHAPTER EIGHT

BATHED IN THE bright December sunshine which flooded
in through the giant windows of their Neapolitan hotel
suite, Molly turned to Salvio, who was just changing
out of the jeans and leather jacket he'd worn for the trip
over, into something a little more formal.

'We still haven't discussed—' Molly hesitated '—
what we're going to tell your parents.'

Pausing in the act of straightening his tie, Salvio
turned to look at his fiancée. She looked…incredible, he
thought. With her shiny hair scooped on top of her head
and her curvy shape encased in a dress the colour of
spring leaves, there was no trace of that shy and frumpy
housekeeper now. They'd just arrived in his home city—
his jet descending through the mountains surrounding the mighty Mount Vesuvius, with all its unleashed
power and terrible history. It was an iconic view which
took away the breath of the most experienced traveller
and he had found himself watching Molly for her reaction. But, oblivious to the beauty which surrounded
them, she had seemed lost in thought. Even when the
car had whisked them to this luxury hotel overlooking

the Castel dell'Ovo and a lavish suite which even *he* could not fault, she seemed barely to register the opulence of their penthouse accommodation.

He wondered if she'd noticed the sideways stares he'd been receiving from the moment they'd stepped off the plane. The double takes and the *'Is it him?'* looks which were as familiar to him as breathing, whenever he returned to his native town. Yet Molly had been impervious to them all.

'We tell them the truth,' he said eventually, giving some thought to her question. 'That you're pregnant and we're getting married as soon as possible.'

She winced a little. 'Do you think we need to be quite so…?'

His gaze bored into her. 'So what, Molly?'

She licked her lips and, mesmerised by the resulting gleam which emphasised their soft beauty, Salvio momentarily cursed himself for not admitting her to his bed last night. Had he really imagined such an action might make him more detached and rational, when he'd been obsessing about her all night long?

'Brutal,' she concluded, pursing her lips together as if it wasn't a word she particularly wanted to use.

'Brutal?'

She shrugged and began walking across the room, pausing only to peer into the elevated stone hot tub which stood at the far end of the enormous suite—an extravagant touch eclipsed only by the tall decorated Christmas tree which was framed in one of the tall windows.

Eventually she came to a halt and perched on an orange velvet chair to look at him. 'You told me you're known as someone who is a commitment-phobe. Someone who doesn't want to get married,' she said.

Salvio gave his tie a final tug. That wasn't the whole story, but why burden her with stuff she didn't need to know? 'What of it?'

'So this sudden marriage is going to come as a bolt out of the blue to your parents, isn't it?'

'And?' he questioned coolly. 'Your point is?'

She studied her left hand warily, as if she couldn't quite get used to the diamond knuckle-duster she was wearing. 'I'd prefer not to say anything about my pregnancy—at least, not yet. It's still very early days. I just thought it might be nice if we could at least *allow* them to think it might be about more than just the unwanted fallout of a…a…'

Her words tailed away and Salvio wondered if, in her innocence, she simply didn't know all the expressions— some of them crude—she could have used to describe what had happened between them that first night. 'A hook-up?' he put in helpfully, before adopting a more caustic tone. 'Are you saying you want to pretend to my parents that this is some great kind of love affair?'

'Of course not.' She flushed before lifting a reproachful grey gaze to his. 'I don't think you're that good an actor, are you, Salvio?'

He inclined his head as if to concede the point. 'Or that good a liar?'

'That's another way of putting it, I suppose.'

He acknowledged her crestfallen expression. 'I don't want to raise your hopes, Molly—or theirs. It's just who I am. And the bottom line is I just don't do emotion. That's all.'

'That's…that's quite a lot,' she observed. 'Do you think…?' She seemed to choose her words very carefully. 'Do you think you were born that way?'

'I think circumstances made me that way,' he said flatly.

'What kind of circumstances?'

Salvio frowned. This was deeper than he wanted to go because he was a man with a natural aversion to the in-depth character analysis which was currently in vogue. But what had he imagined would happen—that he could take an innocent young girl as his wife and present to her the same impenetrable exterior which had made scores of women despair at his coldness in the past? He walked over to the drinks cabinet, ignoring the expensive bottles of wine on display, pouring instead two crystal glasses of mineral water before walking across the room to hand her one. 'You don't know much about me, do you, Molly?'

She shook her head as she sipped her drink. 'Practically nothing. How would I? We haven't exactly sat down and had long conversations since we met, have we?'

He almost smiled. 'You weren't tempted to go and look me up online?'

Molly didn't answer immediately as she met the scrutiny of his piercing black gaze. Of course she'd been *tempted*. Someone like Salvio was high profile enough to have left a significant footprint on the Internet, which she could have accessed at the touch of a computer key, and naturally she was curious about him. But she'd felt as if their lives were unequal enough already. The billionaire tycoon and the humble housekeeper. If she discovered stuff about him, would she then have to feign ignorance in the unlikely event that he wanted to confide in her? If she heard anything about him, she wanted to hear it *from* him—not through the judgemental prism of someone else's point of view.

'I didn't want to seem as if I was spying on you.'

'Very commendable.'

'But it would be useful to know,' she continued doggedly. 'Otherwise your parents might think we're nothing but strangers.'

'And is that what concerns you, Molly?' His black gaze continued to bore into her. 'What other people think?'

Molly bit back her instinctive response to his disdainful question. If she'd been bothered about things like that then she would never have got through a childhood like hers. From an early age she'd learnt there were more important things to worry about than whether you had holes in your shoes or your coat needed darning. She'd learnt that good health—the one thing money couldn't buy—was the only thing worth having. 'I believe it's best to be respectful of other people's feelings and that your parents might be confused and possibly upset if they realise we don't really know one another. But the main reason I need to know about you is because I'm having your baby.' She saw the increased darkening of his eyes—as if she had reminded him of something he would rather forget. But he couldn't forget it, and neither could she. 'I don't know anything about your childhood,' she finished simply. 'Nothing at all.'

He appeared to consider her words before expelling a slow breath of air. 'Very well. First and foremost you must understand that I am a Neapolitan to the very core of my being.' His voice became fierce, and proud. 'And that I have a great passion for this beautiful city of mine.'

So why don't you live here? Molly thought suddenly. *Why do you only ever visit at Christmas?* But she said nothing, just absorbed his words the way she'd absorbed other people's words all her working life.

'I grew up in the Rione Sanità, a very beautiful area, which is rich with history.' There was a pause. 'But it is also one of the poorest places in the city.'

'You?' she echoed disbelievingly, unable to hold back her shocked reaction. 'Poor?'

He smiled cynically as he flicked a disparaging finger towards his sleek suit jacket. 'You think I was born wearing fine clothes like these, Molly? Or that my belly never knew hunger?'

Yes, that was exactly what she'd thought, mainly because Salvio De Gennaro wore his wealth supremely well. He acted as if he'd never known anything other than handmade shoes and silk shirts, and people to drive his cars and planes for him. 'You've come a long way,' she said slowly. 'What happened?'

'What happened was that I had a talent,' he told her simply. 'And that talent was football. The moment my foot touched a ball, I felt as if I had found what I was born to do. I used to play every moment I could. There was nowhere suitable close to my home so I found a derelict yard to use. I marked a spot on the wall and I used to hit that same spot over and over again. Word got out and people used to come and watch me. They used to challenge me to see how long I could keep the ball in the air and sometimes I used to take their bets because many of them thought they could put a ball past me. But I could always score, even if there were two people against me in goal. And then one day the scouts turned up and overnight my whole life changed.'

'What happened?' she prompted as his words faded away.

Salvio stared out of the window, drinking in the sapphire beauty of the bay. Would it sound boastful to tell her he'd been called the greatest footballer of his generation? Or that the superstar lifestyle had arrived far more quickly than expected? 'I trained every hour that God sent, determined to fulfil all that early promise, and very quickly I was signed by one of the country's most prestigious clubs where I scored a record number of goals. I knew success, and fame, and for a while it was a crazy life. Everywhere I went, people would stop me and want to talk about the game and I don't remember the last time I was made to pay for a pizza.'

'But…something went wrong?' she observed. 'I mean, badly wrong?'

He narrowed his eyes. Was her blithe comment about knowing nothing of his past just another of the lies which slipped so easily from women's lips? 'What makes you ask that?'

She hesitated. 'I'm not sure. Maybe the note of finality in your voice. The look of…'

'Of what, Molly?' he demanded. 'And please don't just give me the polite answer you think I ought to hear.'

She met his eyes, surprised at his perception because she had been about to do exactly that. 'Bitterness, I guess,' she said. 'Or maybe disappointment.'

He wanted to deny her accusations—if that was what they were—but he couldn't. And suddenly he found himself resenting her astuteness and that gentle look of understanding which had softened her face. He'd agreed to tell her the basics—not for her to start peeling back the layers so that she could get a closer look at his damned soul. So why did he continue with his story, as if now he'd lifted the lid on it, he found it impossible to put it back?

'I'll tell you what happened,' he said roughly, becoming aware of the heavy beat of his pulse at his temple. 'My life was a fairy tale. It wasn't just the success, or the money—and the chance to do good stuff with all that money—it was the fact that I loved playing football. It was the only thing I ever wanted to do. And then one day I was brought down by an ugly tackle and tore my cruciate ligament. Badly.' His mouth twisted. 'And that was the end of the fairy tale. I never played again.'

Silence followed his stark statement and then she spoke in that soft voice. 'Oh, Salvio, that must have—'

'Please. Spare me the platitudes,' he ground out, hardening his heart to the distress which had made her eyes grow as dark as storm clouds—because he didn't need her sympathy. He didn't need anything from anyone. He'd learnt what a mistake *that* could be. 'The injury I could have learned to live with. After all, every professional sportsman or woman has to accept that one day their career will end—even if that happens sooner than they wanted. What made it worse was the discovery that my manager had been systematically working his way through my fortune before leaving town.' There was a pause. 'Suddenly, everything I thought I had was gone. No job. No money. My fall from grace was...spectacular.'

'So what did you do?' she whispered.

Salvio shrugged. He had raged for several days and thought seriously about going after his manager and pinning him to the nearest wall until he had agreed to pay the money back. Until he'd realised that revenge was time-consuming and ultimately damaging. That he didn't want to spend his life in pursuit of his broken dreams and to dwell on the glories of his past, like some sad loser. And then had come the final blow. The final, bitter straw which had made him feel a despair he had vowed never to repeat. Resolutely, he pushed the memory away. 'I sold all my cars and the fancy apartment I'd bought in Rome,' he said. 'And gave most of the proceeds to my parents. Then I took what was left and bought a plane ticket to the US.'

'That's a long way from Naples,' she observed slowly. 'Why there?'

'Because it was a big enough place to lose myself in and to start again. I didn't want to be defined by a career which had been cut short and I was young and strong and prepared to work hard.' He'd worked to the exclusion of pretty much everything else in order to get the break he'd needed and, when it had come, he had grabbed at it with both hands. Perceptive enough to recognise that people were starting to move downtown and that run-down areas of the city were potential goldmines, he had started buying up derelict properties and then renovating them. On his Christmas trip back to Naples that first year, he had brought his mother a fancy coat from Bloomingdales. These days he could give her the entire store—and frequently tried—but no amount of material success could ever fill the emptiness in his heart.

He stared at Molly, amazed at how much he had told her. More than he'd ever admitted to anyone, even to Lauren. His gaze raked over her and he thought how different she looked from the first time he'd seen her, eating cake in the kitchen, her ripe body looking as if it was about to burst out of her uniform. Her green dress exuded all the class and sophistication which was an inevitable by-product of wearing designer clothes which had been chosen by an expert. Yet it was the softness of her eyes he noticed most—and the dewy perfection of her creamy skin. She still radiated the same wholesome sex appeal which had drawn him to her in the first place and he wondered why he was wasting time talking like this. What would he be doing with any other woman he was sharing a bedroom with—let alone the one who was wearing his ring?

He felt the erratic hammer of his pulse as he glanced down at his watch. 'I don't want to talk about the past any more.'

'Okay,' she said cautiously. 'Then we won't.'

'And we don't have to be at my folks' place for a while,' he said unevenly. 'Do you want a tour of the city?'

'Is that what you'd like to do?' she questioned, with the compliance which was such an essential part of her nature.

'No. That's the last thing I want to do right now. I can think of a much better way to pass the next couple of hours. Can't you?'

Molly thoughts were teeming as she met his dark gaze. So much of what he'd told her hadn't been what she was expecting, yet now she knew the facts they didn't really come as a surprise. The first time she'd seen him she'd noticed the power-packed body of a natural sportsman and the faint limp which he had all but managed to disguise. The single physical flaw in a man who was looking at her now with a question in his eyes.

She was still a relative novice at sex, but already she could recognise the desire which was making his face grow tense. She knew what he wanted. What *she* wanted too. Because she hadn't really enjoyed their night apart, last night. And even though the bed had been amazingly comfortable, she kept thinking about Salvio lying next door. Wondering why he hadn't tried a bit harder to sleep with her. Wondering if he'd gone off her and didn't fancy her any more. And—desire aside—wasn't the truth that she felt *safe* in his arms—even if that feeling passed as quickly as a summer storm? She stared into his molten black eyes and, for once, said exactly what was in her heart.

'Yes, I can think of a few things I'd like to do,' she agreed shyly. 'As long as they involve us being horizontal.'

She was unprepared for the curve of his smile as he walked towards her or for the way he lifted her hand to his, kissing each finger in turn before leading her over to the huge bed which overlooked the famous bay. She was eager to feel his naked skin against hers but this time there was no urgency as he began to undress her. This time his fingers were leisurely as they unclipped her bra and her swollen breasts came spilling out, his moan appreciative as he caught one taut nipple between his teeth. Molly squirmed beneath the teasing flick of his tongue but her frustration didn't seem to have any effect on his lazy pace. And didn't her heart pound with joy when he bent his head to drop a series of tender kisses on her belly as if he was silently acknowledging the tiny life which grew inside her?

'S-Salvio?' she stumbled tentatively as she felt the brush of his lips against her navel.

'It's going to be okay,' he said, his voice growing husky.

What was he talking about—their future, or meeting his parents? Or both?

But suddenly Molly was beyond caring as his movements became more urgent.

She cried out when he entered her and clung to him fiercely as he made each hard thrust. It felt so deep— he seemed to be filling her body completely, as if he couldn't get enough of her. And it felt different, more *intimate* than it had ever been before. Was that because he'd trusted her enough to tell her things she suspected he usually kept locked away—or was this sudden closeness all in her imagination? But the pleasure she was experiencing wasn't imaginary. Her senses felt exquisitely raw and heightened so that when her orgasm came, Molly felt as if rocked by a giant and powerful wave— her satisfaction only intensified by the moan he gave as he spilled his seed inside her. Afterwards she felt as if she were floating on a cloud. His breath was warm and comforting against her neck and she missed his presence when he withdrew from her and rolled to the other side of the mattress.

'That was just…perfect,' she said dreamily, the words out of her mouth before she could prevent them.

But Salvio didn't answer and, although the sound of his breathing was strong and steady, Molly wasn't sure whether or not he was asleep. Was he just lying there ignoring her? she wondered, with a sudden streak of paranoia. Lying there and *pretending*?

But she decided it was pointless to get freaked out by his sudden detachment, even if she'd had the energy to do so. Nestling herself down into the big mound of feathery pillows, Molly gave a little sigh and fell asleep.

CHAPTER NINE

PERHAPS INEVITABLY, THEY slept for longer than they'd intended and Molly woke with a start, looking round in mild confusion as she tried to get her bearings. Maybe they'd been catching up on too many restless nights, or maybe the amazing sex they'd just enjoyed had taken it out of them. Either way, the Neapolitan sky outside their hotel suite was ebony-dark and sprinkled with stars and when she glanced at her watch, she saw to her horror that it was almost seven—and they were due at Salvio's parents for Christmas Eve dinner in just over an hour.

'Wake up,' she urged, giving her sleeping fiancé's shoulder a rough shake. 'Or we're going to be late!'

Hurrying into the bathroom, she had the fastest shower on record before addressing the thorny issue of what to wear when meeting Salvio's parents for the first time. She still wasn't used to having quite so many clothes at her disposal and was more than a little dazzled by the choice. After much consideration, she opted for a soft knee-length skirt worn with a winter-white sweater and long black boots. Taking a deep breath, she did a little pirouette.

'Do you think your mother will approve of what I'm wearing?' she asked anxiously.

Salvio's black gaze roved over her in leisurely appraisal, before he gave a nod of approval. 'Most certainly,' he affirmed. 'You look demure and decent.'

Molly's fixed smile didn't waver as they stepped into the penthouse elevator, but really...*demure* and *decent* didn't exactly set the world on fire, did they?

They reached the lobby and as the doorman sprang forward to welcome them, Molly became aware of the buzz of interest their appearance was creating. Or rather, Salvio's appearance. She could see older men staring at him wistfully while women of all ages seemed intent on devouring him with hungry eyes. Yet despite the glamour of the female guests who were milling around the lobby, Molly felt a sudden shy pride as he took her arm and began guiding her towards the waiting car. Because *she* was the one he'd just been making love to, wasn't she? And *she* was the one who was carrying his child.

The luxury car was soon swallowed up in heavy traffic and before long they drew up outside an elegant house not too far from their hotel. Molly's nerves—which had been growing during the journey—were quickly dissolved when they were met by a tiny middle-aged woman dressed in Christmas red, her eyes dark and smiling as she opened the door to them. She hugged Molly fiercely before drawing back to look at her properly.

'At last! I have a daughter!' she exclaimed, in fluent though heavily accented English, before turning to her son and rising up on tiptoe to kiss him on each cheek, a faint note of reproof in her voice. 'And what I would like to know is why you are staying in a hotel tonight instead of here at home with your parents, Salvatore De Gennaro?'

'Because you would have insisted on us having separate rooms and this is the twenty-first century, in case you hadn't noticed,' answered her son drily. 'But don't worry, Mamma. We will be back again tomorrow.'

Slightly mollified, Rosa De Gennaro ushered them towards a beautiful high-ceilinged sitting room, where her husband was waiting and Molly stepped forward to greet him. Tall and silver-haired, Paolo De Gennaro had handsomely-rugged features which echoed those of his son and Molly got a poignant glimpse of what Salvio might look like when he was sixty. *Will I still know him when he's sixty?* she wondered, unprepared for the dark fear which shafted through her and the sudden shifting sense of uncertainty. But she shelved the useless thought and concentrated on getting to know the older couple whose joy at their son's engagement was evident. As Rosa examined her glittering ring with murmurs of delight, Molly felt a flash of guilt. What if they knew the truth? That the only reason she was here on Christmas Eve, presenting this false front of togetherness with their son, was because one reckless night had ended up with an unplanned baby.

But guilt was a futile emotion and she tried to make the best of things, the way she always did. The house seemed full of light and festivity—with the incomparable air of expectation which always defined the night before Christmas, no matter how much you tried to pretend it didn't. A beautiful tree, laden with gifts, was glittering in one of the windows and she could detect delicious smells of cooking from elsewhere in the house.

It was a long time since she'd been at the centre of a family and Molly found herself wondering what Robbie was doing tonight. She'd tried to ring him earlier that day but he hadn't picked up. *Please don't let him be gambling*, she prayed silently. *Let him have realised that there's more to life than debt and uncertainty and chasing impossible dreams.* Staring down at the nativity set which stood on a small table next to the tree, she focussed on the helpless infant in the tiny crib and tried to imagine what her own baby would look like. Would he or she resemble Salvio, with those dark stern features and a mouth which rarely smiled, but which when it did was like no other smile she'd ever seen?

She remembered the way he'd kissed her belly just before they'd made love and felt a stir of hope in her heart. He'd certainly never done *that* before—and surely that response hadn't been faked? Because the fleeting tenderness she thought she'd detected had meant just as much as the sexual excitement which had followed. And wasn't tenderness a good place to start building their relationship?

Refusing champagne and sipping from a glass of fruit juice, Molly was laughing as she examined a photo of a fourteen-year-old Salvio holding aloft a shining silver trophy, when she felt a brief pain, low in her belly. Did she flinch? Was that why Salvio's mother guided her towards a high-backed brocade chair and touched her gently on her shoulder?

'*Per piacere.* Sit down, Molly. You must be tired after your travels—but soon we will eat. You are hungry, I hope?'

Obediently, Molly took the chair she'd been offered, wondering why people were always telling her to sit down. Did she look permanently tired? Probably. Actually, she *was* a bit tired. She thought about the reason for her fatigue and her heart gave a little skip as she smiled at Salvio's mother.

'Very hungry,' she said.

'Here in Southern Italy we are proud of our culinary traditions,' Rosa continued before directing a smile at her son. 'For they represent the important times that families spend together.'

Soon they were tucking into a feast of unbelievable proportions. Molly had never *seen* a meal so big, as dish followed dish. There was spaghetti with clams and then fried shellfish, before an eel-like fish was placed in the centre of the elegant dining table with something of a flourish.

'*Capitone!*' announced Rosa. 'You know this fish, Molly? No? It is a Neapolitan tradition to eat it on Christmas Eve. In the old days, my mother used to buy it from the market while it was still alive, and then keep it in the bath until it was time to cook it. Do you remember the year it escaped, Salvio—and hid under your bed? And you were the only one brave enough to catch it?'

As his parents laughed Molly sneaked a glance at Salvio and tried to imagine the billionaire tycoon as a little boy, capturing an elusive fish which had slithered underneath a bed. Just as she tried to imagine him cradling an infant in those powerful arms, but that was too big a stretch of the imagination. At times he was so cool and distant—it was only in bed that he seemed to let his guard down and show any real feeling. She stared at the small piece of *capitone* left on her plate, wondering how it was going to work when she had his baby. She'd already established that his London penthouse wasn't particularly child-friendly—but where else would they live? He'd mentioned other houses in different countries but none of them had sounded like home, with the possible exception of his Cotswolds manor house.

They finished the meal with hard little biscuits called *rococo* and afterwards Molly insisted on helping her hostess clear the table. Efficiently, she dealt with the left-over food and dishes in a way which was second nature to her, washing the crystal glasses by hand and carefully placing them on the draining board to dry, while asking her hostess questions about life in Naples. She was just taking off the apron she'd borrowed when she noticed Rosa standing in the doorway of the kitchen watching her, a soft smile on her face.

'Thank you, Molly.'

'It was my pleasure, Signora De Gennaro. Thank you for a delicious meal. You have a wonderful home and you've been very welcoming.'

'Prego.' Rosa gave a small nod of satisfaction. 'I have been waiting many years for a daughter-in-law and I think you will be very good for my son.'

Molly's heart pounded as she hung the apron on a

hook beside the door, hoping Rosa didn't want to hear the romantic story of how she and her son had first met. Because there wasn't one. She suspected the truth would shock this kindly woman but Molly couldn't bear to tell her any lies. *So concentrate on the things you* can *say*, she told herself fiercely. *On all the things you wish would happen.*

'Oh, I hope I will be,' she said, her voice a little unsteady as she realised she meant every word. 'I want to be the best wife I can.'

Rosa nodded, her dark eyes intense and watchful. 'You are not like his other girlfriends,' she said slowly.

Was that a good thing or a bad thing? Molly wondered. 'Aren't I?'

'Not at all.' Rosa hesitated. 'Though he only ever brought one other to meet us.'

Molly stilled, telling herself it would be foolish to ask any more questions. But she hadn't factored in curiosity—and curiosity was a dangerous thing. Wasn't it the key which turned the lock in an invisible door—exposing you to things you might be better not knowing? And the crazy thing was even though she *knew* that, it didn't stop her from prying. 'Oh?' she questioned. Just one little word but that was all it took.

'She was no good for him,' said Rosa darkly, after a brief pause. '*Sì*, she was very beautiful but she cared only for his fame. She would never have helped with the dishes like this. She wanted to spend her Christmases in New York, or Monaco.' She touched her fingertips to the small golden cross at her neck. 'I give thanks that he never married her.'

Married her? Molly's heart constricted. Had Salvio been engaged to someone else? The man who had told her he didn't 'do' emotion? The nebulous twist of pain in her stomach which she'd felt earlier now returned with all the ferocity of a hot spear, which Molly bore behind the sunniest smile in her repertoire. But she was relieved when Salvio phoned his driver to take them back to the hotel, and leaned back weakly against the car seat, closing her eyes and willing the pain to leave her.

'Are you okay?' questioned Salvio beside her.

No, I'm not okay. I discovered tonight that you were going to marry someone else and you didn't tell me. That even though I'm carrying your baby you don't trust me enough to confide in me.

But she couldn't face a scene in the car, so she stuck to the positive. 'I'm fine!' she said brightly, still with that rictus smile in place. 'Your parents are lovely,' she added in a rush.

'Yes,' he said, and smiled. 'They liked you.'

But Molly thought he seemed lost in thought as he stared out at the festive lights of his city. Was he thinking about his other fiancée and comparing the two women? She found herself wondering why they had broken up and wondered if she would summon up the courage to ask him.

But the cramps in her stomach were getting worse. Cramps which felt horribly familiar, but which she tried to dismiss as stress. The stress of meeting his parents for the first time, or maybe the stress of discovering that she wasn't the only woman he'd asked to marry. She found herself breathing a sigh of relief when they arrived back in their penthouse suite and she unbuttoned her coat.

'Would you mind if I checked on my emails?' Salvio said as he removed the coat from her shoulders. 'I just want to see if something has come in from Los Angeles, before everything shuts down for the holidays.'

'No, of course I don't mind,' she said weakly, aware that he was already disappearing towards his computer.

She slipped into the bathroom and locked the door behind her, when she felt a warm rush between her legs and the sudden unexpected sight of blood made Molly freeze. She began to tremble.

It couldn't be.

Couldn't be.

But it was. Of course it was. On a deeper level she'd known all evening that this was about to happen, but the reality was harsher than she ever could have imagined. Her fingers clutched the cold rim of the bathtub as her vision shifted in and out of focus. She found herself wishing she were alone so that she could have given into the inexplicable tears which were welling up in her eyes. But she wasn't alone. She dashed the tears away with the tips of her fingers and tried to compose herself. Out in that fancy hotel room on the night before Christmas was her fiancé…except that the reason he'd slid these diamonds on her finger no longer existed. He would be free now, she thought—as a silent scream of protest welled up inside her.

She found her wash-bag, praying she might find what she needed—but there was no gratitude in her heart when she did, only the dull certainty of what she needed to say to Salvio. But she was loath to go out and face him. To utter the words he would probably be relieved to hear. She didn't think she could face his joy—not when she was experiencing such strange and bitter heartache.

Straightening up, she stared into the mirror, registering the pallor of her face, knowing that she couldn't tell him now. Not tonight. Not when the bells of Naples were peeling out their triumphant Christmas chorus about the impending birth of a baby.

CHAPTER TEN

'SO WHEN…?' THERE was a pause. 'When exactly were you going to tell me, *bedda mia*?'

The words left Salvio's lips like icy bullets but he knew immediately that his aim had been accurate. He could tell by the way Molly froze as she came out of the bathroom, the white towelling robe swathing her curvy body like a soft suit of armour.

'Tell you what?' she questioned.

Maybe if she'd come straight out and admitted it, he might have gone more easily on her but instead he felt the slow seep of anger in his veins as her guileless expression indicated nothing but a lie. A damned lie. His mouth hardened. 'That you aren't pregnant.'

She didn't deny it. She just stood in front of him, the colour leeching from her face so that her milky skin looked almost transparent. 'How did you…?' He saw the sudden flash of fear in her eyes. 'How did you know?'

Her confirmation only stoked the darkness which was building inside him. 'You think I am devoid of all my senses?' he demanded. 'That I wouldn't wonder why you turned away from me last night, then spent hours clinging to the other side of the mattress...pretending to be *asleep*?' he finished with contempt.

'So it's because we didn't have sex,' she summarised dully.

'No, not just because of that, nor even because of the way you disappeared into the bathroom when we got back from my parents' house and refused to look me in the eye,' he iced back. 'I'm not stupid, Molly. Don't you realise that a man can tell when a woman is menstruating? That she looks different. Smells different.'

'How could I ever be expected to match your encyclopaedic knowledge of women?' she questioned bitterly. 'When you're the first man I've ever slept with.'

Salvio felt the pounding of a pulse at his temple. Was she using her innocence as a shield with which to defend herself? To deflect him from a far more disturbing possibility, but one he couldn't seem to shake off no matter how hard he tried. 'Or maybe you were never even pregnant in the first place,' he accused silkily.

She reacted by swaying and sinking down onto a nearby sofa, as if his accusation had taken away her ability to stand. 'You think *that*?' she breathed, her fingers spreading out over her throat as if she was in danger of choking.

'Why shouldn't I think that?' he demanded. 'I've never actually seen any proof, have I? Is that why you didn't want to tell my parents about the baby—not because it was "too early" but because there *was* no baby?'

'You really believe—' she shook her damp hair in disbelief '—that I would lie to you about something as important as that?'

'How should I know what you'd do if you were desperate enough? We both know you were having trouble paying off your brother's debt and that marriage to me would mean the debt would be wiped out overnight.' His gaze bored into her. 'And I was careful that night, Molly. You know I was.'

She was still staring at him as if he were the devil incarnate. 'You're saying that I…made it up? That the whole pregnancy was nothing but an *invention*?'

'Why not? It's not unheard of.' He shrugged. 'It happens less often these days but I understand in the past it was quite a common device, used by women keen to get a wedding ring on their finger.' His mouth hardened. 'Usually involving a wealthy man.'

Her body tensed and Salvio saw the change in her. Saw the moment when her habitual compliance became rebellion. When outrage filled her soft features with an unfamiliar rage which she was directing solely at him. Her eyes flashing pewter sparks, she sprang to her feet, damp hair flying around her shoulders.

'I *was* pregnant,' she flared, her hands gesturing wildly through the empty air. 'One hundred per cent pregnant. I did two tests, one after the other—and if you don't believe me, then that's your problem! And yes, I was waiting until this morning to tell you, because last night I just couldn't face having the kind of discussion we're having now. So if keeping the news to myself for less than twelve hours is harbouring some dark secret, then yes—I'm guilty of that. But I'm not the only one with secrets, am I, Salvio?'

He heard the allegation in her voice as he met her

furious gaze full on and braced himself for what was coming next.

'When were you going to let me know you'd been engaged before?' she continued, her voice still shaking with rage. 'Or weren't you going to bother?'

His eyes narrowed. 'My mother told you?'

'Of course your mother told me—how else would I know?'

'What did she say?'

'Enough.' Her voice wobbled. 'I know the woman you were going to marry was rich and I'm not. I know she was beautiful and I'm not.'

Something about the weariness in her tone made Salvio feel a sharp pang of guilt. He stared at her shadowed eyes. At the milky skin now tinged with the dull flush of fury. At the still-drying shiny hair and the voluptuous curves which had lured him like a siren's call into her arms. And he felt an unexpected wave of contrition wash over him.

'You *are* beautiful,' he stressed.

'Please. Don't,' she said, holding up her hand to silence him. 'Don't make things even worse by telling me lies!'

Her dignified response surprised him. Had he been expecting gratitude for his throwaway compliment about her looks? Was he, in his own way, as guilty as Lady Avery had been of underestimating her? Of treating her like an object, rather than a person—as someone born to serve rather than to participate? Did he think he could behave exactly as he liked towards her and she would just take it?

'You *are* beautiful,' he affirmed, as repentance flowed through him. 'And yes, I was engaged before. I didn't tell you because...'

'Because it's too painful for you to remember, I suppose?'

The pulse at Salvio's temple now flickered. In a way, yes, very painful—though not in the way he suspected she meant. It was more about the betrayal he'd suffered than anything else because, like all Neapolitans, he had an instinctive loathing of treachery. It had come as a shock to realise that Lauren hadn't loved him—only what he represented. He gave a bitter smile. Perhaps he should have had a little more empathy for Molly since he too had been treated like an object in his time. 'It happened a long time ago,' he said slowly. 'And there seemed no reason to rake it up.'

She looked at him in exasperation. 'Don't you know anything about women? On second thought, don't answer that since we've already proved beyond any reasonable doubt that what you don't know about women probably isn't worth knowing. Except maybe you don't know just how far you can push them before they finally snap.' She tugged the towelling belt of her white robe a little tighter. 'Who was she, Salvio?'

Salvio scowled. Did he really have to tell her? Rake up the bitterness all over again? He expelled air from his flared nostrils, recognising from the unusually fierce expression on Molly's face that he had to tell her. 'Her name was Lauren Meyer,' he said reluctantly. 'I met her at an official function on a pre-season tour of America and brought her back here with me to Naples.'

'And she was blonde, I suppose?'

'Yes, she was blonde,' he said, ignoring her sarcastic tone. 'What else do you want to know, Molly? That she was an heiress and that she loved fame and fortune, in that order?'

'Did she?'

'She did. She met me when I had everything.' He gave a short laugh. 'And dumped me the moment I lost it all.'

'So, what…happened?' she said, into the silence which followed.

Salvio's lips tightened, because Lauren had been the catalyst. The reason he had kissed goodbye to emotion and battened up his heart. During his career there had been plenty of women who had lusted after his body and his bank account—but he'd made the mistake of thinking that Lauren was different.

His gaze flicked over to the dark sweep of the bay before returning to the grey watchfulness in Molly's eyes and suddenly he was finding it easy to talk about something he never talked about. 'After the accident, she came to visit me. Every day she sat by my bedside, always in a different outfit, looking picture-perfect. Always ready to smile and pose for the photographers who were camped outside the hospital. She was there when the physiotherapists worked on my leg and she was there when the doctor told me I'd never play professional football again. I'll never forget the look on her face.' His laugh was harsh. 'When I was discharged, she didn't come to meet me, but I thought I knew the reason why. I went home expecting a surprise party because she loved parties, and that's when I discovered she'd flown back to the States and was seeing some all-American boy her parents wanted her to marry all along. And that was that. I never saw her again.'

There was a pause while she seemed to take it all in.

'Oh, Salvio, that's awful,' she said. 'It must have felt like a kick in the teeth when you'd lost everything else.'

'I didn't tell you because I wanted your pity, Molly. I told you because you wanted to know. So now you do.'

'And, did you...did you love her?'

He felt a twist of anger. Why did women always do this? Why did they reduce everything down to those three little words and place so much store by them? He knew what she wanted him to say and that he was going to have to disappoint her. Because he couldn't rewrite the past, could he? He was damned if he was going to tell her something just because it was what he suspected she wanted to hear. And how could he possibly dismiss lies as contemptible if he started using them himself? 'Yes, I loved her,' he said, at last.

Molly hid her pain behind the kind of look she might have presented to Lady Avery if she'd just been asked to produce an extra batch of scones before teatime, and not for the first time she was grateful for all the training she'd had as a servant. Grateful for the mask-like calm she was able to project while she tried to come to terms with her new situation. Because in less than twelve hours she'd lost everything, too. Not just her baby but her hopes for the future. Hope of being a good wife and mother. Hope that a baby might help Salvio loosen up and become more human. And now it was all gone—whipped away like a rug being pulled from beneath her feet. There was no illusion left for her to cling to. No rosy dreams. Just a man who had once loved another woman and didn't love her. A man who had accused her of lying about her baby.

A baby which was now no more.

She wanted to bury her face in her hands and sob out her heartbreak but somehow she resisted the compelling urge. Instead she chose her words as carefully as a resigning politician. 'I don't want to upset your parents but obviously I can't face going for lunch today. I mean, there's no point now, is there? I don't think I'm capable of pretending everything's the same as it was—especially on Christmas Day. I think your mother might see right through me and there's no way I want to deceive her. So maybe it's best if I just disappear and leave you to say whatever you think is best.' She swallowed. 'Perhaps you could arrange for your plane to take me back to England as soon as possible?'

Salvio stared at her, unprepared for the powerful feeling which arrowed through his gut. Was it *disappointment*? Yet that seemed much too bland a description. Disappointment was what you felt if there was no snow on the slopes during a skiing holiday, or if it rained on your Mediterranean break.

He furrowed his brow. After Lauren he'd never wanted marriage. He'd never wanted a baby either but, having been presented with a *fait accompli*, had done what he considered to be the right thing by Molly. And of *course* it had affected him, because, although his heart might be unfeeling, he was discovering he wasn't made of stone. Hadn't he allowed himself the brief fantasy of imagining himself with a son? A son he could teach to kick a ball around and to perfect the *elastico* move for which he'd been so famous?

Only now Molly wanted to leave him. Her womb was empty and her spirit deflated by his cruel accusations and she was still staring at him as if he were some kind of monster. Maybe he deserved that because hadn't she only ever been kind and giving? Rare attributes which only a fool would squander—and he was that fool.

'No. Don't go,' he said suddenly.

She screwed up her eyes. 'You mean you won't let me use your plane?'

'My plane is at your disposal any time you want it,' he said impatiently. 'That's not what I mean.' His mouth hardened. 'I don't want you to go, Molly.'

'Well, I've got to go. I can't hang around pretending nothing's happened, just because you don't want to lose face with your parents.'

'It has nothing to do with losing face,' he argued. 'It has more to do with wanting to make amends for all the accusations I threw at you. About realising that maybe—somehow—we could make this work.'

'Make *what* work?'

'This relationship.'

She shook her head. 'We don't have a relationship, Salvio.'

'But we could.'

She narrowed her eyes. 'You're not making any sense.'

'Aren't I?' He lowered his voice. 'I get the feeling you weren't too unhappy about having my baby.'

She stared down at her feet and as he followed the direction of her gaze, he noticed her toenails were unvarnished. It occurred to him that he'd never been intimate with a woman whose life hadn't been governed by beauty regimes and his eyes narrowed in sudden comprehension. Was that shallow of him? She looked up again and he could see the pride and dignity written all over her face and he felt the twist of something he didn't recognise deep inside him.

'If this is a soul-baring exercise then it seems only fair I should bear mine. And I couldn't help the way I felt about being pregnant,' she admitted. 'I knew it wasn't an ideal situation and should never have happened but, no, I wasn't unhappy about having your baby, Salvio. It would have been...'

'Would have been what?' he prompted as her words tailed off.

Somebody to love, Molly wanted to say—but even in this new spirit of honesty, she knew that was a declaration too far. Because that sounded needy and vulnerable and she was through with being vulnerable. She wished Salvio would stop asking her all this stuff, especially when it was so out of character. Why didn't he just let her fly back to England and let her get on with the rest of her life and begin the complicated process of getting over him, instead of directing that soft look of compassion at her which was making her feel most...peculiar? She struggled to remove some of the emotion from her words.

'It would have been a role which I would have happily taken on and done to the best of my ability,' she said. 'And I'm not going to deny that on one level I'm deeply disappointed, but I'll… I'll get over it.'

Her words faded into silence. One of those silences which seemed to last for an eternity when you just knew that everything hinged on what was said next, but Salvio's words were the very last Molly was expecting.

'Unless we try again, of course,' he said.

'What are you talking about?' she breathed.

'What if I told you that fatherhood was something which I had also grown to accept? Which I would have happily taken on, despite my initial reservations? What if I told you that I was disappointed, too? *Am* disappointed,' he amended. 'That I've realised I *do* want a child.'

'Then I suggest you do something about it,' she said, her words brittle as rock candy and she wondered if he had any idea how much it hurt to say them. Or how hard it was to stem the tide of tears which was pricking at her eyes. Tears not just for the little life which was no more, but for the man who had created that life. Because that was the crazy thing. That she was going to miss Salvio De Gennaro. How was it that in such a short while he seemed to have become as integral to her life as her own heartbeat? 'Find a woman. Get married. Start a family. That's the way it usually works.'

'That's exactly what I intend to do. Only I don't need to find a woman. Why would I, when there's one standing in front of me?'

'You don't mean that.'

'Don't tell me what I mean, Molly. I mean every word and I'm asking you to be my wife.'

Molly blinked in confusion. He was asking her to *marry* him—despite the fact she was no longer carrying his baby? She thought about the first time she'd ever seen him and how completely blown away she'd been. But this time she was no longer staring at him as if he were some demigod who had just tumbled from the stars. The scales had fallen from her eyes and now she saw him for what he was. A flawed individual—just like her. He had introduced her to amazing sex and fancy clothes. They'd made love on a giant bed overlooking the Bay of Naples and he had kissed her belly when a tiny child had been growing there. She had met his parents and they had liked her—treating her as if she were already part of the family. And somehow the culmination of all those experiences had changed her. She was no longer the same humble person who would accept whatever was thrown at her. The things which had happened had allowed her to remove the shackles which had always defined her. She no longer felt like a servant, but a woman. A real woman.

Yet even as that realisation filled her with a rush of liberation, she was at pains to understand why Salvio was making his extraordinary proposition. He was off the hook now. He was free again. Surely he should be celebrating her imminent departure from his life instead of trying to postpone it?

'Why do you want to marry me?' she demanded.

His gaze raked over her but this time it was not his usual sensual appraisal—more an impartial assessment of her worth. 'I like your softness and kindness,' he said slowly. 'Your approach to life and your work ethic. I think you will make a good mother.'

'And that's all?' she found herself asking.

He narrowed his eyes. 'Surely that is enough?'

She wasn't certain. If you wrote down all those things they would make a flattering list but the glaring omission was love. But Salvio had loved once before and his heart had been broken and damaged as a result. Could she accept his inability to love her as a condition of their marriage, and could they make it work in spite of that?

Behind him, Naples was framed like a picture-postcard as he began to walk towards her and for once his limp seemed more pronounced than usual. And although the thrust of his thighs was stark evidence enough of his powerful sensuality, it was that tiny glimpse of frailty which plucked at her heartstrings.

'I wanted this baby,' he said simply.

Her heart pounded—not wanting to be affected by that powerful declaration. But of course she *was* affected—for it was the most human she had ever seen him. 'You had a funny way of showing it.'

He lifted his shoulders as if to concede the point. 'I'm not going to deny that at first I felt trapped. Who wouldn't in that kind of situation? But once I'd got my head around it, my feelings began to change.'

Molly felt the lurch of hope. Could she believe him? Did she dare to? She remembered the way he'd kissed her belly yesterday—and how loving she'd felt towards him as a result. And that was dangerous. When she stopped to think about it, everything about this situation was dangerous. 'So this time you're not asking me to marry you because you have to?' she continued doggedly. 'You're saying you actually *want* to?'

'Yes.' His shadowed jaw tightened. 'I do. For old-fashioned reasons rather than the unrealistic expectations of romantic love. I want a family, Molly. I didn't realise how much until the possibility was taken away from me. I want someone to leave my fortune to— because otherwise what's the point of making all this money? Someone to take my name and my genes forward. Someone who will be my future.'

Molly's heart clenched as she listened to his heartfelt words. She thought of his pain when he'd lost his career and fortune in quick succession. She thought about the woman who had betrayed him at the worst possible time. The woman he had loved. No wonder he had built a wall around his heart and vowed never to let anyone touch that heart again. She drank in the hardness of his beautiful face. Could she dismantle that wall, little by little, and would he allow her close enough to try? She knew it was a gamble—and, despite all the stern lectures she'd given her little brother, a gamble she intended to take, because by now she couldn't imagine a life without him.

But if she was to be his wife then she must learn to be his equal. There had been times in the past when she'd told Salvio what she thought he wanted to hear because that was all part of her training as a servant. But it wasn't going to be like that from now on. From now on they were going to operate on a level playing field.

'Yes, I will be your wife,' she said, in a low and un-emotional voice.

He laughed, softly. 'You drive me crazy, Molly Miller,' he said. 'Do you realise that?'

The look she gave him was genuine. 'I don't know how.'

'I think,' he observed drily, 'that's the whole point. Now come here.'

He was pulling her into his arms and for a moment Molly felt uncertain, because she had her period and surely... But the touch of his fingertips against her cheek was comforting rather than seeking and the warmth of his arms consoling rather than sexual.

'I'm sorry about the baby,' he whispered against her hair, so softly that she might have imagined it.

It was the first time he had ever held her without wanting sex and Molly pressed her eyelids tightly shut, her face resting against his silky shoulder, terrified to move or to speak because she was afraid she might cry.

CHAPTER ELEVEN

THEY WERE MARRIED in Naples in a beautiful church not far from the home of Salvio's parents. The ancient building was packed with people Molly barely knew—friends of the family, she guessed, and high-powered friends of Salvio's who had flown in from all around the world. Most of them she'd met the previous evening during a lavish pre-wedding dinner, but their names had flown in one ear and out of the other, no matter how hard she'd tried to remember them. Her mind had been too full of niggling concerns to concentrate on anything very much, but her main anxiety had been about Robbie.

Because Salvio had quietly arranged for her brother to fly from Australia to Naples as a pre-wedding surprise and Molly's heart had contracted with joy as Robbie had strolled into the restaurant where everyone was eating, flashing his careless smile, which had made many of the younger women swoon.

She had jumped to her feet to hug him, touched by Salvio's unexpected thoughtfulness, as she'd run her gaze over her brother in candid assessment. From the outside Robbie looked good—better than he'd looked in a long time. He was tanned and fit, his golden curls longer than she remembered, and his clothes were surprisingly well chosen. But she'd seen his faintly avaricious expression as he'd taken in the giant ring on her finger and the expensive venue of the sea-view wedding reception.

'Well, what do you know? You did good, sis. Real good,' he'd said slowly, a gleam entering his grey eyes. 'Salvio De Gennaro is *minted*.'

She'd found herself wanting to protest that she wasn't marrying Salvio for his money but Robbie probably wouldn't have believed her, since his teenage years had been dedicated to the pursuit of instant wealth. She'd wondered if his reluctance to maintain eye contact meant that his gambling addiction had returned. And had then wondered if she was simply transferring her own fears onto her brother.

But she wasn't going to be afraid because she was walking into this with her eyes open. She'd made the decision to be Salvio's wife because deep down she wanted to, and she was going to give the marriage everything she could. Who said that such a strangely conceived union couldn't work? She was used to fighting against the odds, wasn't she?

Holding herself tall, she had walked slowly down the aisle wearing the dress which had been created especially for her by one of London's top wedding-dress designers. The whole couture process had been a bit of an ordeal, mainly because a pale, shiny fabric wasn't terribly forgiving when you were overendowed with curves, but Molly had known Salvio wanted her to look like a traditional bride. And in her heart she had wanted that, too.

'Your breasts are very…generous.' The dressmaker had grunted. 'We're going to have to use a minimising bra, I think.'

Molly had opened her mouth to agree until she'd remembered what she'd vowed on the day of Salvio's proposal. That she was going to be true to herself and behave like his equal because the strain of doing otherwise would quickly wear her down. And if she tried to be someone she wasn't, then surely this whole crazy set-up would be doomed.

'I think Salvio likes my breasts the way they are,' she'd offered shyly and the dressmaker had taken the pins out of her mouth, and smiled.

The look on his face when she reached the altar seemed to endorse Molly's theory—and when they left the church as man and wife, the strangest thing happened. Outside, a sea of people wearing pale blue and white ribbons were cheering and clapping and Molly looked up at Salvio in confusion as their joyful shouts filled the air.

'Some of the supporters of my old football club,' he explained, looking slightly taken aback himself. 'Come to wish me *in bocca al lupo.*'

'Good luck?' she hazarded, blinking as a battery of mobile-phone cameras flashed in her face.

'*Esattamente.* Your Italian lessons are clearly paying dividends,' he murmured into her ear, his mouth brushing against one pearl-indented lobe.

Just that brief touch was enough to make her breasts

spring into delicious life beneath the delicate material of her wedding dress and Salvio's perceptive smile made Molly blush. Lifting up her bouquet of roses to disguise the evidence of physical desire, she thought how perfectly attuned he was to her body and its needs. Their sexual compatibility had been there from the start— now all she needed to concentrate on was getting pregnant.

After the wedding they flew to their honeymoon destination of Barbados, where they were shown to a large, private villa in the vast grounds of a luxury hotel. It was the closest thing to paradise that Molly could imagine and as soon as they arrived, Salvio went for a swim while she insisted on unpacking her clothes—because she didn't quite trust anyone else to do it so neatly. *Old habits die hard*, she thought ruefully.

Knotting a sarong around her waist, she went outside where her brand-new husband was lying on a sun lounger the size of a double bed, wearing a battered straw hat angled over his eyes and nothing else. A lump rose in her throat as she watched him lying in the bright sunshine—completely at ease with his bare body which was gleaming with droplets of water drying in the sun. For a moment she couldn't actually believe she was here, with him. His wife. She swallowed. Even her title took some getting used to. Signora Molly De Gennaro.

He turned to look at her, his gaze lazy as it ran a slow and comprehensive journey from her head to the tips of her toes.

'How are you feeling?' he questioned solicitously.

Trying not to be distracted by the very obvious stirring at his groin, she nodded. 'Fine, thank you,' she said politely. 'That sleep I had on the plane was wonderful.'

'Then stop standing there looking so uncertain.' Pushing aside a tumble of cushions, he patted the space beside him on the giant sunbed. 'Come over here.'

It occurred to Molly that if she wasn't careful she would end up taking orders from him just like before, but it was probably going to take a little time to acclimatise herself to this new life. To feel as if she had the right to enjoy these lavish surroundings, instead of constantly looking around feeling as if she ought to be cleaning them.

Aware of the sensual glitter of his eyes, she walked across the patio and sank down next to him. Straight ahead glimmered a sea of transparent turquoise, edged with sand so fine it looked like caster sugar. To her left was their own private swimming pool and any time they wanted anything—*anything at all*, as they had been assured on their arrival—all they had to do was to ring one of the bells which were littered around the place and some obliging servant would appear.

She stuck out her feet in front of her, still getting used to toenails which were glinting a fetching shade of coral in the bright sunshine.

'You've had a pedicure,' Salvio observed.

She blinked and looked up. 'Fancy you noticing something like that.'

'You'd be amazed what I notice about you, Molly,' he murmured. 'Is that the first one you've ever had?'

'I'm afraid it is.' She lifted her chin a little defensively. 'I suppose that shocks you?'

'Not really, no. And anyway—' he smiled '—I like being shocked by you.'

His hand was now on her leg and she felt his fingertips travelling slowly over her thigh. Little by little they inched upwards and her mouth grew increasingly dry as they approached the skimpy triangle of her bikini bottoms. She swallowed as his hand came to a tantalising halt just before they reached the red and white gingham. 'Salvio,' she breathed.

'*Sì*, Molly?' he murmured.

'We're outside. Anyone can see us.'

'But the whole point of having a *private* villa,' he emphasised, 'is that we *can't* be seen. Haven't you ever wondered what it might be like to make love in the open air?'

She hesitated. 'Maybe,' she said cautiously.

'So why don't we do it?'

'What, now?'

'Right now.'

She swallowed. 'If you're *sure* we really can't be seen.'

'I may be adventurous,' he drawled, 'but I draw the line at rampant voyeurism.'

'Go on, then,' she whispered encouragingly.

Salvio smiled as he trailed his lips down over Molly's generous cleavage which smelt faintly of coconut oil and was already warm from the sun. Through her bikini top a pert nipple sprang into life against his lips and he thought how utterly entrancing she could be with that potent combination of shyness and eagerness, despite her lack of experience. 'You are for my eyes only,' he added gravely, hearing her sharp intake of breath as he began to undo the sarong which was knotted around her hips. 'Except you are wearing far too much for me to be able to see you properly.'

The sarong discarded, his finger crept beneath her bikini bottoms to find her most treasured spot, where she was slick and wet. Always wet, he thought achingly. Her enjoyment of sex was so delightfully fervent that it made him instantly hard. He expelled a shuddering breath of air as she responded to his caress by reaching down to touch him intimately, and he moaned his soft pleasure. He liked the way she encircled him within those dextrous fingers and the way she slid them up and down to lightly stroke the pulsing and erect flesh. He liked the way she teased him as he had taught her to tease him and to make him wait, until he felt like her captive slave. But today his hunger would not be tempered and he could not wait, his desire for her off the scale. He had let her sleep on the plane because she had looked exhausted after the wedding, but now his appetite knew no bounds. The bikini was discarded to join the sarong as he wriggled his fingers between her legs. She jerked distractedly as he found her tight bud, her nails digging into his bare shoulders as he increased his rhythmical stroke.

'You like that,' he observed, with a satisfied purr.

'Don't...don't stop, will you?' she gasped.

He gave a low laugh. 'I have no intention of stopping, *bedda mia*. I couldn't stop, even if I wanted to.' But suddenly he no longer wanted to pleasure her with his finger and, positioning himself over her, he parted her thighs and drove into her. He groaned as she matched each urgent thrust with the accommodating jerk of her hips. He revelled in the feel of her, the taste of her and the smell of her. Was it because there was no need for a condom that sex with Molly felt even more incredible than it had done before? Or because he was the one who had taught her everything? She'd never taken a man into her mouth before him, nor sucked him until he was empty and gasping. Just as she'd never had anyone's head between her thighs other than his. He closed his eyes as excitement built at a speed which almost outpaced him. Was he really so primitive that he got some kind of thrill from having bareback sex with his onetime virgin? He drove into her again. Maybe he was.

She began to come, her moans of pleasure spiralling up from the back of her throat and hovering on the edge of a scream, so that he clamped his mouth over hers in an urgent kiss. He felt the rush of her breath in his mouth and the helpless judder of her body clenching around him—and his own response was like a powerful wave which crashed over him and pulled him under. With a groan, he ejaculated, one hand splayed underneath her bottom while the other tangled in her silken hair. Beneath the Barbadian sun he felt the exquisite pulsing of his body as passion seeped away.

For a while he just lay on top of her, dazed and contented, his head cushioned on her shoulder as he dipped in and out of sleep. But eventually he stirred, his fingertips tilting her jaw, enjoying the beatific smile which curved her lips as she opened her eyes to look at him.

'So. We have a choice,' he said slowly. 'We can get

dressed again and ring for drinks, or I can go inside and fix us something and you can stay exactly as you are, which would be my preference.'

She hesitated for a moment. 'I wouldn't mind you waiting on me for a change,' she said. 'Unless you're going to do that helpless man thing of making a mess of it because it's *domestic*, so that you'll never have to do it again.'

His mouth twitched into a smile as he rose from the lounger. 'Is that what men do?'

'In my experience—well, only my working experience, of course. Every time.'

'Not this one.' He picked up the battered straw hat which had fallen off, jamming it down so that the shadow of the brim darkened his face. 'I don't like to fail at anything, Molly.'

She watched him go. Was it that which had hurt the hardest when his life had imploded around him—the fact that he would be perceived as a failure? Had that been at the root of his reluctance to return to Naples very often? Yet he had picked himself up and started all over again. He had made a success of his life in every way, except for one. Just before they'd boarded his private jet to fly here, he'd told her how delighted his parents were that he had chosen her as his bride and she found herself thinking how skewed life could be sometimes. His mother hadn't liked Lauren Meyer, but Salvio had loved her. He'd told her that himself. And if this marriage was to continue, she must resign herself to the fact that she would only ever be second-best.

But that had been her life, hadn't it? It wasn't as

if she wasn't used to it. When you worked in other people's houses you had to put yourself second, because you were only there to help their lives function smoothly. You had to be both efficient yet invisible, because people didn't really see *you*—only the service you provided.

Did Salvio see *her*? she wondered. Or was she simply a vessel to bear his child? The woman he had transformed with his vast fortune, so that she could lie in a Barbadian paradise, looking out over an azure sea as if she'd been born to this life?

The chink of ice made her glance towards the entrance to their villa, where Salvio was standing holding two tall, frosted glasses. As he began to walk towards her she wondered how a man could look so utterly at ease, completely naked save for his sunhat.

Handing her a glass, he joined her on the lounger and for a while they sipped their drinks in silence.

'Salvio,' she said eventually, watching the ice melt in the fruity cocktail.

He turned his face towards her. 'Mmm...?'

'What am I actually going to *do*? I mean, once we get back to England and you go back to work.'

He swirled the ice around in his glass, his fingers dark against the sunlit condensation. 'Weren't we planning to have a baby?'

'Yes, we were. Are,' she corrected. 'But that might not happen straight away, might it? And I can't just sit around all the time just...*waiting*.'

There was a pause. 'You want me to find you something to do?' He studied her carefully. 'There's a charitable arm belonging to my company. Do you think you'd like to get involved in that?'

She hesitated, genuine surprise tearing through her at the realisation he must think her good enough to be a part of his organisation. But it wasn't his validation which pleased her as much as the thought that this would make her a more integral part of his life—and wasn't that what marriage was all about? 'I'd like that very much.' She smiled, but his next words killed her pleasure stone dead.

'You know your brother tapped me for a loan at the wedding?'

The glass she was holding almost slipped from her suddenly nerveless fingers and quickly Molly put it down, her cheeks flaming. *'What?'*

'He said he had an idea for a new business venture and asked if I'd like to invest in it.'

'You didn't say yes?'

'You think I'm in the habit of throwing money away? I asked him how much he had already raised, and how—but he seemed reluctant to answer.' Beneath the shadowed brim of his hat, she saw that his eyes were now as hard and as cold as jet. 'Did you know about this, Molly?'

It hurt that he should ask but, when she thought about it afterwards, why *wouldn't* he ask? Salvio had been a target for women during his playing days and had fallen for someone who saw him as nothing but a trophy husband. He made no secret of not trusting women—so why should he feel any differently about her?

'Of course I didn't know he was going to ask you,'

she said in a low voice. 'And if he'd sought my opinion I would have told him not to even think about it.'

He nodded as he stared out at the bright blue horizon and the subject was closed. But Molly's determination not to let his silky accusation ruin the rest of the day only went so far, and suddenly she was aware of the aching disappointment which made the sunny day feel as if it had been darkened by a cloud.

CHAPTER TWELVE

'So HOW LONG will you be away?' Amid the croissant-crumbed debris of their early-morning breakfast, Molly glanced across the glass dining table at Salvio, who was reading one of the Italian newspapers he had couriered to his London apartment each morning.

'Only a few days,' he said, lifting his dark head to look at her. 'I'm just flying into Los Angeles for back-to-back meetings and then out again.'

'It seems an awfully long way to go,' she observed, taking a final sip of the inky black coffee she'd learned to love and which she now drank in preference to cappuccino. 'For such a short visit.'

'It is. So why don't you come with me?' His eyes gleamed as he put the newspaper down. 'We could add on a few extra days and take the highway to San Francisco. Turn it into a holiday. You've never been to the US, have you?'

She'd never actually been further than the Isle of Wight and that had been years ago. Highly tempted, Molly considered the idea, until she remembered her own responsibilities. 'I can't. I have a lunch with the charity later.'

'You could always cancel it.'

'I can't just *cancel* it, Salvio, or it won't look like I'm committed. Like I'm only playing at being on the board just because I'm your wife.'

A smile played around the edges of his lips as he got up and moved towards her, his dark eyes glittering with an expression she knew so well. 'Which means you'll just have to be patient and wait for me to get back, *mia sposa*, even though it means you'll be without me for four whole nights. In fact, just thinking about it makes me want to kiss you.'

A kiss quickly turned into Molly being carried into their bedroom with a demonstration of that effortless mastery which still dazzled her, no matter how many times it happened. She loved the way he impatiently removed the clothes he'd only just put on and the way he explored her body as if he had just stumbled across a newly discovered treasure. She loved the warm skin-to-skin contact with this man as they tumbled hungrily onto the bed. She loved him, she suddenly realised, as he plunged deep inside her. She just couldn't help herself.

She was still feeling faintly dizzy with pleasure when Salvio returned from the shower wearing the lazy smile of the satisfied predator, and she watched him as he began to dress. 'You are insatiable,' she observed.

'And don't you just hate it?' he mocked, picking up his tie and walking over to the mirror to knot it.

She hardly ever noticed his almost imperceptible limp but she noticed it today—and something about the contrast of frailty and strength which existed in his powerful body stirred a memory in her which she had unwittingly stored away.

'Salvio?'

He stared at her reflected image in the glass. 'Mmm…?'

She hesitated. 'You remember our wedding day?'

'I'm hardly likely to forget it, am I?' he questioned drily. 'And even if I had, it wouldn't be a diplomatic thing to admit after a mere three months of marriage. What about it?'

'Well.' His response didn't sound very promising but Molly forced herself to continue. 'I was wondering whether your charitable organisation ought to include some kind of football sponsorship, which I notice it doesn't do at the moment.'

'Some kind of football sponsorship?' he repeated slowly.

'Yes. You know—you could offer a financial scheme for a promising young player from a poor background.' Again, she hesitated. 'To help the type of boy you once were,' she finished, on a rush.

There was a pause while he finished knotting his tie and when he spoke, his voice was cool. 'But I don't have anything to do with football any more, Molly. You know that. I walked away from that life many years ago.'

'Yes, I know you did. But things have moved on now. You saw all those people wearing your old club's colours who came to wish you luck on your wedding day. They…they love you, Salvio. You're a legend to them and I just thought it would be…nice…' Her words faded away. 'To give something back.'

'Oh, did you?' Moving away from the mirror, Salvio

swept his gaze over his wife, who looked all pink-cheeked and tousled as she lay amid the rumpled mess they'd just made of the bed. A muscle began to work in his cheek. He'd thought that, given her previous occupation, she would have been a rather more compliant partner than she was turning out to be. He'd thought it a generous gesture to give her a seat on the board of his charity and had expected her to be grateful to him for that. But he'd imagined her turning up regularly at meetings and sitting there quietly—not to suddenly start dishing out advice. Surely she, more than anyone, must have realised it was inappropriate as well as unwanted? 'I really don't think it's your place to start advising me on how I spend my money, Molly,' he drawled.

She went very still. 'Not *my place*?' she echoed, the colour leeching from her face and her dark lashes blinking in disbelief. 'Why not? Do you think the one-time servant should remain mute and just go along with what she's been told, rather than ever showing any initiative of her own? Are you making out like there's still all those inequalities between us, despite the fact that I now wear your ring?'

'There's no need to overreact,' he said coolly, even though that was exactly what he *did* think. 'And I really don't want an argument when I'm just about to fly to the States. We'll talk about it when I get back.' He dipped his head towards her with a smile she always found irresistible. 'Now kiss me.'

Knowing it would be childish to turn her face away, Molly attempted a close approximation of a fond kiss, but inside she was seething as the door of the apartment slammed shut behind her departing husband. She felt as if the pink cloud she'd been floating on since the day they'd wed had suddenly turned black. Was it because, behind all the outward appearances of a relatively blissful new marriage, nothing much had changed? Despite him giving her a seat on the board of his charity, it seemed she wasn't allowed to have any ideas of her own. She might be wearing his shiny gold wedding band but at that precise moment she felt exactly like the servant she'd always been. And there was another pressure, too. One she hadn't dared to acknowledge—not even to herself, let alone to Salvio.

Gloomily, she got out of bed and went to stare out of the window, where there was no sign of new life. They were already into April but spring seemed to have been put on hold by the harsh weather. Even the daffodils in the planters on Salvio's roof terrace had been squashed by the unseasonable dump of snow which had ground the city to a halt for the last few days.

No sign of life in her either.

Her hands floating down to her belly, she prayed that this month she might get the news she was longing for, even though the low ache inside her hinted at an alternative scenario. She linked her manicured fingers together, dreading another month of unspoken disappointment. Of cheerfully convincing herself it would happen eventually. Of wondering how long she could continue walking this precarious tightrope of a marriage which had only taken place because her wealthy husband wanted an heir. Because what if she *couldn't* conceive? She'd been pregnant once, yes, but there was no guarantee it would happen again. Life didn't provide guarantees like that, did it?

Forcing herself to get on with the day, she showered and dressed—slithering into a dress she wouldn't have dared to wear a few months ago, even if she could have afforded to. But her body shape had changed since living with Salvio—and not just because she'd checked out the basement gym in this luxury apartment block and discovered she liked it. She ate proper regular meals now because her Neapolitan husband's love of good food meant that he wasn't a great fan of snacks, and as a consequence she was in the best shape of her adult life.

She took a cab to her charity lunch, which was being held in the ballroom of one of the capital's smartest hotels and was today awarding acts of bravery involving animals as well as humans. She particularly enjoyed hearing about the kitten who had been rescued from the top of a chimney pot by a nineteen-year-old university drop-out who had previously been terrified of heights. She chatted to him afterwards and he told her that he'd decided he was going to train as a vet, and Molly felt a warm glow of pleasure as she listened to his story.

She was just chopping vegetables for a stir-fry when Salvio rang from Los Angeles, telling her he missed her and, although she wanted to believe him, she found herself wondering if he was just reading from a script. It was easy to say those sorts of things when he was thousands of miles away, when the reality was that he'd made her feel she'd stepped out of line this morning just because she'd dared express an opinion of her own.

Well, maybe it was time to stop drifting around in a

half-world of pretence and longing. She would sit him down when he returned from his trip and they would talk honestly because, even though the truth could hurt, it was better to know where you stood. And even though her stupid heart was screaming out its objections she couldn't keep putting it off. She would ask him if he really wanted to continue with the marriage and maybe it was better to confront that now, before there *was* a baby.

But then something happened. Something which changed everything.

It started with an email from her brother which arrived on the day Salvio was due to return from America. Robbie was notoriously unreliable at keeping in touch and she hadn't heard from him since the wedding, even though she'd sent several lovely photos of him dancing with one of Salvio's distant cousins at the reception. She hadn't even mentioned the loan he'd asked her husband for—deciding it was an issue best settled between him and Salvio.

So her smile was one of pleasure when she saw new mail from Robbie Miller, which had pinged into her inbox overnight, with the subject line: Have you seen this?

'This' turned out to be an attachment of an article taken from a newspaper website. An American newspaper, as it happened. And there, in sharp Technicolor detail, was a photograph of her husband, sitting outside some flower-decked restaurant with a beautiful blonde, the sapphire glitter of a sunlit sea in the background.

Her fingers clawed at the mouse as she scrolled down the page but somehow Molly knew who Salvio's companion was before she'd read a single word. Was it the woman's poise which forewarned her, or simply the way she leaned towards Salvio's handsome profile with the kind of intimacy which was hard-won? Her heart clenched with pain as she scanned the accompanying prose.

> *Heartthrob property tycoon Salvio De Gennaro was pictured enjoying the sea air in Malibu today.*
>
> *Newly wed to former maid Molly Miller, in a lavish ceremony which took place in the groom's native Naples, the Italian billionaire still found time to catch up with ex-fiancée Lauren Meyer.*
>
> *With the ink barely dry on her divorce papers, perhaps heiress Lauren was advising Salvio on some of the pitfalls of marriage.*
>
> *Either that, or the Californian wine was just too good to resist...*

Hands shaking, Molly stared at the screen, closing her eyes in a futile bid to quell the crippling spear of jealousy which lanced through her like a hot blade, but it was still there when she opened them again, her gaze caught by the glitter of the diamonds at her finger. The diamonds she had once compared to tears, rather than rain. But there were real tears now. Big ones which were splashing onto her trembling fingers. Pushing her chair away from the desk, her vision was blurred as blindly she stumbled into the bedroom. She rubbed her fists into her eyes but the stupid tears just kept on flowing, even though deep down she knew she had no right to feel sorrow. Because it wasn't as if theirs was a *real* relationship, was it? She had no right to be jealous of a husband who had never loved her, did she? Not really. It had only ever been a marriage of convenience—providing each of them with what they wanted.

Or rather, what she'd *thought* she'd wanted… Security and passion with a man she'd begun to care for and, ultimately, a family of her own. Only now the truth hit her with a savage blow as she forced herself to acknowledge what it was she *really* wanted. Not the fancy penthouse or the different homes dotted all around the globe. Not the platinum credit card with its obscene spending limit.

She wanted Salvio's love, she realised—and that was just a wish too far. He didn't do love—at least, not with her. But he *had* loved Lauren. And try as she might, she just couldn't put a positive spin on his reunion with his ex-fiancée in that sunny and glamorous Malibu setting. For the first time in her life she was right out of optimistic options.

There were no tears left to cry as she walked across the bedroom, but she was filled with a strange new sense of calm as she opened up the wardrobe and took out her battered old suitcase, knowing what she intended to do.

She would do the brave thing.

The right thing.

The only thing.

'Molly?' Salvio frowned as he walked into an apartment which instinct told him was empty. Yet he'd texted her to tell her he was on his way home and he'd assumed she would be waiting with that soft smile which always greeted him when he arrived home from work. 'Molly?' he called again, even though the word echoed redundantly through the quiet apartment.

He found the note quickly, as he had obviously been intended to. One of those brief notes which managed to say so little and yet so much, in just a few stark words. And sitting on top of it was her diamond ring.

Salvio.
I've seen the newspaper article about you and Lauren and I want to do the best thing, so I'm staying in a hotel until I can get a job sorted out.

I'll send you my address when I have one, so you can instruct your lawyers.

It's been an amazing experience, so thank you for everything. And...in bocca al lupo.

Crushing the note in an angry fist, he strode over to the computer and saw the article immediately, reading it with a growing sense of disbelief before cursing long and loud into the empty air. Why hadn't any of his staff alerted him to this? Because his assistant had been instructed to treat gossip columns with the contempt they deserved, by ignoring them. He stared at the photo, thinking that whoever said the camera didn't lie must have been delusional. Because it did. Big-time.

He saw Lauren's finely etched profile and the angled bones of her shoulder blades. Her long blonde hair was waving gently in the breeze and she was leaning forward with an earnest expression on her face. It must have been taken just before his response had made her delicate features crumple and her blue eyes darken with disbelief.

Pulling the phone from his pocket, he found Molly's number and hit the call button, unsurprised when it went straight to voicemail over and over again, and his mouth hardened. Did she think she could just walk out on him, leaving nothing but that banal little note?

Scrolling down, he found another number he used only very infrequently. His voice lowered as he began to speak in rapid Neapolitan dialect, biting out a series of terse demands before finally cutting the connection.

CHAPTER THIRTEEN

MOLLY STARED AT the richly embossed walls of the fancy hotel and the dark red lilies which were massed in a silver vase. She'd chosen the five-star Vinoly because she'd heard Salvio mention it, but as from tomorrow she would start searching for somewhere cheaper to stay. No way was she going to try to cling to the high-life she'd enjoyed during her brief tenure as his wife, because that life was over and she needed to get used to it.

The phone rang but she didn't need to look down to see who was calling. Salvio. Again. After yet another brief internal tussle she chose to ignore it, just like she'd avoided reading the texts he'd been sending. Because what was the point in hearing anything he had to say? What if his smooth weasel words tempted her back into his arms and the guarantee of heartbreak? She didn't want to hear excuses or half-truths. She wanted to preserve her sanity, even if her heart had to break in the process.

But first she needed to start looking for a job. A live-in job she could practically do with her eyes closed. She would sign up with an agency in the morning and tell them she wanted a fresh start. Somewhere she'd never been before—like Scotland, or Wales. Somewhere new so she could be completely anonymous while licking her wounds and trying to forget that for one brief shining moment she'd been the wife of a man who...

She bit her lip.

A man she'd fallen in love with, despite all her best efforts to remain immune to him.

But Salvio hadn't wanted her love. Only Lauren's. She swallowed. Was the beautiful heiress willing to give Salvio a second chance? Was that the reason behind their secret liaison when they'd been making eyes at one another in the Californian sunshine?

She didn't feel hungry but she hadn't eaten anything since breakfast and she always used to tell Robbie that your brain couldn't function properly unless you kept it nourished. Ordering a cheese omelette from room service, she thought about her brother. She hadn't replied to his email, mainly because she couldn't think of anything to say. Not yet, anyway. She wondered if he'd acted out of the goodness of his heart. If sending the proof of Salvio's clandestine meeting was a brotherly intervention to protect her from potential hurt. Or had Robbie been motivated by spite—because his wealthy new brother-in-law had refused to give him the loan he'd wanted?

She paced the room, unable to settle. Unable to shift the dark features of her husband from her mind and wondering whether she would ever be able to forget this interlude. Or to—

Her thoughts were interrupted by a loud rap on the door.

'Who is it?' Molly called out sharply.

'Room service!'

She opened the door to the woman's voice, her heart crashing against her ribcage when she saw Salvio standing there, holding a tray dominated by a silver dome. In the distance was the retreating view of a hotel employee, who'd obviously been rewarded for allowing this bizarre role-reversal to take place. Which was exactly what it felt like. Salvio in a subservient role holding a tray, and her opening the door of some swanky hotel room. Except he didn't stay subservient for very long.

'Step aside, Molly,' he clipped out.

'You can't come in.'

'Just try stopping me.'

She didn't dare. She'd never seen him look so determined as he stormed into her room. There was a clatter as he slammed the tray down and Molly shuddered to think what damage he must have inflicted on her cheese omelette. Not that she wanted it any more. How could she possibly have eaten anything when she could barely breathe?

He turned round and she was taken aback by the fury which was darkening his imposing features into an unrecognisable mask. 'Well, Molly?' he snarled.

'Well, what?' she retorted. 'How did you find me?'

'You booked this room with our joint credit card.'

'And?'

'And therefore you were traceable. I had one of my contacts look into it for me.'

She screwed up her brow. 'Isn't that…illegal?'

He shrugged. 'When a man wishes to find his errant wife then surely he will use whatever means are available to him.'

'Well, you've wasted your time because there's nothing to say!'

'I disagree. There's plenty to say, and we're having this out right now.'

And suddenly Molly knew she couldn't let him take over and dominate this situation by the sheer force of his indomitable character. Yes, he was powerful, rich and successful, but she was his wife. His *equal*, despite the inequality of their assets. That was what she'd vowed to be when she had agreed to marry him, but somewhere along the way her resolve had slipped. Was that because the more she'd started to care for him, the harder she had found it to assert herself?

Well, not any more. She needed to make it plain that, although she might not have anything of material value, she valued *herself.* And she would not allow Salvio De Gennaro to make a fool of her, or for her heart to be slowly broken by a man who was incapable of emotion.

'I saw the article from the American newspaper.'

'I know you did. Your brother sent it to you.'

'Did you find *that* out illegally, too?' she scorned.

'No, Molly. You left your computer open.'

'Well, if you'd looked a little harder you'd have seen that I also did a room search for the Vinoly hotel,' she said triumphantly. 'Which wouldn't have involved getting someone to snoop on me!'

Unexpectedly, he sighed and a sudden weariness

touched the corners of his dark eyes as he looked at her. 'What do you think I did in Los Angeles, Molly?' he questioned tiredly. 'Do you think I had sex with Lauren?'

A spear of pain shot through her. 'Did you?'

He winced as he raked his fingers back through his jet-dark hair. 'No, I did not. She heard I was in town and got in touch with me and I agreed to meet her for lunch.'

'Why?'

'Why?' He gave an odd smile. 'I thought it made sense to put away the past for good.'

'Only I suppose she'd suddenly realised the stupid mistake she'd made in letting you go?' accused Molly sarcastically.

He shrugged. 'Something like that. She is recently divorced. She asked for another chance.'

'And you said?'

There was silence for a moment and Molly actually thought that her heartbeat had grown audible—until she realised that the silver clock was thumping out the hour.

'I said I was in love with my wife,' he said simply. 'Only I'd been too stupid to show her how much.'

She shook her head, not believing him. Not believing he would ever admit to love *or* stupidity. 'I don't believe you,' she whispered.

'I know you don't and maybe I deserve that.' He hesitated, like someone who was learning the words of a new language. 'I know that at times I've been cold and difficult.'

'It isn't that, Salvio! It's the fact that you're completely backtracking on everything you said. You told me you didn't *do* love. Not any more. Remember? That you'd loved Lauren and after you broke up, you'd closed off your heart. And if that *was* true—if you really *did* love her like you claim—then how come it has all just died? Is love only a temporary thing, Salvio—which changes like the moon?'

Deeply admiring of her logic at such an intense moment, Salvio took a deep breath. He felt as if he were on a platform in front of a thousand people, about to make the most important speech of his life. And he was. But not to a thousand people. To one. To Molly. The only one who really mattered.

And his whole future hinged on it.

'I thought I loved Lauren because that's how I felt at the time,' he said, in a low voice. 'And surely it is a kind of treachery to deny the feelings we once had? That would be like trying to rewrite history.' There was a pause. 'But I see now it wasn't real love—it was a complex mixture of other stuff which I was too immature to understand.'

'What kind of stuff?' she questioned, as his voice tailed off.

'It was more to do with a young man who wanted to conquer the elusive,' he admitted. 'A man who for a while became someone he wasn't. Someone blinded by an ideal, rather than a real person—and Lauren *was* that ideal. And then I met you, Molly. The most real person in the world. You charmed me. Disarmed me. You crept beneath my defences before I even realised what was happening. You made me feel good—you still do—and not just in the obvious way. It's like I'm the best version of myself whenever you're around. Like I can achieve anything—even if my instinct is to fight against it every inch of the way, because there's a part of me which doesn't really believe that I deserve to be this happy.'

'Salvio—'

'No. Please. Let me finish,' he said and his voice was shaking now. 'You need to understand that all this is true, because there is no way I would say it if it wasn't.' His black eyes raked over her. '*Do* you believe me, Molly? That I would walk to the ends of the earth for you and further, if that's what you wanted? And that I love you in a way I've never loved before?'

Molly stared into the molten darkness of his eyes, but she didn't have to give it a lot of thought, because she did believe him. She could read it in the tender curve of his lips, even if he hadn't uttered those quietly fervent words which had rung so true. But if they were shining a spotlight on their relationship then they couldn't allow any more shadows to lurk in unexplored corners, and she needed the courage to confront what was still troubling her.

'But what about the baby?' she whispered.

'What baby?' he said gently. 'Are you trying to tell me you're pregnant?'

'I don't know. I don't think so. But that's the whole point. What if...?' She swallowed. 'What if, for some reason, I can't give you the child you long for?'

'Then we will go to the best doctors to find out why, or we will adopt. It's not a deal-breaker, Molly. Not even a deal-maker. Not any more. I want you. *You*. That's all.'

That's all? Molly blinked as for the first time she realised that Salvio De Gennaro was truly captivated by her. Her! A flush of pleasure heated her skin and maybe someone else in her position might have briefly revelled in her newly discovered power. But this wasn't about power. It was about love and equality. About consideration and respect. About loyalty and truth.

It was about them.

She smiled, the happiness swelling up in her heart making it feel as if it were about to burst open. 'I believe you,' she said softly. 'And I love you. So much. I think I've always loved you, Salvio De Gennaro, and I know I always will.'

'Then you'd better come here and kiss me,' he said, in a voice which sounded pretty close to breaking. 'And convince me that this is for real.'

EPILOGUE

SALVIO STARED AT the lights as he lay back contentedly. Rainbow-coloured lights which jostled for space among all the glittering baubles which hung from the Christmas tree. Behind the tree glittered the Bay of Naples and, inside the main reception room of their newly purchased home, he lay naked next to his beautiful Molly on a vast velvet sofa which had been chosen for precisely this kind of activity.

'Happy?' he murmured, one hand idly teasing her bare nipple while his lips lazily caressed the soft silk of her hair.

'Happy?' She nuzzled into his neck. 'So happy I can't even put it into words.'

'Well, try.'

Molly traced her finger over the loud rhythm of her husband's heart. Next door their ten-month-old son Marco lay sleeping—getting as much rest as possible in preparation for the excitement of his first Christmas. And this year, everyone was coming to *them*. Salvio's parents would be arriving later for the traditional Eve of Christmas feast. And so would Robbie, who was currently meeting the parents of Salvio's cousin, who he had recently started dating. Molly prayed he wouldn't let anyone down—most of all himself—but she was hopeful that her brother had finally sorted himself out. Much of it was down to Salvio and the well-intentioned but stern advice he had delivered. He'd told Robbie he would support him through college, but only if he kicked his gambling habit for good.

And he seemed to have done just that. Molly had never seen her brother looking so bright-eyed or *hopeful*. It was as if a heavy burden had been lifted from his strong, young shoulders. Was it the presence of a powerful male role model which had been the making of him?

In the very early days of her pregnancy, she'd persuaded Salvio that his London penthouse apartment was no place for a baby and he had surprised her by agreeing. So they'd moved into his sprawling Cotswold manor house where she had fun envisaging Marco and his siblings playing in those vast and beautiful gardens. Salvio had also bought this sea-view home in Naples where they tried to spend as much time as possible.

She sighed against the warmth of his skin. 'You make me so happy,' she whispered. 'I never thought I could feel this way.'

He stroked his fingers through her hair. 'It's because I love you, Molly. You're so easy to love.'

'And so are you. At least, you are *now*,' she added darkly.

He laughed. 'Was I such a terrible man before?'

'Terrible,' she agreed, mock-seriously. 'But terribly sexy too.'

'Are you angling for more sex, Signora De Gennaro?'

'There isn't time, darling. I've got to oversee last-minute preparations for tonight's dinner because there's a lot of pressure when you're cooking for your in-laws for the first time.' She frowned. 'And I'm worried I'm going to ruin the *capitone*.'

His fingertips tiptoed over her belly. 'You're not going anywhere until you tell me you love me.'

'I love you. I love you more than I ever thought possible. I love that you're a brilliant father and husband and brother-in-law and son. I love the fact that you've opened a football academy here in Naples and are giving a chance to poor boys with a dream in their hearts. How's that? Is that enough?'

'Curiously, it leaves me wanting more,' he growled. 'But then you always do.'

'More of wh-what?' she questioned unsteadily, as his hand moved towards her quivering thigh.

'More of this.' He smiled as he found her wet heat and stroked, enjoying her soft moan of pleasure.

'But, Salvio, there isn't time,' she said, her eyes growing smoky as he continued his feather-light teasing. 'What about the *capitone*?'

And then Salvio said something which, as a good Neapolitan, he had never imagined himself saying—but in the circumstances, perhaps was understandable. He pulled her on top of him and touched her parted lips with his own. 'Stuff the *capitone*,' he growled.

* * * * *

THE ITALIAN'S
UNEXPECTED BABY

KATE HEWITT

CHAPTER ONE

'HE'S COMING!'

Mia James's stomach clenched unpleasantly as she hurried to stand behind her desk, shoulders back, chin up, heart pounding.

'He's in the lift now...'

The numbers above the silver doors glowed, one after another. *Two...three...*

Mia watched out of the corner of her eye as her fellow colleagues at Dillard Investments did the same as she had, scurrying to desks, standing up straight. They were like schoolchildren awaiting an inspection by the head teacher. A particularly strict and perhaps even cruel head teacher... the notoriously ruthless Alessandro Costa, self-made billionaire and, as of yesterday, the new CEO of Dillard Investments.

Yesterday the company had been taken over by Alessandro Costa in a calculated and clever manoeuvre that had shocked everyone involved in the company right down to their toes, including Mia's boss and the CEO, Henry Dillard. Poor Henry had looked terribly shaken, aging ten years in a matter of minutes as he realised there was nothing he could do to stop Costa International from gaining controlling shares; it had all happened before he'd even had a chance to realise, Costa stalking the company the way a ruthless predator would a prey.

Four...five... The lift doors pinged open and Mia drew her breath sharply as the new CEO of Dillard Investments stepped through them. She'd seen photos of him online, having done an exhaustive internet search last night when the news had been confirmed that Dillard's had been taken over. What she'd learned had far from reassured her.

Alessandro Costa specialised in hostile takeovers and then stripping the companies of their assets and employees, to be absorbed into his behemoth of a corporation, Costa International.

A few months ago, he'd taken over a company similar to Dillard's—small, family-owned, a bit antiquated. Now it was virtually gone, swallowed up by the man who was striding onto the top floor of the building Dillard's owned in Mayfair.

Mia tried not to make eye contact with Alessandro Costa, but she found she couldn't stop looking at him. The photos on the internet didn't do him justice, she realised with an uneasy pang of physical awareness. They didn't communicate his intense energy, as if a force field surrounded him, as if he *crackled.*

Cropped dark hair, as black as midnight, framed a face that was all angles and hard lines, from his jaw to his nose to the dark slashes of brows over cold, steel-grey eyes. His body, tall and lethally powerful, was encased in a hand-tailored suit of dark grey silk, the silver tie at his throat matching the colour of his eyes. He made Mia think of a laser, or a sword...something powerful and lethal. *A weapon.*

He came onto the floor with its open-plan desks with quick, purposeful strides, his narrowed, hawk-like gaze moving in quick yet thorough assessment around the room, pinning people in place. It felt as if the very air trembled. Mia was afraid she did. Alessandro Costa was incredibly intimidating.

She knew everyone's job was up for grabs, and most likely down the drain as well. In his last takeover, it had been rumoured that Costa had kept three employees out of forty. As personal assistant to the CEO, Mia knew her position would almost certainly be cut. Costa undoubtedly had his own executive assistant already in place, and as he didn't seem likely to keep Dillard's going as a separate entity, her job had most likely become obsolete last night, with the takeover.

Still, she was determined to try to do *something* to keep it. She'd been working for Dillard Investments since she was nineteen, fresh from a B Tech business course, bright-eyed and determined to make something of herself and, most importantly, to finally be independent.

All her childhood she'd been under the controlling thumb of her unbearably autocratic father, having to do as he said and dance to his tune, however discordant its notes. Her mother had been the same, cringing and hopeful in dispiriting turns, and Mia had vowed to gain her freedom as soon as she could—and never make the same kind of mistake her mother had, by marrying a charming yet controlling man…or any man at all.

So now, while Mia knew she could find another job, she resisted the prospect of being fired from this one for no good reason. She'd been here a long time, had worked hard, and had made a few friends along the way.

She might be likely to lose her job anyway, but she'd go down fighting. She had to, as points of both pride and principle.

Alessandro Costa had stopped in the centre of the room, his feet spread wide, his hands on his hips. He looked like the king of an empire, surveying his domain. Like something out of a fairy tale, except in a three-piece suit.

'Who is Mia James?' he asked, his voice slightly accented, the words crisp and precise as they echoed through the open space.

Mia felt every eye on the floor turn instinctively towards her. Like a child in school being called on by a teacher, she raised her hand, hoping her voice would come out strong.

'I am.' She might have overshot it, she realised; she sounded strident. Aggressive, even, to hide her nervousness.

Alessandro Costa's eyes narrowed even further in appraisal, and his lips flattened into a hard line.

'Come with me,' he said, and walked into Henry Dillard's office, the only private space on the floor, an elegant room with wood panelled walls and leather club chairs, tasteful oil paintings and heavy curtains. It felt like a gentleman's club, or the study of an elegant townhouse, which it very well might once have been. Dillard's offices were in a former home, although much of it had been gutted for desk space.

Costa strode towards the big, mahogany desk, inlaid with leather, that Henry had always sat behind while Mia had taken notes or dictation. Henry had been eccentrically old school; he'd only bought a laptop a few years ago, and he'd still depended on Mia to manage emails and spreadsheets, finding both quite beyond him, and not seeming to mind.

It gave her a pang now to think that was all over; Henry had retreated to his estate in Surrey, and Mia half wondered if she'd ever see him again. Last night, as he'd shuffled out of the office, his business in ruins around him, he'd seemed like an old, broken man, and it had wrung her heart right out. And it was this man's fault.

Alessandro Costa stood behind Henry's old desk, his hands placed flat on its surface, fingers spread wide, as he stared at her, his eyes magnetic, his body radiating barely suppressed energy. Although his expression was focused, it wasn't unfriendly. He looked like a man intent on action, and it made Mia tense, something in her kicking up a notch, ready to respond.

'I need you.' Costa spoke the words matter-of-factly, but stupidly they made Mia's heart skip a silly beat. He didn't mean in *that* way, of course he didn't. But perhaps he meant she might keep her job…

'You…do?'

'Yes, for the moment, at least.' Costa straightened, his gaze surveying her with cool appraisal. 'You've been Dillard's PA for how long?'

'Seven years.'

He nodded slowly. 'And, as far as I can see, you were the plug on his life support.'

Mia blinked, absorbing the cruel bluntness of that statement. 'I wouldn't go that far,' she said quietly, although admittedly there was some truth in it. In reality, Henry Dillard would have been happy playing golf and letting the company his father had founded dwindle away to nothing. The company had been ripe for a takeover, even if he hadn't seen it himself, and Mia had never let herself consider such a possibility.

'Perhaps that's a bit harsh,' Costa allowed, 'but Dillard himself admitted he was behind the times. Of course, many of his clients are, as well.'

'Which begs the question why you took it over,' Mia returned. Costa's eyebrows rose as he kept her gaze, and something sparked to life in Mia, something she most certainly wasn't going to acknowledge.

'Yes, it does, doesn't it?' he remarked. 'Fortunately that is not something you need to concern yourself with.'

And that was her, put firmly in her place. 'Very well.' She met his narrowed, steely gaze unflinchingly, although it cost her. Every time she looked at him she felt something in her spark and tingle in a way she definitely didn't like. The man was intense and a little scary, but there was something that drew her to him as well—something in his fierce energy, his incredible focus. 'So why do you need me?' she asked, deciding that keeping things on track was her best bet.

'I need you because I require your knowledge of Henry's clients so I can deal with them appropriately. So as long as you prove useful...'

Which sounded like a barely veiled threat, or perhaps just a statement of fact. Mia couldn't imagine Alessandro Costa putting up with anyone who wasn't useful.

'And when I don't prove useful?' she asked, although she had a feeling she didn't want to know the answer.

'Then you'll be let go,' Costa said bluntly. 'I don't keep useless employees. It's bad business practice.'

'What about the rest of the staff?'

'Again, none of your concern.'

Wow. The man had no hesitation in being blunt, yet Mia didn't sense any cruel relish in his words, just simple bare statements of fact, which she could appreciate, even if she didn't like them.

In any case, needlessly sparring with Alessandro Costa was a fast track to being fired, and she wanted to keep her job. She *needed* to keep her job. It felt like the only thing she had.

'All right.' She straightened, tipping her chin up, determined to stay professional and match his focus. 'What would you like me to do?'

Something silver flashed in Alessandro's grey eyes; it almost looked like approval, and it made a ripple of pleased awareness race through her, treacherous and molten, racing through her fingers and down to her toes. 'I want files on all of Dillard's major clients, with notes about any potential quirks, habits, tendencies, or any other pertinent information within the hour. We'll talk through it all then.'

'All right.' Mia thought she could manage that, if only just.

'Good.' Without another word, Alessandro Costa strode out of the office, closing the door firmly behind him.

Mia let out a gusty breath and then, on watery legs, she sank into a chair in front of the desk. Now that he was gone, she realised afresh how much energy Costa drew from her, how much adrenalin he stirred up so her heart still pounded and her head felt light. Talking with him had felt like a full mental and physical workout. Ten minutes of it and she was, strangely, both exhausted and energised.

She was also...affected. The man's forceful personality was only part of his intense charisma; she'd felt as if she couldn't look away from him—the eyes that almost glowed, the barely leashed energy that radiated from him, the power that was evident in every taut line of his body. Even now she breathed in the faint scent of his aftershave, something with sandalwood in it, and she felt the urge to tremble. Thankfully, she didn't.

On still shaky legs Mia rose from her chair. She needed to show Alessandro Costa she was oh-so-useful, and more than that, she was necessary. Essential, even. Because she wasn't ready to contemplate the alternative.

Quickly Mia left Henry's old office and went to her desk immediately outside of it. The crowds that had been waiting for Alessandro Costa's arrival had dispersed, and people were back at their desks, attempting to at least seem as if they were working.

Alessandro was nowhere to be seen, and Mia wondered what he was doing. Inspecting the ranks? *Firing someone?* If the rumours were true, he'd fire most of Dillard's staff, just as he had countless other times, something she couldn't bear to think about. She had to focus. She had a job to do.

* * *

Dillard Investments was even more of a sorry mess than he'd realised. After a morning of meeting employees and assessing the company's condition, Alessandro Costa felt nothing but a scathing derision for Henry Dillard, a man whose affable exterior hid a terrible weakness—a weakness that had caused the inevitable loss of his company, his clients' assets, and the well-being of his employees. The man had the appearance of a lovable teddy bear, but Alessandro was glad he'd put an end to his benevolent ineptitude.

By refusing to keep up with the times and seek out new opportunities and investments, Henry Dillard had been slowly, or not so slowly, running his company as well as his clients' portfolios into the red, content to live off his dwindling profits and focus on his golf game. If Alessandro hadn't taken over the company, someone else surely would have.

Better, though, that it was him. This was his field of expertise, after all, and what he'd made his life's mission: taking over failing or corrupt companies and turning them into something useful, or else dismantling them completely.

As Alessandro knew and had seen, over and over again, the opportunity of defeating the enemy lay within the enemy himself...discovering his weaknesses and finding his vulnerabilities. It was a concept from Sun Tzu's *The Art of War*, and what Alessandro had learned long ago was that not only was business war, but *life* was war, a battle fought every day, and he had the scars to prove it. Yes, life was war... And he was in it to win.

At least a third of the employees he'd met with today would have to be fired. It seemed as if Dillard had never let anyone go, whether out of sentimentality, stupidity, or just sheer laziness Alessandro didn't know or particularly care.

He always tried to keep redundancies to a minimum, preferring to transfer people to other positions within his portfolio of companies, but many of the staff he'd met here clearly didn't deserve such an opportunity. Dillard's PA, Mia James, being a notable exception...

Surprisingly, reluctantly, Alessandro had been intrigued by her. She was beautiful in a very boring, very English way—straight blonde hair, cornflower blue eyes, a clear, healthy complexion, a tall and athletic figure, without any noticeable curves. *Competent*...in every way, and not the kind of woman that usually sparked his sensual interest.

She was the kind of woman, Alessandro reflected, who had probably been captain of her hockey team at school, who hiked on weekends and had had crushes on horses rather than boys growing up. Who would marry a suitable man and have the requisite two children, a boy and a girl. No one, clearly, whom he would let himself be interested in, much less pursue.

Yet she'd intrigued him. And he didn't like to be intrigued, especially not by a PA whom he would most likely transfer as soon as possible, because he worked best alone. Always had, always would, in every way possible. That was the only way he knew how to conduct his life, learned in childhood and honed to a highly polished skill in adulthood, and he didn't see it changing. Ever.

Mia James was waiting for him in Dillard's office when he walked in an hour after he'd last seen her, to the minute. Alessandro always kept to time, kept his word. Stayed in control, even in such seemingly small, incidental matters, as a point of principle, a matter of pride.

'Well?' he asked. 'Do you have the files?'

She'd risen from her chair as he'd entered, making him notice, rather unwillingly, her long, slender legs encased in sheer black tights, her feet in low black heels. She wore a black pencil skirt and blazer, a crisp white blouse, a simple gold pendant at her throat. Her long, wheat-coloured hair was caught cleanly behind in a clip. He could not fault anything about her, and yet he still felt discomfited. Irritated, even, by his own interest as much as her presence.

He didn't let people affect him. He didn't *do* emotions, and he most definitely didn't act on them. His own unsettled childhood was testament to the power of emotions, as well as the danger, which was why he behaved in a tightly controlled way that made *sense*. Because Alessandro Costa needed to be in control. Always.

'I have everything right here,' Mia said, her voice calm and cool. Unflappable, unlike how he was feeling, which annoyed him further. 'Personal files and relevant information on Dillard's ten most important clients.'

'And how did you determine they were the most important?' Alessandro asked, his voice something close to a snap.

Her clear blue gaze met his; she seemed untroubled by his tone. 'They are the largest investors, and they've been with Dillard's the longest amount of time.'

'Everyone's been with Dillard's since the time of dinosaurs,' Alessandro returned, his irritation making him more callous than he normally would have let himself be. 'That's the nature of the place.'

'Dillard's longevity is one of its points of pride,' Mia agreed, her voice—and what a low, pleasant voice it was—carefully equable. She would not rise to his irritable bait. Another point in her favour, yet unreasonably this just annoyed him further.

He sprawled in the chair behind the desk, beckoning her forward with one hand. 'So show me.'

Mia hesitated for the barest of seconds—hardly noticeable except Alessandro felt so weirdly attuned to her—and then she scooped up the pile of folders and walked around to his side of the desk, placing them in front of him and then flipping the first one open.

'James Davis, a millionaire who set up his own company to manage his financial interests. Inherited money. Generous to a fault. Affable and easy-going but very little common sense. Happy to follow a lead, generally speaking.'

Alessandro was silent, reluctantly impressed by how quickly and clearly she'd summed up the client. Given him all the relevant information, without anything unnecessary, exactly as he would have wanted. So few people impressed him, but Mia James had. *In more ways than one.*

He glanced down at the top sheet detailing the man's investments but the figures blurred in front of him as he inhaled Mia James's scent—something understated and citrusy. She was standing quite close to him, her breasts on a level with his gaze. Not that he was looking, but he did notice how the crisp white cotton with discreet pin tucks highlighted her trim figure. Perhaps curves were overrated.

What was he thinking?

Now seriously annoyed with himself and his unruly thoughts, Alessandro flipped through the pages, skimming all the relevant details with more focus than usual. 'He's operating at a loss,' he observed after a moment.

'Yes.' Another tiny hesitation. 'Many of Dillard's clients are, in the current financial climate. Henry—Mr Dillard—was confident things would bounce back, or at least even out, in the next eighteen months.'

When he would have been retired, with no need to worry about the financial markets or how they were affecting his clients. Alessandro had spoken to Henry Dillard on the phone yesterday, when the takeover had been complete. He always tried to treat his adversaries with dignity, especially when he'd won, which he always did.

Dillard had been furious to be bested by someone he

considered his social inferior—and had made that quite clear. Alessandro had taken it in his stride; it was hardly unusual when he chose to target companies run by men like Henry Dillard—entitled, wealthy, and weak. He almost felt sorry for the man; he hadn't been corrupt, like some of the CEOs Alessandro had taken down, just inept. He'd frittered away his family's company, indifferent to his clients' needs, and now he was angry that someone he didn't think deserved his company had won it fairly. Alessandro had no respect for such people. He'd dealt with too many in his life—first as a child, when he'd had no power, and then as a man, when he'd made sure that he did.

'Eighteen months is a lifetime in the stock market,' he told Mia. 'Henry Dillard should have known that.'

Mia drew a quick breath. 'As I said, longevity—'

'Was one of Dillard's assets. It isn't any more.' He swivelled to face her, tilting his head up to meet her blue, blue eyes. As their gazes met and tangled something clanged inside him, like an almighty bell. He felt it reverberate through his whole body, and he thought Mia did as well, judging from the way her pupils dilated, and she moistened her lips with her tongue.

'Sit down,' he ordered, and surprise flared briefly in her eyes before she complied silently, taking the seat across from him, so the desk was between them.

That was better. Now he wouldn't be distracted. He wouldn't let himself.

'Next, please,' he ordered, and calmly Mia took him through the rest of the clients—all of them old money, with an outdated view of investment, wealth, risk, everything. Dillard Investments was an institution that had lazily rested on its well-worn laurels for far too long…which was exactly why Alessandro had bought it.

Finished with the files, he glanced at Mia, who was sitting perfectly straight in her seat, legs to the side, ankles neatly crossed, her expression deliberately serene. She looked like a duchess. It annoyed Alessandro, as everything about her seemed to, which was a reaction he knew didn't make sense, and yet it *was*. It was, because he'd much rather be annoyed by her than affected. Which he also was. Unfortunately.

'Thank you for this,' he finally said, his voice clipped. 'Will there be anything else?'

'How well do you know Dillard's clients?'

Surprise rippled across the placid expression on her face, like wind on water, and then she gave a tiny shrug. 'Fairly well, I suppose.'

'Do you interact with them often?'

'When they visit the office, yes. I chat with them, give them coffee, that sort of thing.' She paused, her gaze scanning his face, looking for clues as to what he wanted from her. 'I've also organised the annual summer party for clients and their families, held at Mr Dillard's estate in Surrey, every year.'

'You have?' He would have expected Dillard to hire an event planner for such a high-profile event, but perhaps he was too indifferent even for that. 'That must have been quite time consuming.'

'Yes, but rewarding. I enjoy meeting and seeing the families. I've become friends with some of them, in a professional capacity only, of course. But after seven years, I believe I can say that I know many of them quite well.'

Alessandro could picture it—Mia circulating quietly through the crowds, always at the ready to help, providing whatever was needed—a tissue, a glass of champagne, a shoulder to cry on. Learning the secrets and weaknesses of Dillard's clients and their families, as well as their strengths.

Which made Mia James invaluable…for now. She could

help him to get to know Dillard's clients, so he could make a more informed decision about which to pursue or keep.

'So,' Mia asked as he continued to stare at her, his mind clicking over, 'was there anything else you needed?'

'Yes,' Alessandro stated as realisation unfurled and then crystallised inside him. 'Your attendance at a charity gala with me tonight.'

CHAPTER TWO

MIA STARED AT Alessandro's determined, unyielding expression, registering the iron in his eyes, the laser-like focus of his gaze, and tried to make sense of his request.

'Pardon?' she finally said, wishing she didn't feel wrong-footed by his invitation. She'd been doing her best to be the perfect, unflappable PA since he'd stormed into the office, practically vibrating with energy. At moments like this it felt like no more than a flimsy façade.

'A charity gala at the Ritz,' Alessandro clarified, his voice now very slightly edged with impatience, as if she wasn't catching on quickly enough. 'Many of Dillard's clients will be there. I'm attending to reassure them of their assets' safety. You will attend with me.'

A command, then, and one she couldn't afford to disobey. Still, Mia's mind whirled. She'd never attended such a highbrow function, and in what capacity? As his PA? *As his date?*

No, of course not. She was mad to think that way even for a second, and yet somehow the way he'd said *'with me'* had felt…

Possessive. As if he were staking his claim on her, branding her with his words.

But of course that wasn't what he meant. The prospect horrified her, and would undoubtedly horrify him even more. Alessandro Costa most certainly didn't think of her like *that*. And she most certainly didn't want him to.

But why did he need her at such an event? When she'd been Henry Dillard's PA, she'd always had a quiet, unnoticeable presence. Invisible on purpose, gliding through the shadows. She'd attended the summer party, yes, but only as the organiser, slipping quietly behind the scenes, doing her best to be both indispensable and out of the way.

She'd never gone to any other of Henry's many social functions—the balls and cocktail parties, fundraisers and expensive, boozy dinners in Michelin-starred restaurants. Of course she hadn't.

'I'm not sure…' she began, and then stopped, because she wasn't sure what she was trying to say. That she wasn't the kind of person he should ask? That she didn't normally go to these events? That she'd be out of her depth? All three, but the last thing she wanted to do was admit her weakness or unsuitability. Alessandro Costa seemed as if he was simply waiting for her to give him one good reason to fire her, and she was determined not to humour him in that regard.

'You're not sure…?' he prompted, an edge to his voice, as if he was daring her.

Mia lifted her chin. 'When is the gala?'

The tiniest smile quirked the corner of his mouth, electrifying her. The man was devastating already, but heaven help her if he *smiled*. His eyes turned to silver and Mia's insides turned molten. She swallowed audibly and kept her chin up.

'Seven o'clock.'

Mia's mind raced. It was undoubtedly a black-tie event, formal wear absolutely necessary, and her only appropriate outfit was a basic and rather boring black cocktail dress, back at her flat in Wimbledon. It would take nearly an hour to get there, and then back again…

'What is it?' Alessandro demanded, now definitely starting to sound annoyed. 'Why are you looking like this won't be possible, when I can assure you it is?'

'No reason,' Mia said quickly. She'd manage. Somehow she'd manage. 'I'll be ready at seven.'

'Six forty-five,' Alessandro returned. 'On the dot. I like to be punctual.'

Back at her desk Mia couldn't concentrate on anything, not that there was very much for her to do. Like everyone else she was in limbo, waiting to find out how Alessandro Costa decided to handle his new acquisition, and whether they would have jobs come morning.

A few minutes after she'd left the office, Alessandro strode out of it, without sparing her a single glance. As he stepped into the lift, she tried not to notice how the expensive material of his suit stretched across his shoulders, or his dark hair gleamed blue-black in the light. She certainly wasn't going to remember that twang of energy that she'd felt reverberate between them when she'd been standing close enough to inhale the heady scent of his aftershave. No, definitely not noticing any of those things. In fact, she decided, now was as good a time as any to go back to her flat and fetch her dress.

Her heart tumbled in her chest as she grabbed her handbag and headed out, half afraid of running into Alessandro and having to bear the brunt of his ire. It was lunchtime, so she had a reason to be leaving the office, but she still felt nervous about crossing or irritating him in any way. Her job, she acknowledged grimly, was in a very precarious place, no matter how *useful* she seemed to him at the moment.

An hour and a half later, Mia was breathlessly hurrying back into the office, her dress and shoes clutched in a bag to her chest. As the lift doors slid open, she stepped inside—and smack into Alessandro Costa.

The breath left her chest with a startling whoosh, and she would have stumbled had Alessandro not clamped his hands on her shoulders to steady her. For a heart-stopping second his nearness overwhelmed her, the heat and power rolling off him in intoxicating waves. Her mind blurred and then blanked, her palms flat on his very well-muscled chest, fingers stretching instinctively as if to feel more of him. She could not think of a single thing to say. She couldn't even move, conscious only of his powerful, hard body so very near to hers. If she so much as swayed their hips would actually *brush*…

Then Alessandro released her, stepping back, his mouth compressed in a hard line as he raked her with a single, scathing glance. 'Where have you been?'

'I'm sorry, were you looking for me?'

'I wanted the files on Dillard's less impressive clients. Did you think I'd be satisfied with only the top ten?' Even for him, he sounded on edge, his body taut with barely suppressed tension.

'I'm sorry, I was at lunch.'

'For an hour and a half?'

Mia shook her head, a flush fighting its way up her throat and across her face. She'd been afraid of this exact scenario, and now that it was a reality she couldn't handle it. He was still standing so close, and every time she took a breath she inhaled the aroma of his aftershave, felt his heat. 'No, of course not.' She drew herself up, holding onto the last threads of her composure. She could do this. She needed to do this. 'If you must know, I went back to my flat to find a dress to wear this evening. But I will have the other files to you shortly, I promise.'

Alessandro stared at her for another agonising moment before he gave a brief, terse nod. 'Very well. I expect files on all the other clients within the hour. Exactly.'

Mia had no doubt he'd been timing her to the second.

The man was a stickler for detail…among other things. Back at her desk she hung her dress up on the back of a door and hurried to amass the files Alessandro had demanded. She'd be hard-pressed to do it in an hour, but she was determined to show Alessandro she could.

Fingers flying, mind racing, she managed to assemble everything and jot down relevant notes, stepping into Henry's—now Alessandro's—office with one minute to spare. Alessandro glanced at his watch as she stepped through the doors, and then one of his faint smiles quirked his mouth for no more than a second, making her catch her breath.

Heaven help her.

'Impressive,' he said after a moment, sounding both amused and reluctantly admiring. 'I didn't think you could do it in an hour.'

'You underestimate me, Mr Costa.'

His gaze lingered on her, and Mia felt her body start to tingle and hum. 'Maybe I do,' he murmured, and held out his hand for the files.

Mia handed them to him, and then took him through each one, making sure to sit on the other side of the desk as he'd requested before.

It was surely better for her to have a little distance between them; being near him had the troubling side-effect of short-circuiting her brain. She didn't know whether it was his intimidating presence, his undeniable charisma, or the unavoidable fact of his outrageously good looks that turned her mind to slush, but something about him did, and that was definitely not a good reaction to have to her boss, or even to anyone. Mia never wanted another person to have any power over her—not physical, not emotional, and certainly not sensual. Just thinking about it made goose-pimples rise on her flesh. Alessandro certainly had the last one…if she let him.

'Is there anything else you need?' she asked once they'd

gone through all the files, her body tense from holding herself apart and doing her utmost not to notice the powerful muscles of his forearms when he'd rolled up his shirtsleeves, or the stubble now glinting on the hard line of his jaw. No, she was definitely not noticing anything like that.

'Yes,' Alessandro told her shortly. 'Show me your dress.'

Her mouth dropped open before she snapped it shut. 'My...dress?'

'Yes, your dress. I want to make sure it is suitable. As my companion, how you look is important.'

'Your companion...' Her mind spun emptily again. *Surely he wasn't suggesting...?*

'We are attending together,' Alessandro clarified pointedly, as if to highlight the utter impossibility of whatever she might have been thinking. 'You must be suitably attired. Now show me the dress.'

Wordlessly Mia rose from her seat. She had no idea what Alessandro Costa considered *suitably attired*, but she had a feeling her plain black cocktail dress, bought from the bargain rack, wasn't going to be it. Unless he wanted her to be discreet, even invisible, as Henry Dillard had? As she was used to being from childhood, slipping in and out of the shadows, trying not to draw attention to herself, in case she provoked her father's anger? Because in all truth she wasn't sure she knew how to be anything else.

She grabbed the dress and returned to the office, holding it in front of her. 'Will this do?' she asked, unable to keep the faintest tremble from her voice. She'd never had her boss vet her clothing choices before, and she didn't like it. She certainly didn't like feeling controlled, even in as small a matter as this. She'd had enough of that in her life, and she didn't want or need any more, not even by the boss whose good side she was trying to stay on.

'You intended to wear *that*?' Alessandro sounded both

scandalised and completely derisive. 'Did you want to be mistaken for one of the serving staff?'

Mia's chin went up. 'It's perfectly appropriate.'

'It's perfectly dreadful, like something a junior secretary would wear to the office Christmas party.'

She *had* worn it to such a party, and so Mia did not deign to reply to his remark. Alessandro might be offensively blunt, but there was more perception and truth to his remarks than she wanted to acknowledge.

'You can't wear it,' he stated. 'You won't.'

'I don't have anything else,' Mia returned. 'So if you wish for me to attend...'

'Then I will make sure you do have something.' He slid his phone out of his pocket. 'I will not have you on my arm looking like Cinderella still in her rags.'

'So you'll be my fairy godmother?' Mia quipped before she could attempt a more measured reply. What was it about this man that made her hackles rise, everything in her resist? Henry Dillard had certainly never made her respond like this, but then Henry Dillard had never spoken to her in such an arrogant, autocratic way. He'd been affably incompetent, content to let her organise everything.

Alessandro's eyes gleamed like molten silver as his mouth quirked the tiniest bit, making her respond to him. *Again*. A very inconvenient response, when her stomach fizzed and her heart leapt. Mia was determined to ignore it. 'Now, that is the first time anyone has called me that,' he said, his mouth curving deeper, and Mia forced herself to look away.

Alessandro angled his body away from Mia as he spoke into the phone, asking for a personal stylist to be brought to the office immediately. His right-hand man, Luca, took the rather unexpected request in his stride.

Ending the call, Alessandro turned back to face Mia,

trying not to notice the rise and fall of her chest with every agitated breath she took; clearly she didn't like him deciding what she should wear, although she should be thankful he'd vetted her selection. That black bag of a dress looked cheap and boring and was hardly what he needed his companion for the evening to turn up in.

'As your PA, I don't see why I need to wear some fancy dress,' Mia said, clearly striving to moderate her tone. 'Or, in fact, why I need to attend this gala at all. It's highly unusual…'

'You need to attend because many of the guests there will be Dillard's clients,' Alessandro answered. 'And you will know them better than I do. I require your knowledge in this matter.'

'Still…'

'And you need to wear a gown worthy of the occasion,' Alessandro cut across her. He didn't like her protestations; he was used to being obeyed instantly, and Mia James seemed not to have realised that.

'The clients will know I'm Henry's PA,' she protested. 'If I dress up like a proper guest, they'll think I'm putting on airs—'

'You are my PA now, and you are my guest,' Alessandro returned. 'You will wear an appropriate gown. I am sure there will be something you fancy from the selection provided.' He gave her a quelling look. 'Most women I know would be thrilled to have such an opportunity of choice.'

'Somehow I don't think I'm like most women you know,' Mia returned tartly, making him smile.

'That is very true. Even so, I would like you to pick a dress that is suitable.'

Mia nodded, setting her jaw, her eyes sparking like bits of blue ice. 'Very well,' she said, sounding far from pleased about the matter. Despite the difficulties of the situation,

Alessandro would have thought she'd enjoy the opportunity to select a new gown.

'The stylist will be here shortly,' he told her. 'Until then you may return to your work.'

With a brief, brisk nod Mia swivelled on her heel and walked out of the office, closing the door behind her with a firm click that was halfway to becoming a slam. It annoyed and amused Alessandro in equal measure. Normally he didn't like people to oppose him; in fact, he hated any sign of disobedience or disrespect.

As he was a man of both drive and focus, work was a well-oiled machine and rebelliousness was inefficient as well as time-consuming. And, while Mia's rebelliousness did annoy him, that contrary spark of defiance somehow... *enflamed* him.

The knowledge rested uncomfortably with him. He was attracted to her, he acknowledged starkly, and that was something he most certainly could and would control. There was no place for attraction within the workplace, and self-control had always been his personal creed, the way he lived his life. The way he stayed on top.

He would never, ever be like his mother, whose sorry life had been tossed on the waves of other people's whims, her poverty and powerlessness making her constantly vulnerable, searching for love and meaning in shabby, shallow relationships.

Alessandro would never be like that...never at another person's mercy...not even for the sake of a very inconvenient desire.

Still, he was uncomfortably aware of the simple *fact* of his attraction, as well as the realisation that his desire to see Mia attired in an appropriate gown was not quite as professional and expedient as he'd made it seem.

As she'd pointed out herself, she was known as Dillard's PA and a simple, serviceable dress would certainly have been adequate. Yet he hadn't wanted to see his date in something resembling a bin bag. He hadn't wanted to see *Mia* in it.

Still, he told himself, he needed to make the right impression tonight. The last thing he wanted was for people to look at him and think that an impostor had shown up along with his secretary. Because Alessandro had earned the right to be at the party, just as he'd earned the right to be sitting in the office. Just as he'd earned everything he had, fighting for it and winning it, time and time again, a man with a mission. A man who won.

A few minutes later Luca texted him that the stylist had arrived, and Alessandro rose to find Mia. She was at her desk, and as he came to stand behind her, glancing at the screen of her laptop, a cold wave of displeasure and shock rippled through him.

'You're working on your CV?'

She swivelled sharply in her chair, her eyes widening with alarm at the sight of him looking at the screen, but when she spoke her voice was cool. 'For when I'm no longer *useful*.'

'And that is not now.' With one brisk movement Alessandro clicked the mouse to close the document, without saving any changes. Mia's mouth compressed but she did not protest against his action. 'The stylist is here. You may use my office.'

Mia's eyes flashed and he wondered what she objected to—his dismissal of her dress, or his order for a new one? Or simply his manner, which was even more autocratic than usual, because it felt like the best defence against this irritating and inconvenient attraction that simmered beneath the surface, threatening to bubble up?

Even now he found himself sneaking looks at the tantalising vee of ivory skin visible at the all too modest neck of her blouse, and noting the soft curve of her jaw, and the way a wisp of golden hair had fallen against her cheek. He itched to tuck it behind her ear, let his fingers skim to her lobe, a prospect which was too bizarre to be entertained even for a second.

He didn't want to do things like that. *Ever.* Relationships were not on his radar, and sex was nothing more than a physical urge to be sated like any other. He'd always been able to find women who were agreeable to his terms. More than agreeable, so why was he feeling this strange way about Mia James?

He wasn't. Or at least he wouldn't. He wouldn't let himself. Work was too important to risk for a moment's satisfaction, even with someone as annoyingly beguiling as the woman in front of him.

'Are you coming?' he asked tersely, and she nodded, rising from her seat with unconscious elegance, following him with a graceful, long-legged stride. Alessandro found himself watching the gentle sway of her hips before he resolutely turned his gaze away.

A few minutes later the stylist arrived with a flurry of plastic-swathed hangers, an assistant behind her carrying several boxes and bags. Alessandro supervised their setting up before he decided to leave Mia to it.

'Let me see your final choice,' he instructed, and she arched one golden eyebrow.

'To approve it?'

'Of course.' That was the point of this whole exercise, was it not? Still, he decided to temper his reply, for her benefit. 'Thank you for attending to this matter.'

She pressed her lips together. 'It's not as if I had much choice.'

Alessandro frowned. 'I'm offering you a *dress*. Is that so objectionable?'

'It's not the dress and you know it,' she snapped, and surprisingly, he let out a laugh.

'No, I suppose not.'

'It's your entire manner,' she emphasised, and he nodded.

'Yes, I realise,' he said dryly. 'So at least we're in agreement about something.'

For the next few hours he found he could not concentrate on the business at hand, a fact which annoyed him as much as everything else about Mia James had done. What was it about the woman that got under his skin, burrowed deep inside? Was it simply her attractiveness, which was undeniable, or something else? The hint of defiance in the set of her shoulders, the surprising vulnerability he sensed beneath the surface? Why on earth did he *care*?

It was annoying. It was alarming. And it had to stop.

'Mr Costa?' The stylist's fluttering voice interrupted his unruly thoughts; he'd been staring at his laptop screen for who knew how long? 'Miss James has selected her dress and is ready for you to see it.'

'Thank you.' He rose and walked quickly to the office, steeling himself for whatever he was to see. Despite his best intention to remain utterly unmoved, he was still shocked by the sight of her, her slender body swathed in an ice-blue gown of ruched silk that hugged her figure before flaring out around her ankles in a decadent display of iridescent, shimmering material. Instead of back in a sedate clip, her hair was twisted into an elegant chignon. Diamonds sparkled at her ears and throat. She looked like a Norse goddess, an ice queen, everything about her coolly beautiful, icily intoxicating.

Desire crashed over him in an overwhelming wave, unexpected even now in its intensity and force. He wanted to pluck the diamond-tipped pins from her hair. He wanted to tug on the discreet zip in the back of her dress, and count the sharp knobs of her vertebrae, taste the smooth silkiness of her skin.

He *wanted*. And he never let himself want.

'Well?' Mia asked, her voice taut. 'Will I pass?'

'Yes,' he answered after another beat of tense silence, barely managing to get the word out. 'You'll pass.'

She let out a huff of sound, turning away from him, and the stylist's face fell a little bit at his damningly faint praise. Alessandro didn't care. Already he was regretting his command to have Mia accompany him tonight. Already he was looking forward to it far more than he should.

'I'll go and change myself,' he said when a few seconds had ticked by without anyone saying a word. 'Be ready to leave in ten minutes.'

Mia nodded, not quite looking at him, and again Alessandro was captivated by the curve of her jaw, the hollow of her throat, the dip of her waist, each one begging to be explored and savoured. He turned away quickly, striding out of the office without another word.

The sooner this evening was over, the better. This desire he felt was inconvenient and overwhelming and very much unwanted. But, like everything else in his life, he would control it. It would just take a little more effort than he'd anticipated.

CHAPTER THREE

MIA FELT AS if she'd fallen down a rabbit hole into some strange, charmed alternative reality...a reality where she rode in limousines, and drank champagne, and walked into a glittering ballroom on the arm of the most handsome man there.

Of course, as PA to Henry Dillard she'd ridden in plenty of limousines. She'd drunk more than enough champagne. But it had always been as an employee, someone to serve and be invisible while she was at it. Someone to make sure the champagne was flowing, and that the limousine arrived on time. Someone who didn't stride into parties, but sidled along the sidelines, checking that everything was going according to plan and keeping out of the way.

Tonight was entirely different. Tonight, much to her own amazement, she felt like the belle of the ball. It was beyond bizarre. It was also intoxicating, far more than any champagne she might quaff.

It had started with the stylist bringing out several exquisite dresses for Mia to choose from, and then doing her hair and make-up as well, before finishing off her incredible ensemble with the most beautiful diamond earrings and necklace Mia had ever seen.

As someone who had prided herself on always being smart and sensible, no-nonsense and pragmatic, it had felt to her as decadent as an endless dark chocolate sundae to be so pampered and primped. She hadn't expected to enjoy it; she'd been fully intent on chafing at every opportunity, resenting Alessandro's needless autocratic intervention, but then…she hadn't.

She'd submitted to the stylist's every instruction, and then she'd started to enjoy it. To *relish* it. Part of her was horrified by her own acquiescence, and what it might mean. And yet…it was one night. One magical night after a lifetime of having her head down, working hard. Why shouldn't she enjoy it?

At some point she'd let her mind slide into a comforting sort of blurry nothingness, floating on a sea of ease and comfort. As she usually tried to anticipate every possibility, consider every choice, it felt wonderfully relaxing not to overthink this. She wasn't going to wonder what Alessandro Costa wanted with her, or with Dillard Investments, or whether her job, not to mention any of her friends', was secure. She was just going to enjoy a night like no other, because she doubted she'd see another one like it, and that was fine.

And then the moment when Alessandro had come into the room and looked her over…that moment had felt as if the world was tilting on its axis, as if everything was sliding away from the comforting security of its anchor even as it came into glittering focus.

For that one second Mia had seen a flash of masculine approval blaze in his eyes like golden fire and it had ignited her right through, as her blood heated and fizzed and her mind spun out possibilities she'd never dared to dream of.

Then he'd told her she'd pass, his voice as laconic as ever, and she'd wondered if she'd imagined it. She must have. This was *Alessandro Costa*, after all. The ruthless, arrogant CEO she was a little bit scared of. Not a man interested in her. Not her *date*.

It just felt as if he were. And, more alarmingly, she

liked that feeling. She, who had steered clear of love and romance and even anything close to a flirtation, because she did not want someone to have that kind of power over her. Because her mother had fallen in love with her father all those years ago, and look how that had gone.

'*He loves me, Mia. Really. He just has trouble showing it.*'

Mia had listened to far too many of her mother's excuses before she'd died of cancer when Mia was fourteen, too broken and despairing to hold on any longer. Mia had had to wait four more years before she was finally free of her father's sneering control. And since then she'd made it her life's mission to stay strong, independent and alone. *Safe.*

But tonight she let her rules bend and even break. Tonight she let herself forget they existed. It was just a night, after all. Just one wonderful night where she could pretend, for a few hours, that she was a young woman with a gorgeous man, Cinderella with her prince before the clock inevitably struck midnight.

They'd ridden in a limousine to the Ritz, and Alessandro, devastating in black tie, his hair midnight-dark and his hard jaw freshly shaven, had barely said a word, which was fine by Mia because she could barely think. Dressed to the nines and even the tens in a gorgeous gown, on the arm of a beautiful man...going to the kind of party where she'd normally be holding doors or serving champagne... together, all of it, was utterly overwhelming. Intoxicating. *Wonderful.*

A valet had opened the door of the limousine as they'd pulled up to the front entrance of the hotel, and flashbulbs had popped and sparked as Mia had stepped out, blinking in the glare. She wasn't used to the spotlight; she always stood to one side, watched it from afar. It felt very different to be the one basking in the bright light, especially when

Alessandro had slid his arm through hers and smiled for the cameras, their heads nearly touching.

What was he doing? And why?

She still didn't really understand the need for her presence at the ball. Yes, she knew Dillard's clients, but she'd already given Alessandro all the relevant information in the files. And this was a charity event, not a business meeting. Surely he had someone else, a dozen 'someone elses', to accompany him to such a glittering occasion, a supermodel or socialite who would fit in more easily with all this well-heeled crowd? Mia didn't know how to rub shoulders with these people; she was used to fetching them coffee. She was out of her depth, and she never felt it more so than when Alessandro approached a group of people, some of whom she knew, and introduced her as his 'companion'.

Mia clocked the raised eyebrows, the curious smiles, the speculative looks, and like everyone else in the group she wondered what Alessandro Costa was playing at.

'Why don't you just tell people I'm your PA?' she asked when they had a moment alone. She'd drunk two glasses of champagne in quick succession, more to have something to do than because of any desire to be drunk, but now her head was spinning, her tongue loosened.

'Because tonight you are a beautiful woman who is accompanying me to a gala.'

'But…' She shook her head slowly, trying to discern the emotion behind his cool, mask-like exterior, his eyes like blank mirrors. The man gave absolutely nothing away. 'Why?'

He shrugged his powerful shoulders, muscles rippling under the expensive material of his tuxedo. 'Why not?'

'You seem like a man who has a very clear reason for everything he does,' Mia said slowly. 'So your "why not?" doesn't actually hold water with me.'

'Oh?' One dark slash of an eyebrow arched in cool

amusement. 'You surprise me with your perception, Miss James.'

'If I'm your companion, perhaps you should call me Mia.'

Something flickered in his eyes, and Mia felt a shiver through her belly in response. She hadn't meant to sound flirtatious, but she realised she might have…and she didn't actually mind. 'Very well,' Alessandro said after a moment. 'Mia.' His voice, with his slight accent, seemed to caress the two syllables.

'Where are you from?' Mia asked. 'It didn't say when I looked online.'

His eyebrow arched higher. 'You did a search on me?'

She shrugged. 'After I heard you'd taken over the company, yes, of course. Information is power.'

'True.' His gaze held hers, his expression considering. 'And is that what you want? Power?'

'I want to keep my job,' Mia said after a second's pause. 'And knowing my employer helps with that.'

'Mia!' A woman approached them in a flurry of cloying scent, kissing Mia on both cheeks while Alessandro stepped back discreetly. 'Darling, how are you? I heard about poor Henry…'

Mia shot an alarmed look at Alessandro; his expression seemed dangerously neutral. 'Diane,' she said, after she'd returned the woman's tight hug. 'This is Alessandro Costa, the new CEO of Dillard Investments.'

'New…*oh*.' Diane Holley's mouth dropped into a comical 'o' as she swivelled to face Alessandro, her eyes widening in shocked speculation.

'Pleased to meet you…?'

'Diane. Diane Holley.' She took Alessandro's outstretched hand, looking a bit dazed. As Diane shook his hand, Mia saw her expression change from surprise to admiration, her lowered gaze sweeping speculatively, and almost avariciously, over Alessandro Costa's admittedly impressive form. 'Very pleased to meet you too, of course...' she murmured.

Mia felt a sharp tug of jealousy, a reaction which surprised and appalled her in equal measure. *What on earth...?* She had absolutely no reason to feel remotely jealous in any way. She didn't *care* about Alessandro Costa. She didn't even like the man. And jealousy was not an emotion she'd ever let herself entertain. It was so weak and needy. It was also dangerous.

And yet...she was wearing a beautiful dress, and he'd looked at her, for a brief second, with desire in his eyes, and for a single evening she'd felt like someone else entirely, someone transported into a fairy tale, from the shadows to the spotlight.

Perhaps one evening was too much, after all. The last thing she needed to do was lose her head, even for an evening, over Alessandro Costa. The man was too dangerous, and too much was at risk. Not just her job, but her very self. She couldn't let Alessandro Costa affect her. Make her want. Make her weak. Not even for a moment.

Then he put another flute of champagne into her hand, and her fingers closed around the fragile crystal stem automatically. 'You looked as if you were a million miles away,' he murmured, his voice low and honeyed. 'Don't you like hearing about Diane Holley's corgis?'

'Corgis?' Blinking, Mia realised Diane must have been chatting to Alessandro for a few minutes at least and she hadn't taken in a word. The older woman, the wife of one of Dillard's most important clients, had already moved on. 'She told you about her corgis?'

'I asked about them. You mentioned them this afternoon.'

'Did I?'

Alessandro arched an eyebrow, looking more amused

than annoyed—for once. 'You really haven't been paying attention, have you?'

'Of course I have. I always do.' She took a defiant sip of champagne. 'Diane has four corgis, and one of them has digestive issues.'

'She didn't mention those tonight, thankfully.'

'You were lucky, then.' Mia's breath came out in a surprised hiss as Alessandro took her elbow, his hand warm and dry and so very sure as he steered her towards another cluster of people. 'Where…where are we going?'

'To mingle, of course. That's why we're here. You're going to introduce me to all these people, and then tell me their secrets.'

'I thought I'd already done that this afternoon. Besides, I don't know any secrets.'

'I still need to put names to faces. And I think you know more secrets than you realise…always working behind the scenes, listening in the shadows.'

'You make me sound like a snoop.'

'No, someone who is smart.' His gaze lingered on hers for a tantalising second as his hand had moved from her elbow to her waist, his fingers splayed across her hip. Heat flooded Mia's body, and once again she was in danger of drifting along this lovely tide of feeling. 'Mr Costa…'

'You must call me Alessandro.'

'*You* must stop acting like I'm your date.' She knew she never would have said the words if she hadn't had two glasses of champagne, and just chugged half of her third. If she wasn't so afraid of how much he affected her.

'Why? You are my date.' He sounded utterly unruffled, like someone making a simple statement of fact.

'No…' Her breath came out in a rush. Her head spun. People were *looking* at them. Wondering. 'I'm not. Not really…'

'Yes, you are.' They'd reached the group of people, and

Alessandro kept his hand on her waist as he stretched out his other one. 'Alessandro Costa, CEO of Dillard Investments.' In turn, everyone shook his hand, with varying expressions of pleasure, speculation, or snobbery. It made Mia wonder yet again about Alessandro. What was he doing here, exactly? Why did he want her with him? Who *was* this man at her side? And how much did she want to know?

The chit-chat washed over her as she took in Alessandro's easy, urbane manner. The man could be charming when he chose, a fact that alarmed her. If Alessandro Costa affected her when he was blunt and brusque, heaven help her when he was easy and affable.

She knew a few people in the group through Dillard's, and somehow, her mind still spinning, she made chit-chat, introduced Alessandro to a few others, and stumbled through the evening, feeling as if she were acting a part in a play, desperate now to get to the end of the evening without embarrassing herself or losing her head entirely over the man at her side.

When they were alone again, and she was finishing her third glass of champagne, she rather recklessly asked him about it all.

'I can make conversation, if that's what you mean,' he answered as he sipped his own champagne.

'What do you want from these people?' Mia asked, her tongue well and truly loosened by now. 'Why did you buy Dillard Investments, really?'

A guarded look came over his face before he shrugged, the movement clearly meant to be dismissive. 'Why do I buy any company?'

'You tell me.'

The tiniest of pauses. 'For financial gain.'

'But you said yourself Dillard's was operating at a loss.'

'That doesn't mean it always has to.'

'Still…' She shook her head slowly. 'A man like you…'

'A man like me?' Alessandro's voice sharpened. 'What does that mean, exactly?'

'Only that you must always have your eye on the bottom line.'

'True.' He eyed her thoughtfully. 'So what did you learn about me, during that online cyberstalking session?'

Mia let out a choked laugh. 'I was hardly *stalking*.'

'Weren't you?'

'Gathering information. Big difference.'

'Hmm.' She felt dizzy with the turn in their conversation. It almost felt as if…as if they were flirting. But of course they couldn't be. 'So,' Alessandro asked, stepping closer, 'what did you learn about me, Mia?'

Alessandro hadn't meant to ask the question. He surely didn't mean to bother with the answer. He was curious despite his determination never to be curious about anyone. Curiosity implied caring, and he didn't care. And yet… 'Anything interesting?' The words sounded provocative.

Mia licked her lips, her tongue looking very pink as she touched it to her full, lush lips, the instinctive movement causing a dart of desire to arrow through him, unsettling in its intensity. 'Not really.' Her gaze skittered away from his. 'Not much.'

'Tell me.' His voice was low, the words a command, but with a thread of something dark and rich running through it, a promise he hadn't meant to make. Mia turned to look at him, her eyes widening, looking very blue and clear. Eyes he could drown in if he let himself. He stepped closer. 'Tell me,' he said again.

'Well…' Again her tongue touched her lips. 'You have a reputation for being ruthless. You take over companies, strip them of their assets, and fire about ninety percent of the staff before absorbing the company into Costa International.'

That was the gist without being entirely true, but Alessandro wasn't about to defend his actions. They spoke for themselves.

'Are you going to do that with Dillard's?' Her chin lifted a little. 'Fire everyone? Get rid of it all?'

He eyed her for a moment, considering what to tell her. For some contrary reason he didn't like the thought of her thinking badly of him, which was ridiculous, because he'd been thought of far worse by the furious CEOs he'd displaced.

'I'm not going to fire everyone,' he said at last. 'I never do.'

'Ninety percent, then.'

'Your percentages are a bit off.'

'Do you enjoy it?' she asked, her voice choking. 'Ruining people's lives?'

He stared at her for a moment, fighting the urge to explain the truth of his mission. But, no. He was not going to justify himself to her. He was certainly not going to care about her opinion. 'Does it seem as if I do?' he asked, meaning to sound dismissive.

Slowly she shook her head. 'You don't actually seem *cruel.*'

'No?' He tried to keep his voice disinterested.

'The media portrayed you as a bit of a cowboy… someone who came from nowhere and had a meteoric rise. Not entirely respectable, but not cruel.'

'Well, they were wrong,' Alessandro said lightly, even though her words were like razors on his skin. 'I'm not at all respectable.'

'Is that why you took Dillard's over? To seem respectable?'

The question grated. As if he wanted to don Dillard's

shabby suit and call himself a gentleman. 'Not at all. I don't care one iota if I seem respectable or not.'

'Then why bother with them? Where is the profit?'

'In the clients I keep.' Although Alessandro suspected there would be little profit indeed. Profit was not why he did what he did, at least not in regard to companies such as Dillard's.

'And what about all the employees? Innocent people… don't you care about them?'

More than she would ever know. 'You're sounding like a crusader, Mia,' he warned her. He did not wish to discuss this any longer. 'It's quite dull.'

Her eyes flashed. 'So sorry I'm boring you, but people's lives are at stake. Besides… I would have thought you might understand how they felt.'

He tensed, the perception in her eyes like a needle burrowing into his skin. 'Oh?'

'The media said you came from a poor background… the slums of Naples.' He angled his head away from her, not trusting the expression on his face. 'Is that true?'

'Slums is such a pejorative word, but I suppose, in essence, yes.' He did his best to sound bored. He *was* bored.

The last thing he wanted to talk about was his pathetic past…the endless chaos of moving from grotty flat to grotty flat, the stints in foster care when his mother had lost custody of him, the endless jobs she'd taken cleaning office buildings, the countless boyfriends she'd had in a desperate bid to assuage the despairing sadness of her life. A childhood he'd done his best always to remember, to remind him of how he would be different, even as he pretended to forget.

'Then if you know what it's like to be poor, to live from pay check to pay check, how can you fire people like that?'

'Because I know what it's like to work hard,' he said in a steely voice, 'and to earn what I have. And anyone who does those things will have a position with Costa International, that much I guarantee.'

Her eyes widened. 'They will?'

She sounded so hopeful it made him cringe. 'Dillard Investments was dying on the vine. I just plucked it before it fell, withered, to the ground. If anything, I've *saved* people's jobs in the long run.'

'Do you really mean that?'

Impatient now, he shrugged. 'Henry Dillard was charming, I'll grant you that, but he was a terrible businessman. I did his employees a favour.' *Why* had he stooped to justifying himself? 'I'm not the monster you seem to think I am,' he finished levelly. 'Regardless of what you read online.'

She stared at him for a moment, and he felt as if she were seeing right inside him, that blue, blue gaze burrowing deep down inside his soul, reaching places he'd closed off for good. He looked away, shrugging as he took a sip of champagne, struggling to master his wayward emotions.

'No,' she said softly. 'I don't think you are.'

'You've changed your mind?' He'd meant to sound offhand and failed.

'I think you like to present yourself as someone hardened and ruthless,' she said slowly. 'It's the right image for someone who specialises in corporate takeovers, isn't it?'

'I suppose.' What else could he say? She saw too much already.

'I wonder who you really are,' she murmured. 'I wonder what you're hiding.' Alessandro stared at her, unable to look away. He felt a tug low in his belly, pulling him towards her. She wanted to *know* him. It was beguiling, alarming. Nobody knew him, not like that.

'Let's dance,' he said, his voice roughened with emotion. When they danced, they wouldn't talk. She wouldn't say things or see inside him. He would make sure of it.

Wordlessly Mia nodded, and after depositing their

empty champagne flutes on a nearby table, Alessandro took her by the hand and led her to the ballroom's parquet dance floor. The music was a slow, sensuous piece, the sonorous wail of a saxophone wrapping its lonely notes around them as Alessandro took her into his arms.

Her hips bumped his gently and heat flared white-hot, making his hands tense on hers before he deliberately relaxed his grip and began to move her around the floor.

She was elegant in his arms, matching the rhythm of his movements, her hips swaying, her body lithe. Lithe and eager. He felt her tremble and knew, like him, she felt this most inconvenient and heady desire, growing stronger with every second they swayed together. The realisation only stoked his own.

Sex, for him, had always been a matter of expediency, a physical need to be met like any other—food, water, sleep, sex. That was how he'd viewed it. Something to be ticked off, the same as he would with a physical workout or a medical examination.

This felt different. *More.* This desire, twining through him like some dangerous vine, felt capable of overwhelming him. Overtaking the rational thought, common sense and, far worse, the self-control that were the touchstones of his life, the anchors of his soul. And the most alarming part was, in this moment he didn't even think he cared.

The pressures of overseeing the takeover, the twenty-hour work days and the ceaseless striving, for years now, decades…in this moment he sloughed it all off like an old skin, let it slither about him in dead, dried peels, as desire birthed him anew.

The song ended and another started, and still they kept dancing. He pulled her closer, so her body nestled into his. She came willingly, twining her arms around his neck, her breasts brushing his chest. Her head was slightly bowed, so he could see the delicate, vulnerable curve of her neck and he had the nearly irresistible urge to press his lips there, against the skin he knew would be warm and soft and silky.

They twirled around again, and she shifted in his arms, the material of her dress rustling and sliding, pulling taut across her breasts, revealing the pure line of her collarbone. He could press his lips there too.

He could do it, and in the haze of his desire, as well as his exhaustion and the champagne he had drunk, he couldn't remember a single reason not to.

The music swelled and the world around him fell away. There was nothing but this. *Her.* They turned again, her dress flaring out from her ankles, brushing his legs.

Some last, desperate part of him tried to claw back his sanity, his sense. This was a bad idea. A terrible, terrible idea. Mia James worked for him, and he never mixed business with pleasure. Ever. It was far too dangerous. The last thing he needed was a woman at work laying claim to any part of him, or, heaven forbid, accusing him of something.

But there was nothing accusatory in the way Mia was melting into him, her body pliant and willing in his arms. Then she lifted her head, tilting her face upwards, her gaze clashing and then tangling with his.

It felt as if they shared an entire conversation in that silent gaze, a shared yearning and a deeper need, a question and an answer, all encapsulated in a single, burning glance.

Neither of them said a word, but Alessandro felt a shudder run through her as he held her in his arms. The last part of his sanity trickled away. He didn't care.

He didn't care.

'Let's go,' he said, his voice rough with need.

'Where?' Even with her in his arms, he strained to hear her breathy whisper.

'Anywhere.'

Her eyes widened, her lips parting. She swallowed, and he waited for her answer, the one she'd already given in the silent yearning of her gaze. The song ended, and their bodies stilled. Still Alessandro waited, his breath held, his body taut.

Then wordlessly, her eyes wide, Mia nodded.

Alessandro didn't wait for more. Taking her by the hand, he led her from the dance floor and out of the ballroom, out of the hotel, into the warm spring night.

CHAPTER FOUR

THE COOL NIGHT air felt like a slap on her face as Mia left the hotel, Alessandro clasping her hand tightly. It felt like an urgent and much-needed wake-up call.

What on earth was she doing?

What madness had possessed her up there in the ballroom, with the music and the champagne and the slow sway of Alessandro's body in rhythm with hers?

A limousine pulled up to the kerb; Alessandro must have texted his driver while she'd been in this heady daze of desire, a fog that had wrapped her up in its sensuous, blinding warmth, making her immune to everything, including her own common sense. Wordlessly he opened the door and ushered her into the sumptuous leather interior.

Mia slid to the far side of the limo, shivering slightly in the still cool air, despite the sudden blast of warmth from the heater. Now that she was no longer in Alessandro's arms, in that strange, suspended, otherworldly reality... she realised there was no way she could go anywhere or do anything with Alessandro Costa. No matter how she felt. No matter what she'd wanted.

Already she cursed herself for having danced with him at all, swaying in his arms, moving closer, falling under his sensual spell.

What had she been thinking? He was her *boss*, and not a particularly pleasant boss at that, even if she now questioned whether he was as ruthless as he'd been rumoured to be.

Even so, getting involved with him in any capacity would be a serious, serious mistake, and one she had never intended on making with *anyone*. She sneaked a glance at his harsh profile, wondering what he was thinking, now that they were away from the ball, the music and champagne. Was he having second thoughts as she was? Regrets?

'Where…?' Her voice came out scratchy and she licked her lips. 'Where are we going?'

'Back to the office.' Alessandro spoke tersely, and when he turned to her there was something hard and resolute in his face, and his eyes looked dark and flat. Looking at him, taking in that unyielding expression, Mia felt chilled. Clearly he was having second thoughts as well, a thought that should bring sweet, sweet relief, but instead she felt disappointed.

Stupid, stupid.

They rode in silence to the Dillard building in Mayfair, the night a blur of dark sky and city lights all around them. The air in the back of the limo felt taut with tension, and Mia let out a quiet sigh of relief when the limo finally pulled up in front of the office.

'I need to get my things,' she murmured. She'd left her work clothes, coat, and handbag at the office, an oversight she hadn't even considered when she'd been dazzled by being the belle of the ball. The party was well and truly over now, the clock striking midnight, everything turning back to the way it was. There seemed to be no question of their going anywhere together, as Alessandro had hinted at the ball. All Mia wanted to do was go home.

'I need to get my things as well,' Alessandro replied. 'I'll let you go up, and the limo can drive you home.'

'There's no need…' Mia began half-heartedly, feeling

she should take the tube as a matter of principle, and after giving her a hard look, Alessandro shrugged, supremely indifferent.

'As you like.'

He swiped his key card and ushered her inside the building, everything now cloaked in darkness and quiet. Mia had been in the office late at night before, when she'd had to work longer hours for one reason or another, but it felt different now, with Alessandro walking right behind her, and gooseflesh rippling over her skin at the knowledge of him being so close.

The lift had never felt so small or suffocating as they rode up in a silence taut not with expectation but the sudden, unsettling lack of it. Then the doors swished open and they stepped onto the top floor of the building, where Henry's office was located. Mia walked through the dim open-plan space, lit only by the streetlights outside, thankful that this ordeal was almost over.

She'd come so close to losing her mind and heaven knew what else over this man. She could consider herself lucky, she told herself, even if she didn't feel all that lucky right then.

'I left my things in Henry's—I mean your—office,' she said, and Alessandro merely nodded as he opened the door and ushered her through. He flicked on a table lamp, bathing the room in warm light, while Mia hurriedly hunted for her bag and discarded clothes. She hesitated, knowing she didn't want to brave the tube home at ten o'clock at night in a floor-length evening gown.

'Do you mind if I change…?'

Another hard, fathomless look, another shrug. 'As you like.' He left the office, and Mia let out another sigh of relief and pent-up tension as the door closed behind him. Her head still felt fuzzy from the champagne, even though the main part of her was stone-cold sober, longing only to be curled up in her bed with a comforting mug of hot chocolate, this whole evening behind her.

Her fingers fumbled as she unclasped the diamond necklace that now felt heavy and cold around her neck. Carefully she replaced it in the black velvet box the stylist had brandished so proudly just a few short hours ago. It felt like another lifetime. Had she really danced with Alessandro? Flirted with him? Felt she had a connection with him, that something important and intimate had pulsed between them when she'd told him she didn't know who he was? And then she'd twined her arms around his neck and told him she'd go anywhere with him. She'd even believed it.

Her breath came out in a shuddery rush as she acknowledged the folly of her actions. She had done all those things and more, and all she could do now was thank heaven that it hadn't gone any further, and that Alessandro at least seemed to have had the same second thoughts she had.

The best-case scenario now was that they would both pretend to forget everything that had—and hadn't—happened. And really, she told herself, it wasn't as if they'd actually *done* anything. They hadn't even kissed.

But she'd wanted to…

Forcing those pointless, treacherous thoughts away, Mia took off the diamond earrings and put them back as well. Then her heels, silver diamanté-decorated stilettos, and her sheer tights, bundling up the tights and putting the shoes back in the box. Now the dress.

She reached behind her to unzip the dress, her fingertips brushing the top of the zipper but unable to pull it down. Mia groaned under her breath, nearly wrenching her arm out of its socket as she tried again, desperately, to unzip her gown. No luck. She couldn't do it on her own. And she couldn't go on the tube in this. She was going to have to ask Alessandro to help her, a prospect that filled her with dread as well as a tiny, treacherous flicker of excitement she chose to ignore.

Alessandro rapped sharply on the door. 'Are you nearly ready?'

'Yes.' Her voice wavered and she took a deep breath before going to the door and opening it. Alessandro stood there, frowning at the sight of her.

'You haven't changed.' He sounded disapproving.

'I know. I can't manage the zip of the dress.' She met his gaze even though it took effort. 'Do you mind helping me?'

'With the zip?'

Why did he sound so surprised, so scandalised? 'Yes,' Mia answered, and then, pointlessly, 'I'm sorry.'

Wordlessly Alessandro nodded and stepped into the room. Mia took another deep breath as she silently turned around, showing him the zip that ran from the nape of her neck to the small of her back.

Moonlight poured through the windows, bathing everything in silver, as for a hushed moment neither of them moved. A tendril of hair had fallen from her chignon and Alessandro moved it from her neck, making her shudder.

She hadn't meant to, heaven knew, she *hadn't*, but the response rippled through her all the same, visceral and consuming, and more importantly audible.

What was it about this man that made her respond this way? She never had before, not even close. Her romantic and sexual experience was basically nil, and that by her choice. Perhaps that was why she was reacting the way she was now, because she had nothing to compare it to.

And yet Mia knew it wasn't that. It was the man. The man whose sandalwood aftershave she breathed in, making her senses reel. The man who was now tugging the zipper down her back, slowly, so achingly slowly, inch by tempting, traitorous, *lovely* inch. *Tug. Tug.* Mia held her breath as Alessandro's breath fanned her neck, and then her bare back as the dress began to fall away, leaving her skin exposed.

The air was cool on her bared back, but Alessandro's breath was warm. Mia tensed, trying to keep herself from shuddering again, but she failed, a ripple of longing trembling over her skin and right through her. She knew Alessandro saw and heard it, felt it even.

And she felt his response in the sudden stilling of his fingers on the small of her back, the zip almost all the way undone. Still he didn't move, and Mia didn't either.

The world felt stilled, suspended; everything a hushed, held breath as they both remained where they were, *waiting*. Mia knew she should step away, just as she knew she wouldn't. Couldn't. In fact, she did the opposite, her body betraying her as she swayed slightly towards him.

Slowly, so slowly, Alessandro leaned forward. His breath fanned Mia's already heated skin as his lips brushed against the knob of her spine and he pressed a lingering kiss to the nape of her neck.

He hadn't meant to do it. Of course he hadn't. Alessandro didn't know what madness had claimed him as he leaned forward and kissed the back of Mia's neck. Everything about the moment felt exquisitely sensual, as if a honeyed drug was stealing through his veins, obliterating all rational thought, everything but this. Her.

And he didn't even care.

He felt Mia's instant and overwhelming response, her body shuddering again under his touch, and he moved his lips lower, kissing each knob of her spine in turn, letting his lips linger on her silky skin.

The moonlight turned her ivory skin to lambent silver; she was pale, a perfect goddess, like an ancient marble statue, the paragon of classical beauty. He continued to kiss his way down her spine, feeling Mia tremble beneath his feather-light touch. Then he reached the base of her spine and he fell to his knees, anchoring her hips with his hands, as he kissed the small of her back, a place he hadn't even considered sensual or enflaming until this moment, when it was, utterly.

'Alessandro...' The name was drawn from her lips in a desperate plea as the unzipped gown slid from her hips and pooled around her feet, leaving her completely bare. She started to turn and Alessandro rose, pulling her into his arms as his mouth came down hard and hungry and demanding on hers. She responded to the kiss with a frenzied passion of her own as they stumbled backward together, lips locked, hands roving greedily, until they hit Henry Dillard's desk.

Alessandro hoisted her on top of it, stepping between her thighs, as he deepened the kiss. He couldn't get enough of her. He didn't want to. All he wanted was more—more of this, and more of her.

He broke the kiss only to kiss her elsewhere, wanting to claim all her body for his own—her small, high breasts, her tiny waist, her endless legs. Mia's head fell back, her breath coming in desperate pants, as Alessandro explored every inch of her and still felt as if he hadn't had enough, a thirst and craving welling up inside him that could never be slaked.

He ran his hand from the delicate bones of her ankle up her calf, along her inner thigh, before his fingers found the heart of her and she tensed under his touch, her breath hitching as he deftly stroked her.

'Alessandro...' Another plea, and one he answered with his sure caress.

But even that wasn't enough; it wasn't enough when she surrendered entirely to his touch, her voice a broken, shuddering cry. He needed to possess her fully, to make her his own.

Still, one last shred of sanity made him hesitate. 'Mia, are you sure…?' His voice was low, ragged, but certain. He had to know that she wanted this as much as he did.

Her eyes fluttered open, the look in them both dazed and sated as she nodded, her pulse hammering in her throat. 'Yes,' she whispered. *'Yes.'*

Alessandro needed no further encouragement. He spread her thighs wider as he fumbled with his own clothes. Then seconds, but what felt like an eternity, later he thrust inside her, groaning with the pleasure of it.

Mia let out a startled gasp and Alessandro stilled, shock drenching him in icy waves. 'Mia…' He could barely believe what had just happened. 'Mia, are you…' he could barely manage to say the words '…a *virgin*?'

She let out a choked laugh, her fingernails digging into his shoulders as she anchored him in place. 'I *was.*'

Alessandro swore. 'You…' He bit off what he'd been going to say.

You should have told me. I should have known. I never would have…

He'd *asked*, after all. He'd asked her if she was sure. Now, his body aching and still thundering with need, he started to withdraw.

'No. *Don't.*' Mia clutched his shoulders as she wriggled into position underneath him. 'I'm all right.' She shifted again, her body opening beneath him, inviting him in further, and as Alessandro felt her welcoming warmth he knew he was a lost man. He started to move, and Mia gave a breathy sigh of pleasure as she started to match his rhythm.

The regret and uncertainty he'd felt fell away like a mist as they moved together, climbing higher and higher, until they both reached that dazzling apex, and Alessandro let out a shudder of sated pleasure as he pulled her even closer to him, her body wrapping around and enfolding his. He could feel her heart thudding against his own, and he knew he'd never been as close to another person as this.

Seconds ticked by and neither of them spoke or moved. Alessandro had the strange and unsettling feeling that he didn't *want* to move; he didn't want this to end. He had never, ever felt that way before after being with a woman.

Yet of course he had to, and so did Mia, and after another few soul-shaking seconds she started to pull away. Alessandro let her go, tidying himself up as Mia eased off the desk. Her head was bent, her face averted as she walked quickly to her clothes and pulled them on. Alessandro saw that her fingers trembled as she buttoned the now crumpled white blouse he'd admired earlier that day, in what felt like a lifetime ago.

Alessandro knew he should say something, but he had no idea what. Now that the haze of incredible pleasure was no longer clouding his mind, he was realising what an enormous, idiotic mistake he'd just made. Mia James was his PA, and he'd had her on his desk like a…like a…

No. He could barely believe this had happened. This *never* happened to him, because he never let it. He was too self-controlled, too contained, too certain of what he wanted, to let something as stupid as *desire* cloud his mind and guide his actions, even for a few seconds.

And yet that was precisely what had just happened. He could scarcely credit it, and yet it had. It *had*.

Mia had finished dressing and she stood there, her handbag clutched to her chest, her hair in tangles about her pale face, her eyes wide and dazed.

'I should go.' Her voice was a whisper, and guilty regret lashed him like a whip, which made him, unreasonably he knew, feel angry.

'You should have told me you were a virgin.'

Her already wide eyes widened even further, looking huge in her face. 'Would it have mattered?'

'Yes. I'm not accustomed to…' Alessandro gestured to the desk, unwilling to put it into words, furious with himself as well as with Mia. What had she been thinking? *What had he?*

'Well, obviously neither am I.' Her voice was grim, humourless. 'Let's just say the moment got the better of us, and move past it, shall we?'

He stared at her, surprised and a little discomfited that she was offering so pragmatic an approach, and the one he would have suggested but now oddly resented. Minutes before they'd been twined around each other like…but, no. He wasn't going to think about that. Mia was right. They needed to move past this—immediately.

'Yes.' His voice was tight. 'Yes, that is exactly what we shall do.'

Mia nodded, still looking grim, and Alessandro felt the need to gain control of the situation; somehow it had slipped entirely out of his hands, and he needed to come to grips with it. He needed to remind himself what kind of man he was, and it most certainly wasn't one who unzipped a woman's dress and then ended up having her over a desk in a darkened office.

Those were the actions of a man who had no self-control, no common sense, no sense of containment. They were the actions of a man who allowed lust or any other unruly emotion to control him, and that was not who he was. It couldn't be.

'Are you all right?' he asked stiffly. 'You're not…?' The question nearly brought a blush to his face. He'd never slept with a virgin before. 'You're not hurt?'

'I'm fine,' Mia said flatly. She reached for her coat and shoved her arms in. 'I just need to go home.' She made to leave and Alessandro stayed her with one hand; she flinched under his touch, which both shamed and hurt him.

'Mia, please. Don't leave like this.'

Her eyebrows rose. 'How am I supposed to leave?'

Alessandro didn't know how to answer, couldn't even determine what he wanted. For this never to have happened, he supposed, but there was nothing he could do about that. 'Take the limo,' he said at last. 'It will be safer and quicker.' She stared at him for a moment, her face like a mask, and Alessandro realised how little he was offering. *A lift.* But he didn't know what else he could give her.

'Fine,' she said, and then she shook off his arm and walked out through the door.

CHAPTER FIVE

MIA WOKE UP to bright, wintry sunlight streaming through
the window of her bedroom, her head fuzzy and full of
cotton wool from the three glasses of champagne she'd
had the night before, her body aching in all sorts of unexpected places.

For a single second she simply lay there, enjoying the
sunshine, and then memory slammed into her, again and
again, as the events of the last evening played in her mind
in an unwelcome and humiliating reel.

What had she been *thinking*? During the half-hour ride
in Alessandro's limo the night before, she'd been too dazed
to truly consider what had happened or its potential consequences, and so she'd simply blanked her mind, stripping off her clothes and falling into bed as soon as she'd
returned home, surrendering to the welcome numbness of
sleep, except it hadn't claimed her.

She'd tucked her knees up to her chest and scrunched
her eyes shut tight, trying to block out the memories that
insisted on coming anyway, relentless and so awful. So
embarrassing, so full of shame and regret, as well as pleasure and wonder.

She could hardly believe that she'd been so heedless,
welcoming Alessandro's kiss, begging him to touch her…
and losing her virginity on Henry Dillard's desk. How
could she have let that happen? How could she have let

herself be so shameless, so *weak*? What if this ruined everything?

Now, in the cold light of morning, she let out a choked sound, something between a sob and a horrified laugh, as she considered what she'd done.

Of course, it had been amazing. There was no denying or hiding from that stark truth. She'd been transported to a world of pleasure she'd never even known existed, and yet, despite that, she hated how in thrall she'd been to her own body, as well as to Alessandro's touch.

He had a hold over her that she both resented and feared, and the result was she'd lost something precious, something that had been hers, in the blazing heat of a single moment…and to a man who most likely didn't like her and intended to fire her in the foreseeable future.

Stupid, stupid, stupid. Stupid and shameful and wrong.

Slowly, still aching, Mia rolled out of bed and headed for the shower, more than ready to wash away the scent of Alessandro from her skin. She turned the water up to as hot as she could stand and let it beat down on her until her skin turned pink and then red.

She knew she needed to get out, get dressed for work, get *going*. She needed to face Alessandro, even if she dreaded it with every cell of her being. Judging from his reaction last night, he regretted their encounter as much as she did, something which was both a relief and an insult. Still, it was better for them to do their best to move past it, and pretend it had never happened…if they could.

Mia felt as if the memory of Alessandro, the strength of his body, the sureness of his touch, was emblazoned on her brain, branded into her skin. It was going to take a huge act of will even to pretend to forget it. *Him*. And yet she had to. The alternative was inconceivable.

Quickly Mia stepped out of the shower and dressed in a crisp skirt suit of navy blue with a pale grey blouse. She put her hair in a tight bun, determined to look every inch the efficient PA and not the kind of woman who had sex late at night in an empty office. Because she wasn't that person. At all.

Since she was eighteen, Mia had been focused on one thing—finding her freedom and forging a career that would give her independence and security. She'd seen how her mother had been miserably beholden to her father throughout their entire marriage, before the release of her death; she'd lived through the awful ups and downs, her father's sudden, inexplicable rages, his emotional blackmail and silent disapproval, his moods and tempers dictating the unhappy tone of their fractured home, and all the while her mother too scared and unsupported to leave.

Diana James had insisted she loved her husband, even when he'd never shown a reason to deserve that love. Mia had been desperate to escape it herself, as soon as she could. And she had vowed she would never lose her control because of a man—any man—the way her mother had. Yet last night, if just for a few moments, she had lost control, willingly, *joyfully*...and she was horrified by it.

Resolutely Mia gazed at her pale reflection in the mirror, determined to put last night behind her completely. Hopefully Alessandro would do the same, and she would return to being the useful PA he required...and nothing more.

The office seemed quiet as Mia headed up in the lift, everyone working quietly with their heads down, seeming apprehensive. Alessandro hadn't started firing people yet, and perhaps if what he'd implied last night was true, he wouldn't.

But who was the real man? The lover who had shown her a hint of vulnerability in his eyes, or the ruthless tycoon everyone said he was? Who did she want to believe in—and did it matter anyway?

At her desk, Mia let out a little sigh of relief as she looked around and didn't see Alessandro anywhere. In an ideal world, she wouldn't see him all day. She could organise the files he'd requested yesterday, and update her CV, just in case. After that, she'd just have to pretend to look busy until Alessandro issued some directives.

As it happened, Mia had barely sat down and clicked on her computer mouse before the lift doors opened and Alessandro strode onto the floor, emanating power and authority in a navy blue suit, looking freshly showered and shaven, reminding Mia of how he'd smelled. Felt.

She tensed where she sat, memories assaulting her senses, and then his steel-grey gaze clashed with hers before he nodded towards the office doors.

'Miss James...?'

Wordlessly Mia rose on rubbery legs and followed him into the office. Her heart was thudding unpleasantly as she closed the door behind her, trying to avoid looking at the desk. Last night when he'd hoisted her up on it, she remembered papers falling, the phone skittering across the polished surface with a clatter. Now, at least, everything had been neatly replaced and there was no way to tell or even guess what had happened there last night.

But Mia remembered. As much as she was trying to forget, she remembered... Alessandro's hands on her hips, her mouth pressed against his shoulder. The way she'd cried out...

Resolutely she looked away from the desk and fixed her gaze on an innocuous spot on the wall. She wasn't ready to look at Alessandro's face and see what expression resided there, derision, desire, or just remembrance. She couldn't handle any of it.

Alessandro cleared his throat. 'Last night...' he began, and then stopped.

Mia reluctantly forced herself to look at him, even

though everything in her resisted. His face was bland and closed. She couldn't tell what he was thinking, but she shivered just from the coolness in his eyes.

Last night. The two words did not bode well.

Somehow she forced herself to speak, even though her lips were dry, her voice a papery thread. 'Last night didn't happen.'

'While I'd like to agree with you, I can't.' Alessandro met her gaze unflinchingly. 'We didn't use birth control.'

Shock jolted through Mia at the stark realisation but she kept her gaze and voice steady as she answered. 'I'm on the pill.'

Alessandro raised his eyebrows, seeming sceptical. 'You are? Even though you were a—?'

'Yes.' She cut him off. 'It was to regulate my periods, if you must know.' Except she had, in the welter of her own emotions, forgotten to taken it that morning. And now that she thought about it, with the news of the take-over, she hadn't taken one yesterday either. It had hardly seemed important, considering her lack of a sex life, and yet now...

Mia swallowed hard. Surely skipping just two didn't matter so much? She'd take one later today, in any case. The amount of risk wasn't worth telling Alessandro about. She could not possibly handle his reaction to a potential pregnancy right now. She couldn't get her head around it herself.

'Fine,' Alessandro said. 'It's good to know a pregnancy will not be a concern.'

A pregnancy.

No, she really could not handle thinking about that now. And it was surely so very unlikely. 'No, it is not a concern,' she managed.

'And you do not need to worry about any possible disease,' Alessandro continued steadily, starkly. Something else Mia hadn't even considered, not remotely, although if she'd been thinking straight, she surely would have.

'That's good to know. Thank you.'

They stared at each other, the tension in the room ratcheting up with every second until it felt unbearable. 'Then there's nothing more to say,' Mia said finally, desperate to have this over, to move beyond this moment, and more importantly, beyond last night's moment. 'So, as far as both of us are concerned, last night didn't happen. We can move on as if it didn't. We need to, for the sake of…everything.' She drew herself up, determined to do just that. 'Is there anything you need from me today?'

Alessandro stared at her for a long, hard moment, a muscle ticking in his jaw. 'I'm going to write a letter to all of Dillard's clients,' he said at last. 'You can take it down and then show me a draft copy.'

Mia's heart tumbled in her chest as she felt a weird mix of relief and disappointment that she didn't want to understand. Alessandro was doing what she wanted…trying to act normal. 'Very good,' she said, and turned from the room to get her laptop.

A few minutes later Alessandro was sitting behind his desk and Mia was in front of it, the laptop opened on her knees, her fingers poised on the keyboard, as professional a look as she could manage on her face. This was going to work. She was going to make this work.

She was not going to think about how Alessandro had felt or smelled or tasted, how she'd come apart in his arms and was still desperately trying to put herself together. She wasn't. She absolutely wasn't.

And yet the memories still bombarded her as Alessandro began dictating the letter. It took all her mental power, all her energy and willpower, to focus on the words forming on the screen in front of her instead of what had happened between them last night.

It will get better, Mia told herself. *The memory will fade.* This was going to work.

This wasn't working.

Alessandro couldn't keep from the glaringly obvious fact as he dictated his letter to Mia. Twice he had to start over, correcting himself, because he was hopelessly distracted by the sight of her, looking as prim and proper as you please, yet still, amazingly, seeming sexy to him.

That tight topknot made him long to pluck the pins from it and run his fingers through the spill of straight, wheat-gold hair. The crisp grey blouse with the mother-of-pearl buttons seemed to be begging to be undone, button by tiny button. The crisp navy suit would look far better crumpled on the floor.

'Mr Costa?' Her voice, crisp and precise, broke into his scattered thoughts. 'You were saying…?'

'I think, considering the circumstances, you should call me Alessandro.'

Something sparked in her eyes. 'I do not wish to consider the circumstances, and I didn't think you did, either.'

'I meant,' Alessandro clarified, 'as your employer.' But he hadn't been thinking of her as his employee. Not at all.

A faint pink touched Mia's cheeks, making her look all the more delectable. Making him want her all the more. 'Of course,' she murmured, and turned towards back to her laptop, her gaze focused determinedly on the screen.

Alessandro went back to dictating the letter, but again he lost his train of thought, which infuriated him. This was *not* who he was. This was not who he could be.

'Mr… Alessandro?' Mia prompted. Again. Her eyebrows were raised, her eyes so very blue.

'Type up what you have,' Alessandro said abruptly. 'And I'll look at it then. Thank you.'

Wordlessly Mia nodded, rising from her seat in one elegantly fluid movement. Alessandro couldn't keep from watching her as she left the room, noting her long, slim legs in sheer tights, the low navy pumps. As far as he was concerned, she could have been wearing a negligee and stiletto heels. Her staid, puritanical outfit still enflamed him, and that was most definitely a problem.

The door clicked shut softly behind her, and Alessandro swivelled in his chair, too restless to get back to his work, although he certainly had plenty to do. He needed to weed through Dillard's clients and decided which ones were worth keeping. He needed to woo the clients he wanted to stay on and make sure that they did. And he needed to find positions for the employees he intended on keeping, and offer redundancy packages to the ones he didn't.

Which made him think of Mia. He'd intended on keeping her in the office for at least another week, to help smooth the transition period, but that thought felt like torture now. He could at least check on the details for her eventual transfer, to make sure it happened as easily and quickly as possible.

He was always generous with his offers, and so he would be with Mia. It made the most sense. It filled him with relief, that he could be proactive about arranging her inevitable transfer. All it would take were a few phone calls.

Alessandro felt his shoulders loosen at the thought of being free of this alarming obsession he'd developed—and over someone so unprepossessing. He'd been with women, *many* women, who were far more attractive and alluring than Mia James, with her straight hair and English schoolgirl looks. What was it about her that affected him so much, drove him to such irritating distraction?

It didn't matter. His involvement with Mia James was thankfully going to come to an end. He was just reaching for the phone to make the first call when a knock sounded on the door.

'Yes?' he barked.

'It's Miss... Mia. May I speak to you?'

After a second's hesitation he put the phone down. 'Come in.'

She slipped into the office, her blue eyes looking crystal-bright as she met his gaze, a hint of determined challenge to the tilt of her chin.

'I wanted to speak to you.'

'About?'

She angled her chin a bit higher. 'I'd like to request a transfer.'

Shock rooted him to the spot, the phone dangling from his hand. 'A what?'

'A transfer. I don't think it is prudent for us to work together. You mentioned that you found positions for your employees when possible, so I'm asking for you to find me one.' Her eyes blazed as they met his. 'Somewhere preferably not in London.'

She wanted to be shot of him, Alessandro realised dazedly. Just as he wanted to be shot of her...so why did the thought rankle so much?

'Where is this coming from?' he asked, even though he knew. Of course he knew.

'Where do you think?' she returned sharply. 'You mentioned my usefulness as your PA would only be for so long.'

'But it's not finished yet,' he returned, surprised and a bit alarmed by his own annoyance. He'd been planning this very thing, and yet absurdly he resented her suggesting it first.

'I think it is finished,' Mia answered levelly, her tone brooking no disagreement. And, despite the instinctive, gut-level reaction that he had to argue with her, even to in-

sist that she stay, Alessandro held his tongue. Mia wanted
what he wanted. Surely he wasn't so pig-headed as to resist simply because it was now her idea rather than his?

'There are two possibilities, actually,' he said after a
moment. 'I was looking into them myself, for this very
eventuality.'

'I'm sure you were,' Mia returned dryly and Alessandro
had the uncomfortable feeling she'd known what he'd been
thinking, and had simply pre-empted him. 'The first is as
personal assistant to the CEO of the Arras Hotel Group,
based in Los Angeles,' he said. 'It's a property company I
acquired two years ago, running luxury hotels on America's west coast.'

'Los Angeles…' She nodded slowly. 'And the other?'

'Personal assistant to the CEO of a tech company in
Sweden. Or, if you prefer, you can take the standard redundancy package. You'll find I'm very generous.'

'I'm sure.'

'I'll get you the details of both positions.' He leaned
down to his laptop, and a few clicks later he'd printed it
all out and handed Mia the pages.

She took them calmly, scanning them with a cool composure that somehow rattled him.

'Both positions come with accommodation provided,
and the salary is fifty percent higher than yours was here,'
he felt compelled to point out.

'And I can start immediately?'

She couldn't wait to leave, could she? 'If you like. Of
course, you can have some time to pack up and arrange
your travel. All paid for, naturally.'

'Naturally.' She glanced at the paper again. 'I choose
Los Angeles,' she said firmly, although underneath that
conviction he heard a tremble to her voice that unnerved
him. He almost told her that she didn't need to do this,

but of course she did. If not now, then next week, or the week after that. Better for her to feel it was on her terms.

'I'm sure you'll be very happy there,' he said as equably as he could manage. 'Good luck with your move.'

She stared at him for a moment, her lips twisting and then tightening. 'I'll clear my desk, then,' she said, which made it sound as if she'd been fired.

'You don't have to do—' Alessandro began, and she gave him a piercing look.

'I think it's better this way, don't you?'

Yes, he did. Of course he did. Even if he didn't feel like it just then. 'Enjoy LA,' he said stiffly, and she gave him one last accusing look before she nodded and walked out of the room.

CHAPTER SIX

THREE WEEKS AFTER she'd left Alessandro Costa, Dillard Investments, and her home country, Mia came home from work, unlocking the door to her sumptuous apartment in Santa Monica, one of Los Angeles' best neighbourhoods, with a tired sigh as she kicked off her heels.

Choosing to transfer workplaces had been the only way she'd known how to salvage what was left of her pride as well as her working life. She hadn't been able to stand working with Alessandro, and in any case she'd sensed that he would have her transferred or even fired if she'd waited long enough; she was no longer *useful* in the way he required. In fact, she'd become rather inconvenient. Choosing it herself first had felt like the best way to take control.

Since she'd left she'd heard through the grapevine that at least half of Dillard's employees had been made redundant with packages as generous as hers; the other half had been offered positions within Alessandro's portfolio of companies. He wasn't the ruthless tycoon she'd thought he was, at least not in that regard.

It was just in his personal relationships where he was truly ruthless. Because no matter how elegant her apartment, how cushy her job, Mia couldn't escape the feeling that Alessandro had wanted her gone, more even than she'd wanted to go. She hadn't seen him since the day she'd walked out of her office, which was how she'd wanted it—and how Alessandro had seemed to want it, as well.

Sighing, she changed out of her work clothes into more comfy ones, anticipating another evening in front of the TV. She'd been invited out for drinks with some of her colleagues, but for the last few days Mia had been feeling a bit off, tired and nauseous. She hoped she wasn't coming down with the stomach flu, and decided that a good night's sleep, not to mention a healthy dose of Netflix, would knock whatever she was fighting off on its head.

The next morning she woke up with her stomach roiling, and she barely made it to the toilet in time before it emptied its contents. She called in sick, although by the afternoon she was feeling better again. When the same thing happened the next day, and then the next day after that, realisation sliced through her, as sharp as a knife, and just as shockingly painful, even though she'd known all along it had been an admittedly small risk.

She hadn't had a period since she'd come to Los Angeles. Sick in the mornings, better in the afternoons, and so, so tired. She might have been a virgin, but she wasn't completely naïve.

She'd missed two birth control pills, and even though she'd taken one later that day, Mia had read online that she'd opened herself up to a small risk of becoming pregnant. And a small risk was still a risk.

Yet even so, she had trouble believing it.

One night. Two pills. Surely not...

Her heart turned over, an unpleasant sensation, as realisation trickled icily through her.

She couldn't be...

After work that day she went to the nearest pharmacy to buy a pregnancy test, flushing in embarrassment as she paid for it, even though the pimply-faced teenaged boy ringing up her purchase looked completely bored and indifferent.

She took it home, unwrapping it with shaking fingers, staring at the slim white stick in disbelief that she was holding such a thing, needing it.

She couldn't be...

She read the directions twice through, still in a haze of incredulity, and then she took the test, all the while telling herself this was crazy, impossible, nothing more than a needless precaution. The chances of falling pregnant after one time, and just two missed pills...

But she wasn't stupid. She knew it could happen. She just couldn't believe it could happen to her.

And then she turned the test over and stared down at the two blazing pink lines in disbelief.

She couldn't be, but she was.

She spent an hour simply sitting on her sofa, staring into space, having no idea what to think, much less to do. Her mind felt fogged with incredulity, unable to think beyond the reality of those two lines. She couldn't yet consider what they meant or would mean, or how she would respond to them.

Then, at some point, she roused herself from her stupor and made herself a cup of tea. Pregnant. She was pregnant. By Alessandro Costa, a man she barely knew and definitely didn't like, a man known to be ruthless in both personal relationships and the business world. And he was going to be the father of her child.

Realisation slammed into her with that thought; this was her *child*. The family she'd never truly had. And she knew, no matter how inconvenient or unexpected, she was going to keep this baby, this child of her flesh and blood.

And Alessandro's.

Armed with a cup of milky tea, Mia flipped open her laptop and did another internet search on Alessandro. She had deliberately not searched anything personal about him before. She hadn't wanted to know, or to wonder.

Now she blinked as image after image came up on the screen of her laptop of Alessandro. The sight of his commanding profile, those steely eyes, that impressive form... it all battered her senses, made her remember far too many things. The lingering way he'd undone her zip. The press of his lips to the base of her spine...the sudden frenzy of passion they'd both felt, obliterating all thought and reason for those few crucial moments.

As she clicked through the photos, she noticed a common feature, and her expression hardened. In nearly every image, Alessandro was with a woman. A different woman. Over the last month he'd attended a variety of glittering events, in London, in Paris, in Rome, always with a sexy, pouting woman, and usually one who was poured into a dress, on his arm. Clearly he'd completely forgotten about her.

She pushed the laptop away and took a sip of her tea, feeling sick in a way that had nothing to do with the tiny being she nurtured in her womb. That man—that ruthless, arrogant, philandering man—was her baby's father. And she knew she would have to tell him so.

She shuddered with dread at the thought of Alessandro's reaction. Disbelief? Displeasure? He was not going to be pleased, of that Mia was completely certain. And, judging by the way he handled hostile takeovers, he was going to expect Mia to fall in with his plans, whatever they would be.

And what *would* they be? Would he want to, heaven forbid, get rid of their child, considering him or her an inconvenience he couldn't abide? Or would he throw money at her, to make her go away? She knew he would want to do something, but she had no idea what it would be.

And what did *she* want? Never to see Alessandro Costa

again, preferably. Perhaps he wanted the same thing. Hopefully they could come to an agreement, even if this wasn't a scenario either of them had envisioned or wanted.

Of course, she had to get in touch with him first, and Mia didn't really know how to do that. She'd never had his personal information and she certainly wasn't going to find it online. The best she could hope for was to call the headquarters of Costa International and hope the message was passed on. After that…it was surely up to him. The thought comforted her. All she could do was try, surely.

The next morning, Mia made the call to Costa International in Rome, and got the switchboard.

'I'd like to speak to Alessandro Costa, please.' She tried to make her voice sound confident and firm, and had a feeling she failed.

'I'm afraid he's not available.'

'This is important and personal. Is there another number on which I could reach him?'

'I'm afraid not.'

Mia bit her lip, fighting both frustration and a treacherous relief. *She'd tried…* 'Then may I leave a message?' she asked, and the receptionist's voice was toneless as she answered.

'Of course.'

'And can I be sure it will get to him?' Mia pressed, determined to make a good effort. 'It's important.'

'Of course.'

She left her name and number. 'Please do give him the message,' she said, knowing she was probably annoying the receptionist but needing, as a matter of principle, to communicate the urgency of the matter. 'It's important.'

'He'll get the message,' the receptionist assured her in a bored voice, and then disconnected the call.

Mia sat back, feeling the tiniest bit relieved. She'd made

the effort. She'd tried to be in touch. If Alessandro didn't get the message...

Guilt needled her at the thought. She knew she could ask her boss for his personal details, although whether he'd be willing to give them out, she didn't know. Still, she supposed she could try harder.

But the grim truth was, she didn't want to. She knew what it was like to be controlled by a man, someone who dictated what she wore and ate and did. Her father had done all of the above, simply because he could. Mia had lost track of the times he'd insisted she change her clothes, or told her she couldn't go out, or insisted the dinner her mother had made was inedible when it had been fine. Her entire childhood had been one of barely endured oppression, and she could not bear the thought of opening herself up to that again.

Alessandro might not be as odiously domineering as her father, but already in their short relationship he'd told her what to do, what to wear, where to go. It was obvious to Mia that he was someone who liked being in control, not just of his employees, but everyone in his life. And she could not let him be in control of her, or her child. Not like that.

She'd *tried*. She'd left a message, she'd said it was important. And that, Mia told herself, pushing away the guilt that still pricked her, was all she could do.

A year later

He hadn't meant to look her up. He'd excised her from his mind and memory, or done his very best to, even if some nights he still woke up with dreams of her lingering in his mind like an enticing mist, making him remember. Making him want.

In his waking hours, he thought of her not at all, an act

of sheer, determined will, and yet, a year later, as he returned to the office of Dillard Investments that he'd done his best to avoid for the last twelve months, he realised some part of him had been thinking of her all along.

Alessandro had worked hard this last year to incorporate Dillard's clients and assets into his ever-increasing portfolio. He hadn't been back to London in all that time, but now, with another recent British acquisition under his belt, he had needed to return to the former office of Dillard Investments, now part of Costa International.

As he strode through Henry Dillard's old office he tried not to look at *that* desk. Yet even when he was determinedly not looking at it, he was remembering. Remembering Mia's innocent and yet overwhelming response, the way her body had clasped his in complete embrace and surrender. The dazed look in her eyes afterwards, the way her fingers had fumbled as she'd buttoned her blouse. And the next day, when she'd asked for a transfer before he'd been able to order it himself.

A year on, Alessandro could reluctantly acknowledge that perhaps he should have taken a bit more care with Mia's rather abrupt transfer. And now she was on the other side of the world, admittedly by her own choice, but he hadn't even checked whether she'd settled in or was enjoying her job.

It would be the right thing, Alessandro mused, to check on her, just to see how she was doing, that she was enjoying Los Angles and her position with the Arras Hotel Group.

He wouldn't have to talk to her; she wouldn't even have to know. He could ask Eric Foster, the CEO of the Arras Group, a man he'd put in place to run the half-dozen exclusive hotels located on the west coast of America that he'd taken over five years ago. This was nothing more than a courtesy call, a way to clear his conscience…if it needed clearing in the first place.

And yet, as he dialled the number, he felt his heart rate quicken. What if he was put through to Mia herself? What if she was happy to hear from him?

As if, on both counts. He was a fool for thinking it, for wanting it even a little.

'Mia James?' Foster sounded surprised when Alessandro mentioned her. 'She was working out wonderfully, of course. I knew she would, if you'd recommended her.'

'Was?' Alessandro frowned, a sense of unease clenching his gut. 'Isn't she still working for you?'

'Not at the moment.' Taylor let out a little laugh that Alessandro didn't understand. 'She stopped about three months ago, but she's expecting to be back this summer, no pun intended.' He let out another laugh, and Alessandro's frown deepened, his body tensing.

No pun...? What was that supposed to mean? 'Has something happened to make her take such a leave of absence?'

'Has something happened?' Taylor repeated, sounding surprised. 'I guess you don't know...no reason why you would, although I thought she was a personal friend of yours...'

'Know what?' Alessandro demanded, brushing the man's other words aside. He was not about to explain his relationship, or lack of it, to Mia James in any detail whatsoever.

'Sorry, sorry. She's on maternity leave. She had a baby three months ago. A little girl.'

For a second Alessandro couldn't speak. Couldn't think. He felt as if his brain were short-circuiting, misfiring. *A baby.* A baby three months ago...nine months after their night together.

It was impossible. *Impossible.* She'd been on the pill. She would have told him. Surely, no matter what had or hadn't happened between them, she would have told him. *It couldn't be...*

'Right, I must have forgotten that.' His voice, attempting joviality, sounded forced. 'Of course.'

'I hope she comes back,' Taylor said. 'She's a good PA. The best I've ever had.'

'Yes.' Alessandro's mind felt as if it was buzzing, full of static and white noise. He could not form a single coherent thought. 'Yes,' he said again, and then he disconnected the call. He flung the phone across his desk, glad when it clattered noisily across the surface. He half wished it would break, that something would, because he realised he was furious.

Furious, because Mia James might have had his baby and not even told him. Not *ever* told him. His fists clenched as his blood pumped through his body in hectic, vengeful thuds. How dared she? *How dared she?* To not tell him something so critical, so utterly important... To deprive him of knowing his own child...

Unless it wasn't his child?

A little girl. His mind raced as he paced the confines of the room like something caged. Could it be another man's? Yet she'd been a virgin, no other men in the picture as far as he knew, but of course he *didn't* know...anything. And yet he couldn't believe Mia would have gone with another man so soon after. Surely it was his. Surely...

There was only one way to find out.

He took his private jet to Los Angeles that night, cancelling half a dozen meetings without a word of explanation. The flight felt endless, his mind going in pointless circles as he considered what he would say to Mia.

If it was his child, his daughter, then he knew what he wanted, and he knew he'd do anything, *anything*, to see it happen. He'd grown up without a father, and it had tormented him for all his childhood. He would never, ever allow a child of his to experience that same sense of loss, confusion, and grief. He'd never walk away from his own flesh and blood the way his father had, without a single thought or care.

But perhaps the baby wasn't his. A thought that, irrationally, gave him a little lurch of disappointment, even as he recognised that his treatment of Mia had been less than admirable. Could he really blame her if she'd met someone else and forgotten him?

A limo picked him up at the airport and drove him to the address of Mia's apartment that he'd had on file. It was a beautiful, balmy evening, the sun setting over the ocean, its placid surface shimmering with crimson and gold, palm trees silhouetted against a darkening sky.

The apartment building where Mia lived was a two-storey stucco house with an apartment on each floor and a pool in the back. Hers was on the second floor, and he mounted the steps with grim determination. Rapped once, short and hard. Waited.

A few seconds later he heard light footsteps, and then the slip of a chain before the door opened. Mia stood there, the questioning smile on her face morphing into an expression of complete and utter shock.

'Alessandro…' His name came out in a whisper.

'You should have told me.' The words came out before he could stop them.

Her face paled and one hand fluttered to her throat. 'How did you…?'

'So it is mine?' he interjected grimly, and her eyes sparked.

'It is a she, which you probably already know, considering you're here.'

'Yes, I do.' He'd forgotten her fire, and how it annoyed and impressed him in equal measure. 'Are you going to let me in?'

Wordlessly she stepped aside, closing the door behind him. Alessandro looked around the room, noting its bland corporate furnishings softened by familial touches—a co-lourful mat and baby's activity gym on the floor, a pink bouncy seat in one corner, a wicker basket of bright toys by the coffee table.

He turned to Mia, taking in how she had changed. Her hair was pulled back loosely, golden tendrils framing a rounder, softer face. Her figure was rounder and softer too, more womanly. She was dressed in a tunic top and capris, casual clothes he realised he'd never seen her in. Of course, he'd barely seen her at all. He'd known her for two days. Two short, incredible, life-changing days.

Neither of them spoke; she regarded him nervously, wiping her palms down the sides of her flowing top.

'Where is she?' he demanded.

'Sleeping in her nursery. Alessandro…'

'You should have told me.' He couldn't get past that. 'No matter what did or didn't happen between us, you should have told me.' He shook his head. 'I can't forgive that, Mia.'

'You can't *forgive*?' Her nervousness fell away as she stared at him incredulously. 'You have some cheek, Alessandro Costa.'

Now he was glaring as well, both of them with daggers drawn, only moments into their meeting. 'What is that supposed to mean?'

'What makes you think I didn't try to tell you?' She planted her hands on her hips, her eyes furious slits of bright, bright blue. 'Why do you *assume*?'

He shook his head slowly. He wasn't buying that. 'If you'd tried, I would have known.'

'Oh, really? You, the head of a huge, sprawling multi-billion-dollar organisation? You think a message from a nobody PA would have been passed on?'

He frowned. 'So how did you try to reach me?'

'The only way I knew how,' she snapped. 'Through the switchboard of Costa International.'

His frown deepened, but he still couldn't concede the point. 'There must have been a better way…'

'And what way would that have been?' Mia challenged. Now she was the one who sounded angry and aggrieved, the one who was in the right, and yet Alessandro felt she couldn't be. *She couldn't be.* 'You didn't exactly want to keep in touch, did you? I didn't have any of your contact details, and I was under the distinct impression you never wanted to lay eyes on me again. Which was fine by me, because I didn't want to lay eyes on you.'

Which, absurdly, stung, even though he knew it shouldn't have. It wasn't as if they'd had a relationship, or even been friends. 'A baby changes things, obviously,' he snapped. 'A baby changes everything.'

CHAPTER SEVEN

MIA STARED AT ALESSANDRO, a feeling of dread surging along with the anger that had been her instinctive response, even though she knew he had a point. For the last year she'd been fighting a sense of guilt over the fact that she hadn't tried harder to tell him, but she'd always justified it to herself, telling herself at least she had tried to give him a message, and in any case he wouldn't have cared anyway. Presumptions, she realised now, that were utterly wrong, because Alessandro looked as if he cared very much indeed.

Now he was standing there in front of her, she felt overwhelmed by the sheer presence of him, too dazed to hold on to a single coherent thought. When she'd seen him at her door, she'd felt the blood rush from her head, and she'd had to clutch the doorframe to keep herself upright.

She'd never thought she'd see Alessandro again. She'd convinced herself that he would never find out, that he'd never look for her, that he'd never care. Clearly she'd been wrong.

Several times she'd wondered about making more of an effort to let him know he was going to be a father, but she'd never felt brave enough, and as the months had gone on and on it had felt harder and harder to do.

Once Ella had been born, she'd been too tired and overwhelmed to think about Alessandro at all, much less worry about him.

But now he was here, looking furious and wronged, and she had no idea what to do about it. After everything she'd been through—terrible morning sickness, a difficult labour and delivery, and Ella's colicky start to life— she didn't think she could handle Alessandro's outrage on top of it.

'I'm sorry,' she said as she did her best to stand her ground and meet his stony gaze. 'But I did try to reach you.'

'So what are you saying?' Alessandro demanded. 'You left a message with the switchboard saying you were having my baby?' He sounded scathing.

'No, of course not,' Mia answered with dignity. 'I would never be so indiscreet, especially concerning a matter so personal to both of us. I simply said it was urgent and very important that you receive my message, and I asked you to return my call. Which you never did.'

'Because I never got the message!' Alessandro exploded. 'As you very well should have been able to guess.'

Mia drew a steadying breath. 'That is not my fault, Alessandro.'

'No?' Alessandro shook his head slowly. 'Surely there were other ways, Mia. You could have told your boss, Eric Foster. He has my details. You could have got them from him, and contacted me directly.'

Mia looked away, knowing she could have done exactly that. Guilt needled her again, sharp, painful pricks. 'To be honest, Alessandro, I didn't think you'd care.'

The silence that met this statement was thunderous. Alessandro stared at her, his mouth open, his eyes flinty, before he folded his arms across his impressive chest and raked her with a single, scathing glare. 'You didn't *think*? Or you didn't want to know? You hid my own child from me—'

'Yes, I did,' Mia cried. 'I felt I had to.'

'Why?'

'Because…because I was scared.' She hated admitting it, but she didn't know what else to do.

'What were you scared of?'

'You. Sweeping into my life, making demands.'

'Like seeing my own child? Is that such an outrageous demand?'

'I was afraid you might ask for something else,' Mia admitted in a low voice. Alessandro's eyes narrowed to deadly slits.

'Ask for something else…?'

'A termination,' she admitted, unable to look at him as she said it. 'You didn't seem thrilled about a potential pregnancy when you mentioned it to me…' She trailed off, because the absolutely outraged look on Alessandro's face kept her from any speech or thought. She shrank beneath his anger, hating that she was doing so.

She'd promised herself never to cower or cringe, and yet here she was, doing both.

'A termination,' Alessandro said, and then swore. 'How dare you make such decisions for me?'

It seemed a strange twist of irony that in trying not to be controlled, she had come across as controlling. Mia sank onto the sofa, overwhelmed by Alessandro's anger, by the way everything had been turned upside down.

'I'm sorry,' she said in a low voice. 'I see now that I shouldn't have. You just seemed so alarmed by the possibility of a pregnancy…'

'And you assured me you couldn't be pregnant! You were on the pill.'

'I was, but I missed two, because of…well, because of everything.'

'And you didn't think to tell me that? To alert me to the possibility?'

'It seemed such a tiny risk…'

'Obviously not.' He wheeled away from her, his anger making him need to move. 'You made decisions you had no right to make.'

'I thought I was doing what was best. And it isn't as if you were checking up or even thinking of me all year, were you?' she flung at him, tired of being on the defensive. 'I did an internet search on you, you know. And I have to tell you, Alessandro, what I saw made me less inclined to search you out.'

Alessandro turned back to her, his powerful body taut and still. 'What you *saw*?'

'It looked like you were with a different woman every night.' Mia lifted her chin. 'Supermodels and socialites, by the look of them. Your bedroom must have a revolving door.'

'You almost sound jealous,' Alessandro remarked in a low, dangerous tone.

'Hardly,' Mia scoffed. 'But from what I saw, you didn't seem like father material.' As soon as she said the words, she knew she'd gone too far. Something dark and deadly thrummed through Alessandro, tautening his body, flaring in his eyes.

'You are not in a position to judge my parenting skills,' he said in a voice that was all the more frightening in its quiet intensity. 'That was not your right, just as it was not your right to keep this information—and my own child— from me.' Mia opened her mouth, trying to frame a response that was not quite an apology, but Alessandro cut across her before she'd barely drawn a breath. 'In any case, whatever you saw online…those were nothing more than social engagements.'

'Are you saying it never went further?' she scoffed. 'I have trouble believing—'

'I'm not saying one thing or the other,' Alessandro replied, his voice rising, edged with ire. 'It has no relevance. We weren't a couple. *I didn't know.*' He took a step towards her, menacing in his stature, his pure physical presence. Mia held her ground, but only just. 'No matter what photos you saw of me online, you should have told me I was going to be a father. *End of.*'

'Fine.' Her voice quavered as her hands once more bunched into helpless fists at her sides. 'Fine, I should have. I admit that. But…can't you admit your part in this? Getting rid of me the day after…' Her voice trembled and broke. 'The very next day, Alessandro. Can't you realise how that made me feel?'

Colour slashed his cheekbones as he jerked his head in a brief nod. 'It would have happened eventually, but I admit, our…liaison precipitated it. I thought working together would be a distraction. Perhaps I shouldn't have been quite so…abrupt.'

'So that was you making a unilateral decision,' Mia returned, her voice shaking, 'while calling me to account for doing the same.'

'They're entirely different situations, Mia. A job versus a baby. You cannot compare,' Alessandro fired back, taking another step towards her so they were nearly standing toe to toe. Mia felt exhausted by his anger; her daughter was three months old, she'd been going it alone the entire time, and she was hormonal and sleep deprived and very near tears. Still, she took a steadying breath and met his furious, narrowed gaze with a challenging one of her own.

'I'm not comparing, I'm only asking you to understand where I was coming from.'

'I can't understand at all where you're coming from,' he snapped. 'What you did was inexcusable—'

'Did you come here to blame me, Alessandro, for everything? Because I get it. This is all my fault. Message received. Now you can go home.' Her voice trembled and tears she was desperate for him not to see stung her eyes. She turned away from him, too tired to keep battling.

She flopped onto the sofa, tucking her knees up to her chest. She'd just put Ella down for a nap and she'd been hoping for a little sleep herself. Clearly that was now an impossibility, which alone was enough to make her cry.

'I'm not going home.' Alessandro came to sit on the sofa opposite her, his hands resting on his knees. He gave her a level look that Mia could barely summon the energy to return.

'What do you want, then?' she asked tiredly, only to realise how open and dangerous that question was.

Now that she could think about it all properly, the shock of seeing him finally starting to fade, she realised he'd flown a long way for nothing more than a confrontation. He couldn't have come simply for that. He had to want more. A lot more. But what?

'I want my daughter,' Alessandro stated simply, the words icing the blood in her veins and freezing her soul. She stared at him, as trapped as an animal in a snare, as his iron-hard gaze slammed into hers. 'And I'm not leaving without her.'

Alessandro hadn't meant the words as a threat, but he recognised that they sounded like one. He saw it in the flare of Mia's eyes, the pulse that beat in her throat, as her hand crept up to press against her chest as if to still her fast-thudding heart. No, it wasn't a threat. It was a promise.

'Alessandro, be reasonable...'

'Reasonable? What is reasonable about having my child hidden from me for three months—?'

'I didn't *hide*.' Her voice trembled but he still heard a note of quiet dignity in it that struck an emotional chord within him. 'Please, Alessandro, for...for our daughter's sake, can we not play the blame game? Surely we can reach some kind of…of arrangement…'

An *arrangement*?

Was she hoping to fob him off with some half-baked idea of shared custody, parental visitations? 'The only arrangement I'm interested in,' Alessandro told her curtly, 'is to take my daughter back to where she belongs.'

Mia's eyes looked huge and dark in her face. 'Which is where?'

'Home. My villa in Tuscany. It is the perfect place to raise a child.' As he said the words, he knew how much he meant them. His daughter would not have the kind of chaotic, unstable childhood he'd had, filled with strangers and strange places. She would have every need provided for, emotional *and* physical. And that required a home, with two parents fully involved in her life. He would not negotiate on any of those points, as a matter of principle and honour.

Mia pressed her lips together; Alessandro saw the sheen of tears in her eyes, giving them a luminous quality. 'And what are you expecting me to do? Just…just hand her over?'

It took Alessandro a moment to realise what she thought, what she'd assumed—that he would take their daughter, and leave her here. Did she really think him such a monster? Had she thought he'd been threatening *that*? He felt both hurt and shamed by the idea.

'No, of course not. I would never ask or expect such a thing. A child belongs with her mother as well as her father, especially one as young as ours.' *Ours*. A ripple of shock went through him at the thought; he had a *child*. They did. He still couldn't grasp it fully, the implications crashing over him in endless waves.

'Then…' Mia's worried gaze scanned his face. 'You

want me to go with you?' She sounded as if she could scarcely credit such a possibility.

'Yes, of course I do.' It had been obvious to Alessandro from the beginning, considering his own unfortunate background, and one he would never, ever wish on a child of his own. A child belonged with his or her parents. Always.

He could see now from Mia's stunned expression that she had not considered that. No wonder she'd been so hostile; she thought he'd been going to *steal* their child, as if he'd ever do such a despicable thing.

Mia shook her head slowly. 'Go with you…to Tuscany?' she clarified, as if she still couldn't believe it.

'Yes.'

'But…' Mia continued to shake her head, as if she could not imagine such a thing coming to pass.

'There is surely nothing keeping you here,' Alessandro observed. 'You've only lived here a year.'

'As you know so well,' she returned.

'So I fail to see any problem.'

'You just expect me to—to *uproot* myself yet again…'

'For our child.' As if on cue, a faint cry sounded through the flat, making them both still and stare at each other. The moment spun on, both of them frozen, and then she cried again. *His daughter.* 'Where…where is she…?' Alessandro began, barely able to form the words.

Wordlessly Mia rose from the sofa and went down the hallway to the flat's bedrooms. Alessandro followed, his heart starting to thud. *His daughter.*

'Hello, darling.' Mia's voice had softened into an unfamiliar coo as she opened the door to a small bedroom decked out in pale grey and mint green. Alessandro stood in the doorway, transfixed, as Mia went to the cot and bent over it, then scooped up the tiny form that had been inside.

She turned to Alessandro, the baby pressed to her shoulder, one hand cradling her head possessively. She was *tiny*, a mere scrap of humanity, and so very precious, bundled in a white velveteen sleepsuit.

'This is Ella.' Mia's voice trembled. 'Do you…do you want to hold her?'

Hold her?

Alarm warred with a deep longing. Alessandro stared at her for a moment, speechless and uncertain for what felt like the first time in his life.

Did he want to hold her? *Yes.*

Was he terrified? *Yes.*

He nodded, not trusting himself to speak, not sure what to do. How did one hold a baby? He had no idea. He had never held one before.

Mia walked towards him, still cradling their daughter. *Ella.* She came to stand in front of him, close enough that Alessandro was able to breathe in her achingly familiar scent of understated citrus. It assaulted his senses and made him remember far too many things.

'Hold your arms out,' Mia instructed, and Alessandro thrust both arms out stiffly in front of him. 'Not like that,' she said with a small smile, a surprising and strangely gratifying trace of laughter in her voice.

'How?' Alessandro demanded. 'I don't know what to do.' This was a vulnerability he couldn't hide. Knowledge he had never possessed.

'Like this.' Gently, holding Ella with one arm, she guided Alessandro's own, manipulating his limbs as if he were a mannequin, until one arm was bent as if to cradle a football, the other arm to support it. 'Now we just add the baby,' she said softly, and before he knew what she was doing, she put Ella into his arms.

He cradled her to him instinctively, pressing her tiny body gently against his chest as she snuffled into his neck. He breathed in the sweet, milky warmth of her as his heart contracted, expanded, and contracted again. He *felt*. It hurt.

'That's the way,' Mia encouraged him. 'You've got the hang of it now.'

He felt like a complete novice, inexperienced, incapable, and if he were holding the most fragile and yet explosive thing possible—a cross between a stick of dynamite and a Ming vase.

'I don't want to hurt her,' he confessed, undone by this child in his arms, this fragile, precious, *impossible* human being.

'You aren't hurting her,' Mia assured him. Tears sparkled in her eyes and she blinked them back rapidly. 'Trust me, she would let you know if you were.'

'Does she cry? Is she…is she a good baby?' He realised how much he wanted to know—all the details, all he'd missed. It didn't matter now that he'd missed them or why he had, he just wanted to *know*.

'She's a wonderful baby, but she's had her moments.' The smile Mia gave him was weary, and he suddenly noticed how tired she looked. Realised how hard it must have been, to parent alone all these months…which was all the more reason for her to come to Tuscany with him, where she could have help, and comfort, and space.

'You'll come to Tuscany,' he said, and it sounded like an order. Mia's gentle, tired smile faltered as a familiar fire sparked in her eyes.

'Alessandro, you can't order me about…'

'You'll come,' he insisted. 'And Ella, too. You must.' His voice was too strident, his manner too abrupt and autocratic. He knew that, and yet he couldn't keep himself from it, because it was so very important. It was everything.

He saw the remoteness enter Mia's eyes, felt her coolness as she took Ella out of his arms, pressing her against her shoulder as she half turned away from him.

'She needs a feed,' she murmured, but it felt like an

excuse. She slipped past him and went back to the main living area, leaving Alessandro no choice but to follow.

When he came into the room, Mia was sitting back on the sofa, Ella brought to her breast, one tiny fist clutching a tendril of golden hair. Shock jolted through him at the sight of her feeding their daughter, the simple, pure *rightness* of it, followed by a rush of primal possessiveness that nearly felled him with its intensity, its sureness.

This was his *family*. The family he'd never had himself, the family he hadn't even realised he wanted. And he was never letting them go.

CHAPTER EIGHT

MIA WATCHED THE streets of Los Angeles stream by in a colourful blur as the limousine Alessandro had called for her sped towards his luxury hotel in the downtown area of the city. After leaving abruptly the day before, when Mia had begun feeding Ella, he'd commanded she come to where he was staying to discuss their future arrangements...whatever those might be.

Mia had spent a sleepless night, wide-eyed and worried, trying to decide how she was going to respond to Alessandro's suggestion that she move to Tuscany with Ella. Everything in her resisted that notion, and particularly the high-handed manner in which he'd delivered it, as if he expected her to fall in with his plans without so much as a whisper of dissent.

She did not want to be controlled by him, and yet she feared she had no choice. Just like with her father, Alessandro was calling the shots. Just like her father, he had all the power, all the money, all the cards. It had taken years from Mia to break free from her father. She desperately wanted to have the strength to break free from Alessandro now, even as she recognised that Alessandro was a different man from her father, and she'd sensed a kindness beneath his hard exterior that made her want to trust him.

Still, it wasn't enough to move continents for, surely.

And yet... Ella. She couldn't deny Alessandro the right

to see his daughter. After witnessing him holding Ella, the obvious love in his eyes, surprising and powerful, she didn't even want to. So where did that leave her? *Them?*

In the car seat next to her, Ella stirred, blinking wide blue-grey eyes at the world, her thumb finding its way to her mouth, a new discovery. Mia gazed down at her infant daughter, her heart squeezing painfully with love. She hadn't realised just how strong that mother instinct would be, how that natural love would rush in, from the moment she'd felt Ella's first kick. The need to provide, protect, and nurture felt like an unstoppable force. It would make her strong enough to fight this battle with Alessandro...and win. She couldn't contemplate the alternative.

The limo pulled up to a tall, elegant skyscraper, and a white-gloved valet came to open her door. Mia unbuckled Ella's car seat and heaved it out, straightening her tunic top that she'd paired with loose trousers. Three months postpartum, she was still working off the baby weight, something that made her feel self-conscious when she was in Alessandro's hard, honed presence.

Inside the hotel's large and opulent lobby, all marble and crystal, a staff member met her at the door, clearly watching and waiting for her.

'Mr Costa is waiting for you in the penthouse suite,' she informed her crisply, and Mia followed her into a glassed-in lift that soared upwards, her hands slippery on the car seat handle. She wished he hadn't asked—or, rather, commanded—that she come here, to this glamorous place, clearly his turf. It put her at a disadvantage for the battle she knew was coming, and she suspected Alessandro had arranged it for exactly that reason. Still, she would do her best to stand her ground and make her case.

The lift doors opened directly into the penthouse suite, a soaring, open space with floor-to-ceiling windows on every side. As Mia stepped out onto the white marble floor, she felt as if she were flying—or falling. The sight of the city far below all around her made her feel dizzy.

'Mia.' Alessandro's voice was a low, steady thrum as he stepped forward and took the car seat from her, smiling down at a now sleeping Ella. Mia relinquished it unthinkingly as she took a few steadying breaths to combat the sudden feeling of vertigo.

Alessandro looked devastatingly handsome, as usual, in a crisp grey suit with a cobalt-blue button-down shirt and a silver-grey tie. He smelled amazing, too, the same sandalwood aftershave that Mia remembered all too well assaulting her senses and reawakening her memories.

'Would you like a drink?' he asked politely. 'Coffee? Tea? Juice?'

'Just water, please.' On shaky legs she walked to one of the white leather sofas scattered around and sat down. 'This place is amazing.' She glanced around the huge space, noting the king-sized bed, the sunken marble tub, the glittering kitchen with top-notch appliances, all of it open plan, the different areas separated by elegant shelving and tall potted plants.

'The view sold me on it,' Alessandro said as he fetched her a glass of water. 'I wasn't sure about the open plan, but the architect insisted it was the way to go.' He handed her a glass, which Mia took with murmured thanks before sitting opposite her, one leg crossed neatly over the other as he sipped his coffee. Ella sat between them in her car seat, fast asleep.

'So,' Alessandro said, his opening gambit. 'I've arranged a flight to Rome for this evening.'

'What?' Mia nearly dropped her glass, and her surprised squawk made Ella stir in her seat before she settled back to sleep.

'Is that so surprising? I told you what I intended last

night. Why should either of us linger? There's nothing for you here, Mia.'

'How would you even know that?' she demanded. She'd known Alessandro would have a plan, and even that he would insist on it, but she hadn't realised he would enact it so quickly, and without even telling her. It made her furious—and it also made her scared. He had so much more power and money than she did. His will felt like a force of nature. How could she fight it?

'You more or less admitted it yesterday,' he answered evenly. 'You've only been here for a year, and you weren't sure about coming here in the first place. Why stay?'

She'd stayed because it had been worth it financially, and she had no job waiting for her back in London or anywhere else. What friends she'd made in London she'd lost touch with over the last year, and none of them were in a position to help her as a single mother anyway.

She'd been stuck, and Alessandro was right when he said there was nothing keeping her in California, but… that didn't mean she wanted to go to Tuscany with him.

'I'm not committed to LA, it's true,' she said carefully. 'Although I've enjoyed my job here, and I was—*am*—intending to return to it in a few months. But that doesn't mean I want to live in Italy. I don't even know the language, Alessandro.'

He shrugged, dismissive. 'You'll learn. And there's no reason for you to return to work when I will be providing for you.'

'I like working—'

'Then perhaps you can return to it when Ella is a bit older.'

Although she greatly disliked his high-handed manner, Mia wasn't willing to fight that particular battle along with all the others. The truth was, she'd rather stay with Ella when she was so little. But she still didn't want to go to Italy.

'I think we both need to compromise,' Mia said, trying not to sound desperate. 'What if I returned to London? You go there fairly often for business. You could see Ella regularly...' She trailed off at the dark look developing on Alessandro's face, like a storm front coming in, of towering black clouds.

'*That's* your compromise? I see my daughter once a month, if that?'

'Surely you come to London more often than that,' Mia protested. 'To check on Dillard's...'

'Dillard's has been assimilated into Costa International, as I told you it would be. I come to London once or twice a year at most.'

And for that he'd needed to put her on the other side of the world? It was not a point Mia could afford to make now. 'But it's not that far,' she insisted, trying her best to hold on to the plan she'd come up with last night—her in London, living in familiar surroundings with some friends around, and Alessandro safely in Italy or wherever else he travelled, coming by once in a while. She could live with that. Just about.

'Not *far*?' Alessandro's eyebrows rose in incredulity before drawing together in what could only be anger. Mia tried not to shrink back in her seat. 'It's a four-hour plane ride, Mia. How often do you think I want to see my daughter? How much do you think I wanted to be involved in her life?'

She shook her head slowly, afraid to hear his answer. 'I... I don't know.'

'Then I'll tell you. Completely. I want to see her every *day*. Morning and night and even afternoon. I will not have my child growing up without a father in her life. I know what that's like and I will not allow it for Ella, especially when her father wants to be involved.'

He knew what that was like?

The terse statement made Mia realise there were depths

of feeling and conviction to Alessandro's stance that she hadn't anticipated. Hadn't remotely begun to guess. 'So what exactly are you suggesting?' she asked faintly.

'You and Ella live at my villa in Tuscany. It is comfortable, in the country, the perfect place to raise a child. I will live there as well, and commute to Rome or wherever else as needed.'

'So…we'd live together?' She hadn't expected that, somehow. She'd anticipated him tucking her away, controlling her as her father had her mother. But now it almost sounded as if he expected them to play at happy families, something she really could not envision, and she doubted Alessandro had thought it through entirely.

Alessandro's frown deepened. 'Of course we'd live together.' He made it sound as if she'd asked something so obvious as to be absurd.

Mia shook her head slowly. 'That's not a given, Alessandro. I mean…we don't even know each other.'

'We have a baby together.'

'Yes, but…we're strangers.' It hurt to say it, because she'd never, ever have wanted to bring a child into the world the way she had with Ella, and yet she didn't regret her daughter for a single second.

'Then we'll get to know each other.' Again he made it all sound glaringly obvious. 'All the more reason for you to come to Tuscany, Mia.'

'So you expect me to follow you to Italy, to live in your house, without even knowing you?'

'You know enough, surely.'

'What I know I don't even like! You're ruthless, Alessandro, completely ruthless when it comes to the companies you take over—'

'That's business, and in any case, I'm not as ruthless as you think.' He almost sounded hurt. 'I thought you realised that.'

Memories of that night flitted through her brain, the man she'd started to dream he was, as well as what she'd learned about Dillard's former employees. No, he wasn't as ruthless as all that. And yet…

'Still, you've been incredibly overbearing since you blasted back into my life,' she persisted, 'demanding everything and making no compromises—'

'Because I'm right.'

She rolled her eyes. 'Of course you are.'

'And because this is important to me.' He lowered his voice, his hands clenched together, as he struggled with a depth of emotion Mia had never seen before. 'I grew up without a father, Mia. He chose to walk away before I was born. All my life I've wondered…' He paused, cleared his throat. 'I cannot abide the thought of my daughter thinking I would do the same thing, even for a moment. I cannot countenance for a *second* that she might wonder why I don't see her more often, or why I don't live in the same country as she does. I cannot stand the prospect that she might think I don't care.'

Tears, unexpected, unwanted, crowded Mia's eyes. 'I'm sorry,' she whispered. 'I didn't realise.'

He nodded jerkily. 'Now you know.'

'But surely you can still see how much you are asking of me.'

'I am asking just as much of myself. Together we will be parents for Ella. We will put aside our own desires and needs for her sake. It is what any good parent would do.'

And how on earth could she argue with that? Mia felt cornered, and yet she could hardly blame Alessandro for it. She agreed with him…she just wished she didn't. That there was another way, and yet there so clearly wasn't.

'So you want us to live together?' she surmised hesitantly. 'In the same house? What about…what about all your women?'

Alessandro looked at her as if she had sprouted horns. 'I would not have *women.*'

'At least a woman, then,' Mia clarified impatiently. 'I've seen the photos, Alessandro—'

'The only woman I will have on my arm is you,' Alessandro returned, his silver gaze snaring hers and pinning her in place. 'As my wife.'

For a second Alessandro thought Mia might faint. Her face drained of colour and she swayed where she sat, her lips bloodless as she parted them and tried to speak.

'What...?' The word was a scratchy whisper. She shook her head, looking as dazed as if she'd been hit on the head. 'What...are you talking about?'

'I thought it would be obvious.' Although he realised now what had been set in stone in his own mind had not even crossed Mia's. He'd been so sure of the way forward he might have skipped a few rather crucial steps in their conversation. Well, he would cover them now. 'I thought I'd made it clear. For Ella's sake, we will marry. You would live in Tuscany as my wife.'

'Was that a *proposal*?'

Her scathing tone caught him on the raw. He'd just offered to *marry* her, and she was acting offended. 'It was a fact,' he stated rather shortly. 'I accept that neither of us expected or even wished this, Mia, but surely we can put aside our personal preferences for Ella's sake. It's the right thing to do.'

'But you're talking about my whole life.'

'And my whole life.' He met her gaze steadily, refusing to be moved. Mia still looked as if she didn't know what had hit her.

'Alessandro, I can't marry you.'

'I'm not asking you to marry me this very minute.' He tried to ignore the sharp needling of hurt he felt at her blunt refusal. 'I understand we'll want to get to know another before we say any vows, although the sooner we make this official, the better, as far as I am concerned. Again, for Ella's sake.'

'I... I can't.' She looked agonised, strangely torn. 'Alessandro, I can't.'

'Why not?' His voice sharpened. 'Are you already married?'

'No, of course not.' She rose from the sofa, rubbing her arms as if she were cold. 'I just can't. I can't be married. I can't be married to a man like you.'

'A man like me?' His tone had turned icy. 'What is that supposed to mean?' A man of low birth? A bastard? He'd heard it all before, of course, but it still hurt coming from her.

'Just...' Mia shrugged helplessly. 'Someone so...rigid and in control. You've done nothing but order me around since I met you, Alessandro, and I can't live like that. I can't let myself live like that.'

Alessandro absorbed her words, as well as the despairing conviction behind them. 'I understand your concern,' he said finally. 'I don't want you to feel as if you've been railroaded into anything. We can leave the discussion about marriage for now. I'm not about to force you to the altar.' The very thought was distasteful. 'But I hope you can see the rightness of coming to Italy with me.'

'For ever?' Mia flung at him.

Startled, Alessandro shrugged. 'At least for an...interim period.'

'How about three months?' she challenged. 'I can just about live with that.'

'Three months,' he repeated. It wasn't so long, but hopefully long enough. 'So we can get to know one another and make sure a relationship between us will work.'

'A relationship?' She frowned. 'Are you saying that we're...*dating*?' She sounded disbelieving.

'If you are asking if there will be a physical relationship between us,' Alessandro said after a moment, feeling his way through the words, 'then I shall leave that up to you.' He could certainly give her that choice.

'You will?'

'I won't force you to the altar, and neither will I force you to my bed. You will come to it when it's your choice, not my decree.'

Colour touched her cheeks. 'So the offer's open whenever...?' she queried a bit sardonically.

'I won't deny that I still find you attractive,' Alessandro said, meeting her gaze boldly. Perhaps if she remembered just how explosive their chemistry had been, she would be less reluctant to go along with his ideas. 'What we shared was brief, I admit, but it was good, Mia. It was very good.' He held her gaze, felt his own heat, and saw that she remembered just how good it had been... just as he did.

'And what happens after three months?' Mia asked after a long, heated moment. 'If I decide it isn't working?'

Everything in him resisted such a notion, but he still made himself say the words. 'Then we will have to consider alternatives. But I hope, for Ella's sake, such a drastic step will not be necessary.'

'You call *that* a drastic step?' Mia let out a huff of humourless laughter.

'I do,' Alessandro returned evenly. 'Because it would be drastic for Ella, unable to have two loving parents in her life.' His voice rose with the strength of his emotions. He'd only held Ella once, had barely spent any time with her, but she was his and he wanted to raise her right, give her the stability and security and yes, even the love that he'd never had growing up. 'Why should I be content with seeing my daughter only on occasion, a deadbeat dad, and not by my own choosing? Why don't you want Ella to have two parents fully involved in her life, loving and taking care of her? Who doesn't want that for their child?'

'Is that…is that what it would be like?' She sounded so surprised that Alessandro felt stung.

'You don't think I would love my own child?'

'I'm not saying that, it's just…you're so focused on work, Alessandro. As far as I can tell from the tabloids, you've never had a serious relationship.'

'This is different.'

'How?'

'Because of Ella. I admit, I've never been interested in serious relationships before now.'

'And I'm still not,' Mia interjected, surprising him. 'I've never wanted to get married, be tied down—'

'Too bad you had my baby, then.'

They stared at each other, an emotional standoff, and then Mia let out a ragged sigh and sank back onto the sofa. 'I can't keep arguing about this.'

'Then be reasonable. Three months. That's all I'm asking. You wouldn't be going back to work before then anyway.'

She stared into the distance, her expression remote and a bit weary. Then, to his immense satisfaction, she slowly nodded. 'All right. Three months. I can give you that.'

'Good. We can make this work,' he said, with conviction. Mia did not reply. She stared out of the window, her expression so distant and despairing that Alessandro felt something in him shift, turn over. It was as if an emotion he'd long kept buried was stirring to life, and he didn't like it. He realised he wanted to comfort her. He didn't like seeing her sad, but he had no idea how to make her happy. Both realisations were disturbing. She'd given in to his demand and seen the sense in his plan. He should be triumphant, and instead he felt…unsettled.

'You look tired,' he said abruptly. 'Why don't you have a sleep?'

She turned to him, blinking slowly. 'A sleep...?'

'Yes, have a nap. Ella is sleeping, and I can keep an eye on her.' He gestured to the huge bed on the other side of the suite, made into its own cosy enclave with bookshelves and potted palms to give the area privacy without compromising the stunning view. 'Have a rest. You look exhausted, Mia.'

And we fly to Rome tonight.

He didn't say the words, but he had a feeling she heard them anyway.

'All right,' Mia said after a moment. 'I am very tired.'

'Good. Rest.'

He watched as she rose stiffly from the sofa, exhaustion apparent in the slump of her shoulders, the lines on her face. Compassion stirred inside him. She needed help; she needed him. He just needed to make her realise it.

Mia bent over Ella's car seat, tenderly touching her daughter's cheek before she straightened and looked straight at Alessandro.

'I don't like any of this, Alessandro, even if I recognise that our being together is best for Ella. But no matter how you spin it, I still don't feel as if I have any choice.'

'I've given you a choice,' Alessandro protested, and she nodded.

'Exactly,' she said. 'You've *given* me.' Without waiting for his reply, she turned and walked towards the bed, everything about her seeming both proud and defeated. The unsettling combination made Alessandro ache. It also made him feel guilty, as if he were doing something wrong, but he wasn't. He couldn't be.

For Ella's sake, this was how it had to be. Mia would come to accept that in time. He would make sure of it.

CHAPTER NINE

MIA STARED OUT of the window of the private jet as it lifted into the sunset sky. Her stomach clenched with nerves, her insides swooping as the plane rose and then levelled out. She was doing this. She was really doing this.

Because she had to. For Ella's sake, for Alessandro's sake. She'd recognised that this morning, when Alessandro had spoken oh-so-reasonably, but she still resisted. Still hated the thought that she was being backed into a corner.

Three months. She could manage for three months. She could get to know Alessandro. She could try to get along. After that…

Mia had no idea what happened after that.

She glanced across the teakwood table that separated her from Alessandro in the jet's sumptuous living area. Since waking up in Alessandro's penthouse that afternoon, she'd felt as if she'd fallen into a fairy tale, unsure if she was with the prince or the big bad wolf. A little bit of both, perhaps. Alessandro was certainly solicitous of her every need; she couldn't fault him even if she was still on edge.

While she'd been sleeping, something she hadn't even thought she'd be able to do, he'd arranged for all her things to be packed up from her apartment and put onto his private plane. He'd had bags packed for her and Ella with everything they could possibly need for the flight. They'd gone directly from the hotel to the airport, which meant Mia hadn't been able to say goodbye to anyone.

She hadn't made many friends in LA yet, but she still resented his high-handed manner. She didn't think he was even aware of it, which made it worse. Somehow, against everything she believed and hoped for her life, she was ending up with a man like her father. Maybe not in the needless cruelty or sneering manner—Alessandro was certainly better than that. Yet the result was the same—being controlled by a man.

Alessandro, at least, was showing himself to be an attentive father. When she'd stumbled from the sumptuous bed back in the suite, she'd found him on the sofa, cradling Ella in his lap as he cooed down at her, his face softened and suffused with love. Seeing him in that unguarded moment had given Mia the hope that maybe, just maybe, she really was doing the right thing by going to Italy. That maybe it could even be a good thing.

She glanced again at Alessandro, his profile both handsome and hard as he gazed down at his tablet, a faint frown bisecting his patrician brow. He'd shed his suit jacket and rolled up his shirtsleeves, revealing powerful forearms, muscles flexed.

Looking at him now, Mia remembered how irresistible she'd once found him. How Alessandro had informed her it was her choice whether or not she shared his bed. Her choice…and yet she was afraid to make it, afraid of feeling even more under his control, because she knew when he touched her she'd lose her sense of reason completely. And yet she couldn't get the images, the memories, out of her mind.

As if sensing her looking at him, Alessandro glanced up, his frown deepening as their gazes met. 'Is everything all right? Do you need something?'

She shook her head. She'd just fed Ella, and her daughter was asleep in her car seat. 'No, I'm all right.'

'Why don't we have champagne?' Alessandro suggested. 'To toast our future.'

'The next three months, you mean,' Mia couldn't help but correct. She needed to remind herself of that safeguard as much as him. 'I don't know. I shouldn't drink too much whilst I'm breastfeeding…'

'Surely a sip won't hurt.' Alessandro motioned to an aide, and then barked out a command in Italian. Mia watched him silently; he wasn't even aware of how once again he'd exerted his will. It was a small matter, seemingly insignificant, and yet she felt it.

She also felt how, after just one day, she was too weary and defeated to challenge him. What would she be like after a month, a year, a decade? Would she become as worn out and ghost-like as her mother had been, drifting through life, half-heartedly defending her choices, or lack of them?

The staff member came back with a bottle of champagne and two crystal flutes. Alessandro dismissed the man and then expertly opened the champagne, the cork giving a stifled pop before he poured them both glasses.

'To Ella,' he said as he handed her a glass. 'And to us.'

Dutifully Mia clinked her glass against his before taking a tiny sip. The bubbles fizzed through her, pleasantly surprising; it had been over a year since she'd had any alcohol. In fact…

'Do you remember the last time we had champagne?' Alessandro murmured, and Mia stiffened.

'I'm sure you've had champagne last week, if not sooner.'

'I haven't, but I meant when we had it together.'

Together. The word held memory as well as promise. Intent. Mia took another sip of champagne, just to steady her nerves. 'I didn't expect you to talk about that,' she said after a moment.

'Why not?'

'The last time we were *together*, you wanted to forget it, just like I did.' Her voice was unsteady, as was her hand as she put her flute of champagne on the table in front of her.

'Things have changed,' Alessandro answered with a nod towards a still sleeping Ella. 'Obviously.'

'They haven't changed that much,' Mia protested. 'You said I had three months to get to know you...to decide.' Something flickered in his face and she leaned forward. 'Did you mean that?'

'Of course.'

She scanned his taut expression, dark brows drawn together, gaze slightly averted. 'Alessandro,' she said slowly, 'what will happen after three months?'

'My hope is we'll get married.'

'Married...' Was she a fool to think he might have relinquished that notion? 'And if I refuse?'

His eyes gleamed as he leaned forward. 'I will make it my life's mission for the next three months to make sure you don't *want* to refuse.'

His voice was a sensuous caress, yet to Mia the words felt like a threat...and one she suspected he could carry out all too well.

'And how will you do that?' she asked, her voice wobbling. She hadn't meant to direct a challenge, but she realised she had as Alessandro smiled knowingly, his lingering gaze as tangible as if he'd touched her.

'I think you know how.'

'By seducing me?'

'Do I need to remind you how explosive our chemistry was?'

'No, but perhaps I need to remind you there is more to

a relationship—to a *marriage*—than what happens between the sheets.'

'Or on a desk,' Alessandro murmured, his eyes glinting.

Mia's cheeks heated and she looked away. 'Indeed.'

Alessandro settled back in his seat. 'Like I said, we have chemistry, Mia. Let's build on that.'

'That's hardly the foundation for a good marriage.' In fact she feared it could be a disastrous one. What about shared values, aspirations, ideals? And besides, she had never wanted to get married, anyway. She'd never wanted to be so in thrall to another person, so under their control…and yet here she was. It filled her with a feeling of fearful hopelessness.

'Chemistry and a shared love of a child is plenty,' Alessandro returned. 'More than many, or even most, have, and something we can build on.'

'Did your parents love each other?' she asked bluntly, and he stilled, clearly surprised by the question, before he gave a terse shake of his head.

'My mother loved my father, but he did not love her in return.'

'So would our marriage be one of love, eventually? Is that what you would hope for?'

Alessandro stilled, a guarded look coming over his face. 'Our love of Ella…'

'You know that's not what I mean.'

'What do you mean, Mia? Yesterday you told me you had never intended on marrying. Are you now telling me you want something different out of your marriage?'

She deflated, wondering why she'd pursued the point. 'No, I'm not saying that. I've never wanted to fall in love.'

'And neither have I, so I think we're a good match.'

Yet why did that make her feel so despairing, so hopeless? She'd never wanted to marry, yet now that she might, she didn't think she wanted a marriage devoid of affection.

She felt trapped, choiceless, and she hated that. At least it was only for three months. It felt like the only silver lining to an otherwise towering, dark cloud.

'My parents' relationship was stormy and difficult,' Alessandro said after a moment. She had the sense he was telling her something he didn't relate often. 'They never married, and, as I told you once before, my father walked out before I was born. My mother spent the next fifteen years beaten down by life, working dead-end jobs, moving from grotty flat to grotty flat, all in pursuit of some man or other…toxic relationships with wastrels or drunks or men who only wanted one thing.' He sighed heavily, his gaze turning distant, as if he was lost or even trapped in a memory. 'And she gave her heart every time, or so it seemed to me. It was no way to live.' Mia heard a raw note of sadness in his voice that she'd never heard before, and it touched her, made her see him in a new and surprising light.

'That must have been difficult for you,' she said quietly, the aggression gone from her voice.

'It wasn't easy,' Alessandro agreed, a dark note in his voice that made Mia's heart ache. She had an image in her head of a little black-haired boy watching with wide, grey eyes as his mother invited another man into their lives, as they were forced to move, as life upended for him again and again. His childhood had been as challenging as hers, if not more so, just in a different way.

'And so this is the alternative?' she asked after a moment.

'It's *an* alternative.' Alessandro met her gaze directly, his expression now one of firm purpose. 'Give us a chance, Mia. I'm willing to. We can have a marriage of companionship and compatibility. It doesn't have to be some terrible truce, or a sorry stalemate.'

'A loveless marriage?'

'Love is overrated. You must think that yourself, with your own background. Why fall head first into something that spins out of control when you can have something so much better?'

He made it sound so reasonable. So possible. Still Mia hesitated. 'We still don't even know each other, Alessandro.'

'Which is why we're giving it three months.' He smiled and downed the rest of his champagne.

Three months, Mia thought, and then he'd expect her to marry him. And at that point, she had a terrible feeling she'd be the subject of another hostile takeover...impossible to refuse or resist. Alessandro would make sure of it.

Ella stirred in her seat, and Mia rose from where she'd been sitting. 'She needs a top-up,' she said. 'And I'm really tired. I'll feed her in bed and then go to sleep, if you don't mind.'

'All right.' Alessandro had a thoughtful look on his face as he tracked her movements. She unbuckled Ella from her seat and scooped her up, breathing in her sweet baby scent, savouring the innocence of it. All this was for Ella's sake, she told herself. Fighting Alessandro at every turn would only end up hurting Ella. For her daughter's sake, she had to get along with this man. She had to give this—them—a try, even if everything in her still railed against it.

'Please let me or a member of staff know if you need anything,' Alessandro said solicitously. 'Anything at all.'

She nodded, knowing she needed to make an effort even though part of her resisted. 'Thank you, Alessandro,' she said stiffly.

Surprise flashed across his features, followed by a ripple of pleasure, and then he nodded. Mia turned and walked towards the back of the plane with Ella in her arms.

He should have thanked her back, Alessandro realised belatedly as Mia closed the door of the plane's bedroom behind her. She'd thanked him; he should have thanked her, for going along with his plans, for agreeing to so much. But he hadn't thought of it, and the realisation shamed him, an unexpected, unwelcome feeling.

What he was doing was reasonable and generous. He was offering Mia far more than she could ever have on her own—a lifestyle of which she would have never been able even to dream. And yet...in some way he was taking her freedom. He recognised that, just as he recognised she was taking his. Still, it had been his idea, his will. He recognised that too.

Restless, Alessandro rose from his seat to prowl the living area of the plane, knowing he wouldn't be able to work or settle to anything. He should be feeling satisfied, having arranged everything as he'd wanted it. Within twenty-four hours of arriving in California, he had Mia and his daughter back on a plane to Tuscany.

All was going according to his plan. So why did he feel so...restless? So dissatisfied and *hungry*, in a way he didn't expect or understand?

He sat down again, pulling his laptop towards him, determined to work. But after only an hour he realised he hadn't got anything done; he'd been staring at a spreadsheet of profit margins for at least twenty minutes.

With a near growl, he pushed his laptop away and strode towards the back of the plane. He could check on Mia and Ella, at least, and make sure they were okay.

He opened the door as quietly as he could; the bedroom was swathed in darkness, the shades drawn down against the night sky, the only light coming from the adjoining bathroom, the door ajar.

Mia lay on her side, her hair spread across the pillow in a golden sheet, Ella in the middle of the bed, cradled gently in her arm, both of them fast asleep. As Alessandro came closer he saw that Ella had finished feeding; a milk bubble frothed at her lips, one fist flung upwards by her round cheek. His gaze moved to Mia, and something in him jolted as he saw she'd changed into a white cotton nightgown, its buttons undone so she could feed Ella, one creamy breast on display.

All of it together—mother, child—was beautiful to him, and made him ache and yearn even more than he had before. More than he'd ever let himself.

He *wanted* this. Not just Mia, not just Ella. All of it together. *Them.* A family, the family he'd always ached for but never known. Finally, it could be his. He hadn't even realised how much he'd been missing it until it was here, offered up in front of him, tantalising and beautiful.

Resolution crystallised inside him, sharpening into focus. Whatever it took, whatever it meant, he was going to knit them into a family. He would make Mia leave her regrets and fears behind; he would work hard to make her want this as much as he did. He'd worked hard for everything in his life, he could work hard at this too, the most important thing. The most important business deal he'd ever make. Not a hostile takeover as Mia had once suggested, but a true and purposeful merger. A marriage.

Carefully, as quietly as he could, he took off his shoes and belt, leaving his clothes on for form's sake as he stretched out on the bed next to Mia, gently putting his arm around her. She stirred, and he waited, his breath held, wondering what she would do. Then she let out a breathy sigh and relaxed into him, her body softening against his.

Desire and something far, far deeper roared through him, elemental and overwhelming. Yes, he wanted this. He wanted it with every fibre of his being. And he would have it. Eventually he would have it.

Alessandro didn't know how long he slept, but he woke when Mia shifted next to him, gasping as she sat up, her hair tumbled about her shoulders, her face flushed.

'I didn't mean to fall asleep...'

Alessandro blinked the sleep from his eyes as he took in the magnificent sight of her, her body rosy and soft with sleep, her eyes bright, her nightgown still unbuttoned.

'I thought that was your intention when you lay down in bed,' he said, keeping his voice light.

'I was feeding Ella, and then I was going to put her in the Moses basket.' She nodded towards the sleeping basket that had been in her apartment, and had been brought to the plane. It was next to the bed, made up with a fleece-lined blanket.

'She can go in there now.'

'I shouldn't have fallen asleep with her on the bed,' Mia said. She sounded upset. 'It can be dangerous...'

'She's fine, Mia. Look.' With one hand on her shoulder, he turned her so they could both look at their tiny, sleeping daughter. 'She's fine. No harm done.' He rubbed her shoulder, a touch meant for comfort but which made him decidedly less so. Her skin was warm and soft, her nightgown slipping off her shoulder. He fought the urge to slip his hand inside and cup the breast he'd already seen and that was quite, quite perfect.

'Still...' Mia muttered. She sounded half-asleep.

'I'll put her in the basket now.' Awkwardly but tenderly Alessandro scooped Ella up, conscious of her fragility, her utter smallness. He still wasn't used to holding her.

The baby barely stirred as he laid her in the Moses basket, drawing the blanket over her. Then he returned to the bed, where Mia had already fallen back to sleep.

Gently he brushed a tendril of hair away from her cheek, letting his fingers skim along her silky skin. Her breath came out in a soft sigh and she relaxed against him, her body warm and pliant.

Alessandro shifted so he was lying behind her, one arm around her waist. Awareness prickled painfully through him. Sleep, he knew, would be elusive. Then Mia sighed again and wriggled closer to him, so her bottom was nestled against his groin, her head tucked under his chin. Yes, sleep would be very elusive indeed.

Alessandro kept his body relaxed so Mia would stay asleep, savouring her closeness even as it remained an exquisite form of torture. He breathed in her citrusy scent, revelling in her soft warmth, the nearness of her.

He never slept with the women he bedded. He'd always operated alone, on every level. He'd been happy with that. Yet now he found her closeness comforting, a balm as well as an undoubted enticement. He desired her, but he was also content to have her simply lie in his arms. For now, it was enough. It was more than he'd ever had before.

For a few moments he let his mind drift back over the years of his childhood, the loneliness, the uncertainty, the endless turmoil of being moved from one grotty flat to another, the parade of boyfriends who had raged or sneered or used their fists. And his mother…

But that hurt most of all. He tried never to think of his mother, to remember the look of weary defeat on her face, the words she'd said to him, too exhausted by life to be spiteful. They'd been simple truth.

'I wish I'd never had you.'

No, he didn't want to think of that. And he didn't want his daughter to wonder, even for a day, a minute, if he felt that way about her. He would love Ella the way his mother and father had never loved him. And he would build a marriage with Mia that would be better than the candyfloss froth of fairy tales, a solid relationship of affection and companionship without losing control or being vulnerable the way his mother had been. The way he'd so often felt, as a child.

And yet he recognised, as Mia slept in his arms, that he'd already lost control, in some small but elemental way.

Already he'd been more open and vulnerable, more emotional, with her than he ever had with anyone before…not that she would recognise that.

He still did, and it unsettled him. He'd never told anyone about his parents, or how he'd felt as a child. Already she knew more about him than anyone else, ever.

Somehow he was going to have to find a way to have the family he wanted without losing himself in the process. He could not relinquish the solitary independence he'd cultivated since he could remember. He didn't know who he would be without it. And yet he wanted Mia and Ella in his life. He wanted the three of them to be a family.

He must have slept, because bright sunlight was visible underneath the rim of the shades as he stirred in bed, Mia wrapped even more tightly in his arms. In her sleep she'd rolled over to him, and now she was squashed up next to him so he could feel every delectable line and curve of her warm, warm body.

Her eyes fluttered open and she stared straight into his, her body stiffening as she realised how close they were.

'Good morning,' he said softly. 'Ella is still asleep.'

Mia glanced down at their nearly entwined bodies, her breasts spilling out of her nightgown, pressed up against him. Colour flooded her face as she tensed even more.

'What…?'

'You were asleep,' Alessandro said. 'So was I.'

Her cheeks were stained crimson as she scrambled out of his embrace, buttoning up her nightgown with fumbling fingers.

'I didn't…' she muttered, unable to look him in the eye.

'Nothing happened, if that's your concern,' Alessandro said equably. 'I would never take advantage of you, Mia. I promise you that.'

She opened her mouth, and Alessandro braced himself

for what he was sure she would say. *You already have.* But then she closed her mouth and shook her head.

'I'm going to have a shower and get dressed before we land,' she said. 'Can you watch Ella?'

'Of course.'

She looked as if she wanted to say something more, but then she just shook her head again, slipping out of bed and hurrying to the en suite bathroom. The door closed behind her and Alessandro winced as he heard the lock turn with a decisive click.

CHAPTER TEN

MIA HELD ELLA to her as she stepped out of the limo into the warm spring morning. Sunlight glinted off the terracotta tiles of Alessandro's villa, the Tuscan hills now covered in verdant green and bright blossom.

The place was huge and sprawling, made of white stucco, with terraced gardens on the hillside, bursting with colourful blooms. She could hardly credit that she was going to live in such a magnificent place, if just for three months.

Or maybe for ever.

Alessandro gently placed his hand on the small of her back as he guided her towards the imposing entrance. Mia's eyes felt gritty, her body aching with fatigue and jet lag despite the few hours' sleep she'd snatched on the plane, waking up so unsettlingly in Alessandro's arms. For a second, before she'd woken up completely, she'd lain there, warm and comfortable, snuggled and safe.

Happy.

She'd been completely wrong-footed when she'd realised just how much she'd cosied up to Alessandro, and meanwhile forgotten Ella entirely. He still had that devastating effect on her, she realised. Perhaps he always would—the ability to melt her insides like butter, even as he fanned her to flame. It scared her, the power he could have over her if she let him.

After they'd landed, Mia had done her best to find a cordial but formal middle ground, although he suddenly seemed intent on being close to her whenever he had the opportunity, such as now, when he gently pressed his palm to the small of her back, sending shivers of awareness rippling through her, before he took Ella from her.

'I'll hold her for a bit. You look shattered.'

She *was* shattered, but Ella felt like her safety shield. Without her, Mia was exposed, unsure what to do with her arms, how to look or feel. Everything about this was so incredibly strange. Whether for three months or for ever, she couldn't believe she and Ella were going to *live* here, with Alessandro, as a family.

She glanced around the soaring marble foyer in amazed disbelief. Several doors led off to various impressive reception rooms, and a sweeping double staircase led to the second floor.

'This feels like a castle,' she couldn't help but say.

'And you're the princess,' Alessandro told her as he hefted Ella against his shoulder. Already he was starting to handle Ella with more confidence, although he still carried her as if she was so fragile she'd break...or explode.

The flashes of uncertainty Mia saw on his face as he held their daughter made her melt in an entirely different way—he could affect her heart as well as her body. Both were dangerous.

'You may do whatever you like to the place,' Alessandro continued, a look of nervousness crossing his face as Ella began to fuss. 'Redecorate however you want...it is your home, Mia. Yours and Ella's and mine. Ours.' He jiggled Ella uncertainly, and as their baby started to settle down he looked up at Mia with a small smile.

'Do you think she knows me yet?'

'She's starting to.' Ella gave Alessandro a gummy smile that made him grin back in delight.

'She smiled. She actually smiled.'

Mia couldn't help but laugh. 'So she did.' Watching Alessandro and Ella bond over something as simple as a smile made her heart ache. How could she ever contemplate ending this? Walking away from a family life that neither she nor Alessandro had ever had before?

It was just a smile, she told herself, and in any case, she didn't yet know what kind of family life they would have. How it would work. No matter what assurances Alessandro made, she wasn't yet convinced.

'Thank you,' she said. 'Where…where is my room?'

'Our room is at the top of the stairs, to the right.'

She turned to him, appalled even as a treacherous excitement made her stomach flip. '*Our* room?'

'It will be our room,' he amended somewhat reluctantly. 'For now you may have it. But I look forward to the day when we might share it.'

'If,' Mia couldn't help but say and Alessandro gave her a knowing look.

'When,' he repeated firmly. 'Definitely when. Now, why don't you go upstairs and have a bath, relax for a bit? I'll watch Ella, especially since she seems to like me now.' He smiled down at their daughter.

'She needs a feed…' Mia began, torn between wanting to rest and needing her daughter.

'I'll come and get you if she fusses.'

'You mean when,' Mia returned wryly, and Alessandro laughed.

'True enough. When.' He smiled at her, and Mia found herself smiling back. Maybe she needed to relax…not just in a bath, but with everything. With Alessandro. It was going to be a long, tense three months if she didn't.

Upstairs Mia wandered into the first room at the right, gaping at the sheer opulence of what was clearly the master bedroom. As Henry Dillard's PA, and then, briefly, Eric

Foster's, she'd seen more than her fair share of luxury, even if she hadn't partaken in it directly. But this room exceeded all her expectations.

It was enormous, for a start, its tiled floor supplied with underfloor heating so Mia's feet remained toasty warm as she slipped off her shoes with a sigh of relief. A king-sized bed stood on its own dais, piled high with silk and satin pillows. A separate seating area with deep leather sofas had a stunning view of the garden below, with an infinity pool and hot tub large enough to seat twenty. Thick-pile rugs were scattered across the floor, so Mia's toes sank into their exquisite softness as she walked towards the bed.

It looked amazing, inviting, and huge. And one day—if or when—she was meant to share it with Alessandro. Why did that thought not alarm her as it should? She couldn't deny the lick of excitement low in her belly, even as she tensed at the thought. She knew that giving herself to Alessandro again would come at an emotional cost. He might just see it as sex, but she knew she wouldn't. Already she felt herself softening to him, and it scared her. She had too many memories, too many fears, to let herself relax and trust Alessandro…even if he proved trustworthy.

She pushed such thoughts out of her mind as she turned to the bathroom, taking in the sunken marble bathtub, the shower big enough for two, the double sinks. She turned on the taps to fill the tub, and added nearly half a bottle of high-end bubble bath. She was going to have a good, long soak, and try not to think for a while, because if she did, her head might explode.

Twenty minutes later, having submerged herself in hot, soapy bubbles and nearly fallen asleep, Mia sat up suddenly as her breasts prickled and her body tensed. Faintly, so faintly, she heard Ella cry.

With a sigh she pulled the plug on the bath and swathed herself in the thick, velvet-soft terrycloth dressing gown she'd found hanging on the back of the bathroom door. She finger-combed her hair as she walked through the bedroom and then downstairs, following the sound of Ella's now shrill cries.

She wandered through several empty, elegant rooms before she spied Alessandro rocking Ella in the kitchen, a cheerful and comfortable room at the back of the house, with French windows leading out to a wide terrace with steps down to the garden.

Mia paused in the doorway, spellbound by the simple yet heart-warming scene. Ella was crying with determination, while Alessandro danced around the kitchen, jiggling her rather desperately against his shoulder.

'Now, *bambina*, you need to settle down or you'll wake your *mamma*. Why are you upset, eh? What is there to be so sad about?' He pressed a kiss to Ella's cheek. 'Are you hungry, *cara*? Is that the problem? Am I going to have to wake your *mamma*, after all?'

'I'm already awake.'

Mia's voice came out scratchy as she absorbed the scene in front of her, let it squeeze her heart. She'd never seen Alessandro look so gentle, or approachable, or...*loving*. He'd been loving. And it gave her a glimpse of a future that didn't look as unfathomable or impossible as she'd assumed it would be. In a strange and surprising way, for a few seconds it had looked...wonderful. And that scared her too, because it was not what she'd expected, and it made her want things she was afraid to try for or even to dream about.

What if Alessandro was right, and they could have a relationship, a marriage, that was strong and true and good? Based on companionship and affection? What if that was possible?

Why did that thought both terrify and thrill her in equal measure?

Alessandro gave her an endearingly self-conscious smile. 'I guess she is hungry, as you said she would be. I've been trying to calm her, but no luck.'

'You can't provide the goods in this case,' Mia answered as she held her arms out, and Alessandro danced his way over to her, making her smile.

'Here she is.'

'Has she had a change?'

'Her nappy? Yes.'

'You changed it?' Mia couldn't keep the surprise from her voice.

'It took a few tries, I admit. Thankfully there were enough nappies. Those tapes…' He shook his head. 'They were not designed for durability. I might have to take over the company that makes them, to ensure a stronger design.'

Mia laughed at such an outrageous suggestion. 'Is that how you decide what companies to take over?'

'Actually, no.' He looked serious for a moment before he deliberately lightened his expression. 'But perhaps it will be, as far as nappies are concerned.'

'So how do you choose the companies?' she asked as she settled in a sofa in the cosy nook off the kitchen. Alessandro joined her, sitting on the sofa opposite. Conscious of his gaze on her, Mia bent her head, her damp hair falling forward as she brought Ella to her breast. When she was sure she was presentable and Ella feeding discreetly, she looked up, everything in her jolting at the sudden, blazing look in Alessandro's eyes…a look of pride and possession that made her feel a welter of unsettling sensations.

As he caught her gaze, it faded, leaving scorch marks on her soul. He gave her a small smile. 'I choose companies that have corrupt and weak leadership.'

Startled, she shook her head. 'But Henry wasn't…'

'Corrupt? No, perhaps not. But he was weak and lazy, and he was running Dillard's into the red. I estimated that in another eighteen months, none of you would have had jobs.'

'Surely not…'

He shrugged. 'Two years, at the maximum.'

'I always knew he was a bit old-fashioned,' Mia said slowly. 'And he did like his golf game…' But she'd considered those qualities endearing, rather than damaging. Now she wondered.

'As affable as he could be, he was a weak leader,' Alessandro responded firmly. 'And he would have proved disastrous for the company and its employees.'

'And you care about the employees.' Once she would have said as much incredulously, but now there was the lilt of a question in her tone. 'Because I don't understand that—your reputation is so ruthless, firing most of the employees of the companies you take over. And yet…'

Alessandro smiled wryly as he raised his eyebrows. 'And yet?'

'And yet that didn't seem to be the case with Dillard's. Most of the staff were given jobs elsewhere, better jobs by the sounds of it, and the people who were let go had very generous redundancy packages, which has to cut into your profit. But none of that seems to make it into the press.'

'No,' he agreed, sounding unbothered by that fact.

'Why? Don't you mind being portrayed as some ruthless monster?'

'No, because I can hardly be a teddy bear if I'm going to take over a company. Having a reputation helps.'

'But why do you do it?' Mia pressed. 'What are you trying to achieve?' He hesitated for a long moment, and Mia had the sense they were on the cusp of some great and terrible revelation.

'I do it,' he finally said, 'because I cannot abide having weak or corrupt people in leadership, and I will not stand by and allow them to ruin people's lives.' He paused. 'Like my father did.'

Alessandro gazed at Mia, noticing the way her hair, like a golden slide of silk, hid her face, so he couldn't gauge her expression. He hadn't meant to make that admission, but now that he had he was glad he had. He could hardly expect Mia to come to trust him if he didn't share something of his life and past with her...even if doing so made him feel uncomfortably exposed.

'Your father?' she repeated softly. 'How...?'

'He was the CEO of a company in Rome. My mother was a cleaner in his office.' He could not keep the old bitterness from twisting his words. 'It was, as I'm sure you can imagine, a short-lived affair. He made my mother promises he never intended on keeping. And when he found out she was pregnant, he fired her.'

'Oh, Alessandro.' His name was a soft cry of distress. 'I'm so sorry.'

He shrugged one shoulder, half regretting having told her that much. It made him feel scraped raw inside, to have these old wounds on display.

'What did she do?' Mia asked softly.

'She had me, and then worked one dead-end job after another trying to make ends meet, which they rarely did. She told me about my father when I was quite small, and I followed his career, saw how he abused his power and privilege, not just with women like my mother, who had nothing, but in all sorts of ways.' He shifted where he sat, that old determination coursing through him again. 'I determined then that I would never allow people like that to abuse their power. And I've made it part of the mission of my work to take over companies that are showing such signs.'

Mia shook her head slowly. 'I had no idea…'

'You're not meant to. I can't exactly publicise what I'm doing. Hostile takeovers are just that. Hostile.'

'Still, to do something noble and never be known for it…'

The warmth in her eyes both discomfited and awed him. He realised he liked having her look at him like that, feel like that. And that was alarming.

'It's not as much as you think, Mia. Some people are still out of jobs. I have a reputation for a reason.' Why he was trying to dissuade her from thinking well of him, he had no idea. Perhaps simply because he wasn't used to it.

'Still.' She pursed her lips as she gazed down at their daughter. 'I wish I'd known earlier.'

'Well, now you know.'

Alessandro paused, watching as she cradled Ella in her arms, their daughter feeding happily, one fist reaching absently for Mia's hair.

'It occurs to me,' he said conversationally, 'that you know more about me than I know about you.'

Mia looked up, eyebrows raised in surprise. 'What do you want to know about me?'

'Everything. Anything.' He realised he was truly curious. 'But we can start with the basics. Where are you from?'

'The Lake District.'

'A beautiful area.'

'You've been?'

He smiled. 'I've heard.'

'It is beautiful.' She looked away, seeming almost as if she was suppressing a shiver. 'Beautiful and isolated and very cold.'

'That sounds like a rather mixed description.'

She shrugged. 'I didn't like it growing up. I couldn't wait to get away.'

'Why? Just because it was cold?'

She hesitated, and he waited, sensing she had something more important to reveal. 'No, because my father was... well, suffice to say, we didn't get along.' She kept her gaze on Ella, catching their daughter's chubby hand in her own and gently removing it from her hair.

'And your mother?' Alessandro asked quietly.

'She died when I was fourteen. I'd say of a broken heart, but I know how melodramatic that sounds.'

'No.' His mother had wasted away, worn to the bone by work and poverty. It was possible, Alessandro knew, to die of things that ate at you the same way a physical disease did. 'Is your father still alive?'

'I don't actually know.' Mia looked up at him then, her blue eyes icy with a hard anger he'd never seen before, not even in their stormiest moments. 'I haven't seen him in eight years, and that is fine by me.'

'I see.' Although he didn't see the whole picture, he was starting to get a glimpse. Whatever had happened with her father, Mia clearly had emotional scars from it. He didn't know what they were exactly, but at least he knew they were there.

'Anyway.' Mia shrugged, her gaze back on Ella. 'With the background you just told me about, how did you get to be a billionaire by age—what? Thirty-something?'

'Thirty-seven. I worked my way up.'

'From slums to a billionaire lifestyle?' She shook her head slowly, seeming impressed. 'That's quite a steep climb.'

'Yes.'

'How did it happen?'

Alessandro shrugged. 'I was lucky and I worked hard. I started in property, buying rundown buildings and flipping them. It grew from there.'

'It has to have been more than luck.'

'Like I said, I worked hard.'

'Very hard, I imagine. You've always seemed…driven to me.'

'Yes, I suppose I am.' Although, coming from her, he didn't know whether it was a compliment or not.

'What about your mother?' Mia asked. 'Is she still alive?'

'Sadly, no. She died when I was nineteen, just when I was starting, but we'd lost touch a few years before.'

'That's sad.' Mia hesitated. 'It seems as if we have something in common.'

'Yes.' It saddened him, to think that both he and Mia had come from such fractured, damaged families—and it made him more determined to make sure their own little family wasn't. 'Our family doesn't have to be like that, Mia,' he said, a new note of urgency entering his voice. 'This can be a fresh start for the three of us.'

'I'd like to believe that,' she said after a moment, but her tone sounded wistful, even dubious, and that stung.

'Why can't you?'

'It's just… I don't know enough about you, Alessandro. And sometimes the past isn't so easy to overcome.'

'We're getting to know each other,' he persisted. 'And we'll keep doing that. What's your favourite colour?'

'My favourite colour?'

'We've got to start somewhere.'

She let out a little laugh. 'Green.'

'Favourite food?'

'Raspberries.'

'Favourite season?'

'Spring.' She laughed again and shook her head. 'I suppose I have to ask you all the same questions.'

'Only if you want to.'

Her mouth curved, her eyes lightening. Alessandro liked her that way. 'I do.'

'Then it's blue, steak, and autumn.'

'We're practically opposites.'

He raised his eyebrows. 'Is blue the opposite of green?'

'Maybe not. But the others…' Her laugh turned into a sigh as she glanced down at Ella, stroking her downy head. 'I don't know. Do such preferences matter, really? Shouldn't we be asking each other more important things?'

Alessandro caught his breath as he stared at her intently, trying to decipher her mood. He liked what she'd said, but she'd sounded sad. 'Such as?' he asked after a moment.

'I don't even know. Such as what you want out of life. What you value. What you believe.'

'What do you want out of life, Mia?' He spoke quietly, knowing the question was important, the answer even more so.

She looked up, her expression serious, her eyes bright. 'First, I want to keep Ella safe and healthy and happy.'

'Of course. I want that, as well. Utterly.'

'After that, I want to be independent. With my own money, my own choices. That's…very important to me.' Alessandro sensed a wealth of memory and meaning behind her words, and he nodded.

'Understandable.' He'd seen that all along, how she chafed against any autocratic commands…which, he acknowledged wryly, he had a tendency to give. But they could work on all that.

'What do you want out of life, Alessandro?' She glanced around the spacious kitchen, the sunny garden visible through the French windows. 'It seems like you have everything already.'

'I am thankful for what I have,' Alessandro allowed. 'But what I've wanted…what has driven me, as you've said…' He hesitated, feeling his way through the words. 'First, I want to protect and care for my family.'

'Yes.' The word was a soft assent.

'And second…it is similar to what you want, in a way, I suppose. I want to be in control. I don't want to have my life dictated by other people's whims or poor choices, as it was for all my childhood.'

'I can understand that.'

'Yes, it seems you can. So once again we are in accord, Mia. I think you will find we are far more compatible than you once feared.'

'Perhaps.' She didn't sound convinced, but Alessandro knew he could convince her. He had to.

'I mean it, Mia. I want this to work.'

'That's something, then,' Mia said with a small smile, and as their gazes met and tangled Alessandro found himself remembering a whole host of pleasurable things. The feel of Mia in his arms. The taste of her lips. How sleepy and warm she'd been that morning, snuggled up against him. And he thought how much he wanted to experience all of those things again, over and over.

Yet as his own blood heated, Mia's seemed to cool, for she looked away, her hair sliding in front of her face. Alessandro felt her emotional withdrawal like a physical thing.

'I should unpack,' she said as she brought Ella to her shoulder, pulling her robe closed with her other hand. 'And get dressed…'

'Your things will have been brought up to your room by the staff by now, I am sure. Alyssa and Paulo are the couple who run this place. They're very kind.'

'I look forward to meeting them.' She rose, clutching Ella to her a bit like a shield. 'Will you be…returning to Rome? For work?'

'In a few days.' Alessandro couldn't help but be stung by the question. Did she want him gone already? Resolve hardened inside him. He would break down her defences. He would get to know her…in every possible way. 'Shall we have dinner together tonight? Alyssa is happy to sit with Ella.'

Her eyes widened and then slowly, seemingly reluctantly, she nodded. 'Very well.'

It was a grudging acceptance, and one that irked him just a little. Why was Mia so guarded? Why couldn't she enter into the spirit of what he was trying to do?

But what *was* he trying to do? Alessandro asked himself after Mia had gone upstairs and he headed to his study to check his work emails. Mia had asked him a host of serious questions that he had answered honestly, if not fully. What did he want from life? What did he want from this marriage? And how was he going to get it?

Already being with Mia was drawing emotion from him like poison from a wound. He felt it stir inside him, and it alarmed him. He did not want to be ruled by his emotions the way his mother had been, tossed on the turbulent waves of relationships that never delivered what they'd seemed to promise, and left destruction in their wake.

He'd always vowed he would never expose himself to that kind of horrible, humiliating risk. He would never need someone that way, let that need rule and ruin him. He would always stay in control—of himself, and of his emotions.

And he *could* be in control, Alessandro reminded himself. He wasn't that lost little boy, hiding in the cupboard while his mother screamed and fought with one of her many boyfriends, or curled up on a narrow bed, wondering when she'd finally come home after a night out.

He was a man in control of his destiny and his family. His relationship with—and eventual marriage to—Mia would be on his terms. And they would be favourable terms for her, undoubtedly. He would be generous, thoughtful, kind. But they would still be his.

CHAPTER ELEVEN

'AREN'T YOU HAPPY?'

Laughing, Mia tickled Ella's tummy as her daughter grinned and giggled back at her. They were sitting on a blanket in the villa's garden, enjoying the warm spring sunshine. It had been two weeks since Mia had come to Italy, and she was finally starting to relax into this strange and amazing new life of hers. She just wasn't sure whether she could trust it…or Alessandro.

He'd been a model of kindness and consideration since she'd arrived; she couldn't fault him for that. The first night he'd arranged for Alyssa to watch Ella while they'd had a candlelit supper out on the terrace, eating delicious food, drinking fine wine, and enjoying each other's company.

And Mia *had* enjoyed his company… Alessandro had kept the conversation light and sparkling, without any of the heavy issues that seemed poised to drag them down.

She'd even enjoyed the heat she'd seen in his eyes when she'd appeared, having changed into one of her few dresses that fitted her post-pregnancy figure, and when he'd taken her hand, butterflies had risen in a swarm from her stomach to flutter through her whole body and send her senses spinning.

It would be so easy, she'd reflected, to let herself fall. To forget her worries, her fears, her choices. She could just gently bob along on the overwhelming sea that was Alessandro...

And then what?

Fear had knotted in her stomach at the thought. She'd pictured her mother, looking so worn out and defeated, the wedding album open on her lap.

'He was so charming, Mia. So forceful and yet so caring. I fell for him hard... I loved him...'

No matter how many times she told herself Alessandro was not like her father, Mia knew, from both his behaviour and his admission, that he was man who liked to be in control. And that would always be a cause for alarm and even fear.

At the end of that candlelit dinner, Alessandro had brushed a gentle kiss across her lips, like a whisper of a promise.

'For now,' he'd said, and there had been so much intent in his voice that Mia had shivered. It had taken all her strength not to sway into that kiss, not to ask for more. Plead, even, and that scared her along with everything else. She wasn't ready...and she didn't know how long Alessandro would wait.

A fortnight on, Mia still slept alone and Alessandro did no more than kiss her goodnight. The kisses had become a bit more lingering, and last night Mia had found herself clutching his lapels, on her tiptoes, straining for more before she'd finally had the strength of will to wrench herself away.

Alessandro had smiled wryly as he'd cupped her cheek. 'Why are you fighting me so hard, *cara*?' he'd asked gently.

Because I don't know what else to do. How to be. I'm afraid of giving you everything and you taking it. What will happen to me then?

Mia hadn't had the courage to say any of it, and so she'd

just shaken her head and backed away, her body trembling from Alessandro's touch. And he'd let her go, but they'd both known, if he'd wanted to, he could have made her stay.

'Hello to my two gorgeous girls.' Smiling, Alessandro strolled across the lawn to meet them, dropping a kiss on Mia's head before sitting down next to her and tickling Ella's tummy just as she had done. 'She seems happy.'

'Yes, she's very smiley this afternoon.' Mia glanced at him, feeling shy and overwhelmed as she so often did when in his magnetic, compelling presence. He was dressed casually in dark trousers and a grey polo shirt that brought out the silver in his eyes, his hair gleaming blue-black and ruffled by the warm breeze. The sandalwood scent of him still made her senses reel. 'Have you finished your work already?'

'Yes, but I need to go to Rome tomorrow morning, for a few business meetings, as well as a charity ball in the evening.' Alessandro had been working remotely from the villa, with just a few trips to various cities across Europe. Mia wondered how long he could keep such a pattern; he was a very busy, powerful man, with many demands on his time. Surely this idyll couldn't last…and part of her craved a relief from the tension of being with him, even as another part knew she would miss him.

'I think we'll manage to keep ourselves busy,' she said. Over the last few weeks she'd had a few forays into the market town for trips to the shops, and also a baby group that met in a community hall. She was also hoping to start learning Italian, although Mia was wary of putting down too many roots. This still felt temporary rather than like real life, although perhaps that would change the more effort she made.

'Actually,' Alessandro said after a moment, 'I was hoping you would come with me.'

'With you?' Mia was startled. 'But won't Ella and I just be in your way?'

'Not Ella, just you.' His gaze was warm as it met hers and lingered there with intent. 'Just for the evening, so we can spend some time together. Alyssa can watch Ella.'

'You want me to go to a *ball*?'

'Why do you sound sceptical? We've been to one before.'

'I know, but…' Mia felt her cheeks flush as she remembered the last ball they'd been to…and what had happened afterwards. 'I don't have anything to wear.'

'That's easily remedied. I can have a stylist come with a selection of gowns.'

'As you did before?'

He shrugged. 'It's not a problem.'

But it felt like a problem, because Mia wasn't sure she was ready for a night out with Alessandro. Her already wavering defences might crumble completely…and then what?

It was the question that always rose to the front of her mind, popping like a bubble before she could answer it. If she stopped trying to protect herself, keep a safe distance, what would happen?

'What are you scared of, Mia?' Alessandro asked. 'It's just a ball.'

'I know, but…'

'We'll be home before midnight, I promise. And Alyssa will enjoy taking care of Ella.'

'It's not that.'

'Then what?'

He sounded so patient, even tender. How could she doubt him? How could she be so afraid? Mia knew she wasn't being fair, holding back the way she was. Alessandro had been more than generous, more than patient with her. She needed to give something back.

'All right,' she said at last. 'I'll come.'

'Good.' He leaned forward to brush her lips with his, making her whole body tingle. 'I look forward to it. I'll arrange for the stylist now.'

As he left to make the call, Mia realised that, despite her reservations, she wanted to go. She wanted to dress up and walk into a ballroom on Alessandro's arm, just as she had once before. She wanted to spend the evening—and maybe even the whole night—with him. Saying yes had freed her to admit to herself just how much she wanted him, despite her fear. It felt dizzyingly wonderful…as well as incredibly terrifying.

'Here we are.'

Alessandro followed the bellboy into the penthouse suite of the luxury hotel by Rome's Spanish Steps, Mia walking slowly behind them. Since leaving the villa— and Ella—she'd been quiet, even subdued, perhaps wary. Alessandro knew she didn't trust him yet, but at least she'd agreed to come tonight. He hoped to prise her even more out of her shell tonight.

He'd spent the last two weeks trying to gain her trust, win her confidence, and slowly, ever so slowly, he'd felt Mia soften towards him, and he wanted to see—and feel— that even more tonight.

'Wow.' Mia stood in the centre of the large, luxurious living room, with French windows leading out to a wide terrace that overlooked the Spanish Steps. A platter of fresh fruit had been placed on a coffee table, along with bottles of champagne and sparkling apple juice. 'But we're not even staying the night…'

'I own this hotel, and the penthouse is reserved for my exclusive use. I like to have a base while in Rome.' He checked his phone. 'The stylist will be here with a selection of gowns shortly.'

'Will you need final approval, like you did before?' she said, her voice teasing. Alessandro smiled, glad for the bit of banter.

'I think I can leave that to you this time. I look forward to being surprised.'

'All right.' Mia glanced around the living room again, taking in the silk-striped sofas, the original artwork, the marble-topped tables. 'This place really is amazing.'

'I just want you to enjoy everything, Mia,' Alessandro said. 'This evening away is meant to be a break for you, although I know you're worried about leaving Ella.'

'I know it is.' Mia rubbed her arms as if she were cold and then walked to the French windows, before opening them and stepping out onto the terrace. After a second's pause Alessandro followed her, breathing in the balmy air as he joined her at the railing overlooking the city far below.

'What's wrong?' he asked quietly. 'This isn't just about leaving Ella for a few hours.'

'No.' She shook her head. 'It's about…about us.' She glanced at him, her face troubled. 'You've been wonderful these last few weeks, I know. I can admit that.'

'Admit it?' Alessandro tried to keep his voice light, even though he was a bit stung by her words, the reluctance of them. 'You almost sound as if you don't want to.'

'I don't,' Mia admitted. 'It's just… I'm scared, Alessandro. I told you I never wanted to marry or give my life over to another person. A man. And yet here I am.'

'Yes, but…' Alessandro had to feel his way through the words. 'It doesn't have to be something to resist, Mia. We were both in agreement, I thought, about what our relationship could look like. Companionship, trust, affection.'

'And not love.' She spoke flatly, making him hesitate. 'Have you changed your mind on that?'

'No.' She sounded disconcertingly firm. 'It's just difficult to trust you.'

'Have I ever done anything to make you distrust me?' he asked, stung again by her honest admission. What had he done to make her so wary?

'Not recently.'

'What is that supposed to mean?'

'You spend your life taking over other people's businesses,' she said after a moment. 'And sometimes that feels like what you're doing with me.'

Disconcerted, Alessandro did not reply for a moment. Yes, in his own mind he had compared his relationship to Mia in terms of a takeover, although perhaps a merger was a better way of putting it, but it wasn't *hostile*. At least, it didn't have to be.

'I thought you'd agreed this was best for Ella. And I thought you'd enjoyed the last few weeks.' He couldn't keep an edge of affront from entering his voice. It was hardly as if he'd kept her in prison. 'Please believe me, Mia, I am not trying to force you into anything.'

'There are more ways to force someone than strong-arm them.'

'What are you trying to say?'

'I don't *know*,' Mia said helplessly. 'Like I said, I'm scared, Alessandro. You can be ruthless. I know you like to be in control. I understand why you do, but those things scare me.'

'I am hardly going to be ruthless with my family.'

'How do you even know that? You've kept yourself from relationships for so long. Do you even know how to be in a family relationship, one that isn't driven by anger or revenge?'

Hurt flashed through him at her words. 'I can try,' he said quietly, and her face crumpled a little bit.

'Do you really want to?'

'Of course I do,' he snapped, but he heard the anger in his voice and he knew it was wrong. He just didn't know how to show her how he felt. How much he felt. 'I know I like to be in control. But I'm not dictating things to you, Mia. I'm trying to have a real relationship with you, even if I don't understand yet all that it means.' He felt far too vulnerable having admitted that much, and so he pressed his lips together and stayed silent.

'I'm sorry.' She smiled sadly. 'And I need to try, too. I'm sorry I'm so reluctant. It's just…' She paused, and he waited, sensing she was going to say something more. But then she sighed and shook her head. 'I'd better go and choose my dress.' Her lips twisted wryly. 'That's at least one choice I can make.'

The stylist arrived a short while later, and Alessandro busied himself with work while the stylist and her assistants commandeered the bedroom for their beautifying purposes.

As he half listened to the sound of the women chatting in the next room, he found he could not focus on the work in front of him. He kept going over his conversation with Mia in his mind, as if testing it for weaknesses. Why was Mia so wary with him still? What more could he do to gain her trust? He felt as if she questioned his every motive, which made him question them, as well. Was he doing the right thing?

Of course he was. For Ella's sake as well as theirs. He just needed to be more patient. Perhaps Mia just needed more time.

Still, he couldn't keep from feeling a flicker of irritation along with hurt. He'd been trying so hard for the last few weeks, and he'd given Mia everything. What possible cause could she really have to complain? So he liked to be in control. That was hardly the worst thing, was it? It wasn't as if he was abusing his position of power, or forcing her to do something against her will.

Her reluctance annoyed him, but it also made him even more determined. He would win her yet. Whatever aspect of their inevitable relationship Mia was resisting, Alessandro would discover it and deal with it.

Which, he realised uncomfortably, *did* make this all seem a bit like the takeover she'd suggested. But it wasn't, not like that. It was just…strategy. Common sense.

He slid his hand into the pocket of his jacket, his fingers curling around the small black velvet box. Nothing, he told himself. Mia would find fault with nothing. He'd make sure of it.

An hour later, Alessandro had changed into a tuxedo and was waiting for Mia in the living room of the suite, trying to curb his impatience. It felt as if she'd been in the bedroom for ages, and he'd heard the chatter and giggles drift out as he'd wondered just how long it took to find a dress.

'She's ready,' the stylist, Elena, sang out as she came into the living room, followed by her bevy of assistants. 'And she's perfect.' She simpered at Alessandro before she thankfully excused herself, her assistants following, so Alessandro and Mia would be alone. He would be sent the undoubtedly outrageous bill later.

'Mia…?' Alessandro called when she still hadn't come out after Elena had left. 'Are you coming?'

'Yes. Sorry.' With a nervous little laugh, she stepped out of the bedroom. Alessandro sucked in his breath. He'd already seen her in an evening gown, a year ago, when he'd lost his head over the slender woman dancing in his arms.

Tonight he felt himself lose everything else. His mind emptied and his heart tumbled in his chest as Mia smiled uncertainly. 'Do you…do you like it?'

'I love it,' he assured her huskily. The gown was a pale, creamy ivory, with a delicate overlay of gold lace. Strapless, with a full skirt, it reminded him of a wedding dress, and that seemed appropriate indeed. 'Your hair...' he murmured, coming forward to loop one golden curl around his finger.

'She curled it,' Mia said nervously. 'I've never had curly hair before.'

'It's gorgeous.' Half being pinned up, the other half tumbled over her shoulders in glossy, golden waves and curls. Gently, his finger still twined in her hair, Alessandro tugged her towards him. Mia came, a smile trembling on her lips.

'Alessandro...'

'You're so beautiful, Mia. Even more beautiful now that you're a mother.'

'No...' She let out an uncertain laugh. 'I haven't lost all of my baby weight...'

'I don't want you to. You're perfect just as you are.' He knew it sounded like well-worn flattery, but the truth was he meant every word. He wasn't saying it to please her or to get what he wanted, as she so often seemed to suspect, but because he *needed* to. Because it was right, and it was the truth.

Which was why he had to kiss her, as well.

'Mia...' Her name was a question and as she moved closer, her silence was his answer. He placed one hand on her bare shoulder, her skin cool and soft beneath his palm. Then he brushed his lips across hers, softly first, another question.

And she answered again with silence, her mouth opening under his, a thousand times yes. Here was another truth, in the simple purity of their kiss, their lips joining together in a brief moment that spun on and on as Alessandro deepened the kiss, unable to keep himself from it, losing himself in her soft and willing response.

Mia clutched his shoulders as she anchored herself to

him, to their kiss, and the world seemed to spin around them. It was just a kiss, and yet so much more. It felt like a promise as well as a seal.

Finally Alessandro lifted his head, breathing raggedly, dazed by the intensity of the moment. Mia blinked back at him, her fingers at her lips. Neither of them spoke.

Alessandro felt the weight of the black velvet box in his pocket, and he almost reached for it. Now was the perfect moment—and yet perhaps too perfect. The last thing he wanted was for Mia to think he was orchestrating the moment when in truth he'd been felled by it…as she seemed to have been.

So instead he left it where it was, and smiled at her instead. And, needing no words, he took her by the hand and led her from the room, out into the warm, spring night and the promise it surely held.

CHAPTER TWELVE

MIA'S HEAD WAS SPINNING. Her lips were buzzing. And as she and Alessandro moved through the party, meeting and chatting to people, she wondered if she was falling yet again for the fairy tale. Just as before, she was Cinderella for a night, and yet so much more was at stake. Her whole life. Ella's life. Their future together. It all felt as if it hung in the balance now; all she needed to do was say yes.

And for once, with the memory of Alessandro's kiss on her lips, she didn't want to wonder or doubt. She wanted to enjoy the fairy tale; she wanted, at least for tonight, to trust Alessandro's tempting promises. To believe in them and let them sweep her along.

For once she wanted to resist not only Alessandro, but also her own negative history, her persistent belief and fear that keeping herself apart from Alessandro was the only way to stay strong. To feel independent. What if staying strong could mean something else? It could mean choosing him, rather than fighting him. Was it possible?

She pressed her fingers to her lips as she recalled yet again that heart-stopping, breath-stealing kiss. Alessandro had seemed as affected as she'd been. For a few moments, they'd shared something wonderful.

But was it—could it be—real?

Dared she let it be real in her own mind, never mind Alessandro's?

Her thoughts tumbled and shifted in her mind in an ever-changing kaleidoscope that she struggled to make sense of. She felt as if she were teetering on a precipice, but she had no idea what lay ahead—or below.

Then Alessandro took her hand as he drew her towards him, his eyes the colour of smoke, his voice husky as he devoured her in a single glance.

'Dance?'

Mia thought of their dance a year ago, when everything had heightened and changed between them. It had been magical…but it had also been dangerous. Where was the danger now? Was it real—or was she imagining it, because she was so afraid of losing herself the way her mother had? Could she let go of it for a night?

Could she let go of it for ever?

She nodded, her palm sliding across his, fingers twining and tightening as they moved onto the dance floor and began to sway to the sensuous music.

'Are you enjoying tonight?' Alessandro asked as he moved her slowly and languorously around the floor, their hips bumping, heat flaring.

'Yes…'

'You don't sound entirely convinced.' He spoke lightly but Mia saw the flash of concern and even hurt in his eyes, quickly masked.

'I don't know what to think, Alessandro,' she confessed quietly. 'So I'm trying not to think at all. I just want to… feel.'

'Feeling is good,' Alessandro murmured huskily. 'Feeling is very good.' His forehead crinkled in a frown. 'But you don't need to be so wary, Mia. So scared.'

'I'm trying not to be.'

'What exactly is it you are afraid of, *cara*?' The endearment slipped easily from his tongue, caressing her with its intimacy, making her want even more to trust this and believe in it. In him.'

She hesitated, unsure what to say. How much to confess. Yet surely Alessandro deserved to know why she was the way she was, what experiences had formed and shaped her, and that she was becoming desperate to shed now? 'I'm scared of losing myself,' she admitted quietly.

Alessandro's frown deepened, a deep line bisecting his brow. 'Losing yourself?'

'Yes. Losing my...my sense of self, I suppose. My ability to make decisions, to be my own person...' She trailed off, realising how vague and really rather ridiculous she sounded. What did it even mean, to lose yourself? Could she even put what she was so frightened of into concrete ideas and absolutes? Or was it just this vague sense of dread, that life was spinning out of control, that she needed to leave behind her, finally and for ever?

'I don't understand,' Alessandro said as he moved her around the dance floor, one hand warm and sure on her waist. 'Please, will you explain it to me?'

She shook her head. 'I don't know if I can. I know it sounds silly and vague, formless, but...it's what I grew up with. My mother and father...' She faltered, her throat growing tight with memories.

'Your mother and father?' Alessandro prompted gently. 'You mentioned you didn't get along with your father...'

'No, I didn't. He was...very controlling. Mostly of my mother but, after she died, also of me.' She shook her head, unwilling to explain just how cruel her father could be, how domineering. She didn't want to explain about the memories that still tormented her—when he'd locked her in her room, or thrown the meal her mother had made in the bin, claiming it was inedible.

'He's just got high standards, Mia. That's all it is.'

She couldn't explain the choking frustration she'd felt

with her mother, and then later the awful fear she'd felt for herself, knowing she had to get away before her father controlled her completely.

'Controlling,' Alessandro repeated in a neutral voice. 'This is why you have this issue with control? Why you feel I am too controlling?'

'Yes,' she whispered. 'I suppose so. My father was... awful. He told me what I had to do, or say, or even wear. He enjoyed exerting that power, simply because he could.'

'And so you think I am like this man?' Alessandro asked. His voice was even, but Mia felt the hurt emanating from him, and a wave of sorrow and regret rushed through her.

Alessandro was *nothing* like her father. The realisation washed through her in a cleansing flood. Yes, he could be brutal in business, ruthless in his ambition, but he was never cruel. He'd already shown her how his hostile takeovers were, in essence, mercy missions. Although he could be autocratic, he never sneered or insulted or mocked simply to show his power, because he could. His kindness was genuine.

'No,' Mia said quietly. 'I don't think you're like him, Alessandro.' Another realisation was jolting through her, more powerful than the first. No, she didn't think Alessandro was like her father, not really. Not at all.

But maybe she was like her mother.

That, Mia realised, had been her real fear all along. Not that she'd be beholden to a man like her father, but that she would act like her mother. She wouldn't be able to help herself. She'd fall in love with Alessandro, just as her mother had with her father, and give up everything for him—willingly. *That* was what she was afraid of.

Yet how could she admit so much to him now? The last thing she wanted Alessandro to know was the hold he had over her, or that even now she was halfway to falling in love with him, and fighting it all the way.

'I understand why you would be wary, Mia,' Alessandro said. 'Of course I do. But if you know I am not like that...'

Mia shook her head helplessly. The problem was her—her weakness, and her fear. Yet did loving someone have to mean losing yourself? If Alessandro wasn't like her father, was there really any danger? Did she want to be so in thrall to her past and her own fears that she missed out on life, on love?

Yet Alessandro had never said anything about love.

'Mia?' Alessandro prompted gently. 'What is going on inside that beautiful head of yours? Tell me, so I can help.'

'I don't know,' she confessed. 'A million things. I've always believed I would never get married. I'd never...' She hesitated, for she'd been about to say love, and she wasn't ready for that. She was quite sure Alessandro wasn't, either. 'I'd never have that kind of relationship,' she amended. 'And I never wanted it. But now...'

'Now?'

'Now we have to have some kind of relationship, and yes, it scares me. But part of me...wants it, and that scares me, too.'

'All this fear.' The music had ended, and Alessandro stopped their swaying, raising her hand to his lips. He brushed a kiss across her knuckles as his gentle yet determined gaze met hers. 'I will do my best to allay your fears, *cara*. The last thing I want is for you to be afraid—of me, of anyone or anything. I promise never to hurt you, never to take advantage of you, never to make you regret joining your life with mine.'

'Those are big promises, Alessandro,' she whispered shakily. Yet she knew he meant them.

'Yes, they are.' Her hand was still at his lips as he kept

his gaze on her, now fierce and glittering. 'Do you believe me, Mia? Will you trust me?'

Could she?

'I want to,' she whispered.

'Then let yourself. See what can be between us, Mia. Discover how good—how wonderful—it could be, if you let yourself trust. *Fall.* I'll catch you. I promise I will.'

His words were a siren song that she ached to listen to, and believe. If only it could be so easy. If only she could leave her fears behind and step into this bright, glittering future Alessandro promised. *Why not?* Why not at least try, for Ella's sake, for her sake, for *theirs*?

'All right,' she whispered, and Alessandro smiled, victory lighting his eyes as he drew her towards him and kissed her right there on the dance floor, in front of the crowd, his lips on hers like a seal, branding her with his mouth just as he had with his words.

As they broke apart, Mia's lips buzzed and her face flamed. She felt as if she'd just jumped off a cliff, and she couldn't yet tell whether she was flying—or falling.

'Shall we go?' Alessandro murmured, and she knew what he was asking. They'd been on a dance floor before, in thrall to their shared desire, and he'd asked her the same question. And once again, she could agree, she could let herself be caught up in what was spinning out between them, let it sweep her along so she didn't have to think or wonder—or fear.

'Yes, let's,' she whispered, and Alessandro laced his fingers through hers once more as he led her through the crowd, the faceless blur barely registering as they left the ballroom and, just as they had once before, stepped out into the warm spring night.

They were both quiet during the limo ride to the private airport where they took a helicopter back to the villa.

Mia's heart thudded in her chest as she thought about what was ahead of them, what she'd agreed to.

No regrets…

The short helicopter ride seemed over in a moment, and then they were walking up towards the darkened villa, Mia achingly aware of Alessandro's powerful body next to hers. With murmured thanks, he dismissed Alyssa, who assured Mia that Ella had gone to sleep with no problems, and was still sleeping soundly.

At the bottom of the sweeping staircase, Mia paused as Alessandro stood there, his eyes blazing silver as he looked at her, the villa dark and silent all around them.

What was he waiting for?

Why wasn't he taking her in his arms, kissing away the last of her fears and objections? She was ready to be swept up in something bigger than herself, ready to let herself go. At least she hoped she was.

'What now?' she finally asked, when she could bear the silence no longer.

Alessandro met her gaze directly, his hands spread wide. 'You tell me.'

She eyed him uncertainly. 'What do you mean?'

'This moment is yours, Mia. You choose it. You decide what you want now, how far you want this to go.' He drew a shuddering breath. 'Do you want me?' Although his voice was assured, the question held a stark note of painful vulnerability that touched Mia deeply.

For the first time Alessandro was surrendering his control…and in this, the most important and elemental aspect of their relationship.

She'd been fully anticipating him to sweep her into a masterminded and smoothly thought out seduction, and she'd been willing to go along with it, to be caught up in it and, in a way, relieved of any real and active choice… even though that was what she'd been fighting for all along.

But Alessandro wasn't giving her that option. He was making her choose now, making her fully own the decision she thought she'd already made, back in the ballroom. This could be no silent surrender, defeat by acquiescence, overwhelmed by his sheer force of personality and innate authority that she tried to resent and yet somehow craved. Alessandro wouldn't let it be that. He was making this moment hers, making her choose it to be theirs.

He held her gaze, his eyes burning fiercely, his hands still spread open wide, his stance one of acceptance rather than aggression or authority. For once he was giving her all the power, all the control, all she'd said she wanted… so what was she going to do?

Alessandro waited, his body tense, his heart thudding. Everything in him resisted this moment, the utter, revealing weakness of it. He didn't do this. He didn't let someone else choose his fate, even if just for a night, although this was so much more than a night. He'd always, *always* been the architect of his own ambition.

But over the course of the evening, as he'd reflected on what Mia had shared about her family and her past, he'd realised that in this, of all things, she needed to have the control. He needed to surrender it, even if everything in him still fought against it. And so he waited.

Mia stared at him for a long moment, a thousand emotions chasing across her lovely face, making her eyes sparkle and her lips tremble. 'Do I want you?' she repeated slowly, her voice sliding over the syllables, testing them out, and Alessandro tensed even more, waiting, expectant. *Afraid.*

Then, to his deep disappointment and dread, she shook her head. 'Not like that,' she said, with a nod towards the bedroom waiting upstairs, with its sumptuous king-sized bed and all that it beckoned and promised. The sour taste of rejection flooded his mouth, overwhelmed his senses with the unwelcome acid of it.

She didn't want him.

'At least, not *just* that,' Mia clarified, her voice trembling. 'I don't want another night with you, Alessandro, amazing as the last one was, with all of its repercussions.'

She smiled wryly, straightening her shoulders, and Alessandro raised his eyebrows, his stomach clenched hard with anxiety and uncertainty, both which he hated feeling. He'd never felt so vulnerable, so needy, so open to hurt and pain. 'What, then?' he demanded in a raw voice.

'I came up here prepared to be…to be swept away,' she began haltingly. 'I was expecting you to do the sweeping. Then I wouldn't have had to think or wonder or doubt. I could just let myself feel.'

Which sounded pretty good to Alessandro in this moment. Had he made a mistake, in surrendering his own agency? He had been taking a risk, but it was one he had hoped would turn in his favour. Now he wasn't so sure.

'And now?' he made himself ask, although he half dreaded the answer.

'And now I want something else. Something more.'

'More…'

'I don't want a night. I want…' She swallowed, more of a gulp, her eyes huge in her face as she looked at him resolutely, her chin tilted upwards in determination, her slender body trembling with emotion. 'I want for ever.'

Surprise and a far greater relief rippled through him. She wasn't rejecting him. *Them.* 'For ever…'

Her smile trembled on her lips. 'I know you've been hoping or even expecting me to marry you. But I want this to be on my terms, and amazingly you seem to want that, too. So now I'm the one proposing. The one choosing. Will you…will you marry me?'

He laughed, the sound one of shock but also admiration.

He hadn't expected *that*. 'You know I will. In fact...' Fumbling a little, he reached for the small box of black velvet that had nestled in his pocket all evening. 'I was planning to make you a proper proposal tonight, but I didn't want to seem as if I was pressuring you, or arranging things somehow...' He held the box out in the palm of his hand. 'But I can't think of a better moment than this one.'

'Nor can I.' Smiling a little, she reached for it. Alessandro held his breath as she carefully opened the box, her eyes widening at the sight of the simple solitaire diamond nestled amidst its soft velvet folds. 'It's beautiful, Alessandro.'

The ring was stark in its simplicity, a single diamond on a band of white gold. Alessandro had looked at various rings, but they'd all seemed fussy and officious rather than the simple, pure statement of his intent he wanted. *Their* intent, for a life lived together. Mia lifted her face so her eyes, now luminous with the sheen of tears, met his once more. 'Will you put it on me?'

'Of course.' His fingers trembled a little as he took the ring from the box and slid it on her finger, where it winked and sparkled, a promise they were making to each other. He clasped her hand with his own. 'Do you mean this, Mia?'

'Yes.'

'You want this?' he pressed, because somewhere along the way that had become important, too. This wasn't just about winning any more, or getting what he wanted. He needed her to want it, as well. To want *him*.

'Yes.' Her voice quavered. 'I'm scared, Alessandro. I can admit that. I don't know what the future holds, but I also know I don't want to be enslaved to my past. So yes, I want this. For Ella's sake, and perhaps even for...for ours.' Her worried gaze searched his face as she nibbled her lip.

'I know we haven't actually talked about what a marriage between us would look like, besides the obvious...'

No, they hadn't. For a moment Alessandro couldn't speak, as realisation caught up with him and he desperately tried to order his jumbled thoughts. He'd been so focused on Ella, on their being a family, that he hadn't completely considered what their relationship—their *marriage*—would actually look like. What it would mean.

And he was conscious, incredibly so, that in accepting his proposal, or, rather, offering her own, Mia was giving herself to him. Her body, her mind, and yes, perhaps even her heart. Her life. Precious, fragile gifts. And he was even more conscious that in offering them, she'd, inadvertently or not, given him back the power she hated to relinquish, and which he'd always craved.

What if he hurt her?

What if she hurt him?

The second question, he told himself, wasn't a consideration; he would not allow that to happen. He would honour his marriage vows, and give Mia respect and companionship and so much pleasure. Of that he was sure. But as for love? His heart? The ability to reach inside and hurt him?

No. He saw where that led. He'd seen and felt the pain and brokenness all through his childhood. His mother's tears, anger, addictions, helplessness and grief. No. He could not offer Mia that kind of love.

But what he could offer...he'd make sure she'd be happy with. She'd want for nothing. He'd treat her like a queen.

'We'll figure it out as we go along,' Alessandro told her, smiling to soften the prevarication of his words, and what they both knew he wasn't saying. Wasn't promising. He saw it in the cloudy flicker of her eyes, the slight downturn of her mouth before she made herself smile back. 'This is going to work, Mia. I will do my best, my utmost, to give you everything. To never hurt you.' Again he felt the weight of what he wasn't saying.

To love you.

She nodded slowly. 'I know you will, Alessandro.'

'When shall we marry?'

'There's no real rush, is there?'

'Why not make it official?'

'We still could use the time to get to know each other,' Mia protested. 'The three months…'

'It's already been nearly three weeks,' Alessandro returned. Why not marry sooner?'

'At least give it a couple of weeks, so we can plan.'

'Very well.' He could wait that long. 'Are there people you want to invite?'

She shook her head. 'No, not really.'

'Then it will be just us, and Ella, exactly as it should be.' He smiled, liking the thought. 'A family from the beginning.'

'Yes.' She smiled back, but he saw a tiny frown puckering the ivory smoothness of her brow, and he drew her towards him for a lingering kiss. 'We will do this properly, and wait for our wedding night,' he said, savouring the thought. 'Trust me, Mia, our marriage will be the beginning of everything.'

CHAPTER THIRTEEN

SHE WAS A married woman.

Mia gazed down at the two rings now sparkling on her finger, the first the elegant solitaire diamond from the night of her proposal, the second a simple band of white gold that Alessandro had slipped on her finger only moments ago.

They were standing on the terrace at the villa in Tuscany, the gardens and hills spread out before them in all their blossoming glory, the sun shining benevolently down. Alyssa and Paulo had been the witnesses to their wedding, the local priest, a smiling man who spoke no English, the officiant. Ella, clasped in Alyssa's arms and gurgling happily, had been the only guest.

Mia had worn a strapless dress of ivory silk that she'd bought in Rome on an extravagant shopping trip last week; Alessandro had insisted she buy a complete trousseau, including some very sexy lingerie that made her heart race just to look at.

The last three weeks had been a whirlwind, and a wonderful one at that. Mia had let her fears trickle away in the blazing certainty of Alessandro's attention. He doted on Ella and was kind and considerate with her, and the kisses that punctuated each evening had become longer and more lingering, leaving Mia in a welter of unsated desire, wondering why Alessandro insisted they wait, even as she acknowledged she was glad that he had.

He'd given her no reason to doubt the sudden, surprising choice she'd made that night after the ball, when she'd turned down the offer of a night for so much more.

Mia had been shocked by her own audacity and conviction, but in that moment she'd felt the rightness of what she was doing...what *they* were doing.

She could trust Alessandro. That, she realised, was the choice she was making.

With the ceremony finished, Alyssa handed Ella to Paulo, who took the baby with smiling ease, as she went to fetch the refreshments. Alessandro came to stand by Mia, placing a hand on her lower back, warm and sure, as he smiled down at her.

'Happy?' he murmured, and she turned to smile at him, realising that she really was. Over the last few weeks, her fears and doubts had been chipped away until there was very little of them left.

The dread that had taken residence in the pit of her stomach like some fermenting acid no longer pooled there. Yes, she was still afraid, but it was the uncertain nervousness of a new bride rather than the consuming fear of a woman on the brink of some awful abyss.

She *was* on the brink...but perhaps of something wonderful. Mia was trying to stay pragmatic, reminding herself that Alessandro had made no declarations of love, and neither had she. They didn't know each other well enough for that yet, and she still wasn't entirely sure she wanted to give him that much of herself.

And yet, despite her reservations, the possibility remained, in her heart at least, that this could be a marriage not just of convenience and companionship, which Alessandro had already promised, but also of love, something he most certainly had not. Something she'd never let herself consider before, but was now allowing herself to cautiously wonder about, if just a little.

'Yes, I'm happy.' She gazed out at the gardens, burgeoning with blossom and scent. 'It's been a perfect day.'

'You didn't mind not having a big wedding?'

Mia shook her head. 'I never intended on getting married at all, so why would I want a big wedding?' she answered with a little laugh. She glanced again at the rings on her finger, a tremor of excitement rippling through her at the sight of them. There was no going back.

She might have never thought she'd marry, and yet here she was. Here they were...and tonight would be their wedding night. Already nerves sizzled through her at the thought of that.

'Most young girls dream of big, white weddings,' Alessandro remarked.

'Not me. This has been perfect, truly.' She rested one hand on his, curled around the balustrade, the sun warming their skin. 'I couldn't ask for anything more, Alessandro.'

'Nor could I.' He smiled at her, his expression warm and glinting, allaying the last of her fears. This was going to work. It already was working. Then Alessandro nodded towards Alyssa, who was bringing out a magnificent *millefoglie*, the traditional Italian wedding cake of puff pastry, Chantilly cream, icing sugar and strawberries. 'Shall we have cake?'

'I can always have cake.' Mia took Ella from Paulo as Alyssa cut the cake, and Paulo fetched a bottle of champagne. Ella grabbed at her fork as Mia took a bite of the delicious cake, savouring the explosion of sweetness in her mouth. 'Not for you, little one,' she said with a laugh as Ella's chubby fingers latched onto the fork.

'I'll take her.' With relaxed ease born now of experience, Alessandro reached for Ella, cradling her against his shoulder. As it always did, Mia's heart constricted at the sight of father and daughter, husband and child. Her family. A thrill ran through her at the thought, and one that had nothing to do with fear, and all with hope and even joy. This was real now. *They* were.

They ate cake and had champagne in the spring sunshine. Alessandro had planned a dinner for them, and Alyssa insisted on having Ella for the whole night, assuring Mia that the baby could sleep in her cottage.

'Ella is a good *bambina*,' Alyssa said firmly. 'She did not wake up even once. Such a good girl. This is your wedding night, Mia. Enjoy, Signora Costa!'

Signora Costa. Another ripple of surprised excitement shivered through her at the realisation of her new status.

The sun was starting to set, sending golden rays slanting through Mia's bedroom, as she exchanged her wedding gown for a cocktail dress in scarlet with a handkerchief hemline and a halter neck. Her wedding ring flashed as she did her make-up and hair, gazing at her face as if to look for changes. She was a married woman. And by tomorrow morning, she would *truly* be a married woman, in the way that mattered most...

Mia's stomach dipped as she considered the wedding night that loomed ahead of her, exciting and yet terrifying. Her one sexual experience had been short and frenzied, mere moments that had been blurred by passion.

Tonight would be in an entirely different category...and that both excited and scared her, with its promises of both pleasure and intense vulnerability. How would Alessandro be as a husband and lover? How would she be? Would she please him? Ella was only a few months old, and her body had changed since the last time he'd seen it, admittedly for only a brief time. What would he think of her gently rounded stomach, her heavier breasts?

A light knock sounded on the door. 'Ready, *cara*?' Alessandro called.

'I think so.' Mia gave her reflection one last tremulous glance before she went to the door and opened it. Alessandro stood there, looking as devastating as ever in a crisp button-down shirt in dove grey and darker grey trousers. He smelled wonderful.

'You look lovely,' he murmured, putting one hand on her waist as he pulled her to him for a prolonged kiss that made Mia's senses spin and reel. She wondered if kissing him would always make her blood fizz and her heart hum, or if it would become natural, even ordinary.

'So where are we going for dinner, exactly?' Mia asked as they headed downstairs. 'The trattoria in town?'

Alessandro chuckled, shaking his head. 'I think not.'

'There aren't any other restaurants...'

'This is our wedding night, Mia. We will celebrate in style.'

They walked out of the villa, and Mia stopped in surprise at the sight of the helicopter resting on the helipad in the distance, obscured by a few plane trees.

'Where...?'

'Come.' Taking her hand, Alessandro led her to the helicopter.

'But Ella...'

'We'll be back home in a few hours, never fear.' He helped her up into the helicopter as Mia's stomach fizzed with excitement. Where on earth was Alessandro taking her?

She found out an hour later, when they arrived in Venice, the city's many canals gleaming under the setting sun, the wedding-cake roof of San Marco Cathedral blazing with gold. Alessandro had hired out an entire restaurant by Piazza San Marco, the dining room flickering with candlelight, the canal mere steps away, the restaurant secluded and romantic as they were served course after course by a discreet waiter.

'This is amazing,' Mia breathed, in awe of the luxury and romance of it all.

The food was delicious, and she allowed herself a glass of champagne to celebrate, losing herself in the warm and unabashed admiration she saw in Alessandro's eyes. Tonight was made for magic.

And the magic continued as they walked hand in hand along the canal, chatting about everything and nothing. Alessandro had a dry sense of humour that made Mia laugh, and a sensitivity she hadn't expected, even though she'd seen it on display with their daughter. As they enjoyed the sights of the city of bridges, she felt as if her heart were a balloon inside her, filling up with hope, buoying higher and higher. Their marriage could work. Their marriage could even be amazing…

Finally, as twilight settled on the city with deep indigo shadows, the placid surface of the Grand Canal nearly black, they took the helicopter back to the villa.

Moonlight streamed through the windows as they walked quietly, still hand in hand, through the villa, up to the master bedroom Mia had been sleeping in alone for the last few weeks but would share with Alessandro tonight.

In the few hours since she'd been gone, it had been transformed: tall white candles flickered and gleamed, and the bed sheets had been exchanged for a silk duvet, folded back to reveal smooth linen sheets beneath. The nightgown of cobwebby lace and nearly transparent white silk that she'd picked out last week was hanging on the wardrobe door. Mia's heart tumbled in her chest at the sight of it.

'Is all this Alyssa's doing?' she asked.

'And mine.'

It thrilled her to think Alessandro had thought of such romantic touches. 'This is all so romantic…'

'And why shouldn't it be? It is our wedding night, after all.' Alessandro stood behind her, his hands warm on her shoulders. 'It will be different this time, *cara*. So much better.'

Nerves fizzed and popped inside her. 'It was pretty good last time,' she admitted shakily. Now that the moment had come, and they were here together in this beautiful room, intending to consummate their marriage, she felt overwhelmed with both excitement and anxiety.

'Even so.' Alessandro nodded towards the nightgown. 'Do you want to change?'

'All right,' Mia whispered, and, taking the beautiful nightgown, she went into the bathroom.

Alessandro paced the bedroom, feeling restless and eager and, he had to admit, nervous. He was never nervous, and yet he couldn't deny the way his stomach clenched and his heart raced. Yes, he was nervous, but he was also excited. *Very* excited. He'd been waiting a long time for this, and more than once he'd questioned his decision to wait until their wedding night.

The evening had been perfect so far—the food and wine, the company, the romance of it all. Alessandro had never seen the point of such gestures before, but tonight they'd been important, and he'd enjoyed them. He'd wanted them. He'd wanted to make this night special for Mia, and special for him, in a way he'd never remotely wanted to before.

What was happening to him?

He thrust the question away, determined not to think about it tonight. This was just a bit of romance, that was all. It was a way to show Mia he appreciated her. It didn't have to mean anything more than that.

Besides, tonight he only wanted to think about Mia… and what was going to happen between them.

The door to the bathroom opened and then she stood there, her hair loose and golden about her shoulders, her slender body swathed in ivory silk. Alessandro sucked in a hard breath, dazed with desire at the sight of her. The silk was so thin he could see the lush, shadowy curves of her body beneath it, and they enflamed him. The few rushed minutes they'd shared over a year ago were nothing compared to this.

'You're still dressed,' Mia observed with a shaky laugh.

'Not for long.' His hands moved to the buttons of his shirt before they stilled. 'Why don't you do it, Mia?'

Her eyes widened. 'Me?'

'Yes, you.' His voice turned ragged with the force of his feeling. 'I want you to. I want you to touch me.'

She stared at him wide-eyed for a few seconds before she moved towards him, the silk whispering against her body. As she stood before him he breathed in her citrusy scent, felt her hair brush his jaw as her fingers fumbled with the first button.

'I'm nervous,' she whispered.

'So am I.'

She glanced up at him. 'No...'

'Yes.' He clasped her hand in his own and pressed it against his thudding heart. 'Feel.'

She laid her palm flat against his chest, her fingers spread wide. Even that simple touch enflamed him, made him want more. So much more. 'Why are you nervous?'

'Because this feels important.' The words came of their own accord, heartfelt, honest. He didn't care what they revealed of him.

Mia glanced at him uncertainly, her hand still resting against his heart. 'You've been with plenty of women before...'

'Not like this. Never like this.'

'Truly?'

'Truly.'

She pressed her hand lightly against his chest, absorbing his words, the truth of them, and then she resumed unbuttoning his shirt. This time her fingers didn't fumble, and soon she was parting the material, sliding it over his shoulders so he was bare-chested.

'I never did get a good look at you before,' she remarked, her hands resting lightly on the sculpted muscles of his chest. His heart still thudded.

'You can look all you like now.'

'I am.' She ran her hand lightly down his chest, her fingers tracing the hard ridges of muscle, exploring his body in a way that made him feel dizzy with hunger for her even though her fingers were barely skimming his skin.

'Mia, you have no idea what you do to me.'

She ran her fingers along the waistband of his trousers before flicking open his belt as she gave him a mischievous look from under golden lashes. 'Don't I?'

He let out a choked laugh. 'Maybe you do, you imp.' He couldn't stand still any longer, submitting to her intoxicating touch. 'Now perhaps I need to discover what I do to you.' He put his hands on her arms, sliding them up to her shoulders, enjoying the feel of the silk of her skin, before he hooked one finger underneath the spaghetti strap of her nightgown and tugged it down.

Her breath came in a shudder and she swayed as he pressed a kiss to the pure line of her collarbone before moving lower to the soft swell of her breast.

'Alessandro...'

'It seems we affect each other in a similar way,' he murmured. Already he was blazing with need, on fire with it, and they'd barely touched.

'It does seem that way,' she admitted shakily. Her legs nearly buckled as he drew the other strap down, and then with one gentle twist of her shoulders the beautiful gown pooled at her feet, leaving her naked and beautiful. So very beautiful.

'I didn't wear that for very long,' she remarked with an

attempt at wryness, although he could see the pulse beating wildly in her throat, her pupils dark and huge.

'It was in the way.'

'So are these.' She nodded towards his trousers, and Alessandro spread his hands.

'You may do the honours.'

With a gulp, she reached for the button, her fingers fumbling once more as she undid it and then started to tug down the zip, her slender fingers brushing the pulsing length of him, making him groan.

'Mia…' he began, and then he found he couldn't finish his sentence. He drew her into his arms, and in a tangle of naked limbs, he brought her to the bed and laid her on it like a treasure.

He kissed her deeply, drinking her in, feeling how her mouth and her whole body opened to him, an offering freely given—and utterly accepted.

He stretched out on top of her, relishing the feeling of her pressed against every inch of him, her arms wrapped around his shoulders, her breasts pressed to his chest, all his to explore and savour.

And he did, taking his time, coaxing an unfettered and glorious response out of Mia, his wife.

His wife.

The words, the truth of them, reverberated through him as he finally slid inside her welcoming warmth, uniting their bodies in a way they had never been united before, because this was for ever. One flesh, bound by a sacred vow.

For ever.

Mia's cry of pleasure was muffled against his shoulder as he began to move and she joined him, finding a rhythm they claimed for their own as it took them higher and higher, united in this, united in everything.

As one.

The realisation of it thudded through him in the aftermath of their joined explosion as Alessandro rolled onto his back, taking Mia with him. He never wanted to let her go.

He'd never expected this. All along he'd been planning his strategy, wooing his wife, poised for victory, negotiating the terms. She would be his.

He hadn't realised he would be hers.

But he felt it now in every sated fibre of his being, and this union between them that they had just consummated wasn't just special, it was sacred. It was overwhelming. And he knew, as he held her close, that he was in very grave danger of doing that which Mia herself had been so afraid of—losing himself. Giving everything to the woman he now held in his arms.

The woman who held his heart without even realising it. Without him ever having meant to give it to her.

CHAPTER FOURTEEN

IT HAD BEEN one month since she'd become Alessandro's wife, one amazing, incredible, pleasure-filled month. The days had been spent with Ella and often with Alessandro, when he could get away from work, spending time together in easy pleasures, exploring the market town and the surrounding countryside, and simply enjoying getting to know one another.

When Alessandro had to work at his office in Florence, Mia had pottered about the villa, taking over some of the duties from Alyssa, as well as learning Italian and attending a local mums and babies group. She'd been surprised how easy and pleasant it was to fill her days in this way, to simply enjoy being.

And as for her nights…those were filled as well, with a pleasure and intimacy she'd never expected or dared to dream of. Every night she and Alessandro explored each other's bodies, learning the maps of their very selves, and offering themselves to each other in a way that felt like the purest form of communication.

Each night left Mia both sated and shaken, as if she'd flown close to the sun, and been engulfed in its brilliance. It warmed her right through, but she also knew it had the danger to burn her right up.

Because, a month on from their marriage, she knew she was falling in love with her husband. She might have fought against it at the start, had worried all along that it would happen, and now she knew it was.

And she had no idea how her husband felt about her. At night she'd swear on her soul that he loved her, and he showed her he did in a thousand ways. But during the day...

Mia hadn't been able to fault him, at least not until recently. He'd been kind, affectionate, humorous, gentle with Ella. Yet all along she had never been able to escape the sense that he was still keeping some private yet essential part of himself from her. Whenever the conversation turned a little too personal, she felt a distance open up between them, a cool remoteness in Alessandro, as if he had picketed off part of himself and it absolutely wasn't up for grabs.

When she was alone, she told herself she must be imagining it. How on earth could she not be satisfied with all Alessandro gave her? It was such a vague notion, after all. Then, when they were together again, she felt it, like a part of her rubbed raw, always chafing. The words he'd never say, the sense that he wasn't hers, not in the way that she knew she was his. The remoteness was real... and it hurt.

And it had grown worse over the last few days, with Alessandro barely spending any time with her at all. He'd worked late, missing dinner as well as Ella's bedtime, coming to bed when Mia had already succumbed to a restless, unhappy sleep.

She hadn't asked him about his withdrawal; she hadn't, she acknowledged unhappily, been brave enough. Maybe he had some important deal at work. Maybe something else was going on.

But then, why couldn't he tell her about it?

And, more importantly, why couldn't she ask?

Now, with Ella settled in her bouncy chair as Mia prepared dinner, she could pretend, at least, they were just like any other family, any other loving couple. Alessandro had told her this morning he would be home for dinner, and hopefully they would sit and eat, talk and laugh, and everything so easy and simple…at least on the surface.

And when they went up to bed a little while later, it would be even simpler, because between the sheets Mia felt she had all of Alessandro to herself…body and soul.

There Alessandro never became a tiny bit repressive, a little tight-lipped. In bed, she never saw the flash of something in his eyes that reminded her of the man she'd met back in London, cold and autocratic, ruthless and remote. Not the man she married. Not the man she was beginning, to her own wonder and fear, to love.

Alyssa bustled into the kitchen, chucking Ella under her chin before turning to Mia. 'Something smells *molto delizioso!*'

Mia smiled wryly. 'I hope so. That is…*lo spero.*'

Alyssa beamed her approval. '*Molto buona!* Your lessons are coming on, *si*?'

'*Si.*' She'd been having several hours' tuition every day, and she hoped eventually to be fluent, to help Ella be fluent as well. Alessandro already talked to his daughter in Italian, something that made Mia melt inside. At moments like that, she could let herself believe in the fairy tale. She could be carried away by it.

'Is Signor Costa eating at home tonight?' Alyssa asked, and Mia nodded.

'Yes…that is, I hope so. *Lo spero.*' She smiled wryly again. 'He said he would before he left this morning.' Even though he hadn't for the few nights before, with no real explanation.

She was just setting the table, Ella bathed and gurgling in her bouncy chair, when her phone beeped with a text from Alessandro.

Working late.

Two measly words when she'd already prepared dinner, had everything ready. Mia's stomach swirled with disappointment and a far deeper hurt. This was the fourth night in a row. Feeling a bit reckless, she swiped her phone's screen to dial his number.

'Mia?' His voice was terse. 'Didn't you get my message?'

'Yes, but it's so late, Alessandro. I've already made dinner...'

'It will keep, won't it?'

Mia blinked at his brusque tone. No explanations, no apologies, just that edge of impatience to his voice, as if she was wasting his time.

'That's not the point, Alessandro,' she said, trying to keep her voice even. 'This is the fourth night you've missed dinner—'

'I'm working.' There was no mistaking the edge now. 'Surely you can understand that, Mia. I shouldn't have to justify it to you.'

'I'm not asking you to justify it,' she protested, startled by the definite coolness in his voice. 'Alessandro... what's going on?'

'What do you mean by that? Nothing is going on.'

'You've been so distant...'

'I'm *working*.'

Gone was even the pretence of the gentle, kind and attentive lover Mia had grown to know and love these last few weeks, making her wonder if it had all been a mirage.

'I know that,' she said quietly.

'Then there's no problem,' Alessandro answered, his voice clipped, and before Mia could say another word he disconnected the call.

She stood there for a moment, stunned by what had just

happened, and yet somehow not surprised at all. Hadn't some part of her been waiting for this? For the mask to fall away, the true man to be revealed? All her fears to be realised?

She hadn't had the courage to confront Alessandro, and when she'd tried, he'd put her in her place, brushing off her concerns as if they were of no importance. The same way her father had.

It didn't have to be a big deal, Mia told herself. It was one phone conversation. All couples had arguments. She was overreacting, she *knew* that. And yet…

But she knew it wasn't one conversation; it was everything that had and hadn't happened in the last month. On their wedding day—and night—she'd felt so wonderfully close to him, and the last month had been a sliding away from that, inch by infinitesimal inch.

Alessandro had been becoming more remote, and, worse, she had become more needy. More desperate. She'd heard it in her voice; she felt it in herself.

Drawing in a ragged breath, Mia reached for the pan of sauce simmering on the stove and recklessly she scraped it all into the bin.

She didn't want it to *keep*. Alessandro would most likely come home late tomorrow night as well. And the night after that…the night after that…

She couldn't live this way.

The realisation came suddenly, starkly, and was completely overwhelming, every fear she'd ever had rising restlessly to the fore. Here she was, just like her mother, miserable and alone, having just been told off by the man she was coming to love.

In her seat, Ella let out a happy gurgle, startling Mia out of her unhappy thoughts. She picked Ella up, pacing the kitchen, before she decided she couldn't stay in this villa for another moment. It felt like a mausoleum—a mausoleum of her fragile, fledgling hopes and dreams. As melo-dramatic as she knew that sounded, even in her own head, she also knew she needed some space.

Quickly Mia went upstairs and packed a case for both her and Ella. She needed to get out of here, get some per-spective. And, she acknowledged, she wanted to show Alessandro that he wasn't the only one who could change plans.

It didn't take long to pack what she needed and ring a taxi. While waiting for the car to arrive, she'd checked out a family-friendly hotel in nearby Assisi. She'd go there for the night, she decided. Perhaps in the morning, things would feel and look better, and she'd know what to do. How to feel.

As the taxi sped away from the villa, Ella dozing in her car seat by her side, Mia glanced down at her phone. Alessandro hadn't called or texted again, but she knew he deserved at least some explanation as to her absence.

Needed to think, she texted,

And then waited for a reply that never came.

Alessandro glanced moodily at his phone. *Needed to think?* What was that supposed to mean? He hadn't bothered to reply, because he didn't know what to say. In truth, he hadn't known what to say for weeks now, as he fought the feeling that had been growing between them, stronger every day, and more alarming.

After the soul-changing encounter on their wedding night, when he'd realised just how far he'd fallen, he'd found himself inexorably withdrawing, trying to create a safe distance between him and Mia while pretending to her that it wasn't there.

It had been easy at night, when their bodies took over, and yet he knew that those earth-shattering nights were actually drawing them closer together. Making him want even more from Mia—and for her to want more than he was able to give.

Because during the day, when she asked about his family, or looked at him with so much expectation in her eyes, when he felt a welling of need inside him, a need that felt overwhelming and consuming...he started to freeze. To fear.

He was falling in love with Mia; hell, he was already in love with her, and he knew what happened when you loved someone. They rejected you. Eventually, always, they rejected you.

In his mind's eye he could see his mother's haggard face, the weary resignation in her face giving truth to her words.

'I wish I'd never had you.'

His own mother had wished him out of existence. His father hadn't wanted to know him at all. How on earth could he expect Mia to love him the way he knew he loved her...especially when she'd said she'd never wanted to love anyone at all? That had suited him admirably...once.

Now the only choice he felt he had was to keep himself safe. Separate. But the result was this restless ache, this impossible anxiety.

Needed to think?

He didn't like the sound of that at *all*.

Snatching up his phone and his coat, Alessandro decided he'd confront Mia directly, ask her just what she needed to think about. Even if he didn't like the answer, it was surely better to know.

It took an hour to drive back to the villa, and with each minute Alessandro felt his insides coil tighter and tighter, till everything in him was ready to snap and break. What did Mia need to think about? What was going on?

He'd tell her he loved her, he decided recklessly. He'd admit the truth he'd been trying to hide from himself, even if the thought made his stomach cramp even more. Did he dare be that vulnerable? Open himself up to that much pain?

But what was the alternative? To live in this welter of frustration and fear, walking a tightrope between staying safe and being real? Gaining nothing or risking everything?

He'd always been willing to take a risk in business, and here was the biggest risk of all. He would be man enough to take it.

Filled with determination, powered by adrenalin, he drove up the sweeping lane to the villa, only to find it darkened and empty.

Perhaps she'd gone to bed already, he thought as he hurried upstairs.

'Mia…?' he called softly as he opened the door to their bedroom. It was empty, the bed still made up and untouched. Frowning, Alessandro walked down the hall to Ella's nursery, his blood freezing to ice in his veins at the sight of the empty cot, the open drawers, the missing clothes. Back to the master bedroom, and he saw that a suitcase was gone, along with some of Mia's clothes.

She'd left him, he realised hollowly. She'd actually left him. And she'd taken his daughter with him.

He sank onto the bed, caught between grief and rage. So this was why Mia had needed to *think*? To think about whether she was leaving him—for a night, or perhaps, heaven help him, even for good? He couldn't see any other possibility. Memories of his childhood, of empty apartments, lonely nights and constant uncertainty, tormented him, and made him unable to think clearly, or even at all. All he knew was he was alone, and he hated it.

Alessandro dropped his head into his hands, overcome with emotion. Thank heaven he hadn't told her he loved her.

CHAPTER FIFTEEN

A NIGHT AWAY hadn't given Mia much rest. The hotel had been small and noisy, and Ella had had an unsettled night. Mia had, as well, missed the strong, solid presence of her husband in her bed. She'd gone away hoping to order her own thoughts, gain a bit of her independence back, but the time apart had only made her realise how much she missed Alessandro—and, yes, loved him.

The truth was stark and real, and she couldn't hide it from herself any longer. As she climbed in the taxi to head home the next morning, she let that realisation rest and then grow inside her, filling up all the empty space.

She loved him.

She hadn't meant to, hadn't wanted to, but she'd fallen in love with a man who most likely didn't feel the same way about her.

The realisation thudded dully inside her. This was the exact scenario she'd once feared, the one thing she'd never wanted to come to pass, and yet here she was, knowing it was true and having to deal with it.

How?

By telling Alessandro she loved him? The thought filled Mia with frightened panic, and yet she also knew, intrinsically and instinctively, that it was the right thing to do. What kind of love was it if she couldn't even admit to it?

And if he was horrified, if he told her flat out he didn't love her back…well, then at least she'd know.

As the taxi came up the villa's drive, hope warred with icy terror. Could she really do this? What if, improbably, impossibly, Alessandro told her he loved her back? Dared she even dream…?

Mia held on to that hope as she climbed out of the taxi, Ella in her arms. She'd just paid the driver and started towards the steps when the front door was thrown open.

'Where the *hell* have you been?'

Mia froze at the sound of Alessandro's condemning voice, the cold rage she heard in it, as he strode towards her, everything about his taut form and angry voice catapulting her back to her childhood.

'I told you…' she began, faltering at the sight of the thunderous look on her husband's face.

'You told me you needed to *think*! And then I came home to an empty house, no explanation, my daughter *gone…*'

'I went away for a night, that's all…'

'Without telling me so. Without telling me where.' Alessandro shook his head, his eyes dark, his lips compressed. 'How could you, Mia? How could you do such a thing?' He shook his head again before she could form a reply. 'I don't care. No reason is good enough.'

'Then I won't bother giving you one,' Mia snapped, goaded into her own rage by his high-handed manner. To think she'd been about to tell him she loved him! 'It seems you can come and go as you please, but I can't.'

'That's completely different. I was working.'

'While I was playing with the fairies? Never mind.' Anger and hurt choked her voice. 'I don't care. I'm going inside.' She pushed past him, only to have him reach for her arm.

'Mia—'

'Leave me alone.' She shrugged off his hand, her eyes blinded by tears, and hurried inside. It was, she realised as she headed upstairs, the first argument they'd had since they'd been married, and it felt as if it might be the last one as well. How had everything gone so disastrously wrong so quickly? Except it hadn't been quick at all. It had been happening all month. This was just the result.

Ella was fussing, so Mia fed and changed her before putting her down for a nap. Then she had a shower, hoping it might make her feel better, but everything only made her feel worse. She thought of going in search of Alessandro, but couldn't bear the thought of another argument, or, worse, a freezing silence.

How had it got this bad between them? Was there any way to make it better?

'Mia.' Alessandro stood in the doorway of the bedroom as she came out of the bathroom, finger-combing her damp hair. She stilled as she saw him, everything in her poised for flight.

'What is it?' she asked warily.

He shook his head slowly. 'I've been thinking.'

That didn't sound good. 'Thinking? About what?'

'About us.'

Her hands stilled and she turned to face him fully, lowering her hands from her hair. 'Alessandro…?'

'I never gave you a choice, Mia.'

What…?

'You did,' she protested, scanning his face for clues to what he was feeling.

'Not really. I as good as sent you to California, and then I took you from there, without you being able to do much about it. I practically forced you to marry me…'

Mia gazed at him, trying to figure out where he was going with this. 'But you asked me to choose, Alessandro. I was the one who proposed, after all—'

'Do you really think that was any choice at all? If you'd said no, I would have seduced you. I would have had my way. I was always determined about that. There was absolutely no way you weren't going to marry me, Mia.' He met her gaze bleakly, and Mia shook her head.

'Why are you telling me this now?'

'Because I realise I can't do this any more. I can't give you what you need, what you deserve.'

'Which is what?' Mia whispered.

'Love.' He spoke the word flatly. 'It's too hard for me, Mia. With my childhood…my parents… I can't do it.'

'Did I ever say I wanted you to love me?' Mia asked in a shaking voice, even though it hurt to say the words, because in her heart and mind she'd been asking him, begging him every day. Had he been able to see that? Had it horrified him?

'A marriage needs love as its foundation,' Alessandro stated. 'Without it, it will always crumble at one point or another. It won't be strong enough to endure. I've realised that now…and I realise that what we have isn't enough.'

'So what are you really saying?' Mia asked, her voice hardening. 'You want a divorce?'

'We could probably arrange an annulment, or otherwise, yes, a quiet divorce.'

'And what about Ella?' Mia demanded, her voice catching on her daughter's name. 'What about her needing a father? You insisted on that—'

'We'll arrange visits. I can still be part of her life. I want to be. That won't change.'

'Visits.' Mia felt faint suddenly, her vision blurring, as the awful import of everything Alessandro was saying slammed into her. Slowly she walked to the bed and sank onto its edge, blinking the world back into focus. 'Why are you telling me this now? Is it because of our argument?

What made you realise all this so suddenly?' Her voice rose and then broke. 'Was none of this real?'

'How could it have been?' Alessandro returned rawly. 'Considering?'

Tears stung her eyes then and she did her best to blink them back. She felt as if her heart was being wrung like a rag inside her, squeezing out its last painful drops of love. 'So all this time, you've just been pretending? Orchestrating a takeover? You are known to be subtle,' she added bitterly. 'Even when it's hostile.'

'Don't think of it like that, Mia...'

'How am I supposed to think of it?' she demanded. 'Either our marriage was real or it wasn't. Either the vows you made were sacred and binding or they weren't.'

'I'm trying to be fair and give you your freedom—'

'Some freedom. What am I supposed to do now?'

He spread his hands. 'Whatever you want. I'll make sure you have a generous settlement. You'll want for nothing—'

'I'll want for everything.' Mia's voice broke. 'Why are you doing this, Alessandro?'

'Because I told you, I realised that a marriage needs more than what we have to grow—'

'And you're so sure you can never, ever love me? Learn to love me, if it's so important?' Her voice broke as the full force of rejection hit her. He stayed silent, and she looked up, and for the first time she saw the torment on his face. 'Or are you worried that I can't love you?' she whispered, barely daring to say the words. 'Is that what this is about, Alessandro? Are you afraid?'

'I'm not afraid.'

'Then say the words,' she demanded. 'Say, "Mia, I don't love you and I never will."' He stayed silent and she rose, her hands balled into fists by her sides, risking everything on this. '*Say* them.'

'Mia...' He stopped and shook his head. 'I don't want to hurt you.'

'Well, you're failing miserably at that, because you already have. Immeasurably. And what I think, Alessandro, is that *you* don't want to be hurt. So tell me now that you don't love me. Make it real.'

He sighed heavily, his gaze averted. 'I'm not sure I know how to love.'

'So...'

A hesitation, endless, awful, as he searched her face, steeling himself. 'No,' Alessandro said finally. 'I don't love you. I... I never will.'

Mia had been bracing herself for it, expecting it, but those two simple, stark words still held the power to fell her. She swayed where she sat and two tears slipped quickly and coldly down her cheeks before she could stop them. She dashed her eyes with the back of her arm and then stood up on wobbly legs.

'Fine. I'll pack in the morning.'

'It's better this way...'

No, it wasn't. It wasn't at all. But at least she knew now. With a leaden heart, Mia walked out of the bedroom—and away from her husband.

He was a coward. Alessandro lay in bed, gritty-eyed as he stared at the ceiling. Mia was sleeping in a guest bedroom, and he missed her presence with a ferocity that undid him...but even more overwhelming and shaming was the truth pounding through him that he hadn't been brave enough to admit.

I don't love you.

Except he did. Of course he did. And in the moment she'd asked he'd known what a pathetic coward he was, because he'd been afraid to admit it. The most crucial moment of his life, and he'd blown it out of fear. He'd lied, because it had seemed easier. It had felt safer. Because letting her walk away now was surely better than letting her hurt him later…or, heaven forbid, hurting her.

Except he'd just hurt her unbearably.

I don't love you. The cruellest words he could have said, as terrible as the words his mother had said to him, which had tormented him for decades. How could he have done it? How could he have let himself?

It would have been worse later, he told himself for the tenth time. *Surely it would have been worse later.*

Except right now it felt like hell.

He shifted in the bed, knowing sleep would never come. Would she really leave in the morning, with Ella? Had he just fractured his family, and for what purpose? He'd convinced himself he'd been noble, saving her from a loveless marriage. How deluded was he, thinking that was the right choice? Mia had seen through him, of course. She'd known what this was really about.

It wasn't about him not loving her…it was about him loving her too much. It was about how loving someone meant losing yourself, just as they'd both feared, in their own ways. And gaining so much more…if Mia loved him back.

Why was he so scared to risk it? Risk himself? Could this really, possibly, be better?

It had to be.

The next morning, after a sleepless night, Alessandro came downstairs to find Mia already packed, Ella in her arms.

'You're going already…' Even though he'd been expecting it, he could scarcely believe the sight in front of him.

'It seems better.' Mia's voice was flat, her shoulders slumped. She looked as if all the life had drained out of her, as if the very will to live had been sucked from her soul.

He'd done this, Alessandro realised. This was his fault.

This was all going so horribly wrong, simply because he hadn't had the courage to take the biggest risk you could in this life...loving someone else. Giving them your heart. Accepting theirs in return.

And he knew he couldn't let it end this way. He wouldn't. He wouldn't live life as a coward, unwilling to take the biggest risk of all, to let go of control and hand someone his heart. 'Mia, wait.'

She looked at him with lifeless eyes, Ella clutched in her arms. 'Do you love me?' he asked, the words raw, his voice quavering.

She stared at him blankly, her face so weary and sad, tears nearly stung his eyes. 'Why are you asking that now, Alessandro?'

'Because...because it's important. Because I should have asked last night, when you asked me.'

'Why do you care, when you've already told me how you feel?' Mia responded quietly. 'Do you just want to pour salt into my wound? Isn't it enough that you don't love me?'

He hesitated, poised to fly, afraid to fall. Even now, with everything at stake, he held back. And in his silence was his condemnation.

'I've called a taxi,' Mia said. 'It should be here now.'

Alessandro glanced at her one small travel bag. 'Where are your bags?'

'I'm leaving everything here. I... I don't want it. I certainly don't need all those fancy gowns and things.' From outside they heard the crunch of tyres on gravel. Mia hoisted her bag in one hand, Ella in her car seat in the other.

This was it. The end. She was really leaving, because he was going to let her.

Do you love me?

She hadn't answered the question, and Alessandro couldn't blame her, considering what his own response had been last night.

He'd said he wasn't capable of love, or even that he knew what it was, and yet…what if he did?

What if in this moment he really did?

What if real love wasn't a safe landing, but a dangerous fall? What if it was risking everything, not knowing the result? Letting yourself get hurt, because that was part of the whole, terrifying, incredible deal?

Mia was at the door, one hand reaching for the handle, the seconds sliding past far too fast.

'Mia!' His voice came out in a shout of command that made her stiffen. 'Mia,' he said more softly. 'Please wait.'

'Why? What is there left to say?'

He swallowed hard, his throat impossibly tight. Now. He needed to say it now. She reached for the handle again.

'I love you.'

The words fell into the stillness, and even now part of him wanted to snatch them back. The last time he'd said them had been to his mother, and she'd wearily told him she wished she'd never had him. He'd vowed never to say them again. Never to want or need to say them again.

But Mia had changed him. Loving Mia had changed him.

'Alessandro…' She shook her head slowly. 'Why are you saying this now? You can't mean it…'

'I do. I was too much of a coward to say it before. But the truth is I've been falling in love with you for months now, and fighting it all the way.' His words came faster and more assuredly, and the release of finally being open and honest was strangely wonderful. Freeing in a way he'd never expected. 'I never wanted to love anyone, Mia. My mother didn't love me, and I wanted her to, desperately. She told me she wished she'd never had me…she forgot about and neglected me time and again, and still I wished she'd love me. I loved her.' He swallowed hard, the words coming faster and faster as he tried to explain. 'At a young age I told myself I'd never let someone have that kind of control over me. I'd be the one who was in control, always, and I made that my life's mission. Yet here I am, risking everything because it's too important not to. Because I love you too much, and I don't want to be a coward any more. I love you, Mia. I love you.'

He spread his hands wide, his heart thudding as he waited for her response.

'You...love me?' She sounded incredulous as she turned from the door and put down her bag and Ella's car seat.

'With all my soul. All my heart. I'm terrified, Mia. I'm shaking.' He let out a ragged laugh. 'And yet here I am, giving everything I have to you. You can do with it as you will. You can walk out that door as you were intending to, or you can come over here and slap my face and tell me what an arrogant imbecile I am.' He took a quick, steadying breath. 'Or you can tell me you love me back, or even that you could learn to love me, like you asked me to last night, and you'll give us a chance even though I've been so very stupid and scared. I wasn't giving you your freedom... I was trying to find mine. I'm sorry. I don't want you to go. I love you.'

He was babbling, but he didn't care. He'd say anything to make her stay...even, *especially*, the truth.

'I've been afraid too,' Mia said after a long moment. 'I've been fighting it too, because I was scared of losing myself, like I said. So scared, and yet it happened anyway.'

'Yes.' Alessandro's voice was fervent. 'But I realised last night that loving someone means losing yourself—to another person. Entrusting them with everything that you are. And that's terrifying, but it's also so good and right. I know I'll mess up, Mia, so many times. I'll be angry or thoughtless or bossy or...something. But I'll try. And I hope you'll forgive me. And learn to love—'

'Oh, Alessandro, you idiot,' Mia said with tears in her

voice. 'I already love you. I've loved you for ages. I just thought you'd never love me. You'd never do what you just said, and offer me everything. Ever since our wedding I've felt you've been holding something back…'

'I know. I have been. But it's yours now. All of it—me—is yours. I'll tell you whatever you like. I'll give you the parts of myself I've been trying to hide, the ones that are dark and ugly and needy. And hopefully you won't be put off—'

'Never,' Mia whispered. Tears trickled down her face, and with a jolt Alessandro realised he was crying too.

'So you'll stay?'

'Yes.' Mia walked towards him, her arms held out, so all it took were two steps for Alessandro to catch her up in his, pulling her body closely to his. Home. He was home. 'I'll stay,' Mia whispered as he lowered his head to kiss her. 'I'll stay. For ever.'

EPILOGUE

Three years later

SUN BEAMED DOWN on the terrace as Mia stepped out, baby Milo in her arms. It was her son's christening, three months after his birth. Just like Ella, he had Alessandro's grey eyes and her blonde hair. He gurgled up at her now before catching sight of his father and reaching out chubby arms to him.

'Hello, *caro*,' Alessandro said, scooping up his son easily and planting a kiss on his plump cheek. 'It's your special day.'

'She's been good as gold,' Alyssa said as she joined them on the terrace, holding Ella, now three and a half, by the hand. 'A very proud big sister.'

Mia smiled at Ella, and then shared a loving look with Alessandro. The last three years had been so wonderful, so blessed. Admittedly, it hadn't always been easy. They'd had their battles and struggles, both of them learning day by day to let go of control, of their very selves, as they committed themselves to each other in small yet significant ways.

Now Alessandro brushed a kiss across her lips as he cradled their son. 'Happy?' he asked softly, his eyes full of warmth and tenderness that, even after three years, made Mia melt inside.

She reached for his free hand, lacing her fingers through his. 'Yes,' she told him, thankful for so much, and especially this man by her side who had chosen to share his life, his very self, with her. 'Very, very happy.'

* * * * *

UNWRAPPING HER ITALIAN DOC

CAROL MARINELLI

CHAPTER ONE

'ANTON, WOULD YOU do me a favour?'

Anton Rossi's long, brisk stride was broken by the sound of Louise's voice.

He had tried very hard not to notice her as he had stepped into the maternity unit of The Royal in London, though, of course, he had.

Louise was up a stepladder and putting up Christmas decorations. Her skinny frame was more apparent this morning as she was dressed in very loose, navy scrubs with a long-sleeved, pale pink top worn underneath. Her blonde hair was tied in a high ponytail and she had layer after layer of tinsel around her neck.

She was also, Anton noted, by far too pale.

Yes, whether he had wanted to or not, he had noticed her.

He tended to notice Louise Carter a lot.

'What is it that you want?' Anton asked, as he reluctantly turned around.

'In that box, over there…' Louise raised a slender arm and pointed it towards the nurses' station '…there's some gold tinsel.'

He just stood there and Louise wondered if possibly he didn't understand what she was asking for.

'Tin-sel...' she said slowly, in the strange attempt at an Italian accent that Louise did now and then when she was trying to explain a word to him. Anton watched in concealed amusement as she jiggled the pieces around her neck. 'Tin-sel, go-o-old.'

'And?'

Louise gave up on her accent. 'Could you just get it for me? I've run out of gold.'

'I'm here to check on Hannah Evans.'

'It will only take you a second,' Louise pointed out. 'Look, if I get down now I'll have to start again.' Her hand was holding one piece of gaudy green tinsel to the tired maternity wall. 'I'm trying to make a pattern.'

'You are *trying*, full stop,' Anton said, and walked off.

'Bah, humbug,' Louise called to his departing shoulders.

Anton, had moved to London from Milan and, having never spent a Christmas in England, would have to find out later what that translated as but he certainly got the gist.

Yes, he wasn't exactly in the festive spirit. For the last few years Anton had, in fact, dreaded Christmas.

Unfortunately there was no escaping it at The Royal—December had today hit and there were invites galore for Christmas lunches, dinners and parties piling into his inbox that he really ought to attend. Walking into work this morning, he had seen a huge Christmas tree being erected in the hospital foyer and now Louise had got in on the act. She seemed to be attempting to singlehandedly turn the maternity ward into Santa's grotto.

Reluctantly, *very* reluctantly, he headed over to the box, retrieved a long piece of gold tinsel and returned to Louise, who gave him a sweet smile as she took it.

Actually, no, Anton decided, it was far from a sweet smile—it was a slightly sarcastic, rather triumphant smile.

'Thank you very much,' Louise said.

'You're more than welcome,' Anton responded, and walked off.

Anton knew, just knew that if he turned around it would be to the sight of Louise poking her tongue out at him.

Keep going, he told himself.

Do not turn around, for it would just serve to encourage her and he was doing everything in his power to discourage Louise. She was the most skilled flirt he had ever come across. At first he has assumed Louise was like that with everyone—it had come as a disconcerting, if somewhat pleasant surprise to realise that the blatant flirting seemed to be saved solely for him.

Little known to Louise, he enjoyed their encounters, not that he would ever let on.

Ignore her, Anton told himself.

Yet he could not.

Anton turned to the sight of Louise on the stepladder, tongue out, fingers up and well and truly caught!

Louise actually froze for a second, which was very unfortunate, given the gesture she was making, but then she unfroze as Anton turned and walked back towards her. A shriek of nervous laughter started to pour from Louise because, from the way that Anton was walking, it felt as if he might be about to haul her from the ladder and over his shoulder. Wouldn't that be nice? both simultaneously thought, but instead he came right up to her, his face level with her groin, and looked up into china-blue eyes as she looked down at the sexiest, most aloof, impossibly arrogant man to have ever graced The Royal.

'I got you your tinsel.' Anton pointed at her and his voice was stern but, Louise noted, that sulky mouth of his was doing its level best not to smile.

'Yes, Anton, you did,' Louise said, wondering if he could feel the blast of heat coming from her loins. God knew, he was miserable and moody but her body responded to him as if someone had just thrown another log on the fire whenever he was around.

On many levels he annoyed her—Anton checked and re-checked everything that she did, as if she was someone who had just wandered in from the street and offered to help out for the day, rather than a qualified midwife. Yet, aside from their professional differences, he was as sexy as hell and the sparks just flew off the two of them, no matter how Anton might deny that they did.

'So why this?' Anton asked, and pulled a face and poked his tongue out at her, and Louise smiled at the sight of his tongue and screwed-up features as he mimicked her gestures. He was still gorgeous—olive-skinned, his black hair was glossy and straight and so well cut that Louise constantly had to resist running her hands through it just to see it messed up. His eyes were a very dark blue and she ached to see them smile, yet, possibly for the first time, while aimed at her, now they were.

Oh, his expression was cross but, Louise could just see, those eyes were finally smiling and so she took the opportunity to let him know a few home truths.

'It's the way that you do things, Anton.' Louise attempted to explain. 'Why couldn't you just say, "Sure, Louise," and go and get the tinsel?'

'Because, as I've told you, I am on my way to see a patient.'

'Okay, why didn't you smile when you walked into the unit and saw the decorations that I've spent the last two hours putting up and say, "Ooh, that looks nice"?'

'Truth?' Anton said.

'Truth.' Louise nodded.

'I happen to think that you have too many decorations...' He watched her eyes narrow at his criticism. 'You asked why I didn't tell you how nice they looked.'

'I did,' Louise responded. 'Okay, then, third question, why didn't you say hello to me when you walked past?'

For Anton, that was the trickiest to answer. 'Because I didn't see you.'

'Please!' Louise rolled her eyes. 'You saw me—you just chose to ignore me, as I'm going to choose to ignore your slight about my decorations. You can never have too much tinsel.'

'Oh, believe me Louise, you can,' Anton said, looking around. The corridor was a riot of red, gold and green tinsel stars. He looked up to where silver foil balloons hung from the ceilings. Then he looked down to plastic snowmen dancing along the bottom of the walls. Half of the windows to the patients' rooms had been sprayed with fake snow. Louise had clearly been busy. 'Nothing matches.' Anton couldn't help but smile and he *really* tried to help but smile! 'You don't have a theme.'

'The theme is Christmas, Anton,' Louise said in response. 'I had a very tinsel-starved Christmas last year and I intend to make up for it this one. I'm doing the nativity scene this afternoon.'

'Good for you,' Anton said, and walked off.

Louise didn't poke out her tongue again and even if

she had Anton wouldn't have seen it because this time he very deliberately didn't turn around.

He didn't want to engage in conversation with Louise. He didn't want to find out why she'd had a tinsel-starved Christmas the previous year.

Or rather he *did* want to find out.

Louise was flaky, funny, sexy and everything Anton did not need to distract him at work. He wasn't here to make friends—his social life was conducted well away from the hospital walls. Anton did his level best to keep his distance from everyone at work except his patients.

'Hannah.' He smiled as he stepped into the four-bedded ward but Hannah didn't smile back and Anton pulled the curtains around her bed before asking his patient any questions. 'Are you okay?' Anton checked.

'I'm so worried.'

'Tell me,' Anton offered.

'I'm probably being stupid, I know, but Brenda came in this morning and I said the baby had moved and I'm sure that it did, but it hasn't since then.'

'So you're lying here, imagining the worst?'

'Yes,' Hannah admitted. 'It's taken so long to get here that I'm scared something's going to go wrong now.'

'I know how hard your journey has been,' Anton said. Hannah had conceived by IVF and near the end of a tricky pregnancy she had been brought in for bed rest as her blood pressure was high and the baby's amniotic fluid was a little on the low side. Anton specialised in high-risk pregnancies and so he was very comfortable listening to Hannah's concerns.

'Let me have a feel,' Anton said. 'It is probably asleep.'

For all he was miserable with the staff and kept himself to himself, Anton was completely lovely and open with his patients. He had a feel of Hannah's stomach and then took out a Doppler machine and had a listen, locating the heartbeat straight away. 'Beautiful,' Anton said, and they listened for a moment. 'Have you had breakfast?' Anton asked, because if Hannah had low blood sugar, that could slow movements down.

'I have.'

'How many movements are you getting?'

'I felt one now,' Hanna said.

'That's because I just nudged your baby awake when I was feeling your stomach.'

He sat going through her charts. Hannah's blood pressure was at the higher limits of normal and Anton wondered for a long moment how best to proceed. While the uterus was usually the best incubator, there were times when the baby was safest out. He had more than a vested interested in this pregnancy and he told Hannah that. 'Do you know you will be the first patient that I have ever helped both to conceive through IVF *and* deliver their baby?'

'No.' Hannah frowned. 'I thought in your line of work that that would happen to you all the time.'

'No.' Anton shook his head. 'Remember how upset you were when I first saw you because the doctor you had been expecting was sick on the day of your egg retrieval?'

Hannah nodded and actually blushed. 'I was very rude to you.'

'Because you didn't want a locum to be taking over your care.' Anton smiled. 'And that is fair enough. In Italy I used to do obstetrics but then I moved into reproductive endocrinology and specialised there. In my opinion you can't do both simultaneously, they are completely different specialties—you have to always be available for either. I only helped out that week because Richard was sick. I still cover very occasionally to help out and also because I like to keep up to date but in truth I cannot do both.'

'So how come you moved back to obstetrics?'

'I missed it,' Anton admitted. 'I do like the fertility side of things and I do see patients where that is their issue but if they need IVF then I refer them. Obstetrics is where I prefer to be.'

The movements were slowing down. Anton could see that and with her low level of amniotic fluid, Hannah would be more aware than most of any movement. 'I think your baby might be just about cooked,' Anton said, and then headed out of the ward and asked Brenda to come in. 'I'm just going to examine Hannah,' Anton said, and spoke to both women as he did so. 'Your cervix is thinning and you're already three centimetres dilated.' He looked at Brenda. 'Kicks are down from yesterday.'

Anton had considered delivering Hannah last night and now, with the news that the kicks were down combined with Hannah's distress, he decided to go ahead this morning.

'I think we'll get things started,' Anton said.

'Now?'

'Yes.' Anton nodded and he explained to Hannah his reasoning. 'We've discussed how your placenta is coming to the end of its use-by date. Sometimes the baby does better on the outside than in and I think we've just reached that time.' He let it sink in for a moment. 'I'll start a drip, though we'll just give you a low dose to help move things along.'

Hannah called her husband and Anton spoke with

Brenda at the nurses' station, then Hannah was taken around to the delivery ward.

All births were special and precious but Anton had been concerned about Hannah for a couple of weeks as the baby was a little on the small side. Anton would actually be very relieved once this baby was out.

By the time he had set up the drip and Hannah was attached to the baby monitor, with Luke, her husband, by her side, Anton was ready for a coffee break. He checked on another lady who would soon deliver and then he checked on his other patients on the ward.

Stephanie, another obstetrician, had been on last night and had handed over to him but, though Anton respected Stephanie, he had learnt never to rely on handovers. Anton liked to see for himself where his patients were and though he knew it infuriated some of the staff it was the way he now worked and he wasn't about to change that.

Satisfied that all was well, he was just about to take himself to the staffroom when he saw Louise, still up that ladder, but she offered no snarky comment this time, neither were there any requests for assistance. Instead, she was pressing her fingers into her eyes and clearly felt dizzy.

Not my problem, Anton decided.

But, of course, it was.

CHAPTER TWO

'LOUISE...' HE WALKED over and saw her already pale features were now white, right down to her lips. 'Louise, you need to get down from the ladder.'

The sound of his voice created a small chasm between the stars dancing in her eyes and Louise opened her eyes to the sight of Anton walking towards her. And she would get down if only she could remember how her legs worked.

'Come on,' Anton said. This time he *did* take her down from the ladder, though not over his shoulder, as they had both briefly considered before. Instead, he held his hand out and she took it and shakily stepped down. Anton put a hand around her waist and led her to the staffroom, where he sat her down and then went to the fridge and got out some orange juice.

'Here,' he said, handing the glass to her.

Louise took a grateful gulp and then another and blew out a breath. 'I'm so sorry about that. I just got a bit dizzy.'

'Did you have breakfast this morning?'

'I did.' Louise nodded but he gave her a look that said he didn't believe a word. Anton then huffed off, leaving her sitting in the staffroom while he went to the kitchen. Louise could hear him feeding bread into the toaster.

God, Louise thought, rolling her eyes, here comes the lecture.

Anton returned a moment later with two slices of toast smothered in butter and honey.

'I just told you that I'd already had breakfast,' Louise said.

'I think you should eat this.'

'If I eat that I'll be sick. I just need to lie down for a few minutes.'

'Do you have a photo shoot coming up?' Anton asked, and Louise sighed. 'Answer me,' Anton said.

'Yes, I have a big photo shoot taking place on Christmas Eve but that has no part in my nearly fainting.'

Louise was a part-time lingerie model. She completely loved her side job and took it seriously. Everyone thought that it was hilarious, everyone, that was, except Anton. Mind, he didn't find anything very funny these days.

'You're too thin.' Anton was blunt and though Louise knew it was out of concern, there was no reason for him to be. She knew only too well the reason for the little episode on the ladder.

'Actually, I'm not too thin, I'm in the healthy weight range,' Louise said. 'Look, I just got dizzy. Please don't peg me as having an eating disorder just because I model part time.'

'My sister is a model in Milan,' Anton said, and Louise could possibly have guessed that, had Anton had a sister, then a model she might be because Anton really was seriously beautiful.

Louise lay down on the sofa because she could still see stars and she didn't want Anton to know that. In fact, she just wanted him gone. And she knew how to get rid of him! A little flirt would have him running off.

'Are my hips not childbearing enough for you, Anton?' Louise teased, and Anton glanced down and it wasn't a baby he was thinking about between those legs!

No way!

Louise had used to work in Theatre—in fact, she had been the nurse who had scrubbed in on his first emergency Caesarean here at The Royal. It had been the first emergency Caesarean section he had performed since losing Alberto. Of course, Louise hadn't known just how nervous Anton had been that day and she could not possibly have guessed how her presence had both helped and unsettled him.

During surgery Anton had been grateful for a very efficient scrub nurse and one who had immediately worked well with him.

After surgery, when he'd gone to check in on the infant, Louise had been there, smiling and cooing at the baby. She had turned around and congratulated him on getting the baby out in time, and he had actually forgotten to thank her for her help in Theatre.

Possibly he had snapped an order instead—anything rather than like her.

Except he did.

A few months ago Louise had decided to more fully utilise her midwifery training and had come to work on Maternity, which was, of course, Anton's stomping ground.

Seeing her most days, resisting her on each and every one of them, was quietly driving him insane.

She was very direct, a bit off the wall and terribly

beautiful too, and if she hadn't worked here Anton would not hesitate.

Mind you, if she hadn't worked here he wouldn't know just how clever and funny she was.

Anton looked down where she lay, eyes closed on the sofa, and saw there was a touch of colour coming back to her cheeks and her breathing was nice and regular now. Then Anton pulled his eyes up from the rise and fall of her chest and instead of leaving the room he met her very blue eyes.

Louise could see the concern was still there. 'Honestly, Anton, I didn't get dizzy because I have an eating disorder,' Louise said, and, because this was the maternity ward and such things were easily discussed, especially if your name was Louise, she told him what the real problem was. 'I've got the worst period in the history of the world, if you must know.'

'Okay.' He looked at her very pale face and her hand that moved low onto her stomach and decided she was telling the truth.

'Do you need some painkillers?'

'I've had some,' Louise said, closing her eyes. 'They didn't do a thing.'

'Do you need to go home?' Anton asked.

'Are you going to write me a note, Doctor?'

He watched her lips turn up in a smile as she teased but then shook her head. 'No, I'll be fine soon, though I might just stay lying down here for a few minutes.'

'Do you want me to let Brenda know?'

'Please.' Louise nodded.

'You're sure I can't get you anything?' Anton checked.

'A heat pack would be lovely,' Louise said, glad that her eyes were closed because she could imagine his expression at being asked to fetch a heat pack, when surely that was a nurse's job. 'It needs two minutes in the microwave,' she called, as he walked out.

It took five minutes for Anton to locate the heat packs and so he returned seven minutes later to where she lay, knees up with her eyes closed, and he placed the heat pack gently over her uterus.

'You make a lovely midwife,' Louise said, feeling the weight and the warmth.

'I've told Brenda,' Anton said, 'and she said that you are to take your time and come back when you're ready.' He went to go but she still concerned him and Anton walked over and sat down by her waist on the sofa where she lay.

Louise felt him sit down beside her and then he picked up her hand. She knew that he was checking her nails for signs of anaemia and she was about to make a little tease about her not knowing he cared, except Anton this close made talking impossible. She opened her eyes and he pulled down her lower lids and she wished, oh, how she wished, those fingers were on her face for very different reasons.

'You're anaemic,' Anton said.

'I'm on iron and folic acid...'

'You're seeing someone?'

'Yes, but I...' Louise had started to let a few close friends know what was going on in her personal life but she wasn't quite ready to tell the world just yet. She ached to discuss it with Anton, not on a personal level but a professional one, yet was a little shy to. 'I've spoken to my GP.' His pager went off and though he read it he still sat there, but the moment had gone and Louise decided not to tell him her plans and what was going on.

'He's told you that you don't have to struggle like this.

There is the Pill and there is also an IUD that can give
you a break from menstr—'

'Anton,' Louise interrupted. 'My GP is a she, and I
am a midwife, which means, oh, about ten times a day
I give contraceptive advice, so I do know these things.'

'Then you should know that you don't have to put up
with this.'

'I do. Thanks for your help,' Louise said, and then,
aware of her snappy tone, she halted. After all, he was
just trying to help. He simply didn't know what was going
on in her world. 'I owe you one.' She gave him a smile.
'I'll buy you a drink tonight.'

'Tonight?' Anton frowned.

'It's the theatre Christmas do,' Louise said, and Anton
inwardly groaned, because another non-work version of
Louise seared into his brain he truly did not need! Anton
had seen Louise dressed to the nines a few times since
he had started here and it was a very appealing sight. He
had braced himself for the maternity do in a couple of
weeks—in fact, he had a date lined up for that night—
but it had never entered his head that Louise would be
at the theatre do tonight.

'So you will be going tonight?' Anton checked. 'Even
though you're not feeling well?'

'Of course I'm going,' Louise said. 'I worked there
for five years.' She opened her eyes and gave him a very
nice smile, though their interlude was over. Concerned
Anton had gone and he was back to bah, humbug as he
stood. 'I'll see you tonight, Anton.'

Stop the drip! Anton wanted to say as he went in to
check on Hannah, for he would dearly love a reason to
be stuck at the hospital tonight.

Of course, he didn't stop the drip and instead Hannah
progressed beautifully.

* * *

'Louise, would you be able to go and work in Delivery after lunch?' Brenda came over as Louise added the finishing touches to her nativity scene during her lunch break. She'd taken her chicken and avocado salad out with her and was eating it as she arranged all the pieces. 'Angie called in sick and we're trying to get an agency nurse.'

Louise had to stop herself from rolling her eyes. While she loved being in Delivery for an entire shift, she loathed being sent in for a couple of hours. Louise liked to be there for her patient for the entire shift.

'Sure,' Louise said instead.

'They're a bit short now,' Brenda pushed, and Louise decided not to point out that she'd only had fifteen minutes' break, given the half-hour she'd taken earlier that morning. So, instead, she popped the cutest Baby Jesus ever into the crib, covered him in a little rug and headed off to Delivery.

She took the handover, read through Hannah's birth plan then went in and said hello to Hannah and Luke. Hannah had been a patient on the ward for a couple of weeks now so introductions had long since been done.

Hannah was lying on her side and clearly felt uncomfortable.

'It really hurts.'

'I know that it does,' Louise said, showing Luke a nice spot to rub on the bottom of Hannah's back, but Hannah kept pushing his hand away.

'Do you want to have a little walk?' Louise offered, and at first Hannah shook her head but then agreed. Louise sorted out the drip and got her up off the delivery bed and they shuffled up and down the corridor, sometimes silent between contractions, when Hannah leant against the wall, other times talking.

'I still can't believe we'll have a baby for Christmas,' Hannah said.

'How exciting.' Louise smiled. 'Have you shopped for the baby?''

'Not yet!' Hannah shook her head. 'Didn't want the bad luck.' She leant against the wall and gave a very low moan and then another one.

'Let's get you back,' Louise said, guiding the drip as Luke helped his wife.

Hannah didn't like the idea of sitting on a birthing ball—in fact, she climbed back onto the delivery bed and went back to lying on her side as Louise checked the baby's heart, which was fine.

'You're doing wonderfully, Hannah,' Louise said.

'I can't believe we're going to get our baby,' Hannah said. 'We tried for ages.'

'I know that you did,' Louise said.

'I'm so lucky to have Anton,' Hannah said. 'He got me pregnant!'

Louise looked over at Luke and they shared a smile because at this stage of labour women said the strangest things at times, only Louise's smile turned into a slight frown as Luke explained what she'd meant. 'Anton was the one who put back the embryo…'

'Oh!' Louise said, more than a little surprised, because that was something she hadn't known—yes, of course he would deal with infertility to a point, but it was a very specific specialty and for Anton to have performed the embryo transfer confused Louise.

'He was a reproductive specialist in Milan, one of the top ones,' Luke explained further, when he saw Louise's frown. 'We thought we were getting a fill-in doctor when Richard, the specialist overseeing Hannah's treatment, got sick, but it turned out we were getting one of the best.' He looked up as Anton came in. 'I was just telling Louise that you were the one who got Hannah pregnant.'

Anton gave a small smile of acknowledgement of the conversation then he turned to Louise. 'How is she?'

'Very well.'

Anton gave another brief nod and went to examine Hannah.

Hannah was doing very well because things soon started to get busy and by four o'clock, just when Louise should be heading home to get ready for tonight, she was cheering Hannah on.

'Are you okay, Louise?' Brenda popped her head in to see if Louise wanted one of the late staff to come in and take over but instead Louise smiled and nodded. 'I'm fine, Brenda,' Louise said. 'We're nearly there.'

She would never leave so close to the end of a birth, Anton knew that, and she was enthusiastic at every birth, even if the mother was in Theatre, unconscious.

'How much longer?' Hannah begged.

'Not long,' Louise said. 'Don't push, just hold it now.' Louise was holding Hannah's leg and watched as the head came out and Anton carefully looped a rather thin and straggly umbilical cord from around the baby's neck.

She and Anton actually worked well in this part. Anton liked how Louise got into it and encouraged the woman no end, urging her on when required, helping him to slow things down too, if that was the course of action needed. This was the case here, because the baby was only thirty-five weeks and also rather small for dates.

'Oh, Hannah!' Louise was ecstatic as the shoulders

were delivered and Anton placed the slippery bundle on Hannah's stomach and Louise rubbed the baby's back. They all watched as he took his first breath and finally Hannah and Luke had their wish come true.

'He's beautiful,' Hannah said, examining her son in awe, holding his tiny hand, scarcely able to believe she had a son.

He was small, even for thirty-five weeks, and, having delivered the placenta, Anton could well see why. The baby had certainly been delivered at the right time and could now get the nourishment he needed from his mother to fatten up.

Anton came and looked at the baby. The paediatrician was finishing up checking him over as Louise watched.

'He looks good,' Anton said.

'So good,' Louise agreed, and then smiled at the baby's worried-looking face. He was wearing the concerned expression that a lot of small-for-dates babies had. 'And so hungry!'

The paediatrician went to have a word with the parents to explain their baby's care as Louise wrapped him up in a tight parcel and popped a little hat on him.

'How does it feel,' Louise asked Anton, 'to have been there at conception and delivery?' She started to laugh at her own question. 'That sounds rude! You know what I mean.'

'I was just saying to Hannah this morning that it has never happened to me before. So this little one is a bit more special,' Anton admitted. 'I'm going to go and write my notes. I'll be back to check on Hannah in a while.'

'Well, I'll be going home soon,' Louise said, 'but I'll pass it all on.' She picked up the baby. 'Come on, little man, let's get you back to your mum.'

She didn't rush home then either, though. Louise helped with the baby's first feed, though he quickly tired and would need gavage top-ups. Having put him under a warmer beside his parents, she then went and made Hannah a massive mug of tea. Anton, who was getting a cup of tea of his own, watched as she went into her pocket and took out a teabag.

'Why do you keep teabags in your pocket?'

'Would you want that…' she sneered at the hospital teabags on the bench '…if you'd just pushed a baby out?'

'No.'

'There's your answer, then. I make sure my mums get one nice cup of tea after they've given birth and then they wonder their entire stay in hospital why the rest of them taste so terrible after that,' Louise said. 'It's my service to women.' She went back into her pocket and gave him a teabag and Anton took it because the hospital tea really was that bad. 'Here, but that's *not* the drink I owe you for this morning. You'll get that later.'

He actually smiled at someone who wasn't a patient. 'I'll see you tonight,' Louise said, and their eyes met, just for a second but Anton was the one who looked away, and with good reason.

Yes, Anton thought, she would see him tonight but here endeth the flirting.

CHAPTER THREE

LOUISE LIVED FAIRLY close to the hospital and arrived at her small terraced home just after five to a ringing phone.

She did consider not answering it because she was already running late but, seeing that it was her mum, Louise picked up.

'I can't talk for long,' Louise warned, and then spent half an hour chatting about plans for Christmas Day.

'Mum!' Louise said, for the twentieth time. 'I'm on days off after Christmas Eve all the way till after New Year. I've told you that I'll be there for Christmas Day.'

'You said you'd be there last year,' Susan pointed out.

'Can we not go through that again,' Louise said, regretting the hurt she had caused last year by not telling her parents the truth about what had been going on in her life. 'I was just trying to—'

'Well, don't ever do that again,' Susan said. 'I can't bear that you chose to spend Christmas miserable and alone in some hotel rather than coming home to your family.'

'You know why I did, Mum,' Louise said, and then conceded, 'But I know now that I should have just come home.' She flicked the lights of her Christmas tree to on, smiling as she did so. 'Mum, I honestly can't wait for Christmas.'

'Neither can I. I've ordered the turkey,' Susan said, 'and I'm going to try something extra-special for Boxing Day—kedgeree...'

'Is that the thing with fish and eggs?' Louise checked.

'And curry powder,' Susan agreed.

'That's great, Mum,' Louise said, pulling a face because her mother was the worst cook in the world. The trouble was, though, that Susan considered herself an amazing cook! Louise ached for her dad sometimes, he was the kindest, most patient man, only that had proved part of the problem—the compliments he'd first given had gone straight to Susan's head and, in the kitchen, she thought she could do no wrong. 'Mum, I'd love to chat more but I have to go now and get ready, it's the theatre Christmas night out. I'll call you soon.'

'Well, enjoy.'

'I shall.'

'Oh, one other thing before you go,' Susan said. 'Did you get the referral for the specialist?'

'Not yet,' Louise sighed. 'She says she wants me to have a full six months off the Pill before she refers me...' Louise thought for a moment. She really wasn't happy with her GP. 'I know I said that I didn't want to go to The Royal for this but it might be the best place.'

'I think you're right,' Susan said. 'I didn't like to say so at the time but I don't think she took you very seriously.'

Louise nodded then glanced at the clock. So much for a quick chat!

'I have to get ready, Mum.'

'Well, if you do go to The Royal, let me know when and I'll come with you...'

'I will,' Louise said, and then there were all the *I love you*s and *Do you want a quick word with Dad?*

Louise smiled as she put down the phone because, apart from her cooking, Louise knew that she had the best mum and possibly the best family in the world.

Her dad was the most patient person and Louise's two younger sisters were amazing young women who rang Louise often, and they all got on very well.

This was part of the reason why she hadn't wanted to spoil Christmas for everyone last year and had pretended that something had happened at work. At the time it had seemed kinder to say that they were short-staffed rather than arrive home in such a fragile state on Christmas morning and ruin everyone's day.

Her sisters looked up to her and often asked her opinion on guys; it had been hard, admitting how badly she had judged Wesley. Even a part of the truth had hurt them and her dad would just about die if he knew even half of what had really gone on.

Louise lay on her bed while her bath was running, thinking back to that terrible time. Not just the break-up with Wesley but the horrible lonely time before it.

Louise's wings had been clipped during their relationship. *Seriously* clipped, to the point that she had given up her modelling side job, which she loved. Somehow, she wasn't quite sure how it had happened, her hems had got lower, her hair darker until her sparkle had almost been extinguished.

At a work function Wesley had loathed that she had chatted with Rory, an anaesthetist who was also ex-boyfriend of Louise's from way back.

She and Rory had remained very good friends up to that point.

Louise had given Wesley the benefit of the doubt after that first toxic row. Yes, she'd decided, it wasn't unreasonable for him to be jealous that she was so friendly with her ex. She had severed things with Rory, which had been hard to do and had caused considerable hurt when she had.

It hadn't stopped there, though.

Wesley hadn't liked Emily, Louise's close friend, either. He hadn't liked their odd nights out or their phone calls and texting and gradually that had all tapered off too.

Finally, realising that she had been constantly walking on eggshells and that she'd barely recognised herself any more, Louise had known she had to end things. It had been far easier said than done, though, knowing, with Wesley's building temper, that the ending would be terrible.

It had been.

On Christmas Eve, when Wesley had decided that her family didn't like him and perhaps it should be just the two of them for Christmas, Louise had known she had to get the hell out. An argument had ensued and the gentle, happy Louise had finally lost her temper.

No, he hadn't taken it well.

It would soon be a year to the very day since it had happened, and in the year that had followed Louise had found herself again—the woman she had been before Wesley, the happy person she had once been, though it had taken a while.

Louise's confidence had been severely shaken around men but her dad, her uncles, Rory, Emily's now-husband, Hugh, all the people Wesley had been so jealous of had been such huge support—insisting that Wesley wasn't in the regular mould men were cast from. Finally convincing her that she should simply be her sparkling, annoying, once irrepressible self.

Without her family and friends, Louise did not know how she'd have survived emotionally.

She'd never turn her back on them again.

Anton had appeared at The Royal around March and the jolt of attraction had been so intense Louise had felt her mojo dash back. Possibly because he was so aloof and just so unobtainable that it had felt safe to test her flirting wings on him.

Anton never really responded, yet he never stopped her either. He simply let her be, which was nice.

It was all for fun, a little confidence boost as she slowly returned to her old self, yet in the ensuing months it had gathered steam.

Nope!

Louise got of the bed and looked around her room. It was a sexy boudoir indeed, thanks to a few freebies from a couple of photo shoots. There was a velvet red chair that went with the velvet bedspread, and it made Louise smile every time she sat in it. She smiled even more at the thought of Anton in here but she pushed that thought aside.

In the flirting department he was divine but his arrogance, the way he double-checked everything Louise did at work, rendered him far from relationship material.

Not that she knew if he even liked her.

To Louise, Anton was a very confusing man.

Still, flirting was fun!

Not that she felt particularly sparkly tonight.

After her bath, Louise did her make-up carefully,

topped it off with loads of red lipstick and then started to dry her hair.

It still fell to the right, even after nearly a year of parting it to fall to the left.

Louise examined the shiny red scar on her scalp for a moment. She could still see the needle marks. Thanks to her delay in getting sutured, the stitches had had to stay in for ten days. Unable to deal with the memory, she quickly moved on and tonged her hair into wild ringlets. She put on the Christmas holly underwear that she'd modelled a couple of months ago, along with the stockings from the same range, which were a very sheer red with green sprigs of holly and little red dots for berries.

They were fabulous!

As were the red dress and high-heeled shoes.

Hearing Emily blast the horn outside, Louise pushed out a smile, determined to enjoy all the celebrations that took place at her very favourite time of the year, however unwell she felt.

'God help Anton!' Hugh said, as Louise stepped out of her house and waved to him and Emily.

'Why haven't they got it on?' Emily asked, as Louise dashed back in the house to check that she'd turned off her curling tongs.

'I don't know,' Hugh mused. 'Though I thought that Louise had sworn off men.'

'She's sworn off relationships,' Emily said, 'not joined a nunnery.'

Hugh laughed. No, he could not imagine Louise in a nunnery.

'Is Anton seeing anyone?' Emily asked, but Hugh shook his head.

'I don't think so—mind you, Anton's not exactly friendly and chatty.'

'He is to me.'

'Because you're six months pregnant and his patient,' Hugh pointed out, as Louise came down her path for the second time. 'Maybe you could ask him if he's seeing someone next time you see him.'

'That's a good idea.' Emily smiled. 'I'll just slip that question in while he examines me, shall I?'

She turned and smiled as Louise got into the back of the car.

'Hi, Emily. You make a lovely taxi driver—thank you for this,' Louise said. 'Hi, Hugh, how lucky you are to have a pregnant wife over Christmas!'

'Very lucky,' Hugh agreed, as Emily drove off.

'You look gorgeous, Louise,' Emily said.

'Thank you, but I feel like crap,' Louise happily admitted. 'I've got the worst period and I can only have one eggnog as I'm working in the morning.'

Hugh arched his neck at Louise's openness and Emily smiled.

They both loved her.

As they arrived at the rather nice venue, Louise got her first full-length look at Emily.

'You look gorgeous and I want one...' she said, referring to Emily's six–months-pregnant belly, which was tonight dressed in black and looking amazing.

'You will soon,' Emily said, because Louise had shared with her her plans to get pregnant next year.

'I hope so.'

Louise's eyes scanned the room. It had been very tastefully decorated—there were pale pinkish gold twigs in vases on the tables and pale pinkish gold decorations and lights that twinkled, and there was Anton, talking to Alex, who was Hugh's boss, and Rory was with them as well.

Perfect, Louise thought as the trio made their way over and all the hellos began.

'Aren't the decorations gorgeous?' Emily said, but Louise pulled a face.

'Some colour would be nice. Who would choose pink for Christmas decorations?' As a waiter passed with a tray, she took a mini pale pink chocolate that the waiter called a frosted snowball but even the coconut was pink. 'They have a *theme*,' she said, and smiled at Anton, but it went to the wall because he wasn't looking at her.

'No Jennifer?' Hugh checked with Alex, because normally his wife Jennifer accompanied him on nights such as this.

'No, Josie's got a fever.' Alex explained things a little better for Anton. 'Josie's our youngest child. You haven't yet met my wife Jennifer, have you?'

'Your wife?' Anton said. 'I have heard a lot of nice things.'

Perhaps because Louise was close to PhD level in Anton's facial features, Anton's accent, Anton's words, oh, just everything Anton, she frowned just a little at his slightly vague response. Still, she didn't dwell on it for long because he simply looked fantastic in an evening suit. Her eyes swept his body, taking in his long legs, his very long black leather shoes and then, when her mind darted to rude places, she looked up. His olive complexion was accentuated by the white of his shirt and he was just so austere that it made her want to jump onto his lap and whisper in his ear all the things she wanted him to do to her for Christmas.

Oh, a relationship might not be on the agenda but so pointed was his dismissal of her tonight that they were clearly both thinking sex.

'Is that holly on your stockings?' Rory asked, and everyone looked down to examine Louise's long legs.

Everyone, that was, but Anton.

'Yes, I got them free after that shoot I did a couple of months ago,' Louise said. 'I've been dying to wear them ever since. Got to get into the Christmas spirit. Speaking of which, does anyone want a drink?'

'No, thank you,' Alex said.

'I'll have a tomato juice,' Emily sighed. 'A virgin bloody Mary.'

'Hugh?' Louise asked.

'I'd love an eggnog.'

'Yay!' Louise said. 'Anton?'

'No, thank you.'

'Are you sure?' Louise said. 'I thought I owed you one.'

'I'm fine,' he responded, barely looking at her. 'I think Saffarella is getting me a drink. Here she is…'

Here she was, indeedy!

Rippling black hair, chocolate-brown eyes, a figure to die for, and she was so seriously stunning that she actually made Louise feel drab, especially when her thick Italian accent purred around every name as introductions were made.

'Em-il-ee, Loo-ease.'

On sight the two women bristled.

It was like two cats meeting in the back yard and Louise almost felt her tail bush up as they both smiled and nodded.

'Sorry, I didn't catch your name,' Louise said.

Saffarella was already getting on her nerves.

'Saffarella,' she repeated in her beautiful, treacle voice, and then was kind enough to give Louise a further explanation. 'Like Cinderella.'

With a staph infection attached, Louise thought, but thankfully Rory knew Louise's humour and decided to move her on quickly!

'I'll come and help you with the drinks.' Rory took Louise's arm and they both walked over to the bar.

'Good God!' Louise said the second they were out of earshot.

'No wonder you've got nowhere with him.' Rory laughed. 'She's stunning.'

'Oh!' Louise was seriously rattled, she was far too used to being the best-looking woman in the room. 'What sort of name is Saffarella? Well, there goes my fun for the night. I thought I'd at least get a dance with him. I don't have anyone to fancy any more,' Louise sighed. 'And I'm going to look like a wallflower.'

'Don't worry, Louise.' Rory smiled. 'I'll dance with you.'

'You have to now,' Louise said. 'I'm not having him seeing me sitting on my own. I was so positive that he liked me.'

Louise returned with Emily's virgin bloody Mary but then she caught sight of Connor and Miriam and excused herself and headed over for a good old catch up with ex-colleagues. It was actually a good, if not brilliant night—Rory was as good as his word and midway through proceedings he did dance with her.

Rory was lovely, possibly one of the nicest men that a woman could know.

In fact, Rory was the last really nice boyfriend that Louise had had.

There was absolutely nothing going on between them. Their parting, three years ago, had been an amicable one. Though most people lied when they said that, in Rory and Louise's case it had been true. Just a few weeks into their relationship Louise had, while undergoing what she'd thought were basic investigations for her erratic menstrual cycle, received the confronting news that, when the time came, she might not fall pregnant very easily.

It hadn't been a complete bombshell, Louise had known things hadn't been right, but when it had finally dropped Louise had been inconsolable. Rory had put his hands up in the end and had said that, as much as he liked her, there wasn't enough there to be talking baby, baby, baby every day of the week.

They were far better as exes than as a couple.

'How's Christmas behaving?' Rory asked, as they danced.

'Much better this time.'

'You look so much happier.'

'I'm sorry we stopped being friends,' Louise said.

'We never stopped being friends,' Rory said. 'Well, I didn't. I was so worried when you were with him.'

'I know,' Louise said. 'Thanks for being there for me.' She gave him a smile. 'I might have some happy news soon.'

'What are you up to, Louise?'

'I'm going to be trying for a baby,' Louise admitted, 'by myself.'

'How did I not guess that?' Rory smiled.

'Please don't ask me if I've thought about it.'

'I wouldn't. I know that it's all you think about.'

'It's got worse since I've gone back to midwifery,' Louise said. 'My fallopian tubes want to reach out and steal all the little babies.'

'It might end any chance of things between you and Anton,' Rory said gently, but Louise just shrugged.

'He's the last person I'd go out with, he's way too controlling and moody for my taste. I just wanted a loan of that body for a night or two.' Louise smiled. 'Nope...' She had made up her mind. In the three years since she and Rory had broken up she had made some poor choices when it came to men. The news that she might have issues getting pregnant had seriously rocked Louise's world, leaving her a touch vulnerable and exposed. She was so much stronger now, though her desire to become a mother had not diminished an inch. 'I want a baby far more than I want another failed relationship.'

'Fair enough.'

They danced on, Louise with her mind on Anton. She was seriously annoyed at the sight of them laughing and talking as they danced and the way Saffarella ran her hands through his hair and over his bum had Louise burn with jealousy. Worse, though, was the way Anton laughed a deep laugh at something she must have said.

'I don't think I've ever seen him laugh till now, and I know that I'm funnier than her,' Louise grumbled. 'God, why does she have to be so, so beautiful? What did he introduce her as?'

'Saffarella.'

'Did he say girlfriend when he introduced her?' Louise pushed. 'Or my wife...?' She was clutching at straws as she remembered that his sister was a model. 'It's not his sister, is it?'

'If it's his sister then we should consider calling the police!' Rory said. 'Sorry, Louise, they're on together.'

But then a little while later came the good news!

She and Rory were enjoying another dance, imagining things that could never happen to John Lennon's 'Imagine'. Louise was thinking of Anton while Rory was thinking of a woman who couldn't be here tonight. He glanced up and saw that Anton was watching them, and then Anton looked over again.

'Anton keeps looking over,' Rory whispered in Louise's ear.

'Really?'

'He does,' Rory said. 'I don't think he likes me any more—in fact, I'd say from the look I just got he wants to take me out the back and knock my lights out.'

'Seriously?' Louise was delighted at the turn of events.

'Well, not quite that much, but I think you may be be right, Louise, Anton does like you.'

'I told you that he did. Is he still looking?'

'He's trying not to.'

'You have to kiss me,' Louise said.

'No.'

'Please.' Louise was insistent. 'Just one long one—it will serve him bloody right for trying to make me jealous. Come on, Rory,' she said when, instead of kissing her, he still shook his head. 'It's not like we never have before and I do it all the time when I'm modelling. It doesn't mean anything.'

'No,' Rory said.

'I got off with you a couple of years ago when Gina got drunk and was making a play for you!' Louise reminded him.

Gina was an anaesthetist who had had a drink and

drug problem and had gone into treatment a few months ago. A couple of years back Rory had been trying to avoid Gina at a Christmas party. Gina had tended to make blatant plays for him when drunk, so he and Louise had had a kiss and pretended to leave together.

'Come on, Rory.'

'No,' he said, and then he rolled his eyes and reluctantly admitted the reason why not. 'I like someone.'

'Who?' Louise's curiosity was instant.

'Just someone.'

'Is she here?'

'No,' Rory said. 'But I don't want it getting back to her that I got off with my ex.'

'Do I know her?'

'Leave it, Louise,' Rory said. 'Please.'

It really was turning out to be the most frustrating night! First Anton and Saffarella, now Rory with his secret.

Hugh and Emily watched the action from the safety of the tables, trying to work out just what was going on.

'Anton is holding Saffarella like a police riot shield,' Hugh observed, but Emily laughed just a little too late.

'Are you okay?' Hugh checked, looking at his wife, who, all of a sudden, was unusually quiet.

'I'm a bit tired,' Emily admitted.

'Do you want to go home?' Hugh checked, and Emily nodded. 'But I promised Louise a lift.'

'She'll be fine,' Hugh said, standing as Louise and Rory made their way over from the dance floor. 'We're going to go,' Hugh said. 'Emily's a bit tired.'

'Emily?' Louise frowned as she looked at her friend. 'Are you okay?'

'Can I not just be tired?' Emily snapped, and then corrected herself. 'Sorry, Louise. Look, I know that I said I'd give you a lift—'

'Don't be daft,' Louise interrupted. 'Go home to bed.'

'I'll see Louise home,' Rory said, and Hugh gave a nod of thanks.

They said their goodnights but as Hugh and Emily walked off, Rory could see the concern on Louise's face.

'Louise!' Rory knew what she was thinking and dismissed it. 'Emily's fine. It isn't any wonder that she's feeling tired. She's six months pregnant and working. Theatre was really busy today...'

'I guess, but...' Louise didn't know what to say. Rory didn't really get her intuition where pregnant women were concerned. She wasn't about to explain it to him again but he'd already guessed what she was thinking.

'Not your witch thing again?' Rory sighed.

'Midwives know.' Louise nodded. 'I'm honestly worried.'

'Come on, I'll get you a drink,' Rory said. 'You can have two eggnogs.' But Louise shook her head. 'I just want to go home,' she admitted. 'You stay, I can get a taxi.'

'Don't be daft,' Rory said, and, not thinking, he put his arm around her and they headed out, followed by the very disapproving eyes of Anton.

Rory dropped her home and, though tired, Louise couldn't sleep. She looked at the crib, still wrapped in Cellophane, that she had hidden in her room, in case Emily dropped round. It was a present Louise had bought. It was stunning and better still it had been on sale. Louise had chosen not to say anything to Emily, knowing how superstitious first-time mums were about not getting anything in advance.

Emily had already been through an appendectomy at six weeks' gestation, as well as marrying Hugh and sorting out stuff with her difficult family. She was due to finish working in the New Year and finally relax and enjoy the last few weeks of pregnancy.

Louise lay there fretting, trying to tell herself that this time she was wrong.

It was very hard to understand let alone explain it but Emily had had that *look* that Louise knew too well.

Please, no!

It really was too soon.

CHAPTER FOUR

ANTON WAS RARELY uncomfortable with women.

Even the most beautiful ones.

He and Saffarella went back a long way, in a very loose way. They had met through his sister a couple of years ago and saw each other now and then. He had known that she would be in London over Christmas and Saffarella had, in fact, been the date he had planned to take to the maternity Christmas evening.

'Where are we going?' Saffarella frowned, because she clearly thought they were going back to his apartment but instead they had turned the opposite way.

'I thought I might take you back to the hotel,' Anton said.

'And are you coming in?' Saffarella asked, and gave a slightly derisive snort at Anton's lack of response. 'I guess that means, no, you're not.'

'It's been a long day...' Anton attempted, but Saffarella knew very well the terms of their friendship and it was *this* part of the night that she had been most looking forward to and she argued her case in loud Italian.

'Don't give me that, Anton. Since when have you ever been too tired? I saw you looking at that blonde tart...'

'Hey!' Anton warned, but his instant defence of Louise, combined with the fact that they both knew just who he was referring to, confirmed that Anton's mind had been elsewhere tonight. Saffarella chose to twist the knife as they pulled into the hotel. 'I doubt that she's being dropped off home by that Rory. They couldn't even wait for the night to finish to get out of the place.' When the doorman opened the door for her Saffarella got out of the car. 'Don't you ever do that to me again.' She didn't wait for the doorman, instead slamming the door closed.

Anton copped it because he knew that he deserved it.

His intention had never been to use Saffarella, they were actually good together. Or had been. Occasionally.

Anton had never, till now, properly considered just how attracted he really was to Louise. Oh, she was the reason he had called Saffarella and asked if she was free tonight, and Saffarella had certainly used him in the same way at times.

But it wasn't just the ache of his physical attraction to Louise that was the problem. He liked her. A lot. He liked her humour, her flirting, the way she just openly declared whatever was on her mind, not that he'd ever tell her that.

But knowing she was on with Rory, knowing he had taken her home, meant that Anton just wanted to be alone tonight to sulk.

It's your own fault, Anton, he said to himself as he drove home.

He should have asked Louise out months ago but then he reminded himself of the reason he hadn't, couldn't, wouldn't be getting involved with anyone from work ever again.

Approaching four years ago, Christmas Day had suddenly turned into a living nightmare. Telling parents on

Christmas Day that their newborn baby was going to die was hell at the best of times.

But at the worst of times, telling parents, while knowing that the death could have been avoided, was a hell which Anton could not yet escape from and he returned to the nightmare time and again.

The shouts and the accusations from Alberto's father, Anton could still hear some nights before going to sleep.

The coroner's report had pointed to a string of communication errors but found that it had been no one person's fault in particular. Anton could recite it off by heart, because he had gone over and over and over it, trying to see what he could have done differently.

But the year in the between the death and the coroner's report had been one Anton could rarely stand to recall.

He took his foot off the brake as he realised he was speeding and pulled over for a moment because he could not safely think about that time and drive.

His relationship hadn't survived either. Dahnya, his girlfriend at the time, had been one of the midwives on duty that Christmas morning and when she hadn't called him, the continual excuses she had made instead of accepting her part in the matter, had proved far too much for them.

Friends and colleagues had all been injected with the poison of gossip. Everyone had raced to cover their backs by stabbing others in theirs and the once close, supportive unit he had been a part of had turned into a war zone.

Anton had been angry too.

Furious.

He had raged when he had seen that information had not been passed on to him. Information that would have meant he would have come to see and then got the labouring mother into Theatre far sooner than he had.

The magic had gone from obstetrics and even before the coroner's findings had been in, Anton had moved into reproductive endocrinology, immersing himself in it, honing his skills, concentrating on the maths and conundrum of infertility. It had absorbed him and he had enjoyed it, especially the good times—when a woman who had thought she never would get pregnant finally did, and yet more and more he had missed obstetrics.

To go back to it, Anton had known he would need a completely fresh start, for he no longer trusted his old colleagues. He had come to London and really had done his best to put things behind him.

It was not so easy, though, and he was aware that he tended to take over. He sat there and thought about his first emergency Caesarean at The Royal. Louise just so brisk and efficient and completely in sync with him as they'd fought to get the deteriorating baby out.

He had slept more easily that night.

That hurdle he had passed and perhaps things would have got better. Perhaps he might have started to hand over the reins to skilled hands a touch further had Gina not rear-ended him in the hospital car park.

Anton had got out, taken one look at her, parked her car, pocketed the keys and then driven her home.

Twenty minutes later he'd reported her to the chief of Anaesthetics and Anton had been hyper-vigilant ever since then.

Anton looked down the street at the Christmas lights but they offered no reprieve; instead, they made it worse. He loathed Christmas. Alberto, the baby, had missed out on far too many.

Yep, Anton reminded himself as he drove home and then walked into his apartment, which had not a single shred of tinsel or a decoration on display, there was a very good reason not to get involved with Louise or anyone at work.

He took out his work phone and called the ward to check on a couple of patients, glad to hear that all was quiet tonight.

Anton poured a drink and pulled out his other phone, read an angry text from Saffarella, telling him he should find someone else for the maternity night out, followed by a few insults that Anton knew she expected a response to.

He was too tired for a row and too disengaged for an exchange of texts that might end up in bed.

Instead, he picked up his work phone and scrolled through some texts. All the staff knew they could contact him and with texting often it was easy just to send some obs through or say you were on your way.

He scrolled through and looked at a couple of Louise's messages.

BP 140/60—and yes, Santa, before you ask, I've read your list and I've checked it twice—it's still 140/60. From your little helper

He'd had no idea what that little gem had meant until he'd been in a department store, with annoying music grating in his ears, and a song had come on and he'd burst out laughing there and then.

He had realised then how lame his response at the time had been.

Call me if it goes up again.

Her response:

Bah, humbug!

Followed by another text.

Yes, Anton, I do know.

He must, Anton thought, find out what 'bah, humbug' meant.

Then he read another text from a couple of months ago that made him smile. But not at her humour, more at how spot-on she had been.

I know it is your weekend off, sorry, but you did say to text with any concerns with any of your patients. Can you happen to be passing by?

Anton had *happened* to be passing by half an hour later and had found Louise sitting on the bed, chatting with the usually sombre Mrs Calini, who was in an unusually elated mood.

'Oh, here's Anton.' Louise had beamed as he had stopped by the bed for a *chat*.

'Anton!' Mrs Calini had started talking in rapid Italian, saying how gorgeous her baby was, just how very, very beautiful he was. Yes, there was nothing specific but Anton had been on this journey with his patient and Louise was right, this was most irregular.

Twelve hours and a lot of investigations later, Mrs Calini had moved from elation to paranoia—loudly declaring that all the other mothers were jealous and likely to steal her beautiful baby. She had been taken up to the psych ward and her infant had remained on Maternity.

Two weeks later the baby had been reunited with Mrs Calini on the psychiatric mother and baby unit and just a month ago they had gone home well.

Anton looked up 'bah, humbug' and soon found out she wasn't talking about odd-looking black and white mints when she used that term.

He read a little bit about Scrooge and how he despised Christmas and started to smile.

Oh, Louise.

God, but he was tempted to text her now, by accident, of course. In his contacts Louise was there next to 'Labour Ward' after all.

He loathed that she was with Rory but, then again, she had every right to be happy. He'd had his chances over the months and had declined them. So Anton decided against an accidental text to Louise, surprised that he had even considered sending one.

He wasn't usually into games.

He just didn't like that the games had now ended with Louise.

Louise checked her phone the second she awoke, just in case Emily had called or texted her and she'd missed it, but, no, there was nothing.

It had been a very restless night's sleep and it wasn't even five. Louise lay in the dark, wishing she could go back to sleep while knowing it was hopeless.

Instead, she got up and made a big mug of tea and took that back to bed.

Bloody Anton, Louise thought, a little embarrassed at

her blatant flirting when she now knew he had the stunning Saffarella to go home to.

Had it all been one-sided?

Louise didn't think so but she gave up torturing herself with it. Anton had always been unavailable to her, even if just emotionally.

After a quick shower Louise blasted her hair with the hairdryer, and as a public service to everyone put some rouge on very pale cheeks then wiped it off because it made her look like a clown.

She took her vitamins and iron and then decided to cheer herself up by wearing the *best* underwear in the world to work today. She had been saving it for the maternity Christmas party but instead she decided to debut it today. It was from the Mistletoe range, the lace dotted with leaves of green and embroidered silk cream berries topped with a pretty red bow—and that was just the panties. The bra was empress line and almost gave her a cleavage, and she loved the little red bow in the middle.

It was far too glamorous for work but, then, Louise's underwear was always far too glamorous for work.

Instead of having another cup of tea and watching the news, Louise decided to simply go in early and hopefully put her mind at rest by not finding Emily there.

She lived close enough to walk to work. It was very cold so she draped on scarves and walked through the dark and damp morning. It was lovely to step into the maternity unit, which was always nice and warm.

There was Anton sitting sulking at the desk, writing up notes amidst the Naughty Baby Club—comprising all the little ones that had been brought up to the desk to hopefully give their mothers a couple of hours' sleep.

Louise read through the admission board, checking for Emily's name and letting out a breath of relief when she saw that it wasn't there.

'How come you're in early?' she asked Anton, wondering if he was waiting for Emily.

'I couldn't sleep,' Anton said, 'so I thought I'd catch up on some notes.'

They were both sulking, both jealous that the other had had a better night than they'd had.

'I'm going to make some tea,' Louise said. 'Would you like some?'

'Please.' Anton nodded.

'Evie?' Louise asked, and got a shake of the head from the night nurse. 'Tara?'

'No, thanks, we've just had one.'

Louise changed into her scrubs then headed to the kitchen and made herself a nice one, and this time Anton got a hospital teabag.

He knew he was in her bad books with one sip of his tea.

Well, she was in his bad books too.

'You and Rory left very suddenly,' Anton commented. 'I didn't realise that the two of you...'

'We're not on together,' Louise said. 'Well, we were three years ago but we broke up after a few weeks. We're just good friends now.'

'Oh.'

'Rory took me home early last night because I'm worried about Emily,' Louise admitted. She was too concerned about her friend to play games. 'She hasn't called you, has she? You're not here, waiting for her to come in?'

'No.' Anton frowned. 'Why are you worried? She seemed fine last night.'

'She was at first but then she was suddenly tired and went home. Rory said that she'd had a big day at work but…'

'Tell me.'

'She snapped at me and she had that look,' Louise said. 'You know the one…'

'Yep,' Anton said, because, unlike Rory, he did know what Louise meant and he took her concerns about Emily seriously.

'How many weeks is she now?'

'Twenty-seven,' Louise said.

'And how many days…?' Anton asked, pulling Emily's notes up on his computer. 'No, she's twenty-eight weeks today.' Anton read through his notes. 'I saw her last week and all was fine. The pregnancy has progressed normally, just the appendectomy at six weeks.'

'Could that cause problems now?' Louise asked.

'I would have expected any problems from surgery to surface much earlier than this,' Anton said, and he gave Louise a thin smile. 'Maybe she *was* just tired…'

'I'll ring Theatre later and find out what shift she's on,' Louise said. 'In fact, I'll do it now.'

She got put through and was told that Emily was on a late shift today.

'Maybe I am just worrying about nothing,' Louise said.

'Let us hope so.'

A baby was waking up and Tara, a night nurse, was just dashing off to do the morning obs.

'I'll get him.'

Louise picked up the little one and snuggled him in. 'God, I love that smell,' Louise said, inhaling the scent of the baby's hair, then she looked over at Anton.

'Did Saffron have a good night?'

She watched his lips move into a wry smile.

'Not really,' Anton said, and then added, 'And her name is Saffarella.'

'Oh, sorry,' Louise said. 'I got mixed up. Saffron's the one you put in your rice to make it go yellow, isn't it?' Louise corrected herself. 'Expensive stuff, costs a fortune and you only get a tiny—'

'Louise,' Anton warned, 'I don't know quite where you're going there but, please, don't be a bitch.'

'I can't help myself, Anton,' Louise swiftly retorted. 'If you get off with another woman in front of me then you'll see my bitchy side.'

Anton actually grinned; she was so open that she fancied him, so relentless, so *aaagggh*, he thought as he sat there.

'I didn't *get off*, as you say, with Saffarella. We danced.'

'Please,' Louise scoffed.

Maybe he wanted to share the relief he had felt when he had just heard that she and Rory were only friends but, for whatever reason, he put her out of her misery too.

'I took Saffarella back to the hotel she is staying at last night.'

He gave her an inch and, yep, Louise took a mile.

'Really!' Louise gave a delighted grin and covered the baby's ears. 'So you didn't—'

'Louise!'

'The baby can't hear, I've covered his ears. So you and she didn't…?'

'No, we didn't.'

'Did she sulk?' Louise asked with glee, and he grimaced a touch at the memory of the car door slamming.

'Yes.'

'Oh, poor Saffron, I mean Saffarella—now that I know you and she didn't do anything, I can like her.'

They both smiled, though it was with a touch of regret because last night could have been such a nicer night.

'Thanks so much,' Tara said, coming over and looking at the baby. 'He's asleep now, Louise. You can put him back in his isolette.'

'But I don't want to,' Louise said, looking down at the sleeping baby. He was all curled up in her arms, his knees were up and his ankles crossed as if he were still in the womb. His little feet were poking out of the baby blanket and Louise was stroking them.

'They're like kittens' paws,' Louise said, watching his teeny toes curl.

'You are so seriously clucky,' Tara said.

'Oh, I'm more than clucky,' Louise admitted. 'I keep going over to the nativity scene just to pick up Baby Jesus. I have to have one.'

'It will ruin your lingerie career,' Tara warned, but Louise just laughed.

'I'm sure pregnant women can and do wear fabulously sexy underwear—in fact, my agent's going to speak to a couple of companies to see what sort of work they might have for me if I get pregnant.'

'Surely you're missing something if you want a baby...' Tara said, referring to Louise's lack of a love life, but now she had told her mum, now she'd told Rory and Emily knew too, Louise had decided it was time to start to let the world know.

'No, I'm not missing anything.' Louise smiled. 'In fact, I might have to pay a visit to Anton.'

She was referring to the fact she'd found out he was

a reproductive specialist too and he gave a wry smile at the ease of her double entendre.

'I have an excellent record,' Anton said.

'So I've heard.' Louise smirked.

Then Anton stopped the joking around and went to get back to his notes. 'You don't need to be rushing. How old are you?'

'Thirty next year!' Louise sighed.

'Plenty of time. You don't have to be thinking about it yet,' Anton said, but it turned out that the ditzy Louise ran deep.

'I think about it a lot,' she admitted. 'In all serious-ness, Anton,' she continued, as Tara headed off to do more obs, 'I'm actually confused by the whole thing. I recently saw my GP but she just told me to come off the Pill for a few months.'

Anton frowned, fighting the urge to step in while not wanting to get involved with this aspect of Louise, so he was a little brusque in response. 'The fertility cen-tre at this hospital runs an information night for single women,' Anton offered. 'Your questions would be best answered there.'

'I know they do,' Louise said. 'I've booked in for the next one but it's not till February. That's ages away.'

'It will be here before you know it. As I said, there's no rush.'

'There might be, though,' Louise said, and told him the truth. 'A few years ago I found out I'd probably have problems getting pregnant. That's why I'm off the Pill and trying to sort out my cycle. I know quite a bit but even I'm confused.'

'You need a specialist. Perhaps see an ob/gyn and have him answer your questions, but I would think, from the little you've told me, that you would be referred to a fertility specialist. Certainly, if you are considering pregnancy, you need to get some base bloods down and an ultrasound.'

'Can I come and see you?' Louise was completely serious now. 'Make an appointment, I mean, and then if I did get pregnant...'

'There is a long wait to see me.'

'Even for colleagues?' Louise cheekily checked.

'Especially for colleagues,' Anton said, *really* not liking the way this conversation was going.

'What about privately?' Louise asked, and she was serious about that because all her money from modelling was going into her baby fund.

'Louise.' Anton was even brusquer now. 'Why would you want to be a single mother?'

'I'm sure that's not the first thing you ask your patients when they come to see you,' Louise scolded. 'I don't think that's very PC.'

'But you're not my patient,' Anton pointed out, 'so I don't have to watch what I say. Why would you want to be a single mother?'

'How do you know I'm not in a relationship?' Louise said.

'You just told me that you and Rory were only friends.'

'Hah, but I could have an infertile partner at home.'

'Do you?'

'Lorenzo,' Louise teased, kicking him gently with her foot. 'And he's very upset that he can't give me babies.'

He knew she was joking, though he refused to smile, and he wanted to capture her foot as she prattled on.

'Or,' Louise continued, 'I might be a lesbian in a very happy relationship and we've decided that we want to have a baby together.' She loved how his lips twitched as she continued. 'I'm the girly one!'

'You're not a very good lesbian,' Anton said, 'given the way that you flirt with me.'

'Ha-ha.' Louise laughed. 'Seriously, Anton—' and she was '—about seeing you privately. You're right, I need to get an ultrasound and some bloods done. I'm going in circles on my own—fertility drugs, artificial insemination or IVF. I'm worried about twins or triplets or even more...' Louise truly was. 'I want someone who knows what they are doing.'

'Of course you do,' Anton agreed. 'If you want, I can recommend someone to you. Richard here is excellent, I can speak with him and give you a referral and get you seen quickly—' Anton started, but Louise interrupted him.

'Why would I see someone else when we both know you're the best?' she pushed. 'Look, I know we mess around...'

'*You* mess around,' Anton corrected.

'Only at work.'

Louise *was* serious, Anton realised. She had that look in her eyes that Anton recognised on women who came to his office. It was a look that said she was determined to get pregnant, so he had no real choice now but to be honest.

No, this conversation wasn't going well for him at all.

'It would be unethical for me to see you,' Anton said, and stood.

'Unethical?' Louise frowned. 'What, because we work together?'

'Professionally unethical,' Anton said, and rolled his

eyes as a delighted smile spread across her face. 'I can't say it any clearer than that.'

Ooooh!

She hugged the baby as Anton walked off.

'He *has* got the hots for me,' Louise whispered to the baby, and then let out a loud wolf whistle to Anton's departing back.

No, Anton did not turn around but he did smile.

CHAPTER FIVE

'I NEED SOMEONE to buddy this,' Beth called, and Louise went over to the nurses' station to look at the CTG tracing of one of Beth's patients.

The policy at The Royal was that only two experienced midwives could sign off on a tracing and so a buddy system was in place.

It was way more than a cursory look Louise gave to the tracing. They discussed it for a few moments, going over the recordings of the contractions and foetal heart rate before Louise signed off.

It was a busy morning and it sped by. At lunchtime, as Anton walked into the staffroom, had he had sunglasses then he would have put them on. There was a silver Christmas tree by the television and it was dressed in silver balls. There were silver stars hanging from the ceiling—really, there was silver everything hanging from every available space.

'Have you been at the tinsel again?' Anton said to Louise, who was eating a tuna salad.

'I have. I just can't help myself. I might have to go and speak with someone about my little tinsel problem— though I took up your suggestion and went with a theme in here!'

'I cannot guess what it was.'

Anton chose to sit well away from her and, for something to do, rather than listen to all the incessant gossip, he picked up a magazine.

Oh, no!

There she was and Louise was right—the underwear was divine.

'Christmas Holly' said the title and there a stunning Louise was in the stockings she'd had on last night but now he got the full effect—bra, stockings and suspenders. Anton turned the page to the Mistletoe range, and the shots, though very lovely and very tasteful, were so sexy that Anton felt his body responding, like some sad old man reading a porn magazine, and he hastily turned to the problem page, just not in time.

Oh, God, he was thinking about swiping the magazine, especially when he glimpsed the Holly and the Ivy shots.

'Ooooh.' Louise looked over and saw what he was reading. 'I'm in that one.' She plucked it from his hands and knelt at the coffee table and turned to the section in the magazine as a little crowd gathered around.

She was so unabashed by it, just totally at ease with her body and its functions in a way that sort of fascinated Anton.

'You've got a cleavage,' Beth said, admiring the shot.

'I know,' Louise said. 'Gorgeous, isn't it?'

'But how?'

Anton closed his eyes. These were women who spent most of their days dealing with breasts and vaginas and they chatted with absolute ease about such things, an ease Anton usually had too, just not when Miss Louise was around.

'Well,' Louise said as Anton stared at the news, 'they

take what little I have and sort of squeeze it together and then tape it—there's a lot of scaffolding under that bra,' Louise explained. 'Then they pad the empty part and then they edit out my nipples.'

'Wow!'

'I wish they *were* real,' Louise sighed.

'Would you ever get them done?' Beth asked.

'No,' Louise said, as Anton intently watched the weather report. 'I did think about it one time but, no, I'll stick with what I've been given, which admittedly isn't much. Hopefully they'll be *massive* when I get pregnant and then breastfeed.'

'Anton!' Brenda popped her head in to save the day. 'I've got the husband of one of your patients on the phone. Twenty-eight weeks, back pain...'

'Who?'

'Emily Linton.'

'Merda.' Anton cursed under his breath and then took the phone while trying to ignore Louise, who was now standing over him as Hugh brought him up to speed.

'Okay,' Anton said, as Louise hopped on the spot. 'I'll come down now and meet you at the maternity entrance.'

'Back pain, some contractions,' Anton said. 'Her waters are intact...' As Louise went to follow him out Anton shook his head. 'Maybe Emily needs someone who is not close to her,' Anton said.

'Maybe she needs someone who *is* close to her,' Louise retorted. 'You're not getting rid of me.'

Anton nodded.

'Brenda, can you let the paediatricians know?'

'Of course.'

They stood waiting for the car and Anton looked over. Louise was shivering in the weak winter sun and her teeth were chattering. 'Emily isn't the most straightfor-ward person,' Louise said. 'She acts like she doesn't care when, really, she does.'

Anton nodded and watched as, even though she was terrified for her friend, Louise's lips spread into a wide smile as the car pulled up.

'Come on, trouble,' Louise said, helping her friend into a wheelchair.

'I'm sure it's nothing,' Emily said, as Louise gave di-rections.

'Hugh, go and park the car and meet us there.'

Once Hugh was out of earshot, Emily let out a little of her fear. 'It's way too soon,' Emily said. Her expres-sion was grim but there were no tears.

'Let's just see where we are,' Anton said.

Though Anton would do his level best to make sure that the pregnancy remained intact, Emily was taken straight through to the delivery ward, just in case.

'I had a bit of a backache last night,' Emily admitted. 'At first I thought it was from standing for so long yes-terday. Then, late this morning, I thought I was getting Braxton-Hicks...'

Louise was putting on a foetal monitor as Anton put in an IV line and took some bloods, and then, as Hugh arrived, Anton looked at the tracing. 'The baby is look-ing very content,' Anton said, and then he put a hand on Emily's stomach as the monitor showed another contrac-tion starting.

'I'm only getting them occasionally,' Emily said.

But sometimes you only needed a few with a baby this small.

'Emily,' Anton said when the contraction had passed, 'I am going to examine you and see where we are.'

But Emily kept panicking, possibly because she didn't *want* to know where they were, and nothing Hugh or Anton might say would reassure her.

'I need you to try and relax,' Anton said.

'Oh, it's so easy for them to say that when they come at you with a gloved hand!' Louise chimed in, and Anton conceded Louise was right to be there because Emily let out a little laugh and she did relax just a touch.

'How long are you here for?' Emily asked Louise, because even though Louise had yesterday told her she was on an early today, clearly such conversations were the last thing on Emily's mind at the moment and it was obvious that she wanted her friend to be here.

'I've just come on duty,' Louise lied, 'so I'm afraid that you're stuck with me for hours yet.'

Anton examined Emily and Louise passed him a sterile speculum and he took some swabs to check for amniotic fluid and also some swabs to check for any infection.

'You are in pre-term labour,' Anton said. 'You have some funnelling,' Anton explained further. 'Your cervix is a little dilated but if you think of a funnel...' he showed the shape with his hands '...your cervix is opening from the top but we are going to give you medication that will hopefully be able to, if not halt things, at least delay them.' He gave his orders to Louise and she started to prepare the drugs Anton had chosen. 'This should taper off the contractions,' he said as he hooked up the IV, 'and these steroids will help the baby's lungs mature in case it decides to be born. You shall get another dose of these in twenty-four hours.'

Louise did everything she could to keep the atmosphere nice and calm but it was all very busy. The paediatricians came down and spoke with Anton. NICU was notified that there might be an imminent admission. Anton did an ultrasound and everything on there looked fine. Though the contractions were occasionally still coming, they started to weaken, though Emily had a lot of pain in her back, which was a considerable concern.

'Content,' Anton said again, but this time to the screen. 'Stay in there, little one.'

'And if it doesn't?' Emily asked.

'Then we have everything on hand to deal with that if your baby is born,' Anton said. 'But for now things are settling and what I need for you to do is to lie there and rest.'

'I will,' Emily said. 'First, though, I need a wee.'

'I'll get you a bedpan!' Louise said.

'Please no.'

'I'm afraid so.' Louise smiled. 'Anton's rules.'

Anton smiled as he explained his rules. 'Many say that it makes no difference. If the baby is going to be born then it shall be. Call me old-fashioned but I still prefer that you have complete bed rest, perhaps the occasional shower...'

'Fine.' Emily nodded, perhaps for the first time realising that she was going to be there for a while.

Hugh and Anton waited outside as much laughter came from the room, mainly from Louise, but Emily actually joined in too as they attempted to get a sterile specimen and also to check for a urinary tract infection.

Bedpans were not the easiest things to sit on.

But then Emily stopped laughing. 'Louise, I'm scared if I wee it will come out.'

'You have to wee, Emily,' Louise said, and gave her friend a cuddle. 'And you have to poo and do all those things, but I'm right here.'

It helped to hear that.

'I've got such a bad feeling,' Emily admitted, and Hugh gave a grim smile to Anton as outside they listened to Emily expressing her fears out loud. 'I really do.'

'Okay.' Louise was practical. 'How many women at twenty-eight weeks sit on that bed you're on, having contractions, and say, "I've got a really good feeling"? How many?' Louise asked.

'None.'

'I had a bad feeling last night,' Louise admitted. 'You can ask Anton, you can ask Rory, because I left five minutes after you and I came in early just to look at the board to see if you had been admitted, but I don't have a bad feeling now.'

'Honest?'

'Promise,' Louise said. 'So have a wee.'

'I'm going to give her a sedative,' Anton said to Hugh.

'Won't that relax her uterus?' Hugh checked, and then stopped himself because he trusted Anton.

'I want her to sleep and I want to give her the best chance for those medications to really take hold,' Anton said. 'You saw that her blood pressure was high?'

Hugh nodded—Emily's raised blood pressure could simply be down to anxiety but could also be a sign that she had pre-eclampsia.

'We'll see if there's any protein in her urine,' Anton said. If she did that would be another unwelcome sign that things were not going well.

Louise came out with the bedpan and urine sample, which would be sent to the lab.

'Can you check for protein?' Anton asked.

Louise rolled her eyes at Hugh. 'He thinks that because I'm blonde I'm thick,' she said to a very blond

Hugh, who smiled back. 'Of course I'm going to check for protein!'

'He's blondist,' Hugh joked, but then breathed out in relief when Louise called from the pan room.

'No protein, no blood, no glucose—all normal, just some ketones.'

'She hasn't eaten since last night,' Hugh said, which explained the ketones.

'I've put dextrose up but right now the best thing she can do is to rest.'

It was a very long afternoon and evening.

Louise stayed close by Emily, while Anton delivered two babies but in between checked in on Emily.

At eight, Louise sat and wrote up her notes. It felt strange to be writing about Emily and her baby. She peeled off the latest CTG recording and headed out.

'Can you buddy this?' Louise asked Siobhan, a nurse on labour and delivery this evening.

'Sure.'

They went through the tracing thoroughly, both taking their time and offering opinions before the two midwives signed off.

'It's looking a lot better than before,' Siobhan said. 'Let's hope she keeps improving.'

Around nine-thirty p.m. Anton walked into the womblike atmosphere Louise had created. The curtains were closed and the room was in darkness and there was just the noise of the baby's heartbeat from the CTG. Emily was asleep and so too was Hugh. Louise sat in a rocking chair, her feet up on a stool, reading a magazine with a clip-on light attached to it that she carried in her pocket for such times, while holding Emily's hand. She let go of the magazine to give a thumb's-up to Anton, and then she put her finger to her lips and shushed him as he walked over to look at the monitors—Louise loathed noisy doctors.

All looked good.

Anton nudged his head towards the corridor and Louise stepped outside and they went into the small kitchenette where all the flower vases were stored and spoke for a while.

'She's still got back pain,' Louise said, and Anton nodded.

'We'll keep her in Delivery tonight but, hopefully, if things continue to improve we can get her onto the ward tomorrow morning.'

'Good.'

'You were right,' Anton said. 'There *was* something going on with her last night.' He saw the sparkle of tears in Louise's eyes because, despite positive appearances, Anton knew she was very worried for her friend.

'I'd love to have been wrong.'

'I know.'

'Anton…' Louise spilled what was on her mind. 'I bought a crib for the baby a few days ago.'

'Okay.'

'It was in a sale and I couldn't resist it. I didn't tell Emily in case she thought it bad luck…'

'Louise!' Anton's firm use of her name told her to let that thought go.

She took a breath.

'Louise,' he said again, and she met his eye. 'That's crazy. I've got Mrs Adams in room two, who's forty-one weeks. She's done everything, the nursery is ready…'

'I know, I know.'

'Just put that out of your mind.'

Louise did. She blew it away then but a tear did sneak out because Louise cared so much about Emily and she was also pretty exhausted. 'Why did it have to be now?' she asked.

'I would love to know that answer,' Anton said, and Louise gave a small smile as he continued. 'It would save me many sleepless nights.'

'I wasn't asking a medical question.'

'I know you weren't.'

Anton stood in the small annexe and looked at Louise. Today she had been amazing, though it wasn't just because she was Emily's friend. Every mother got Louise's full attention. It was wrong of him to compare her to Dahnya, Anton realised. It was futile to keep going back to that terrible day.

Louise was too worried about Emily to notice his silence and she rattled on with her fears.

'I know twenty-eight weeks isn't tiny tiny but...'

'It is far too soon,' Anton agreed. 'She's *just* into her third trimester but we'll do all we can to prolong it. It looks like we've just bought her another day and those steroids are in. The night staff have arrived, Evie is on and she is very good.'

Louise nodded. 'I know she is but I'm going to sleep here tonight.'

'Go home,' Anton said, because Louise really did look pale, but she shook her head at his suggestion. 'Louise, you have been here since six.'

'And so have you,' Louise pointed out. 'I didn't think you were on call tonight, Anton, so what's your excuse for being here?'

'I'll be a lot happier by morning. I just want to be close if something occurs.'

'Well, I'm the same. If something happens tonight then I want to be here with Emily.'

'I get that but—Louise, I never thought I'd say this to you, but you look awful.'

It was a rather backhanded compliment but it did make her smile. 'I'll go and lie down soon,' Louise said, and looked over as Hugh came out.

'Is she awake?'

'Yes, they're just doing her obs. Thanks for today,' Hugh said to them both. 'I'm going to text and ring five thousand people now. Emily told her mum and, honestly, it's spread like wildfire…'

'I get it,' Louise said, because she knew about Emily's very complex family and the last thing she needed now was the hordes arriving. 'I've put her down as no visitors.'

'Thanks for that,' Hugh said. 'I'm going to ring for pizza—do you want some?'

'No, thanks.' Louise shook her head and yawned. 'I'm going to go and sleep.'

'Anton?'

'Sounds good.'

Louise handed over to Evie, the night nurse who would be taking care of Emily. 'Promise, promise, promise that you'll come and get me if anything happens.'

'Promise.'

'I'm going to take a pager,' Louise said, 'just in case you're too busy, so if you page him…' she nodded to Anton '…page me too.'

Louise went to the hotbox and took out one of the warm blankets that they covered newly delivered mums in. Brenda would freak if she knew the damage that Louise singlehandedly did to the laundry budget but she was too cold and tired to care about that right now.

'I'll be in the store cupboard if anything happens.'

'Store cupboard?' Anton said.

'Where all the night nurses sleep.' Louise nodded to the end of the corridor. ''Night, guys. 'Night, Hugh. I'll just go and say night to Emily if she's awake.'

She popped in and there was Emily half-awake as Evie fiddled with her IV.

'You've done so well today.' Louise smiled, standing wrapped in her blanket. 'I'm just going to get some shut-eye but I'm just down the hall, though I have a feeling I shan't be needed.'

'Thanks so much for staying,' Emily said.

'Please.' Louise gave her a kiss goodnight on her fore-head. 'Hopefully we'll move you to a room tomorrow. I'm going to have a jiggle with the beds in the morning and give you one of the nice ones.' She spoke then in a loud whisper. 'One of the private ones!'

'You're such a bad girl.' Evie smiled.

'I know.' Louise grinned. 'Sleep!' Louise said to Emily and then stroked her stomach. 'And you, little one, stay in there.'

'Do you know what I'm having?' Emily asked, and Louise just smiled as Emily spoke on. 'Hugh knows and when I said that I didn't want to find out, he said that he wouldn't tell me even if I begged him.'

'Do you want to know?' Louise asked.

'No, yes, no,' Emily admitted. 'But I want to know if you know.'

'I do,' Louise said, and then burst into Abba. '"I do, I do, I do, I do, I do,"' Louise sang, just as Anton and Hugh walked in. 'But I'm not telling. If you want to know you can speak to Anton.'

'She's mad,' Emily said, when Louise had gone but she said it in the nicest way.

'Completely mad,' Anton agreed. 'How are you feeling now?'

'A bit better.'

'Any questions?' Anton checked, but Emily shook her head.

'I think you've answered them all. Presumably you know what I'm having?'

'Of course I do,' Anton said. 'You know you are allowed to change your mind and find out if you want to.'

'I want it to be a surprise.'

'Then a surprise it will be.'

'Are you going home now?' Emily asked, because she had been told he was only here till six and she felt both guilty and relieved when Anton shook his head.

'Stephanie is the on-call obstetrician tonight and she will be keeping an eye on you so that I can get some rest as I am working tomorrow. I am staying here tonight, though, and if anything changes, I have asked her to discuss it with me.'

'Thank you.'

The store cupboard was actually an empty four-bedded ward at the front of the unit and was used to store beds, trolleys, stirrups, birth balls and all that sort of stuff. Louise curled up on one of the beds and lay there with her eyes closed, hoping that they would stay that way till morning.

She was exhausted, she'd barely had any sleep last night, but now that she finally could sleep, Louise simply could not relax. There was that knot of worry about Emily and another knot between her legs when she thought about Anton and the fact that he actually liked her.

In *that* way!

After half an hour spent growing more awake by the minute Louise padded out with her blanket around her.

Anton gave her a smile and she couldn't really remember him smiling like that, unless to a patient. In fact, he didn't smile like *that* to the patients.

'Food should be here soon,' Anton said.

Louise shook her head and instead of waiting for the pizza to arrive she had a bowl of cornflakes in the kitchen. Anton looked up as she returned with a bottle of sparkling water and a heat pack for her cramping stomach and then took two painkillers.

She tossed her now cold blanket into the linen skip and took out a newly warm one.

'If Brenda knew…' Anton warned, because the cost of laundering a blanket was posted on many walls, warning staff to use them sparingly.

'I like to be warm at night,' Louise said, and, no, she hadn't meant it to be provocative but from the look that burnt between them it was.

She headed back to the storeroom but sleep still would not come.

Then she heard the slam of the door. Louise climbed out of the bed to tell whoever it was off for doing that but then a delicious scent reached her nose.

Pizza.

OMG.

She could almost taste the pepperoni.

Louise hadn't said no to Anton because of some diet, she had said no because…

Well.

Because.

No, she did not want to be huddled up at the desk with him—she might, the way she was feeling this moment, very possibly end up licking his face.

God, he was hot.

Her stomach was growling, though, and it was the scent of pizza that was at fault, not her, Louise decided as she smiled and pulled out her phone.

Anton had two phones and one of the numbers she was privy to. It was his work phone and she'd call him on it at times if one of his patients weren't well while he was off duty, or she might text him sometimes for advice.

She wondered if he'd tell her off for using it for something so trivial.

Or if he'd ignore her request, perhaps?

Anton sat eating pizza as Hugh fired off texts to family to let them know that Emily was doing well.

When his work phone buzzed, indicating a text, Anton read it and decided it might be best to ignore it.

For months he had done his best to ignore her yet since he'd see her up that stepladder it had been a futile effort at best.

He did try to ignore it. In fact, he said goodnight to Hugh and then went into the on-call room, grimly determined to sleep.

Then he read her text again and gave up fighting. He went back to the desk, picked up two slices of pizza and headed off to where perhaps he shouldn't.

CHAPTER SIX

'PIZZA MAN!' ANTON said, as he came into the dark room.

'Oh, my, and an authentic Italian one too!' Louise smiled in the dark and sat up and then took out her light from her pocket and shone it up at him. 'And so good looking.'

'You changed your mind about the pizza?'

'I did,' Louise said. 'A bowl of cornflakes wasn't going to cut it tonight.'

'I could have told you that half an hour ago—you need to eat more.'

'I do eat.'

Anton shook his head very slowly. 'With my sister's line of work I know all the tricks, *all* of them,' Anton said. 'Tell me the truth.'

'Okay, I do watch my weight,' Louise admitted, 'a lot! But I am not anorexic.'

'I can see that you're not anorexic but you do seem to live off salad.'

'Ah, so you notice what I eat, Anton, how sweet!' Louise teased, and then she answered him properly. 'I love my modelling work,' Louise said. 'I mean I *love* it and it is my job to present at a certain weight but I don't do the dangerously thin stuff. Yes, for the most part I have to watch what I eat but, in saying that, I eat very well. I'm nearly thirty. I can't believe I'm still working...'

'I can.' Anton smiled.

'Anyway, I've got a huge photo shoot on Christmas Eve,' Louise explained, as she ate warm pizza. 'It's for Valentine's Day and I'm going to pay a small fortune to get dressed up to the nines and have my hair and make-up done so, yes, I'm being careful.' Her slice of pizza was finished and he handed her the other one. 'I'm just not being very careful tonight.'

'If you are looking at trying for a baby...'

'I would never jeopardise that for work, Anton. I'm just eating healthily. What happened this morning is un-related to that.'

'Good to know.'

He glanced at the stirrups over the bed. 'You really sleep here?'

'Of course,' Louise said, and then she looked to where his gaze fell. 'Do you want me in stirrups, Anton?'

He actually laughed. 'No. It is that I *don't* want you in stirrups that means you can't be my patient.' He ex-plained as best he could. 'Louise, I know I have given mixed messages. Yes, I like you but I never wanted to get involved with someone at work.'

'We're not at work.' Louise smiled a provocative smile. 'Officially we're both off duty.'

'Louise, the thing is—'

'Please, please, don't,' Louise said. 'Please spare me the lecture, because, guess what, I'm the same. The last thing I want now is a full-on relationship, particularly with you.'

Anton frowned in slight surprise. He'd come in having finally given in and deciding that they should perhaps give it a go, only to find out that a relationship with him was far from her mind.

'Why *particularly* not with me?'

'Okay, I think you're as sexy as hell and occasionally funny but I think you'd be very controlling, and that's fine in the bedroom perhaps—'

'I am not controlling,' Anton immediately interrupted. 'Well, I know that I am at work but not when I'm in a relationship.'

'Oh, they all say that.' Louise put on an Italian accent. 'I do not want my woman posing in her underwear...'

'That is the worst Italian accent ever.' He frowned at her opinion of him. 'I happen to think your work is very beautiful.'

'Really?'

'Of course it is.' He was still frowning. 'Have you had trouble in the past—?'

'I have,' Louise said quickly, hurrying over that part of her life, 'and so I keep things on my terms. The only thing I want to focus on right now is myself and becoming a mum. I'm not on a husband shop.'

A flirt, some fun, was all she was prepared to give to a man right now.

Though she had fancied Anton for ages.

Ages.

Pizza done, Louise went into her pocket, peeled off some baby wipes from a small packet she carried and wiped her hands. Then she went into her pockets again and pulled out a breath spray.

'What the hell have you got in those pockets?'

'Many, many things—basically my pockets are designed so that I don't have to get up if I'm comfy.' Louise smiled and settled back on the pillow. 'The breath spay is so that I don't submit a labouring woman to my pizza breath, and,' she added, 'it's also terribly convenient if you want to kiss me goodnight.'

'Louise,' Anton warned. 'We're not going to be skulking around in the shadows.'

'I know,' Louise sighed regretfully. 'How come you left fertility?' She yawned, but was pleased when Anton sat on the edge of the bed.

'I missed obstetrics,' Anton admitted, though he too chose to avoid the dark stuff.

'Is it nice to be back doing it?'

'Some days,' Anton said, 'like yesterday with Hannah's son—that was a really good day. Today...' He thought for a moment. 'Yes, it is still good. Thanks for your help today, you were right to stay—it is good for Emily to have you nearby.'

'You're making me nervous, Anton—you're being too nice.'

Anton smiled and watched as she put her hand under the blanket and turned the hot pack on her stomach.

'Still hurt?'

'Yep.'

He wanted his hand there.

Louise wanted the same thing.

She wanted him to lean forward and Anton actually felt as if her hand were at the back of his head, dragging him down, but it wasn't her hand that was pressuring him, it was want.

'I'm going to go,' Anton said. 'I just wanted to clear the air.'

'It doesn't feel very clear,' Louise said, because it was thick with sexual tension, a tension that had come to a head last night but had had no outlet for either of them.

'You're right, it doesn't,' Anton agreed. 'You are such a flirt, Louise,' he said, his mouth approaching hers.

'I know.' She smiled then asked a question as his lovely mouth approached. 'If you were intending to just pop in to clear the air, why did you brush your teeth before you came in?'

'I was *hoping* to clear the air but you have worn me down.'

They were far from worn down as their mouths finally met. It was supposed to break the tension but instead it upped it as, in the dark, Louise found out how lovely that sulky mouth could be.

The mixture of soft lips and rough stubble had her break on contact.

Anton had decided on one small kiss to chase away a wretched day but small was relative, Anton told himself as he slipped in his tongue and met the caress of hers, for it was still a small kiss if he compared it to the one he really wanted to give.

For Louise, it was bliss. She could not remember a kiss that had been nicer, and her hands moved up to his head and their kiss deepened from intimate to provocative. As he moved to remove her hands and halt things he changed his mind as his thumb grazed her breast. Anton heard the purr and the nudge of her body into his palm, like a cat demanding attention, and so he stroked her through the fabric, until for both of them he had to feel her.

Anton went to lift her top, just to get to her breast, but the heat pack slipped off and she willed his hand to change direction, her tongue urging him on as Anton obliged.

He could feel the ball of tension of her uterus as his

hand slipped down instead of up, stroking her tense stomach as he kissed her more deeply.

Louise lifted her knees to the bliss and the sensation but then she peeled her mouth from his.

'Anton…'

'I know that you do,' he said, not caring a bit. 'What colour underwear?' he asked, as he toyed with the lace.

'Cream and green, with a red bow—it's from the Mistletoe collection.'

She loved his moan in her mouth and the feel of his fingers creeping lower. His warm palm massaged low on her stomach as his finger hit the spot and Louise felt her face become red and hot as she kissed now his neck then his ears. One of his hands was behind her head, supporting it, while beneath the other she succumbed.

The tension hit and his mouth suckled hers as he stroked her through the deepest come of her life and then she felt the bliss abate as her stomach lay soft beneath his palm. Her intimate twitches stilled and Louise lay quiet for a moment.

'Better?' Anton asked.

'Positively sedated.'

She lay in sated bliss, pain free for the first time today, and trying to tell herself it was just the sex she wanted as she moved her hand and stroked his thick erection.

'Poor Anton,' she said.

'There have been way too many poor Antons of late,' Anton said. 'I'm going to go and you're going to sleep and—'

'We never discuss this again.' Louise smiled. 'Got it!'

How was she supposed to sleep after that? Louise thought as Anton made his way out.

It took about forty-seven seconds!

CHAPTER SEVEN

LOUISE AWOKE TO the sound of the domestic's floor polisher in the hallway and the even happier sound of no pager, which meant nothing had happened with Emily and so she padded out to the ward.

'How is she?' Louise asked Evie.

'Very good,' Evie said. 'She's slept mostly through and her back ache has eased and the contractions have stopped.' She looked at Louise, who was yawning. 'Why don't you go home?'

'I'm going to have a shower and then I'll see Emily over to her room before I do just that.'

'Well, the royal suite is empty.' Evie smiled as she used the name they all called it. 'I'll go and set it up.'

'I'll do that when I've had my shower,' Louise said, smiling when she heard Anton's voice.

'Morning, Louise,' Anton said, looking all the more handsome for not having shaven. 'How did you sleep?'

'Oh, I went out like a light,' Louise answered. She headed off to the shower and had to wash with the disinfectant soap used for washing hands. Smelling like a bathroom cleaner commercial, she headed out to set up the room for Emily.

It was hardly a royal suite but it had its own loo and

was more spacious than others and there was a trundle bed if Hugh wanted to stay. Louise checked the oxygen and suction and that there were pads and vomit bowels and suchlike.

Anton checked in on Emily and was very happy with her lack of progress and agreed that she could be moved.

'Every day that you don't go into labour is a good day,' Anton said, as Louise helped her onto the bed. 'For now you are on strict bed rest and that means bedpans.'

'Okay.' Emily nodded. She wasn't going to argue if it meant her baby stayed put. 'I feel much more positive today.' She looked over at Louise. 'You can go home now.'

'I am,' Louise said. 'But you're to text me with anything you want me to bring in for you. I can visit tonight or tomorrow. I'm off for two days now but—'

'I'll text you,' Emily interrupted, because Louise lived by her phone and they texted each other most days anyway.

As they headed out—Anton to start his shift, Louise to commence her days off—he asked if he could have a word with her in his office.

'Sure,' Louise said.

She knew what was coming and immediately she broached it. 'Don't worry, I get that last night was an aberration.' She saw him frown. 'A one-off.'

Anton wasn't so sure. He had no regrets about last night and he looked at the woman standing before him and wanted to get to know her some more, but before he did there was something that he first needed to know.

'This referral, are you sure that now is the right time?'

'Very sure,' Louise said. 'I've been thinking about it for close to a year.'

'Okay…' Anton said, because that alone was enough for him to ensure last night remained an *aberration*, although still he would like to give them a chance. 'Why don't you wait a while? Maybe we can—?'

'Anton, I already have waited a while. I'm twenty-nine years old and for twenty-eight of those years I have wanted a baby. I didn't just dress up my dollies and put them in a pram, Anton, I used to put them up my dress…' Anton smiled as she carried on. 'I'm not brilliant at relationships.'

'Why would you say that?'

'Oh, I've gathered quite a list of the reasons over the years.' Louise started to tick off on her fingers. 'I'm high maintenance, vain, obsessed with having a baby, inappropriate at times… I could go on but you get the drift. And, yes, I am all of those things and shall happily continue to be them. But, while relationships may not be my forte, I do know for a fact that I shall be a brilliant mum. So many women do it themselves these days.'

'Even so…'

'It's not a decision I've come to lightly. I've sat on it for close to a year and so, if I could have that referral, it would be completely brilliant.'

He wrote one out for her there and then. 'I'll let his secretary know this morning. When you call ask to speak to her because Richard is very booked up too.'

'Thank you.'

'Louise…'

'Anton.' She turned round. She did not want to hear now how they might stand a chance, and she did not want to be put off her dream. One of the reasons she was attracted to him perhaps was that he had been so unobtainable and she wanted that to remain the same. 'Don't be such a girl!'

Six feet two of testosterone stood there and smiled as she continued.

'It was fun, there can be more fun, just as long as it's conducted well away from work, but I *am* going ahead with this.'

He said nothing as she stepped out and Louise didn't really want him to. She didn't want to hear that maybe they could give it a go. She had fancied him for ever, since the moment she had first laid eyes on him, and now, when the year she had given herself to come to her decision was almost up, when her dream was in sight, Anton was suddenly interested.

Why couldn't he have left it at sex?

That, Louise could deal with.

It was the relationship part that terrified her.

Louise went and visited her family that morning and told them what was going on with Emily. When she got home Emily texted, asking her to go shopping for some nightwear but that there was no rush. And she added…

Something suitable, Louise!!!

Louise killed a couple of happy hours choosing nightwear for a pregnant, soon-to-be breastfeeding woman, while pretending she was shopping for herself. She did her level best to buy not what she'd like but what she guessed Emily would like, and, finally home, she thought about Anton and what had happened.

Not just their kiss and things, more the revelation that he liked her.

She had always been herself with him. Almost, since the day they had met, she had actually *practised* being herself with him. Anton had no idea just how much he had helped her. Not once had he told her to tone it down as she'd gradually returned to the woman she once had been.

She didn't particularly want Anton to know just how bad things had been. In fact, as her fingers traced the scar on her scalp and her tongue slid over the crown on her front tooth, she could not imagine telling him what had happened in her past—it would be a helluva lot to dump on him.

Louise let out a breath as she recalled her family's and friends' reactions.

It had been Emily she had called on Boxing Day and Rory too.

Rory, whose friendship she had dumped, had, when she'd needed him, patched her up enough to go and face her parents at least.

No, she did not even want to think of Anton's reaction to her tale so she pushed all thoughts of that away and pulled out the referral letter and made the call she had been waiting for ever to make.

Anton must have rung ahead as promised because when Louise spoke to the secretary she was told that there had been a cancellation and that she could see Richard the following Wednesday at ten a.m. Louise checked her diary on her phone and saw that she was on a late that day.

Perfect!

Louise put down the phone and did a little happy dance.

Finally, possibly, her baby was on the way!

CHAPTER EIGHT

EVERY QUESTION THAT Louise had, and there were many, was answered.

Susan had come to Louise's appointment with her and Louise was very glad to have her mother by her side. She knew she would probably forget half of what was said later. Also it was easier if her mother understood what was happening first hand.

Richard ordered a full screening, along with a pelvic ultrasound, and did a thorough examination, as well as looking through the app she had on her phone that charted all her dates.

'We have counsellors here and I really suggest that you take up my suggestion and make an appointment. The next step is to await all the blood results and then I'll see you in the new year and we'll look at the ways we can go ahead.'

Louise nodded.

'But you think I'll probably end up having IVF?' Louise said, because that was the impression she had got during the consultation. She was nervous that the fertility drugs might produce too many eggs but with IVF it was more controlled and Louise only wanted one embryo put back. Richard had even discussed egg sharing, which would give Louise one round of IVF free.

'I'm leaning that way, given your irregular cycle and that you want to avoid a multiple pregnancy, but right now I'd suggest you carry on with the iron and folic acid till we get the results back. We might put you on something stronger once they're in. For now, go and have a good Christmas.'

Louise made an appointment for the second week in January, when Richard returned from his Christmas break, and she made an appointment for an ultrasound and then went and had all the bloodwork done as well.

'Aren't you going to book the counsellor?' Susan asked.

'Why would I need to see one?' Louise said. 'You didn't have to see one before you had your three children.'

'True,' Susan responded, 'but before we went in you said that you were going to do *everything* he suggests.'

'And I am,' Louise said, 'apart from that one.'

Louise's cheeks were unusually pink as they walked down the corridor. Her mind was all ajumble because even as little as a couple of weeks ago she'd have happily signed up to talk to someone. She was one hundred per cent sure that she wanted this.

Or make that ninety-nine point nine per cent positive.

'Have you got time for a quick lunch before your shift?' Susan asked.

She did have time but unfortunately that point one per cent, or rather Anton, was already in the canteen and Louise was very conscious of him as they got their meals. Fortunately the table that Susan selected was quite far away from where Anton sat.

'Well, all I can say is that he was a lot better than the GP,' Susan said. 'Do you feel better for having seen him?'

'I do.'

'You're very quiet all of a sudden.'

Louise didn't know whether or not to say anything to her mum.

Actually, she didn't know if there even was anything to discuss. She and Anton had returned to business as usual after the other night. She was being far less flirtatious and Anton was checking up on her work even more than usual, if that was possible.

'I think I like someone, Mum,' Louise admitted. 'I'm a bit confused, to be honest.'

'Does he know that you like him?'

Louise nodded. 'And he also knows I'm doing this but I think if I continue to go ahead then it takes away any chance for us. I don't even know if I want us to have a chance.'

Susan asked what should have been a simple question. 'What's he like?'

'I don't really know.' Louise gave a wry laugh. 'I know what he's like at work and I find him a bit...' She hesitated. 'Well, he's very thorough with his patients and I'm pretty used to doctors dismissing and overriding midwives...' Louise thought for a long moment before continuing. 'I've just fancied him for a long time but nothing ever happened and now, when I've decided to do this, he seems to want to give us a try.'

'How long have you liked him for?' Susan asked.

'About six months.'

'And if he'd tried anything six months ago, what would you have done?'

'Run a mile.'

'If he'd tried anything three months ago, what would you have done?'

'Run a mile,' Louise admitted.

Only now was she truly healing.

'Do you want to give it a try?'

'I think so,' Louise said, 'but I want this so much too.'

She wanted back her one hundred per cent and her unwavering certainty she was finally on the right path. Unthinkingly she looked across the canteen and possibly the cause of her indecision sensed it, because Anton glanced over and briefly met her gaze.

'I don't see a problem.' Susan picked up her knife and fork and brought Louise back to the conversation. 'You don't have an appointment till the second week of January and Richard did say to go and enjoy Christmas. Have some fun, heaven knows, you deserve it. Maybe just try not to think about getting pregnant for a few weeks.'

Louise nodded, though her heart wasn't in it. Her mum tried, she really did, but she simply couldn't get it. Getting pregnant wasn't something Louise could shove in a box and leave in her wardrobe and drag it out in a few weeks and pick up again— it was something she had been building towards for a very long time.

She glanced over and saw that Anton was walking out of the canteen. There had been so little conversation of late between them that Susan could never have guessed the topic of their conversation had just walked past them.

'Think about counselling,' Susan suggested again.

'Why would I when I've got you?' Louise smiled.

'Ah, but since when did you tell me all that's going on?'

Her mother was right, she didn't tell her parents everything. 'Maybe I will,' Louise said, because this year had been one of so many changes. Even as little as a month or so ago she'd have died on the spot had Anton responded to one of her flirts. She was changing, ever changing, and every time she felt certain where she was heading, the road seemed to change direction again.

No.

Louise refused to let go of her dream.

'I need to get to my shift.'

'And I need to hit the shops.' Susan smiled. 'Come over at the weekend, I'll make your favourite.'

'I shall,' Louise said, and gave her mum a kiss good-bye. 'I'll give you a call. Thanks for coming with me today.'

Louise's patient allocation was a mixed bag between Stephanie and Anton's patients and all were prenatal patients, which meant no baby fix for Louise this shift.

'Hi, Carmel, I'm Louise,' she introduced herself to a new patient. Carmel had been admitted via the antenatal clinic where she had been found to have raised blood pressure. 'How are you?'

'Worried,' Carmel said. 'I thought I was just coming for my antenatal appointment and I find out my blood pressure's high and that the baby's still breech. I'm trying to sort out the other children.'

'This is your third?'

Carmel nodded. 'I've got a three- and a five-year-old. My husband really doesn't have any annual leave left and I can't ask my mum.' Carmel started to cry and, having taken her blood pressure, Louise sat on the chair by her bed.

'There's still time for the baby to turn,' Louise said.

'You're not due till January...' she checked her notes '...the seventh.'

'But Stephanie said if it doesn't turn then I'll have a Caesarean before Christmas.'

Louise nodded because, rather than the chance of the mother going into spontaneous labour, Caesareans were performed a couple of weeks before the due date.

'I just can't be here for Christmas. I know the baby might have come then anyway but at least with a natural labour I could have had a chance to be in and out...' Carmel explained what was going on a little better. 'My mum's really ill—it's going to be her last Christmas.'

Poor Carmel had so much going on in her life at the moment that hospital was the last place she wanted to be. Right now, though, it was the place she perhaps needed to be, to concentrate on the baby inside and let go a little. Louise sat with her for ages, listening about Carmel's mum's illness and all the plans they had made for Christmas Day that were now in jeopardy.

Finally, having talked it out, Carmel calmed a bit and Louise pulled the curtains and suggested she sleep. 'I'll put a sign on the door so that you're not disturbed.'

'Unless it's my husband.'

'Of course.' Louise smiled. 'The sign just says to speak to the staff at the desk before coming in.'

She checked in on Felicity, who was one of Anton's high-risk pregnancies, and then she got to Emily.

'How's my favourite patient?' Louise asked a rather grumpy Emily.

Emily was very bored, very worried and also extremely uncomfortable after more than a week and a half spent in bed. She was relying heavily on Louise's chatter and humour to keep her from the dark hole that her mind kept slipping into. 'I'm dying to hear how you got on at your appointment.'

'It went really well,' Louise said, as she took Emily's blood pressure.

'Tell me.'

'He was really positive,' Louise explained, 'though not in a false hope sort of way, just really practical. I'm going to be seeing him in the new year, when all my results are in, to see the best direction to take, but I think it will be IVF.'

'Really!'

'I think so.' Louise nodded. 'He discussed egg sharing, which would mean I'll get a round of IVF free...'

'You don't feel funny about egg sharing?' Emily asked, just as Anton walked in.

'God, no,' Louise said, happy to chat on. 'I'd love to be able to help another woman to get her baby. It would be a win-win situation. I think egg sharing is a wonderful thing.'

She glanced over as Anton pulled out the BP cuff.

'I've done Emily's blood pressure,' Louise said.

'I'm just checking it for myself.'

Louise gritted her jaw. He did this all the time, *all the time*, even more so than before, and though it infuriated Louise she said nothing.

Here wasn't the place.

'Everything looks good,' Anton said to Emily. 'Twenty-nine weeks and four days now. You are doing really well.'

'I'm so glad,' Emily said, 'but I'm also so...' Emily didn't finish. 'I hate that I'm complaining when I'm so glad that I'm still pregnant.'

'Of course you are bored and fed up.' Anton shrugged. 'Would a shower cheer you up?'

'Oh, yes.'

'Just a short one,' Anton said, 'sitting on a chair.'

'Thank you,' Emily said, but when Anton had gone she looked at Louise. 'What's going on with you two?'

'Nothing,' Louise said.

'Nothing?' Emily checked. 'Come on, Louise, it's me. I'm losing my mind here. At least you can tell me what's going on in the real world.'

'Maybe a teeny tiny thing *has* gone on,' Louise said, 'but we're back to him sulking at me now and double-checking everything that I do.'

'Please, Louise, tell me what has happened between you.'

'Nope,' Louise said, but then relented a touch. 'We got off with each other a smudge but I think the big chill is from my getting IVF.'

'Well, it wouldn't be the biggest turn-on.'

'I guess.'

'Can you put it off?'

'I don't want to put it off,' Louise said. 'Then again, I sort of do.' She was truly confused. 'God, could you imagine being in a relationship with Anton? He'd be coming home and checking I'd done hospital corners on the bed and things…'

'He's nothing like that,' Emily said.

'Ah, but you get his hospital bedside manner.'

'Why not just try?'

'Because I've sworn off relationships, they never work out… I don't know,' Louise sighed, and then she looked at her friend and told her the truth. 'I'm scared to even try.'

'When's the maternity do?' Emily asked.

'Friday, but I'm on a late shift, so I'll only catch the end.'

'If you get changed at work I want to see you before you go.'

'You will.' Louise gave a wicked smile. 'Let's see if he can rustle up another supermodel.'

'Or?'

Louise didn't answer the question because she didn't know the answer herself. 'I'll go and set up the shower for you,' Louise said instead, and opened Emily's locker and started to get her toiletries out. 'What do you want to wear?'

'Whatever makes me look least like a prostitute,' Emily said, because, after all, it was Louise who had shopped for her!

'But you look gorgeous in all of them,' Louise said, 'and I promise that you're going to feel gorgeous too once you've had a shower.'

Emily actually did. After more than a week of washing from a bowl, a brief shower and a hair wash had her feeling so refreshed that she actually put on some make-up and her smile matched the scarlet nightdress that Louise had bought her.

'Wrong room!' Hugh joked, when he dropped in during a lull between patients, please to see how much brighter Emily looked.

In fact, Emily had quite a lot of visitors and Anton glanced into her room as he walked past.

'Is she resting?' Anton asked Louise.

'I'm going to shoo them out soon,' Louise said. 'She's had her sister and mum and now Hugh's boss and his wife have dropped in.'

Alex and Jennifer were lovely, just lovely, but Emily really did need her rest and so, after checking in on Carmel, who seemed much calmer since her sleep and a visit from her husband and children, Louise popped in on Emily, dragging the CTG monitor with her.

'How are you?' Louise asked.

'Fine!' Emily said, but she had that slightly exhausted look in her eyes as she smiled brightly.

'That's good.' Louise turned to the visitors. She knew Alex very well from the five years she had worked in Theatre and she knew Jennifer a little too. 'I'm sorry to be a pain, but I've got to pop Louise on the monitor.'

'Of course,' Jennifer said. 'We were just leaving.'

'Don't rush,' Louise said, while meaning the opposite. 'I'm just going to get some gel.'

That would give them time to say goodbye.

Of course Emily was grateful for visitors but even a shower, after all this time in bed, was draining, and Louise would do everything and anything she had to do to make sure Emily got her rest. By the time she returned with the gel Alex and Jennifer had said their goodbyes and were in the corridor.

'How are you, Louise?' Alex asked. 'Missing Theatre?'

'A bit,' Louise admitted, 'although I simply love it here.'

'Well, we miss you,' Alex said kindly, and then glanced over to the nurses' station, where Anton was writing his notes. 'Oh, there's Anton. Jennifer, I must introduce you—'

'Not now, darling,' Jennifer said. 'We really do have to get home for Josie.'

'It will just take two minutes.' Alex was insistent but as he went to walk over, Jennifer caught his arm.

'Alex, I really am tired.'

'Of course.' Alex changed his mind and they wished Louise goodnight before heading off the ward.

Louise looked at Anton, remembering the night of the theatre do and Anton's stilted response when Alex had said he hadn't yet met his wife. Even if she and Anton were trying to keep their distance a touch, Louise couldn't resist meddling.

'She's gone,' Louise said, as he carried on writing.

'Who?'

'Jennifer.'

'That's good.'

'She's nice, isn't she?' Louise said, and watched his pen pause for a second.

'So I've heard,' Anton responded, and carried on writing.

'Have you met her?'

Anton looked up and met Louise's eyes, which were sparkling with mischief. 'Should I have?'

'I don't know.' Louise smiled, all the more curious, but, looking at him, properly looking at him for the first time since he had handed her the referral, she was curious now for different reasons. 'Why aren't we talking, Anton?'

'We're talking now.'

'Why are you checking everything I do?'

'I'm not.'

'Believe me, you are. I might just as well give you the obs trolley and follow you around and simply write your findings down.'

'Louise, I like to check my patients myself. It has nothing to do with you.'

'Okay.' She went to go but changed her mind. 'We're not talking, though, are we?'

He glanced at the sticking plaster on her arm from where she had had blood tests. 'How was your appointment?'

'He was very informative,' Louise said.

'You're seeing him again?'

'In January.' Louise nodded.

'May I ask…?' Anton said, and Louise closed her eyes.

'Please don't.'

'So I just sit here and say nothing?' Anton checked. He glanced down the corridor. 'Come to my office.'

Louise did as she wanted to hear what he had to say.

'I want to see if we can have a chance and I don't think we'll get one with you about to go on IVF.'

'Oh, so I'm to put all my plans on hold because you now think we might have a chance.'

'I don't think that's unreasonable.'

'I do,' Louise said. 'I very much do. I've liked you for months,' she said, 'months and months, and now, when I'm just getting it together, when I'm going ahead with what I've decided to do, you suddenly decide, oh, okay, maybe I'll give her a try.'

'Come off it, Louise…'

'No, you come off it,' Louise snapped back. A part of her knew he was right but the other part of her knew that she was. She'd cancelled her dreams for a man once before and had sworn never to do it again and so she went to walk off.

'You won't even discuss it?'

'I need to think,' Louise said.

'Think with me, then.'

'No.'

She was scared to, scared that he might make up her mind, and she was so past being that person. Instead, she gave him a cheeky smile. 'Richard told me to have a *very* nice Christmas.'

Her smile wasn't returned.

'I'm not into Christmas.'

'I meant—'

'I know what you meant, Louise,' Anton said. 'You want some gun for hire.'

'Ooh, Anton!' Louise smiled again and then thought for a moment. 'Actually, I do.'

'Tough.'

Anton stood in his office for a few moments as she walked off.

Maybe he'd been a bit terse there, he conceded.

But it was hearing Louise talk about egg sharing with Emily that had had him on edge. From the little Louise had told him about her fertility issues he had guessed IVF would be her best option if she wanted to get pregnant. Often women changed their minds after the first visit. He had hoped it might be the case with Louise while deep down knowing that it wouldn't be.

He had seen her sitting in the canteen with her mother today—and it had to have been her mum as Anton could see where Louise had got her looks from—but even that had caused disquiet.

Louise had talked this through with her family. It was clearly not a whim.

It just left no room for them.

Anton wanted more than just sex for a few weeks.

Then he changed his mind because a few weeks of straight sex sounded pretty ideal right now.

Perhaps they should try pushing things aside and just seeing how the next few weeks unfolded.

He walked out of his office and there was Louise, walking with a woman in labour. She caught his eye and gave him a wink.

Anton smiled in return.

The tease was back on.

CHAPTER NINE

'I AM SO, so jealous!' Emily said, as Louise teetered in on high heels on Friday night, having finished her shift and got changed into her Christmas party clothes.

'It's fine that you're jealous,' Louise said to Emily, 'because I am so, so jealous of you. I'd love to be in bed now, nursing my bump.'

'You look stunning,' Hugh said.

Louise was dressed in a willow-green dress that clung to her lack of curves and she had her Mistletoe range stockings on, which came with matching panties, bra and suspenders. As they chatted Louise topped her outfit off with a very red coat that looked more like a cape and was a piece of art in itself.

'God help Anton,' Hugh said openly to Louise.

'Sadly, he's stuck on the ward.' Louise rolled her eyes. 'So that was a waste of six pounds.'

As she headed out Hugh turned to Emily, who was trying not to laugh at Hugh's reaction.

'Was she talking about condoms?' Hugh asked.

'She was.'

Oh, Louise was!

As she approached the elevator, there was Anton and his patient must have been sorted because he had changed out of scrubs and was wearing black jeans and a black jumper and looked as festive as one might expect for Anton. He smelt divine, though, Louise thought as she stood beside him, waiting for the lift. 'You've escaped for the weekend,' Louise said.

'I have.'

'Me too!'

She looked at the clothes he was wearing. Black trousers, a black shirt and a very dark grey coat. He looked fantastic rather than festive. 'I didn't know they did out-of-hours funerals,' Louise said as they stepped into the elevator and her eyes ran over his attire.

'You would have me in a reindeer jumper.'

'With a glow stick round your neck,' Louise said as she selected the ground floor. 'It will be fun tonight.'

'Well, I'm just going to put my head in to be polite,' Anton said. 'I don't want to stay long.'

'Yawn, yawn,' Louise said. 'You really are a misery at Christmas, Anton. Well, I'm staying right to the end. I missed out on far too many parties last year.'

She leant against the wall and gave him a smile when she saw he was looking at her.

'You look very nice,' Anton said.

'Thank you,' Louise responded, and she felt a little rush as his eyes raked over her body and this time Anton did look down, all the way to her toes and then back up to her eyes.

She resented that the lift jolted and that the doors opened and someone came in. They all stood in silence but this was no socially awkward nightmare. His delicious, slow perusal continued all the way to the ground floor.

'Do you want a lift to the party?' Anton offered.

'It's a five-minute walk,' Louise said. 'Come back later for your car.'

They stepped out and it was snowing, just a little. It was too damp and not cold enough for it to settle but there in the light of the streetlamps she could see the flakes floating in the night and he saw her smile and chose to walk the short distance.

It was cold, though, and Louise hated the cold.

'I should have worn a more sensible coat,' Louise said through chattering teeth because her coat, though divine, was a bit flimsy. It was the perfect red, though, and squishy and soft, and she dragged it out every December and she explained that to Anton. 'But this is my Christmas party coat. It wasn't the most thought-out purchase of my life.'

'You have a Christmas coat?'

'I have a Christmas wardrobe,' Louise corrected. 'So, you're just staying for a little while.'

'No,' Anton said.

'Oh, I thought you said—'

'You ruined my line. I was going to suggest that you leave five minutes after me but then you said that you were looking forward to it.'

'Oh!'

'I think you are right and that we should enjoy Christmas, perhaps together, and stop concerning ourselves with other things.' He stopped walking and so did she and they faced each other in the night and he pulled her into his lovely warm coat. 'Can you be discreet?'

'Not really,' Louise said with a smile, 'but I am discreet about important things.'

'I know.'

'And having a nice Christmas is a very important thing,' she went on, 'so, yes, I'll be discreet.'

Pressed together, her hands under his coat and around his waist there was nothing discreet about Anton's erection.

'I would kiss you but…' He looked down at her perfectly painted lips for about half a second because he didn't care if it ruined her make-up and neither did she. It had been a very long December, all made worth it by this.

After close to two weeks of deprivation Louise returned to his mouth. His kiss was warm and his lips tender. It was a gentle kiss but it delivered such promise. His tongue was hers again to enjoy. His hands moved under her coat and stroked her back and waist so lightly it was almost a tickle, and when their lips parted their faces barely broke contact and Louise's short breaths blew white in the night. She was ridiculously turned on in his arms.

'We need get there,' Anton said.

'Should we arrive together?' Louise asked. 'If we're going to be discreet?'

'Of course,' Anton said, 'we left work at the same time.'

She went into her bag, which was as well organised as her pockets at work, and did a quick repair job on her face and handed Anton a baby wipe.

'Actually, have the packet,' Louise said, and Anton pocketed it with a smile.

He might rather be needing them.

It was everything a Christmas party should be.

The theme was fun and midwives knew how to have it. All the Christmas music was playing and Louise was the happiest she had been in a very, very long time amongst her colleagues and friends. Anton was there in the background, making her toes curl in her strappy stilettoes as she danced and had fun and made merry with friends while he suitably ignored her. Now and then, though, they caught the other's eye and had a little smile.

It was far less formal than the theatre do and everyone let off a little seasonal steam, well, everyone but Anton.

He stood chatting with Stephanie and Rory, holding his sparkling water, even though he was off duty now until Monday.

'Louise,' Rory called to her near the end of the evening, 'what are you doing for Emily at Christmas?'

'I don't know,' Louise said. 'I've been racking my brains. She's got everything she needs really but I'm going Christmas shopping tomorrow. I might think of something then.'

'Well, let me know if you want to go halves,' Rory said. 'Or if you see something I could get, then could you get it for me?'

'I shall.'

'I'm going to take Stephanie home,' Rory said, and as Stephanie went to get her coat, even though Anton was there, Louise couldn't resist, once Stephanie had gone, asking Rory a question.

'Is it Stephanie?'

'Who?'

'The woman you like.'

'God.' Rory rolled his eyes. 'Why did I ever say anything?'

'Because we're friends.'

'Just drop it,' Rory said. 'And, no, it's not Stephanie.'

He let out a laugh at Louise's suggestion. 'She's married with two children.'

'Maybe that's why you have to keep it so quiet.'

'Louise, it's not Stephanie and you are to leave this alone.' He looked at Anton. 'She's relentless.'

'She is.'

Louise pulled a face at Rory's departing back and then turned and it was just she and Anton.

'Do you want a drink?' Anton asked.

'No, thanks,' Louise said. 'I've had one snowball too many.'

'What *are* you drinking?' Anton asked, because he had seen the pale yellow concoction she had been drinking all night.

'Snowballs—Advocaat, lemonade and lime juice,' she pulled a face.

'You don't like them?'

'I like the *idea* of them,' Louise said, and then her attention was shot as a song came on. 'Ooh, I love this one...'

'Of course you do.'

'No, seriously, it's my favourite.'

It was dance with her or watch her dance alone.

'I thought we were being discreet?' Louise said.

'It's just a dance,' Anton said, as she draped her arms round his neck. 'But Rory's right—you are relentless.'

'I know I am.' Louise smiled.

They were as discreet as two bodies on fire could be, just swaying and looking at each other and talking.

'I want to kiss you under the mistletoe,' Anton said.

'I assume we're not talking about the sad bunch hanging at the bar.'

'No.'

'Did you know these stockings come with matching underwear?'

'I do,' Anton said, 'I saw your work in the magazine.'

'Did you like?'

'I like.' Anton nodded. 'As I said, I want to kiss you under the mistletoe.'

'I am so turned on.' She stated the obvious because he could feel every breath that blew from her lips, he could see her pulse galloping in her neck as well as the arousal in her eyes.

'Good.'

'We need to leave,' Louise said.

'I'm going to go and speak to Brenda and then leave, and you're going to hang around for a little while and then we meet at my car.'

'I live a two-minute walk from here,' Louise said.

'Okay...'

She loved his slow smile as she gave him her address. 'I'll slip the key into your coat pocket,' Louise said. 'You can go and put the kettle on.'

'I shall.'

'Please don't,' Louise said. 'I meant—'

'Oh, I get what you meant.'

Anton said his goodbyes and chatted with Brenda for an aching ten minutes, though on the periphery of his vision he could see Louise near the coats but then off she went, back to the dance floor.

Anton headed out into the night and found her home very easily. Louise had left the heating on. She loathed coming home to a cold house and a furnace of heat hit Anton as he opened the door as well as the dazzle of decorations, which were about as subtle as Louise.

And as for the bedroom!

Anton couldn't help but smile as he stepped inside Madame Louise's chamber. He looked at the crushed velvet bed that matched the crushed velvet chair by the dressing table and he looked at the array of bottles and make-up on it.

Anton undressed and got into her lovely bed. He had never met someone so unabashed and he liked that about her, liked that she was who she was.

Louise had never been more in demand than in the ten minutes at the end of the party. Everyone, *everyone* wanted her to stop for a chat, and just as she finally got her coat on and was leaving, Brenda suggested they drop over to Louise's as some work dos often ended up there.

'I can't tonight,' Louise said. 'Mum's over.'

'Your mum?'

'I think she and Dad had a row,' Louise lied, but she had to, as her mind danced with a sudden vision of a naked Anton in the hallway greeting half of the maternity staff. 'It's a bit of a sensitive point.'

Louise texted him as she walked out.

I just told the biggest lie

Should I be worried that there is a crib in your bedroom? Anton texted back.

She laughed because she had already told him it was for Emily's baby and it was wrapped in Cellophane too, so she continued the tease.

Aren't we making a baby tonight? Louise fired back. Get here!!!

She waved as a car carrying her friends tooted, trying not to run on shaky, want-filled legs, and almost breaking her ankle as she walked far too fast for her stilettoes.

She could barely get the key in the door, just so delighted by the turn of events—that they were going to put other things on hold and simply enjoy. Her coat dropped to the floor as she stepped into the bedroom and there he was, naked in her bed and a Christmas wish came true.

'Who's been sleeping in my bed?' Louise smiled.

'No sleeping tonight,' Anton said. 'Come here.'

Louise was not shy; she went straight over, kneeling on her bed and kissing him without restraint.

It was urgent.

Anton was at the tie of her dress as their mouths bruised each other's. He tried to peel it off over arms that were bent because she was holding his head, tonguing him, wanting him, but there was something she first had to do.

'I have to take my make-up off.'

'I'll lick it off.'

'Seriously.' She could hardly breathe, she was somehow straddling him, her dress gaped open and it would be so much easier not to reach for the cold cream. 'It's not vanity, it's work ethic—I'll look like a pizza for my photo shoot otherwise…'

She climbed off the bed and shed her dress and Anton got the full effect of her stunning underwear, and as beautiful as the pictures had been he far preferred the un-airbrushed version.

Louise sat on her chair and slathered her face in cold cream, quickly wiping it off and wishing she hadn't worn so much mascara. Just as she had finished she felt the chair turn and she was face to groin with a naked Anton.

'Poor Anton,' Louise said.

'Not any more,' Anton said, as she started to stroke him. She went to lower her head but he was starting to kneel.

'Stay…' Louise said, because she wanted to taste him.

'You can have it later.'

He caressed the insides of her thighs through her stockings then the white naked flesh so slowly that she was twitching. He stroked her through her damp panties till he moved them aside and explored her again with his fingers till she could almost stand it no more. Her thighs were shaking and finally his hands went for her mistletoe panties and slid them down so slowly that Louise was squirming. Anton pulled her bottom right to the edge of the chair and then took one stockinged leg and put it over his shoulder and then slowly did the same with the other. Such was the greed in his eyes she was almost coming as finally he did kiss what had been under the silken mistletoe.

Louise looked down but his eyes were closed in concentration and her knees started to bend to the skill of his mouth but hands came up and clamped her legs down, so there was nowhere to go but ecstasy.

She felt the cool blowing of his breath and then the warm suction of his mouth and then another soft blow that did nothing to put the fire out. In fact, her hips were lifting, but his mouth would not allow them to.

'Anton…' She didn't need to tell him she was coming, he was lost in it too, moaning, as her thighs clamped his head and she pulsed in his mouth. Anton reached for his cock on instinct. He was close to coming too. He raised himself up, and was stroking himself at her entrance.

They were in the most dangerous of places, two people who definitely should know better.

Louise was frantically patting the dressing table behind her, trying to find a drawer, while watching the silver bead at his tip swelling and drizzling.

'Here...' She pulled out a foil packet and ripped it open. She slid it onto his thick length and there was no way they could make it to the bed, but Anton took a turn in the lucky chair and she leapt on his lap. His mouth sucked her breast through her bra as she wriggled into position.

She hovered provocatively over his erection, revelling for a brief moment in the sensation of his mouth and the anticipation of lowering herself. Anton had worked the fabric down and was now at her nipple, her small breast consumed by his mouth, and then his patience expired. His hands pulled her hips down and in one rapid motion Louise was filled by him, a delicious searing but, better still, his hands did not leave her. Her bedroom was like a sauna and the sheen on her body had her a little slippery but his hands gripped her and did not relent, for she would match his needs.

It had her feeling dizzy—the sensation of being on top while being taken. Louise rested her arms on his shoulders as he pulled her down over and over, and then his mouth lost contact with her breast as he swelled that final time. Her hands went to his head and she ground down, coming with him, squealing in pleasure as they hit a giddy peak. They shared a decadent, wet kiss as he shot inside her, a kiss of possession as she pulsed around his length and her head collapsed onto his shoulder.

Louise kissed his salty shoulder as her breathing finally slowed down.

She could feel him soften inside her and she lifted her head and smiled into his eyes.

'Ready for bed?'

CHAPTER TEN

AFTER ONE HOUR and about seven minutes of sleep they woke to Louise's phone at six.

'I thought you were off today,' Anton groaned.

'I am, but I'm going Christmas shopping.'

'At six a.m.?'

'I want to get a book signed for Mum so I have to line up,' Louise said. 'Stay,' she said, kissing his mouth .'Get up when you're ready, or you can come shopping with me.'

'I'll give it a miss, thanks.'

'Have you done your Christmas shopping?'

'I'll do it online. The shops will be crazy.'

'That's half the fun.' She gave him a nudge. 'Come on.'

She went into the shower and Anton lay there, looking up at the ceiling. He had a couple of things to get. Something for the nurses and his secretary and, yes, he might just as well get it over and done with.

'We'll stop by my place and I can get changed,' Anton said, as she came out of the shower.

'Sure.' Naked, she smiled down at him and lifted her hair. 'Check me for bruises,' she said, while craning her neck and looking down at her buttocks where his fingers had dug in, but, no, they were peachy cream too.

'No need to check,' Anton said, for he had been careful, knowing that she had her photo shoot coming up.

Neither could wait till it was over!

Louise dressed while Anton showered. She pulled on jeans and boots and a massive cream jumper and then she tied up her hair and added a coat.

Anton put on the clothes he had worn last night, though they were stopping by his place so he could get changed.

'Ready to do battle?' she asked, thrilled that Anton had agreed to come along with her. She was determined to Christmas him up, especially when they arrived at his apartment.

'You really are a misery,' Louise said, stepping in. She didn't care about the view or the gorgeous furnishings in his apartment—what she cared about was that there wasn't a single decoration. There were a few Christmas cards stacked with his mail on the kitchen bench but, apart from that, it might just as well have been October, instead of just over a week before Christmas.

'Aren't you even going to get a tree?' Louise asked.

'No.'

'Don't you have Christmas trees in Italy?'

'Some,' Anton said, 'but we go more for nativity scenes and lights.'

'You have to do something.'

'I'm hardly ever here, Louise,' Anton said.

'It's not the point. When you come home—'

'I don't like Christmas,' Anton said, but then amended, 'Although I am starting to really enjoy this one.'

'What do you have to get today?'

'I need to get something for my secretary,' Anton said.

'Perfume?'

'Maybe,' Louise said. 'What sort of things does she like?'

Anton spread out his hands—he really had no idea what Shirley liked.

'What sort of things does she talk about?'

'My diary.'

'God, you're so antisocial,' Louise said.

'Oh, she likes cooking,' Anton recalled. 'She's always bringing in things that she's made.'

'Then I have the perfect present,' Louise said, 'because I'm getting it for my mum. That's what we're going to line up for.'

It wasn't just a book. The first twenty people had the option to purchase a morning's cooking lesson with a celebrity chef. It was fabulous and expensive and with it all going to charity it was well worth it.

Celebrating their success at getting the signed books and cookery lessons, at ten a.m., having coffee and cake in an already crowded department store, they chatted.

'If your mother can't cook, why would you spend all that money? Surely it will be wasted?'

'Oh, no.' Louise shook her head. 'If she learns even one thing and gets it right, my dad will be grateful for ever—the poor thing,' she added. 'He has to eat it night after night after night. I usually wriggle out of it when I go and visit. I'll go over tomorrow and say I've just eaten, but you can't do that on Christmas Day.'

'How bad is it?'

'It's terrible. I don't know how she does it. It always looks okay and she thinks it tastes amazing but I swear it's like she's put it in a blender with water added, burnt it and then put it back together to look like a dinner again...' She took out her list. 'Come on, off we go.'

Louise was a brilliant shopper, not that Anton easily fathomed her methods.

'I adore this colour,' Louise said, trying lipstick on the back of her hand. 'Oh, but this one is even better.'

'I thought we were here for your sisters.'

'Oh, they're so easy to buy for,' Louise said. 'Anything I love they want to pinch, so anything I love I know they'll like.'

Make-up, perfume, a pair of boots... 'I'm the same size as Chloe,' she explained, as she tried them on. 'It's so good you're here, I'd have had to make two trips otherwise.'

Bag after bag was loaded with gifts. 'I want to go here,' Louise said, and they got off the escalator at the baby section. 'I'm going to get something for Emily and Hugh's baby,' Louise said. 'Hopefully it will be a waste of money and I can give it to NICU.' She looked at Anton. 'Do you think she'll get to Christmas?'

'I hope so,' Anton said. 'I'm aiming for thirty-three weeks.'

Louise heard the unvoiced *but* and for now chose to ignore it.

They went to the premature baby section and found some tiny outfits and there was one perk to being the obstetrician and midwife shopping for a pregnant friend, they knew what colour to get! Louise said yes to gift-wrapping and they waited as it was beautifully wrapped and then topped with a bow.

'I'll keep it in my locker at work,' Louise said.

It was a lovely, lovely, lovely day of shopping, punctuated with kisses. Neither cared about the grumbles they caused as they blocked the pavement or the escalators when they simply had to kiss the other and by the end Louise was seriously, happily worn out.

'You want to get dinner?' Anton offered.

'Take-out?' Louise suggested. 'But we'll have it at my place. I'm not going to your miserable apartment.'

'I have to go back,' Anton said. 'I have to do an hour's work at least.'

'Fine,' Louise conceded, 'but we'll drop these back at my place first and I'll get some clothes.'

'You won't need them,' Anton said, but Louise was insistent.

All her presents she put in the bedroom. 'I can't wait to wrap them,' Louise said. 'I'll just grab a change of clothes and things, you go and make a drink.'

Louise grabbed more than a change of clothes. In fact, she went into her wardrobe and pulled out some leftover Christmas decorations and stuffed them all into a not so small overnight bag. She also took the tiny silver tree that she'd been meaning to put up at the nurses' station but kept forgetting to take.

'How long are you staying for?' Anton asked, when she came out and he saw the size of her overnight bag.

'Till you kick me out.' Louise gave him a kiss. 'I like to be prepared.'

Anton really did have work to do.

A couple of blood tests were in and he went through them, and there was a patient at thirteen weeks' gestation who was bleeding. Anton went into his study and rang her to check how things were.

Louise could hear him safely talking and quickly set to work.

The little tree she put on his coffee table and she draped some tinsel on the window ledges and put up some stars, a touch worried she might leave some marks on his walls but he'd just have to get over it, Louise decided.

She took out her can and sprayed snow on his gleaming windows, and oh, it looked lovely.

'What the hell have you done?' Anton said, as he came into the lounge, but he was smiling.

'I need nice things around me,' Louise said, 'happy things.'

'It would seem,' Anton said, looking not at her handiwork now but the woman in his arms, 'that so do I.'

CHAPTER ELEVEN

'WHAT HAPPENED LAST Christmas?' Anton asked, late, late on Sunday night. They'd started on the sofa and had watched half a movie and now they lay naked on the floor bathed by the light from the television. 'You said it was tinsel-starved.'

She really would prefer not to talk about it. They had had such a lovely weekend but there were so many parts of so many conversations that they were avoiding, like IVF and Anton's loathing of Christmas, that when he finally broached one of them, Louise answered carefully. There was no way she could tell him all but she told him some.

'I broke up with my boyfriend on Christmas Eve.'

'You said it was tinsel-starved before then, that you didn't go to many parties.'

'It wasn't worth it.'

'In what way?'

'I know you think I'm a flirt...'

'I like that about you.'

'But I'm only really like that with you,' Louise said. 'I mean that. I used to be a shocking flirt and then when I started going out with Wesley...well, I got told off a lot.'

'For flirting with other men?'

'No!' Louise said, shuddering at the memory. 'He decided that if I flirted like that with him, then what was I like when he wasn't there? I don't want to go into it all, but I changed and I hate myself for it. I changed into this one eighth of a person and somehow I got out—on Christmas Eve last year. It took months, just months to even start feeling like myself again.'

'Okay.'

'Do you know the day I did?' Louise asked, smiling as she turned to face him.

'No.'

'We were going to Emily's leaving do and I saw you in the corridor and I asked you to come along...'

'You were wearing red,' Anton easily recalled. 'You were with Emily.'

'That's right, it was for her leaving do. Well, even when I asked if you wanted to come along, I deep down knew that you wouldn't. I was just...' She couldn't really explain. 'I was just flirting again...sort of safe in the knowledge that it wouldn't go anywhere.'

'But it has,' Anton said.

'I guess.' Louise smiled. 'Have you ever been married?' Louise asked.

'Why do you ask?'

'I just wondered.'

'No,' Anton said. 'Have you?'

'God, no,' Louise said.

'Have you ever come close?'

'No,' Louise admitted.

'You and Rory?'

Louise laughed and shook her head. 'We were only together a few weeks. Just when we started going out I found that it was likely that I was going to have issues getting pregnant. It was terrible timing because it was all I could think about. Poor Rory, he started going out with a happy person and when the doctor broke the news I just plunged into despair. It wasn't his baby I wanted, just the thought I might never have one. It was just all too much for him...' She looked at Anton. 'I think I was just low at that time and that's why I must have taken my bastard alert glasses off. I've made a few poor choices with men since then.' She closed her eyes. 'None worse than Wesley, though.'

'How bad did it get?' Anton asked, but Louise couldn't go there and she shook her head.

'What about you?' Louise asked. 'Have you been serious with anyone?'

'Not really, well, there was one who came close...' It was Anton who stopped talking then.

Anton who shook his head.

He simply couldn't go there with someone who might just want him for a matter of weeks.

CHAPTER TWELVE

'CAN YOU KEEP a close eye on Felicity in seven?' Anton asked. 'She's upset because her husband has been unable to get a flight back till later this evening.'

Felicity was one of Anton's high-risk pregnancies and finally the day had arrived where she would meet her baby, but her husband was in Germany with work.

'How is she doing?' Louise asked.

'Very slowly,' Anton said. 'Hopefully he'll get here in time.' He picked up a parcel, beautifully wrapped by Louise. 'I'm going to give this to Shirley now. She's only in this morning to sort out my diary before she takes three weeks off. Then I will be in the antenatal clinic. Call me if you have any concerns.'

'Yes, Anton,' Louise sighed.

Anton heard her sigh but it did not bother him.

Things were not going to change at work. In fact, he was more overbearing if anything, just because he didn't want a mistake to come between them.

'This is for you,' Anton said, as he went into Shirley's office. 'I just wanted to thank you for all your hard work this year and to say merry Christmas.'

'Thank you, Anton.' Shirley smiled.

'I hope you have a lovely break.'

He went to go, even as she opened it, but her cry of surprise had him turn around.

'How?'

Anton stared. His usually calm secretary was shaking as she spoke.

'How did you manage to get this—there were only twenty places.'

'I got there early.'

'You lined up to get me this! Oh, my...'

Anton felt a little guilt at her obvious delight. It really had been far from a hardship to be huddled in a queue with Louise, but it was Shirley's utter shock too that caused more than a little disquiet.

'I never thought...' Shirley started and then stopped. She could hardly say she'd been expecting some bland present from her miserable boss. 'It's wonderful,' she said instead.

God, Anton thought, was he that bad that a simple nice gesture could reduce a staff member to tears?

Yes.

He nodded to Helen, the antenatal nurse who would be working alongside him, and he saw that she gave a slightly strained one back.

Things had to change, Anton realised.

He had to learn to let go a little.

But how?

'How are things?' Louise asked, as she walked into Felicity's room with the CTG machine.

'They're just uncomfortable,' Felicity said. She was determined to have a natural birth and had refused an epidural or anything for pain. 'I'm going to try and have a sleep.'

'Do,' Louise said. 'Do you want me to close the curtains?'

Felicity nodded.

Brenda popped her head in the door. 'Are you going to lunch, Louise?'

'In a minute,' Louise said. 'I'm just doing some obs.' Both Felicity and the baby seemed fine. 'I'll leave this on while I have my lunch,' Louise said about the CTG machine, and Felicity nodded. 'Then later we might have a little walk around, but for now just try and get some rest.'

She closed the curtains and moved a blanket over Felicity, who was half-asleep, and left her to the sound of her baby's heartbeat. Louise would check the tracing when she came back from her break and see the pattern of the contractions.

'Press the bell if you need anything and I'll be here.'

'But you're going to lunch.'

'Yep, but that buzzer is set for me, so just you press it if you need to.'

'Thanks, Louise,' Felicity said. 'What time are you here till?'

Louise thought before answering. 'I'm not sure.'

Louise left the door just a little open so that her colleagues could easily pop in and out and could hear the CTG, then headed to the fridge and got out her lunch.

'Fancy company?' Louise asked Emily as she knocked on her open door.

'Oh, yes!' Emily sat up in the bed. 'How was the party?'

'Excellent.'

'Why didn't you text me all weekend?'

'I did!' Louise said.

'Five-thirty on a Sunday evening suggests to me you were otherwise engaged.'

'I was busy,' Louise said, 'Christmas shopping!'

'You lie,' Emily said.

'Actually, I need to charge my phone,' Louise said, because she hadn't been back home since being at Anton's. 'Can I borrow your charger?'

'Sure.' Emily smiled. 'That's not like you.'

Louise said nothing. She certainly wasn't going to admit to Emily her three-night fest with Anton. As she plugged in her phone and sat down, the background noise of Felicity's baby's heartbeat slowed. Louise was so tuned into that noise, as all midwives were, and she didn't like what she had just heard.

'Are you okay?' Emily asked.

'I think I've got restless leg syndrome.' Louise gave a light response. 'I'm just going to check on someone and then I'll be back.'

She went quietly into Felicity's room. Felicity was dozing and Louise warmed her hand and then slipped it on Felicity's stomach, watching the monitor and patiently waiting for a contraction to come.

'It's just me,' Louise whispered, as Felicity woke up as a contraction deepened and Emily watched as the baby's heart rate dipped. She checked Felicity's pulse to make sure the slower heart rate that the monitor was picking up wasn't Felicity's.

'Turn onto your other side for me,' Louise said to the sleepy woman, and helped Felicity to get on her left side and looked up as Brenda, alerted by the sound of the dip in the baby's heart rate, looked in.

'Page Anton,' Louise said.

Even on her left side the baby's heart rate was dipping during contractions and Louise put some oxygen on Felicity. 'We'll move her over to Delivery,' Brenda said.

'Have you heard from Anton?'

'I've paged him but he hasn't answered,' Brenda said. 'I'll see if he's in the staffroom.'

Louise raced around to check but Anton wasn't there.

She paged him again and then they moved Felicity through to the delivery ward. They were about to move her onto the delivery bed but Louise decided to wait for Anton before doing that as she listened to the baby's heart rate. The way this baby was behaving, they might be running to Theatre any time soon.

She typed in an urgent page for Anton but when there was still no response Louise remembered her phone was in Emily's room. 'Text him,' Louise said to Brenda, and, ripping off a tracing, Louise left Felicity with Brenda and swiftly went to a phone out of earshot.

'Are the pagers working?' she asked the switchboard operator. 'I need Anton Rossi paged and, in case he's busy, I need the second on paged too, urgently.'

She then rang Theatre and, because she had worked there for more than five years, when she rang and explained they might need a theatre very soon, she knew she was being taken seriously and that they would immediately be setting up for a Caesarean.

'I can't get hold of Anton,' Louise said, but then she saw him, his phone in hand, racing towards them. 'Anton! Felicity's having late decelerations. Foetal heart rate is dropping to sixty.'

'How long has this been going on?'

'About fifteen minutes.'

'And you didn't think to tell me sooner! Hell! If Brenda hadn't texted me...' Anton hissed, taking the tracing and looking at it in horror, because time was of the essence. With pretty much one look at the tracing the decision to operate was made. For Anton it was a done deal.

It was like some horrific replay of what had happened two years ago.

'I paged you when it first happened,' Louise said, but there wasn't time for explanations now. As Anton went into the delivery room the overhead speakers crackled into life.

'System error. Professor Hadfield, can you make your way straight to Emergency? Mr Rossi, Delivery Ward, room two.'

Anton briefly closed his eyes.

'Mr Rossi, urgently make your way to Delivery, room two. System error—pagers are down.'

And so it repeated.

'Is that for me?' Felicity cried, terrified by the urgency of the calls overhead.

'Hey…' Louise gave Felicity a cuddle as Anton examined her. 'It's just that the pagers are down and so I had to use my whip a bit on Switchboard to get Anton here.'

'Felicity.' Anton came up to the head-end of the bed. 'Your baby is struggling…' Everything had been done. She was on her side, oxygen was on and she was still on the bed so they could simply speed her to Theatre. 'We're going to take you to Theatre now and do a Caesarean section.'

'Can I be awake at least?'

'We really do need to get your baby out now.'

'I'll be there with you,' Louise said, as the porter arrived. 'I am not leaving your side, I promise you. I can take some pictures of your baby if you like,' Louise offered, and Felicity gave her her phone.

'Can you let Theatre know?' Anton said, before he raced ahead to scrub.

It took everything she could muster to keep the bitterness from her voice. 'I already have, Anton.'

Louise and the porter whisked the bed down the corridor. There was no consent form to be signed—that had been taken care of at the antenatal stage.

'I'm so scared,' Felicity said, as they wheeled her into Theatre.

'I know,' Louise said, cleaning down her shoes and popping on shoe covers, then she put on a theatre hat and gown. 'You've got the best obstetrician,' Louise said. 'I've seen him do many Caesareans and he's brilliant.'

'I know.'

The bed was wheeled through and Louise's old colleagues were waiting. Connor and Miriam helped Louise to get Felicity onto the theatre table and she smiled when she saw Rory arrive. He was a bit breathless and as he caught his breath Louise spoke on. 'You've got an amazing anaesthetist too. Hi, Rory, this is Felicity.'

Rory was lovely with Felicity and went through any allergies and previous anaesthetics and things. 'I'm going to be by your side every minute,' he said to Felicity. 'Till you're awake again, here is where I'll be.'

'I'll be here too,' Louise said.

Theatre was filling. The paediatric team was arriving as Rory slipped the first drug into Felicity's IV.

'Think baby thoughts,' Louise said with a smile as Felicity went under.

Louise was completely supernumerary at this point. She was simply here on love watch for one of her mums. And so, once Felicity had been intubated, Louise simply closed her mind to everything, even bastard Anton. She just sat on a stool and thought lovely baby thoughts.

She heard the swirl of suction and a few curses from Anton as he tried to get one very flat baby out as quickly as possible.

Then there was silence and she looked up as a rather floppy baby was whisked away and she kept thinking baby thoughts as they rubbed it very vigorously and flicked at its little feet. She glanced at Rory as another anaesthetist started to bag him.

But then Rory smiled and Louise looked round and watched as the baby shuddered and she watched as his little legs started to kick and his hands started to fight. His cries of protest were muffled by the oxygen mask but were the most beautiful sounds in the world.

Louise didn't look at Anton, she just told Felicity that her baby was beautiful, wonderful, that he was crying and could she hear him, even though Felicity was still under anaesthetic.

Anton did look at Louise.

She did that, Anton thought.

She made all his patients relax and laugh, and though Felicity could not know what was being said, still Louise said it.

He could have honestly kicked himself for his reaction but, God, it had been almost a replica of what had happened back in Italy.

'He's beautiful,' Louise said over and over.

So too was Louise, Anton thought, knowing he'd just blown any chance for them.

Louise *was* beautiful, even when she was raging.

Not an hour later she marched into the male changing room and slammed the door shut.

'Hey, Louise,' called Rory, who was just getting changed. 'You're in the wrong room.'

'Oh, I'm in the right room,' Louise said. 'Could you excuse us, Rory, please?'

'We will do this in my office,' Anton said. Wet from the shower, a towel around his loins, he did not want to do this now, but Louise had no intention of waiting till he got dressed. She was far, far beyond furious.

'Oh, no, this won't keep.'

'Good luck,' Rory called to Anton as he left them to it.

And then it was just Louise and Anton but even as he went to apologise for what had happened earlier, or to even explain, Louise got in first.

'You can question my morals, you can think what you like about me, but don't you ever, ever—'

'Question your morals?' Anton checked. 'Where the hell did that come from?'

'Don't interrupt me,' Louise raged. 'I've had it with you. What you accused me of today—'

'Louise.'

'No!' She would not hear it.

'I apologise. I did not realise the pagers were down.'

'I did,' Louise said instantly. 'When you didn't come, or make contact, it was the first thing I thought—not that you were negligent and simply couldn't be bothered to get here…'

Her lips were white she was so angry. 'I'm going to speak to Brenda and put in an incident report about the pagers today, and while I'm there I'm going to tell her I don't want to work with you any more.'

'That's a bit extreme.'

'It's isn't extreme. I've thought about doing it before.' She saw him blink in surprise. 'Everything I do you check again—'

'Louise…' Anton wasn't about to deny it. He checked on her more than the other midwives, he was aware of that. In trying to protect her, to protect *them*, from what had happened to him and Dahnya, he had gone over the top. 'If I can explain—'

But Louise was beyond hearing him. She lost her temper then and Louise hadn't lost her temper since that terrible day. 'You don't want a midwife,' Louise shouted, 'you want a doula, rubbing the mums' backs and offering support. Well, I'm over it, Anton. Have you any idea how demoralising it is?' she raged, though possibly she was talking more to Wesley than Anton. 'Have you any idea how humiliating it is…?'

Anton took a step forward, to speak, to calm her down, and then stood frozen as he heard the fear in her voice.

'Get off me!' She put her hands up in defence and there was a shocked moment of silence when she realised what she had said, what she had done, but then came his calm voice.

'I'm not touching you, Louise.'

She pressed her hands to her face and her fingers to her eyes. 'I'm sorry,' Louise said, 'not for what I said before but—'

'It's okay.' Anton was breathless too, as if her unleashed fear had somehow attached to him. 'We'll talk when you've calmed down.'

'No.' Louise shook her head, embarrassed at her outburst but still cross. 'We won't talk because I don't want to hear it, Anton.' And then turned and left.

She was done.

CHAPTER THIRTEEN

'WHAT HAPPENED?' EMILY asked, when Louise returned a couple of hours later to the ward.

'Sorry, I just got waylaid.'

'Louise?'

'I'm fine.'

'You've been crying.'

'There's nothing wrong.'

'Louise?' Emily frowned when she saw Louise's smile was wavering as she took Emily's blood pressure. 'What's going on? Look, I'm bored out of my mind. I mean, I am so seriously bored and I'm fed up with people thinking I can't have a normal conversation, or that they only tell me nice things.' Emily was truly concerned because she hadn't seen red eyes on Louise in a very long time. 'Wesley isn't contacting you again?'

'No, no.' Louise sat down on the bed, even though Brenda might tell her off.

'Tell me.' Emily took her hand.

'Anton.' Louise gulped. Certainly she wasn't going to scare Emily and tell her all that had gone on with Felicity's baby but they really were speaking as friends.

'Okay.'

'Personal or professional?'

'Both,' Louise admitted. 'He checks and double-checks everything, you know what he's like…'

'I do,' Emily said.

'It's like he doesn't trust any of the staff but he does it more with me.'

'Louise.' Emily didn't know whether she should say anything but it was pretty much common knowledge what had happened a few months ago. 'Remember when Gina had her meltdown and went into rehab?'

'Yep, I know, Hugh reported her…' Louise looked at Emily, remembering that there had been more than one complaint, or so the rumours went. 'Did Anton report her as well?'

'I'm saying nothing.'

'Okay.' Louise squeezed her hand in gratitude as Emily spoke on.

'So maybe he feels he has reason to be checking things.'

'Hugh doesn't, though,' Louise pointed out. 'Hugh isn't constantly looking over the nursing staff's shoulders and assuming the worst.'

'I know.' Emily sighed. She adored Anton but had noticed that he was dismissive of the nurses' findings and she could well understand that things might have come to a head. 'So, what's the personal stuff?'

'Do you really need to know that your obstetrician got off with your midwife?'

'Ooh.' Emily gave a delighted smile. 'I think I did really need to know that.'

'Well, it won't be happening again,' Louise said. 'We just had the most terrible row, or rather I did…'

'And what did Anton do?' Emily gently enquired.

'He apologised,' Louise said, and then she frowned

because she wasn't very used to a guy backing down. For too long it had been the other way around. 'Emily...' Louise's eyes filled with tears. 'I shouted for him to get off me and the poor guy was just standing there.'

'Oh, Louise...' Emily rubbed Louise's shoulder. 'It must have been terrifying for you to have a big row. Rows are normal, though. What happened to you wasn't.'

'I know.' Louise blew her nose and recovered herself and gave Emily a smile. 'I really let rip.' Louise let out a small shocked laugh.

'She really did!' Anton was at the door and came over to the bed. 'Your latest ultrasound is back. All looks well, there is a nice amount of fluid.' He had a feel of Emily's stomach.

'Nice size,' Anton said.

'Really?'

'Really.' Anton nodded. 'Now is the time they start to plump up and your baby certainly is.'

They headed out of Emily's room and he turned to Louise. 'What is her blood pressure?'

'Ha-ha,' Louise said. 'Check it yourself.'

Anton gave a wry smile as Louise flounced off but it faded when he saw she went straight up to Brenda.

Louise hadn't been lying when she had said she didn't know when she'd be going home.

Something, something had told her she'd be around for the delivery, which meant she wanted to be around when Felicity was more properly awake, and at four she sat holding a big fat baby who had given everyone a horrible scare.

'Your husband just called and he's at Heathrow and is on his way,' Louise said. 'And your mum is on her way too.' Felicity smiled. 'And you have the cutest, most gorgeous baby. In fact, he's so cute I don't think I can hand him over...'

Felicity smiled as Louise did just that and placed the baby in her arms.

'He's gorgeous.'

'I was so scared.'

'I know you were but, honestly, he gave us a fright but he's fine.' She stared at the baby, who was gnawing at his wrist. 'He's beautiful and he's also starving,' Louise said.

'Can I feed him?'

'You can,' Louise said, 'because he's trying to find mine and I've told him I've got nothing...' She looked up as Anton came in and then got back to work, helping a very hungry baby latch on.

'Louise, can I have a word before you leave?' Anton asked.

Louise's response was a casual 'Sure', but Anton knew that was for the sake of the patient.

'Felicity,' Anton said. 'Your mother has just arrived...'

'Do you want me to tell her to wait while you feed?' Louise checked, but Felicity shook her head.

'No, let her in.'

Louise stayed for the first feed. She just loved that part and then when finally the baby was fed and content and in his little isolette she gave Felicity a cuddle. 'I'll come by tomorrow and we'll talk more about what happened today, if you want to. I took some photos with your phone, if you want to have a look through them with me.'

'Thank you.'

She popped in to see Emily on her way out, as she always did, but she was just about all smiled out. She just wanted to go home for a good cry, a glass of wine and then bed.

She didn't even pretend to smile when she knocked on Anton's office door and went in.

'Can we talk?'

Louise shook her head. 'I don't want to talk to you, Anton,' Louise said. 'I'm tired. I just want to go home.'

'Louise, what happened today was not about you. I had an incident in Milan...'

'I don't want to hear it, Anton,' Louise said, and then relented. 'Imelda's, then,' Louise said. 'I'm just going to get changed.'

'Sure.'

'I'll meet you over there.'

There was Anton with his sparkling water but there was a glass of wine and some nachos waiting for Louise. Really, she shouldn't because she had the bloody photo shoot in less than a week but Louise shovelled them in her mouth, getting hungrier with each mouthful.

'Do you want to get something else?'

'These are fine,' Louise said, and then looked at him. 'Well?'

'I am so very sorry for today. You did everything right, from ringing Theatre to keeping her on the bed. She was very lucky to have you on duty and I apologise for jumping to the worst conclusion.'

Louise gave a tight shrug. It wasn't just today she was upset about. 'What about the other days?' she challenged. 'I don't think you trust me.'

'No.' Anton shook his head. 'That is not the case.'

'It's very much the case,' Louise said. 'Everything I do you double-check, or you simply dismiss my findings...

Aside from the repeated wallops to my ego, it's surely doubling up for the patient.' Louise let out a breath. 'So what happened in Milan?'

'A few years ago, on Christmas morning, I took a handover, and I was told everything was fine, but by lunchtime I had a baby dead—' Louise was about to say something but Anton spoke over her. 'It *was* the hospital's fault,' Anton said. 'Apparently the night midwife had told a junior doctor she had concerns; I took the handover from the registrar and those concerns hadn't been passed on to her. It was just complete miscommunication. I went in to see my patient at ten, and there were many things that I should have been paged about but hadn't been. I took her straight to Theatre and delivered the baby but he only lived for a couple of hours.

'The coroner did not blame me, thank God, but I have never seen friendships fall so rapidly. There was blame, accusations, it was hell. So much so that when the finding came in I no longer trusted anyone I worked with, and I knew I had to make a fresh start, which was why I moved into fertility.'

'But you came back.'

'Yes, I never thought I would but the last months I was there, the parents of Alberto, the baby who had died, came in to try for another baby. It was a shock to us all. I offered to step aside but by then I had quite a good reputation and they asked that I remain. I was very happy when they got pregnant and it was then that I realised how much I had missed obstetrics. I knew I needed a fresh start so I applied to come here. I had always had a good rapport with colleagues until Alberto's death. I wanted to get that back and I tried, but within a few weeks of being here there was an incident...' He looked at Louise and she was glad that Emily had filled her in about Gina because Anton didn't. 'I'm not giving specifics but it shook me and from that point I have been cautious…'

'To the extreme,' Louise said.

'Yes.'

'Terrible things happen, Anton. Terrible, terrible things…'

'I know that. I just wish I had not taken a handover that morning and had checked myself…'

'You can't check everyone, you can't follow everyone around.'

'I'm aware of that.'

'Yet you do.'

'I've spoken to Brenda and I have told her what went on, not just today but in the past. I also told her that I am hoping things will be different in the future.'

'Did you get her "There's no I in team" lecture?' Louise asked, and Anton smiled and nodded.

'I've had it a few times from Brenda already and, yes, I got it again today.'

'Well, I disagree with her,' Louise said. 'There should be an I in team. I am responsible, I am capable, I know I've got this, and if I stuff up then I take responsibility. If we all do that, which we seem to do where I work, then teams do well. We look out for each other,' Louise said. 'We have a buddy system. I don't just glance at CTGs when they're given to me and neither do my colleagues. We take ages discussing them, going over them…'

'I know that.'

'It doesn't feel like it,' Louise said.

'I am hoping things will be different now.'

'Good,' Louise said. 'Is that it?'

'No, I want to know what you meant about me judging you on your morals.'

'This isn't a social get-together, Anton. I'm here to talk about work.'

'Louise.'

'Okay, just because I'm not on a husband hunt, just because I fancied you...'

'Past tense?'

'Oh, it is so past tense,' Louise said. 'So very past tense.'

'Louise,' Anton said, and she must have heard the tentative tone to his voice because immediately her eyes darted away, even before his question was voiced. 'What happened that made you so scared back there?'

'That isn't about work either.' She got up and hoisted up her bag. 'I'm sorry you went through crap and I'm so sorry for the baby and its family.'

'Louise.' He halted her as she went to go. 'The midwife on that morning, I was going out with her. She was busy, meant to go back and check, meant to call, but got waylaid. Can you see why I was very reluctant to get involved with you?'

'I can.' She stood there but didn't give him the answer he was hoping for. 'Well, at least you don't have that problem with me now—we're no longer involved.' She gave him a tight smile. 'Goodnight, Anton.'

Louise got home, closed the door and promptly burst into tears. Despite her tough talk with Anton she could think of nothing worse than losing a baby under those circumstances and at Christmas too.

Then she went into the bath and cried some more. She'd been raging at him and he'd simply stood there.

She was beyond confused and all churned up from her loss of control.

Why couldn't it just be sex? Louise thought. Why did she have to really, really like him?

As she got out of the bath her phone bleeped a text from Emily.

U OK?

Louise gave a rapid reply.

Bloody men! How's baby?

Kick-kicking, or maybe he's waving to you.

Louise sent back a smiley face, knowing what was to come.

Maybe SHE'S waving???? Emily texted, hoping that Louise would give her a clue.

Not telling, came Louise's reply. Ask Hugh.

He won't tell me, Emily replied. Bloody men!

CHAPTER FOURTEEN

ANTON REALLY DID make an effort at work, though Louise wasn't sure if it was temporary. At least he had stopped double-checking everything that she did. Brenda had a word with some of the staff, as Anton had asked her to do. They in turn rang him a little sooner than usual with concerns, and slowly the I in team was working, except Louise was no longer a part of his team.

'Phone for you, Louise,' someone called, and Louise headed out to the desk. It was the IVF clinic, which had been unable to reach her on her mobile or at home, and Louise took out her phone and saw that the battery was flat.

'Are you okay to talk, or do you want to call us back?'

'No, now's fine,' Louise said.

'Richard wanted to let you know that your iron levels are now normal but to keep taking the supplements, especially the folic acid.'

'I shall. Thank you,' Louise said.

'Have a lovely Christmas and we'll see you in the new year.'

Louise's stomach was all aflutter as she ended the call.

'Good news?' Brenda asked, but Louise didn't answer. Her *lovely Christmas* was walking past and this time when he sat down and ignored her it was at Louise's request.

Of course, she still dealt with his patients—after all, Emily was one of them—but the distance she had asked for was there. As far as was reasonable she was allocated other patients and when they spoke it was only about work.

'Can you buddy this?' Beth asked, and Louise nodded and sat down. 'What are you working over Christmas?' Beth asked.

'Tomorrow's my last shift,' Louise said, 'and then I'm off till after New Year.'

'Lucky you!'

'I know.' Louise smiled. 'I can't wait.'

She lied.

They looked at the CTG together and Anton could hear them discussing it, Louise asking a couple of questions before they both signed off on it.

What a mistrusting fool he had been.

He had never worked anywhere better than here. The diligence, the care, was second to none but he'd realised it all too late.

'Do you need anything, Anton?' Beth asked, as Anton signed off on a few prescriptions and then stood.

'Nope, I'm heading home. Goodnight, everyone.'

When Anton stepped into his apartment a little later he felt like ripping the bloody tinsel down, yet he left it.

Louise had been in his apartment for three nights in total yet she was everywhere.

From lipstick on the towels and sheets to long blonde hairs in his comb.

Even the bed smelt of her perfume and Anton woke to his phone buzzing at three-thirty a.m. and, for a second, so consuming was her scent he actually thought she was in bed beside him.

Instead, it was the ward with news about Emily.

'I'm so sorry...' Emily said, as Anton came into the room at four a.m.

'No apologies,' Anton said, taking off his jacket, and then smiled at Evie, who had set up for Anton to examine Emily.

'I thought I'd wet myself,' Emily said. 'Maybe I did...'

'It is amniotic fluid,' Anton said, taking a swab. 'Your waters are leaking. We will get this swab checked for any signs of infection and keep a close eye on your temperature.'

'How long can I go with a leak?'

'Variable. Do you have any discomfort?'

'My back aches,' Emily said, 'but I'm not sure if that's from being in bed...'

'Have you told Hugh?'

'Not yet,' Emily said. 'He was paged at midnight and he's in Theatre. He'll find out soon enough.'

When Louise came on for her shift she saw Anton sitting at the desk and duly ignored him. She headed around to the kitchen and made herself a cup of tea, trying to ignore the scent and feel of him when he walked into the kitchen behind her.

'Emily's waters are leaking,' Anton said. 'I just thought I'd tell you now, rather than you hear it during handover.'

Louise turned round.

'I've ordered an ultrasound to check the amniotic levels and she is on antibiotics...'

'But?'

'Her back is hurting again. There are no contractions but her uterus is irritable.'

'She's going to have it.'

'You don't know that's the case…'

'I do know that this baby is coming soon,' Louise said, and Anton nodded.

'I don't think she'll hold off for much longer.'

Louise felt her eyes fill up when Anton spoke on.

'I miss working with you, Louise.'

Louise didn't say anything.

'I miss *you*,' Anton said.

She looked at him and, yes, she missed him too.

'Can we start again?' Anton said.

'I don't know.'

'Louise, you seem to have it in your head that I'm controlling. I get that I have been at work, I still will be…' He looked at her. 'Do you know why I've been on water at all the parties over Christmas? It's because I have Hazel who is due to deliver soon and I believe Emily will have that baby any day. I want to be there for them both. Yes, I am fully in control at work, and I get you have seen me at my worst here, but you know why now.'

Louise breathed out and looked at him, the most diligent person she knew, and then he continued speaking.

'You explained you are dieting because you have a photo shoot, that you know what you're doing with your weight, and not once since then have I said anything. I was worried about you because my sister has been there but when you said you knew what you were doing, I accepted that.'

He had.

'My ex…' she didn't want to say it here but it was time to tell him a little, if not all. 'He was so jealous, he didn't get that I could be friends with Rory. He didn't even like Emily…'

'And…?' Anton pushed, but Louise shook her head so he pushed on as best he could, but he was a non-witness after the fact and Louise kept him so.

'I would never come between you and your friends.'

'You weren't exactly friendly towards Rory on the night of the theatre do—you were giving him filthy looks.'

'Oh, that's right,' Anton said. 'And you were so sweet to *Saffron*. I was jealous when I thought you were on together, just as you were with me.'

Louise swallowed, she knew he was right.

'I like your friends. I like it that you can be friendly with an ex. And you can flirt, you can be funny, and I have no issue with it, but what I will not do is go along with the notion that I like you going for IVF so early in our relationship.'

Louise turned to go.

'Wrong word for you, Louise?'

It was.

'I need to think, Anton,' Louise said, and possibly the nicest thing he did then was not to argue his case or demand that they speak. He simply nodded.

'Of course.'

Louise took handover and she was allocated Stephanie's patients, all except for Emily, who was asleep when she went in to her.

'Just rest,' Louise said. 'I'm only doing your blood pressure.'

'When are you going for lunch?' Emily asked sleepily.

'About twelve. Do you want me to have it here with you?'

Emily nodded. 'Unless you need a break from the patients.'

'Don't be daft—of course I'd love to have lunch with you.'

When lunchtime came Louise went and got her salad from the fridge and it was so nice to close the door and sit down with her friend.

'It's going to be strange, not having you around,' Emily admitted.

'I'll be visiting, texting…'

'I know,' Emily said, 'it just won't be the same. Are you excited about your photo shoot tomorrow?'

'I am, though you're to promise you'll text me if anything happens.' Louise went into her pocket and handed Emily a business card. 'This is the hotel I'm at, just in case there's nowhere to put my phone!'

'Louise, you are not leaving your photo shoot,' Emily said, handing her back the card.

'But I want to be here if anything happens.'

'I know you do and I'd love you to be here, but I've got Hugh.'

Louise took back the card and stared at it.

Emily had Hugh.

Yes, Louise could do this alone and she would, but for a moment there she reconsidered. Hugh had been here every day, making Emily laugh, letting her relax, an endless stream of support.

It would be so hard to do this alone.

Louise cleared her throat. She didn't like where her mind was heading. 'Well, if you can hold off tomorrow,

Christmas Day would be fine.' Louise gave her friend a wide smile as she teased her. 'At least that would get me out of dinner at Mum's.'

Emily laughed,

'Have you seen what you're wearing for the photo shoot?' Emily asked.

'Oh, it's so nice, all reds and black—Valentine's Day stuff, seriously sexy,' Louise said. 'We've got the presidential suite and I think I'm his girlfriend or wife, the model's Jeremy...' Louise rattled on as, unseen, Anton came in and checked Emily's CTG. 'He's so gorgeous but so gay. Anyway, we wake up and why I'm wearing a bra and panties and shoes at six a.m. I have no idea, but then there are to be photos with me waving him off to work...'

'Still in your undies and shoes?' Emily asked, and Louise nodded.

'Then he comes home with flowers and I'm in my evening stuff then, and I think he takes me over the dining table...'

Emily wished Louise would turn around and see Anton's smile as she spoke.

'Everything is looking good,' Anton said, and Emily watched as Louise jumped, wondering how much he had heard. Emily's heart actually hurt that Louise expected to be told off for being herself, and she watched her friend make herself turn around and smile.

'Hiya,' Louise said. 'I'm just asking Emily to cross her legs tomorrow, but any time after that is fine.'

'How Emily's temperature?'

'All normal. I'm actually on my lunch break.'

'Oh,' Anton said, and left them to it. 'Sorry for interrupting.'

'Why won't you give the two of you a chance?' Emily said. 'Why can't you believe—?'

'Because I stopped believing,' Louise said. 'I want to believe—I want to believe that we might be able to work, that we're as right for each other, as I sometimes feel we are. I just don't know how to start.'

'Have you told him what happened last Christmas?'

'I don't know how to.'

'He needs to know, Louise. If you two are to stand a chance then you have to somehow tell him.'

Louise shook her head. 'I don't want to talk about it ever again.'

'Why don't you ask Anton to come along tomorrow?'

'Good God, no!'

'Think about it—you at your tarty best. What would Wesley have done?'

'I shudder to think,' Louise said. 'Look, I know Anton's not like that. I'm just so scared because I'd have sworn Wesley wasn't like that either.'

'Well, there's one very easy way to find out.'

'I think he's working tomorrow,' Louise said. 'Anyway, don't you want him here?'

'Oh, believe me, if I go into labour I'll be calling him, so you'd know anyway, but please don't leave your photo shoot for me. I know how important it is to you.'

'Okay,' Louise said. 'I still want to know, though.'

'Ask Anton.'

Louise shook her head. 'He's not going to take a day off for that.'

'He's not going to if you don't ask him.'

Louise checked on a patient who was sleeping but in labour and she put her on the CTG machine and took a footstool and climbed up onto the nurses' station where she sat, watching her patient from a distance, listening to the baby's heartbeat.

Anton walked onto the unit and saw Louise sitting up on the bench, back straight, ears trained, like some elongated pixie.

'What are you doing?' Anton asked, as he walked past.

'Watching room seven,' Louise said, and smiled and looked down.

'Are you okay?' Anton said, referring to their conversation in the kitchen that morning.

'I don't know.'

'I know you don't and that's okay.'

'Can you help me down?' Louise asked cheekily, and watched as he glanced at the footstool. 'Whoops!' She kicked away the footstool and Anton smiled and helped her down. The brief contact, the feel of his hands on her waist stirred her senses and made her long to break her self-imposed isolation. She just didn't know how.

'I know we need to talk,' Louise said. 'I just don't know when.'

'That's fine.'

A patient buzzed and he let her go.

'Hello, Carmel,' Louise said, and then saw that Carmel wasn't in bed but in the bathroom, and the noise she was making had Louise instantly push the bell before even going to investigate.

'There's something there,' Carmel said. She was deep-squatting and Emily pulled on gloves with her heart in her mouth. Carmel's baby was breech, and if it was a cord prolapse then it was dire indeed.

Louise pressed the bell in the bathroom in three short bursts as she knelt.

Thankfully it wasn't the cord. Instead two little legs

were hanging out. 'Call Stephanie,' Louise said, as Brenda popped her head in the door.

'She's delivering someone,' Brenda said. 'I'll get Anton and the cart.'

'You,' Louise said to Carmel, 'are doing amazingly.' The baby was dangling and it was the hardest thing not to interfere. Instinct meant you wanted traction, to get the head out, but Louise breathed through it, her hands hovering to catch the baby.

She heard or rather sensed that it was Anton who had come in and she went to move aside but he just knelt behind Louise. 'Well done, Carmel,' Anton said.

Louise felt his hand on her shoulder as patiently they waited for Mother Nature to take her course.

It was just so lovely and quiet. Brenda came in with the cart and stood back. There was a baby about to be born and everyone just let it happen.

Patience was a necessary virtue here.

'That's it,' Louise said. 'Put your hands down and feel your baby,' she said, as the baby simply dropped, and Carmel let out a moan as her baby was delivered into her own and Louise's hands.

'Well done,' Anton said, as Brenda went and got a hot blanket and wrapped it around the mother and infant.

Stephanie arrived then, smiling delightedly.

'Well done, Carmel!'

It had been so nice, so lovely and so much less scary with Anton there—a lovely soft birth. Louise's eyes were glittering with happy tears as finally Carmel was back in bed with her husband beside her and her baby in her arms.

It was lovely to see them all cosy and happy.

'It looks like you might get that Christmas at home after all.' Louise smiled.

'Oh, I'm going home tomorrow,' Carmel said. 'Nothing's going to stop us having the Christmas we want now.'

Later, in the kitchen, pulling a teabag from her scrubs to make Carmel her only fantastic cup of hospital tea, she saw the hotel card that she had brought in to give Emily.

Was it a ridiculous idea to ask him to be there tomorrow? Did she really have to put him through some strange test?

Yet a part of Louise wanted him to see the other side of her also.

She walked out and saw Anton sitting at the desk, writing up his notes.

'Are you working tomorrow?' Louise asked.

'I am.'

She put the card down.

'It's my photo shoot tomorrow from ten till seven— see if you can get away for an hour or so. I'll leave your name at Reception.'

Anton read the address and then looked up but Louise was gone.

CHAPTER FIFTEEN

IT REALLY WAS the best job in the world.

Well, apart from midwifery, which Louise absolutely loved, but this was the absolutely cherry on the cake, Louise thought as she looked in the mirror.

Her hair was all backcombed and coiffed, her eyes were heavy with black eyeliner and she had lashings of red lipstick on.

All her body was buffed and oiled and then she'd had to suffer the hardship of putting on the most beautiful underwear in the world.

It was such a dark red that it was almost black and it emphasised the paleness of her skin.

And she got to keep it!

Louise smiled at herself in the mirror.

'Okay, they're ready for you, Louise.'

Now the hard work started.

She stepped into the presidential suite and took off her robe and there was Jeremy in bed, looking all sexy and rumpled but very bored with it all, and there, in the lounge, was Anton.

Oh! She had thought he might manage an hour, she hadn't been expecting him to be here at the start.

He gave her a smile of encouragement and Louise let out a breath and smiled back.

'On the bed, Louise,' Roxy, the director said.

'Morning, Jeremy.' Louise smiled. She had worked with him many times.

'Good morning, Louise.'

It was fun, though it was actually very hard work. There were loads of costume changes and not just for Louise—Jeremy kept having to have his shirt changed as Louise's lipstick wiped off. Cold cream too was Jeremy's friend as her lips left their mark on his stomach.

And not once did Anton frown or make her feel awkward.

As evening fell, the drapes were opened to show London at its dark best, though the Christmas lights would be edited out. This was for Valentine's Day after all.

'He's just home from work,' Roxy said. 'Flowers in hand but there's no time to even give them…'

'Okay.'

Jeremy lifted her up and she wrapped her legs around his hips and crossed her ankles as Roxy gave Jeremy a huge bouquet of dark red roses to hold.

'A bit lower, Louise.'

Louise obliged and as she wiggled her hips to get comfortable on Jeremy's crotch she made everyone, including Anton, laugh as she alluded to his complete lack of response. 'You are so-o-o gay, Jeremy!'

Anton had stayed the whole day. Louise could not believe he'd swapped shifts for her and, better still, clearly Emily's baby was behaving.

At the end of the shoot she put on her robe, feeling dizzy and elated, clutching a huge bag of goodies and ready to head to a smaller room to get changed. Anton joined her and they shared a kiss in the corridor.

'Do you want me to hang up my G-string?' Louise asked, between hot, wet kisses.

'God, no,' Anton said.

'You really don't mind?'

'Mind?' Anton said, not caring what he did to her lipstick.

They were deep, deep kissing and she loved the feel of his erection pressing into her, and then she pulled back and smiled—they must look like two drunken clowns.

'I've booked a room,' Anton said.

'Thank God!'

They made it just past the door. Her robe dropped, her back to the wall, Louise tore at his top because she wanted his skin. Louise worked his zipper and freed him, still frantically kissing as she kicked her panties off. Anton's impatient hands dealt swiftly with a condom and then he lifted her. Louise wrapped her legs around him and crossed her ankles far more naturally this time. She was on the edge of coming as she lowered herself onto him but he slowed things right down as he thrust into her because what he had to say was important.

'I am crazy for you, Louise, and I don't want to change a single thing.'

'I know,' Louise said, 'and I'm crazy about you too.'

She couldn't say more than that because her mouth gave up on words and gave in to the throb between her legs. The wall took her weight then as Anton bucked into her, a delicious come ensuing for them both. Then afterwards, instead of letting her down, he walked her to the bed and let her down there.

'We're going to sort this out, Louise.'

'I know we will.' Louise nodded, except she didn't want to ruin their day with tales of yesterday and it was Christmas tomorrow and Louise didn't want to ruin that again, so instead she smiled.

'I need carbs.'

They shared a huge bowl of pasta, courtesy of room service, and then Louise, who had been up since dawn, fell asleep in his arms. Better than anything, though, was the man who, when anyone else would have been snoring, lay restless beside her and finally kissed her shoulder.

'I'm going to pop into the hospital,' Anton said. 'I've got two women—'

'Go,' Louise said, knowing how difficult it must have been to swap his shift today. 'Call me if something happens with Emily.'

'You don't mind me going in?'

She'd have minded more if he hadn't.

CHAPTER SIXTEEN

TWO PATIENTS WERE on his mind this Christmas Eve and Anton walked into the ward and chatted with Evie.

'Hazel's asleep,' Evie said, as he went through the charts. 'I'd expect you to be called in any time soon, though.'

'How about Emily?'

'Hugh's in with her, he's on call tonight. Stephanie looked in on her an hour ago and there's been no change.'

'Thanks.'

He let Hazel sleep. Anton knew now he would be called if anything happened but, for more social reasons, he tapped on the open door of the royal suite.

'Hi, Anton,' Hugh said. 'All's quiet here.'

'That's good.'

'How was your day off?' Emily asked.

'Good.'

'I was just going to check on a patient.' Hugh stood and yawned.

'I could say the same,' Anton said, 'but I wanted to check in on Emily too.'

'Is this a friendly visit, Anton?' Emily asked when Hugh had left.

'A bit of both,' Anton said, and sat on the bed. 'How are you?'

'I don't know,' Emily admitted. 'I think I've given up hoping for thirty-three weeks.'

'Thirty-one weeks is considered a moderately premature baby,' Anton said. 'Yours is a nice size. I would guess over three pounds in weight and it's had the steroids.'

'How long would it be in NICU?'

'Depends,' Anton said. 'Five weeks, maybe four if all goes well.' He knew this baby was coming and so Anton prepared Emily as best he could. 'All going well with a thirty-one-weeker means there will be some bumps—jaundice, a few apnoea attacks, runs of bradycardia. All these we expect as your baby learns to regulate its temperature and to feed...' He went through it all with her, and even though Emily had been over and over it herself he still clarified some things.

Not once had she cried, Anton thought.

Not since he had done the scan after her appendectomy had he seen Emily shed a tear.

'You can ask me anything,' Anton offered, because she was so practical he just wanted to be sure there was nothing on her mind that he hadn't covered.

'Anything?' Emily said.

'Of course.'

'How was the photo shoot?'

Anton smiled. 'I walked into that one, didn't I?'

'You did.'

'Louise was amazing.'

'She is.'

'Yet,' Anton ventured, 'for someone who is so open

about everything, and I mean *everything*, she's very private too…'

'Yes.'

'I'm not asking you to tell me anything,' Anton said.

'You just want her to?'

Anton nodded and then said, 'I want her to feel able to.'

CHAPTER SEVENTEEN

LOUISE OPENED HER eyes to a dark hotel room on Christmas morning and glanced at the time. It was four a.m. and no Anton.

She lay there remembering this time last year but even though she was alone it didn't feel like it this time, especially when the door opened gently and Anton came in quietly.

'Happy Christmas,' Louise said.

'Buon Natale,' Anton said, as he undressed.

'How's Emily?'

'Any time now,' Anton said. 'I was just about to come back here when another patient went into labour.'

'Hazel?' Louise sleepily checked.

'A little girl,' Anton said. 'She's in NICU but I'm very pleased with how she is doing.'

'A nice way to start Christmas,' Louise said, as he slid into bed and spooned into her.

His hands were cold and so was his face as he dropped a kiss on her shoulder.

'Scratch my back with your jaw.'

He obliged and then, without asking, scratched the back of her neck too, his tongue wet and probing, his jaw all lovely and stubbly, and his hand stroking her very close to boiling.

'Did you stop for condoms?'

'No,' Anton said. 'We have one left.'

'Use it wisely, then.' Louise smiled, though she didn't want his hand to move for a second and as Anton sheathed himself Louise made the beginning of a choice—she would have to go on the Pill. They were both so into each other that common sense was elusive, but she stopped thinking then as she felt him nudging her entrance. Swollen from last night and then swollen again with want, it was Louise who let out a long moan as he took her slowly from behind. His hand was stroking her breast and she craned her neck for his mouth.

He could almost taste her near orgasm on her tongue as it hungrily slathered his. He was being cruel, the best type of cruelty because she was going to come now and he'd keep going through it. She almost shot out of her skin as it hit, and she wished he would stop but she also wished he wouldn't. It was so deliciously relentless, there was no come down. Anton started thrusting faster, driving her to the next, and then he stilled and she wondered why because they were just about there…

'No way,' Louise said, hearing his phone. 'Quickly…'

Oh, he tried, but it would not stop ringing. 'Sorry…' Anton laughed at her urgency, because sadly it was his special phone that was ringing. The one for his special Anton patients. And a very naked Louise lay there as he took the call.

'Get used to it,' Anton said as he was connected, and then he hesitated, because if he was telling Louise to get used to it, well, it was something he'd never said before. There was no time to dwell on it, though, as he listened to Evie.

'I'll be there in about fifteen minutes. Thank you for letting me know.' He ended the call. 'Are you coming in with me to deliver a Christmas baby?'

'Emily!'

'Waters just fully broke…'

'Oh, my goodness…'

'She's doing well. Hugh's on his way in but things are going to move quite fast.'

They had the quickest shower ever and then Anton drove them through London streets on a wet, pre-dawn Christmas morning and he got another phone call from the ward. He asked for them to page the anaesthetist for an epidural as that could sometimes slow things down and also, despite the pethidine she'd been given, Emily was in a lot of pain.

'She'll be okay,' Louise said, only more for herself. 'I'm so scared, Anton,' Louise admitted. 'I really am.'

'I know, but she's going to be fine and so is the baby.' There was no question for Anton, they *had* to be okay. 'Big breath,' Anton said.

'I'm not the one in labour.'

It had just felt like it for a moment, though.

Oh, she was terrified for her friend but Louise was at her sparkly best as she and Anton walked into the delivery ward.

'Oh!' Emily smiled in delighted surprise because it was only five a.m. after all.

'The mobile obstetric squad has arrived,' Louise teased. 'Aren't you lucky that it's us two on?' She smiled and gave Emily a cuddle. 'Oh, hi, Hugh!' Louise winked and noted he was looking a bit white. 'Merry Christmas!'

'Hi, Louise.' Hugh was relieved to see them both too.

'I want an epidural,' Emily said.

'It's on its way. I've already paged Rory. We want to slow this down a little,' Anton explained while examining her, 'and an epidural might help us to do that. You've got a bit of a way to go but because the baby is small you don't have to be fully dilated.'

'I'm scared,' Emily admitted.

'You're going to meet your baby,' Louise said, and she gave Emily's hand a squeeze. 'Let us worry for you, okay? We're getting paid after all.'

Emily nodded.

'NICU's been notified?' Anton checked, and then gave an apologetic smile when Evie rolled her eyes and nodded, and Anton answered for her. 'Of course they have.'

There was a knock on the door and Emily's soon-to-be-favourite person came in.

'Hi, lovely Emily,' Rory said. 'We meet again.'

'Oh, yes,' Louise recalled. 'Rory knocked you out when you had your appendix.'

'Hopefully this will slow things down enough that I miss Christmas dinner,' Louise joked, though they all knew this baby would be born by dawn.

A little high on pethidine, a little ready to fix the world, very determined not to panic about the baby, Emily decided she had the perfect solution, the perfect one to show Louise how wonderful and not controlling or jealous Anton was.

And the man delivering your premature baby had to be seriously wonderful, Emily decided!

'Tell them about your Christmas dinner last year,' Emily said, as Louise sat her up and put her legs over

the edge of the bed and then pulled Emily in for an epidural cuddle.

'Relax,' Hugh said, stroking Emily's hair as she leant
on Louise, while Rory located the position on Emily's
spine.

But Emily didn't want to relax, she wanted this sorted
now!

'Tell them!' Emily shouted, and Louise shared a little
'yikes' look with Hugh.

Never argue with a woman in transition!

'I'm going to have a word with you later,' Louise
warned. She knew what Emily was doing.

'Okay!' Louise said, as she cuddled Emily. 'Well,
I'd broken up with Wesley and I checked myself into
a hotel—the most miserable place on God's earth, as it
turned out, and I couldn't face the restaurant and families so I had room service and it was awful. I think it was
processed chicken...'

'Stay still, Emily,' Rory said.

'She's having a contraction,' Anton said, and Louise
rocked her through it and after Rory got back to work
she went on with her story.

'Well, I was so miserable but I cheered myself up by
realising I'd finally got out of having Christmas dinner
at Mum's.'

'It's seriously awful food,' Rory said casually, thread-
ing the cannula in.

'You wouldn't know,' Louise retorted. 'The one time
you came for dinner you pretended you'd been paged
and had to leave. Anyway, I arrived at Mum's on Boxing
Day and she'd *saved* me not one but about five dinners,
and had decided I needed a mother's love and cooking...'

Anton laughed. 'That bad?'

'So, so bad,' Louise said, and her little tale had got them through the insertion of the epidural and she'd managed not to reveal all.

She looked at Anton and there wasn't a flicker of a ruffled feather at her mention of Rory once being at her family's home.

He was a good man. She'd always known it, now she felt it.

'You'll start to feel it working in a few minutes, Emily,' Rory said.

'I can feel it working already.' Emily sighed in relief as Louise helped her back onto the delivery bed.

Rory left and Louise told Evie she'd got this and then suggested that Anton grab a coffee as she set about darkening the room.

'Sure,' Anton said, even though he didn't feel like leaving, but, confident that he would be called when needed and not wanting to make this birth too different for Emily, he left.

The epidural brought Emily half an hour of rest and she lay on her side, with Hugh beside her as Louise sat on the couch out of view, a quiet presence as they waited for nature to take its course, but thirty minutes later Louise called Anton in.

The room was still quiet and dark but it was a rather full one—Rory and the paediatric team were present for the baby as the baby began its final descent into the world.

'Do you feel like you need to push?' Anton asked, and Emily shook her head as her baby inched its way down.

'A bit,' she said a moment later.

'Try not to,' Anton said. 'Let's do this as slowly as we can.'

'Head end, Hugh,' Louise said, because he looked a bit green, and she left him at Emily's head and went down to the action end, holding Emily's leg as Anton did his best to slow things down.

'Do you want a mirror?' Louise asked.

'Absolutely not.'

'Black hair and lots of it.' Louise was on delighted tiptoe.

'Louise, can you come up here?' Emily gasped. 'I don't want you seeing me...'

'Oh, stop it.' Louise laughed and then Emily truly didn't care what anyone could see because, even with the epidural, there was the odd sensation of her baby moving down.

'Oh!'

'Don't push,' Anton said.

'I think I have to.'

'Breathe,' Hugh said, and got the F word back, but she did manage to breathe through it as Anton helped this little one get a less rapid entrance into the world. And then out came the head and Louise gently suctioned its tiny mouth as its eyes blinked at the new world.

'Happy Christmas,' Anton said, delivering a very vigorous bundle onto Emily's stomach.

Emily got her hotbox blanket wrapped around her shoulders and then another one was placed over a tiny baby whose mum and dad were starting to get to know it.

Anton glanced over at the paediatrician and all was well enough to allow just a minute for a nice cuddle.

'A girl,' Emily said.

The sweetest, sweetest girl, Louise thought. She stood watching over them, holding oxygen near her little mouth as Emily and Hugh got to cuddle her and Louise cried happy tears, baby-just-been-born tears, but then she did what she had to.

'We need to check her...'

And finally Emily started to cry.

CHAPTER EIGHTEEN

LOUISE TOOK THE baby over to the warmer and she was wrapped and given some oxygen and a tube put down her to give her surfactant that would help with her immature lungs.

'We're going to take her up,' Louise said, as Emily completely broke down.

'Can't I go with her?'

'Not yet,' Anton said, 'but you'll be able to see her soon.'

'I'll go with her,' Hugh assured his wife, but Louise could see how upset Emily was. She had been holding onto her emotions for weeks now, quietly determined not to love her baby too much, though, of course she did.

'Hugh, you stay with Emily and I'll stay with the baby,' Louise suggested. 'She's fine, she's beautiful and you'll see her very soon, Emily. I promise I am not going to leave her side.'

Louise did stay with her, the neonatal staff did their thing and Louise watched, but from a chair, smiling when an hour or so later Hugh came in.

'Hi, Dad,' Louise said, watching as Hugh peered in. 'How's Emily?'

'Upset,' Hugh said. 'She'll be fine once she sees her

but Anton says she needs to have a sleep first and she won't.' He took out his phone and went to film the baby, who was crying and unsettled.

'Why don't you go and get some colostrum from her?' Ellie, the neonatal nurse, suggested to Louise. 'Mum might feel better knowing she's fed her.'

'Great idea.' Louise smiled and headed back to the ward.

Emily was back in her room, the door open so she could be watched, but the curtains were drawn.

'Knock-knock,' Louise said, and there was her friend, teary and missing her baby so much. 'She's fine, Hugh's with her,' Louise went on, and explained her plans.

'You just need to get a tiny bit off,' Louise said, 'but she's hungry and it's so good to get the colostrum into them.'

'Okay.'

Emily managed a few drops, which Louise nursed into a syringe, but Louise reassured her that that was more than enough. 'This is like gold for your baby.' Louise was delighted with her catch.

As Louise headed out she glanced at the time and realised she would have to ring her mum, who was going to be incredibly worried, given what had happened last year.

As Anton walked into the kitchen on the maternity unit it was to the sight of Louise brightly smiley and taking a selfie with her phone.

'Forward it onto me,' Anton said.

Louise smiled. He didn't care a bit that she was vain, though in this instance he was mistaken. 'Actually, this is for Mum. She's all stressed and thinks I've made up Emily's baby. Well, she didn't say that exactly...' She texted her mum the photo and then picked up the small syringe of colostrum. 'Christmas dinner for Baby Linton. I can't believe she's here.'

'Relieved?' Anton asked.

'So, so relieved. I know she's going to get jaundice and give them a few scares but she is just so lovely and such a nice size…'

'Louise.' Anton caught her arm as she went to go. 'How come you didn't go home last Christmas?'

'I told you, I was pretty miserable.'

'Your family are close.'

'Of course.' She shrugged. 'I just didn't want to upset them…'

'You couldn't put on an act for one day?'

'No…' Her voice trailed off. She hadn't wanted to upset her family on Christmas Day and neither did she want to upset him now. Yet her family had been so hurt by her shutting them out. Louise looked into his eyes and knew that her silence was hurting him too. Everyone in the delivery room except Anton knew what had happened last year and if they were going to have a future, and she was starting to think they might, then it was only fair to tell him.

'I couldn't cover up the bruises. I waited till Boxing Day and called Emily, who came straight away. When I wouldn't go to hospital she called Rory and he came to the hotel and sutured my scalp.'

Louise didn't want to see his expression and neither did she want to go into further details of the day right now. She had told him now and she could feel his struggle to react, to suppress, possibly just to breathe as he fathomed just what the saying meant about having the living daylights knocked out of you. The light in Louise had gone out that day and had stayed out for some months, but it was fully back now. 'I'm going to get this up to the baby.' She kissed his taut cheek. 'You need to shave.'

They had a small, fierce cuddle that said more than words could and then Louise said she was heading up to NICU, still unable to meet his eyes.

Hugh watched and Louise did the filming as Baby Linton was given the precious colostrum and a short while later was asleep.

Have a sleep now, Louise texted. Your daughter is and she attached the film and sent it.

A few moments later Hugh's phone buzzed and he smiled as Emily gave him the go-ahead.

'Thanks,' Hugh said, and then he took out a pen and crossed out the 'Baby' on 'Baby Linton'. He wrote the word 'Louise' in instead.

Louise Linton.

'Two Ls means double the love,' Louise said, trying not to cry. 'Thanks, Hugh, that means an awful lot.'

More than anyone could really know.

When Hugh went back to Maternity to be with Emily, Louise sat there, staring at her namesake, and the thought she had briefly visited that morning returned.

She'd have to go back on the Pill. It wouldn't be fair to Anton if there were any mistakes, however unlikely it was that she might naturally fall pregnant. But that ultimately meant, when she came off the Pill again, another few months of the horrible times she'd just been through simply trying to work out her cycle.

Louise knew she was probably looking at another year at best. Could she do it without sulking? Louise wondered. Just let go of her hopes for a baby and chase the dream of a relationship that actually worked?

She walked over and looked at the little one who had

caused so much angst but who had already brought so many smiles.

'How's Louise?' Anton came up a couple of hours later and saw Louise standing and gazing into the incubator.

'Tired,' Louise said, still not able to meet his eyes after her revelation. 'Oh, you mean the baby? She's perfect.' She glanced over to where Rory and several staff were gathered around an incubator. Louise knew that it was Henry, a baby she had delivered in November. He had multiple issues and was a very sick baby indeed. She looked down at little Louise, who was behaving beautifully. 'You're a bit of a fraud really, aren't you?'

'Emily's asleep,' Anton said. 'When she wakes up she can come and visit.'

'I'll stay till then.' Louise smiled. 'Can you just watch Louise while I go to the loo?'

Anton glanced over at the neonatal nurse but that wasn't what Louise meant. 'No, you're to be on love watch,' Louise said.

Anton took a seat when usually he wouldn't have and looked at the very special little girl.

'Thank you!' Louise was back a couple of minutes later. 'I really needed that!'

Anton rolled his eyes as Louise, as usual, gave far too much information. When Anton didn't get up she perched on his knee, with her back to him, watching little Louise asleep. She had nasal cannulas in but she was breathing on her own and though she might need a little help with that in the coming days, for now she was doing very well.

'Emily's here,' Anton said, and Louise jumped up and smiled as Emily was wheeled over.

Yes, Louise was far from the tiniest infant here but

the machines and equipment were terrifying and Ellie talked them through it.

'I'm going to go,' Louise said, and gave Emily a kiss. 'I'll come and see you tomorrow. Send me a text tonight. Oh, and here…' She handed over a little pink package. 'Open it later. Just enjoy your time with her now.'

She gave her friend a quick cuddle then she and Anton left them to it.

'Do you want to come to Mum and Dad's?' Louise asked, as they stopped by his office to get his laptop.

'Will it cause a lot of questions for you?'

'Torrents,' Louise said, but then the most delicious smell diverted her and she peeked out the door, to see Alex and Jennifer heading onto the ward with two plates and lots of containers.

'Alex,' Louise called, and they turned round.

'They're up seeing the baby,' Louise explained.

'Oh, we didn't come to see them,' Jennifer said, and Louise jumped in.

'How sweet of you to bring Christmas dinner for the obstetrician and midwife,' Louise teased, watching Jennifer turn purple as Anton stepped out.

'Anton.' Alex smiled warmly. 'Merry Christmas.'

'Merry Christmas,' Anton said.

'You haven't met Jennifer…'

'Jennifer.' Anton smiled. 'Merry Christmas.'

'Merry Christmas,' Jennifer croaked, and then turned frantic eyes to Louise. 'We don't want to disturb Emily and Hugh, we were just going to leave them a dinner for tonight…' She was practically thrusting the plates at Louise. 'We'll leave these with you.'

But Louise refused to be rushed.

'That's so nice of you,' Louise said, but instead of taking the plates she peeked under the foil. 'Jennifer, Emily didn't just give birth to a foal—there's enough here to feed a horse.'

It looked and smelt amazing and Louise was shameless in her want for a taste, not just for her but for Anton too. 'That's what a traditional Christmas dinner looks like, Anton.' Louise smiled sweetly at Jennifer. 'It's Anton's first Christmas in England,' Louise explained, and of course she would get her way. 'What a shame he's never tasted a really nice one.'

'I'm sure there's enough for everyone,' Alex said, oblivious to his wife's tension around Anton, and Jennifer gave in.

'Luckily my husband's good with a scalpel!'

It was a very delicate operation.

They went into the kitchen and got out tea plates.

Louise and Anton got two Brussels sprouts each, one roast potato and two slivers of parsnips in butter as Anton watched, fascinated by the argument taking place.

'I don't think Emily needs six piggies in blankets,' Louise said.

'Piggies in blankets?' Anton checked.

'Sausages wrapped in bacon,' Alex translated.

'Two each, then,' Jennifer said, and Alex added them to the tea plates.

'How much turkey can they have?' Alex asked.

'A slice each,' Jennifer said. 'Emily needs her protein.'

Louise shook her head.

'Okay, one and a half,' Jennifer relented.

Alex duly divided.

They got one Yorkshire pudding each too, as well as home-made cranberry and bread sauce, and finally dinner was served!

'You can go now.' Louise smiled. 'Merry Christmas.'

She put sticky notes on Hugh and Emily's plates, warning everyone to keep their greedy mitts off, then Louise closed the kitchen door.

She found a used birthday candle among the ward's Christmas paraphernalia and stuck it in a stale mince pie as their Christmas dinners rotated in the microwave and then she turned the lights off.

'Do you want to pull a cracker?'

'Bon-bon,' Anton said, but they cracked two and sat in hats and, oh, my, Jennifer's cooking was divine, even if you had to fight her to taste it.

'How do you know Jennifer?' Louise asked, as she smeared bread sauce over her turkey.

'I don't.'

'Anton!' Louise looked at his deadpan face. 'No way was that the first time you two have met. Is she pregnant again?' Louise frowned. 'She must be in her mid-forties...'

'I don't know what you're on about,' Anton said, though his lips were twitching to tell.

'Are you having an affair with Jennifer?' Louise asked, smiling widely.

'Where the hell did you produce that from?' Anton smiled back.

'Anton, Jennifer went purple when she saw you and I just know you've seen each other before.'

'I don't know if I like this bread sauce,' was Anton's response to her probing.

'It's addictive,' Louise said, and gave up fishing.

It was the nicest Christmas dinner ever—perfect food, the best company and a baby named Louise snug and safe nearby. After they had finished their delectable meal

Louise went over and sat on his knee. 'Thank you for a lovely Christmas, Anton.'

'Thank you,' Anton said, because what she'd told him, though upsetting, hadn't spoiled his Christmas. Instead, it had drawn them closer.

'We both deserve it, I think.'

She felt his arms on her back, lightly stroking the clasp of her bra and as she rested her head on his shoulder it felt the safest place in the world.

'Do you understand why I'm so wary?'

'Now I do,' Anton said. 'I'm glad you were able to tell me and I am so sorry for what happened to you.'

It was then Louise let her dreams go; well, not for ever, but she put them on hold for a while.

'I'm going to cancel my appointment,' Louise said, and she didn't lift her head, not now because she couldn't look him in the eye but because she didn't want Anton to see her cry. 'Well, I'm going to go and get the test results back but I'm not going to go for the IVF.'

He could hear her thick voice and knew there were tears and he rubbed her back.

'Thank you,' Anton said, and they sat for a moment, Anton glad for the chance for them, Louise grateful for it too but just a bit sad for now, though she soon chirped up.

'When I say cancelling the IVF I meant that I'm post-poning it,' Louise amended. 'No pressure or anything but I'm not waiting till I'm forty for you to make up your mind whether you want us to be together.'

'You have to make your mind up too,' Anton pointed out.

'Oh, I did yesterday,' Louise said, and pulled her head

back and smiled into his eyes. 'I'm already in.' She gave him a light kiss before standing to head for home.

'You're stuck with me now.'

CHAPTER NINETEEN

As THEY WALKED out they bumped into Rory, who was on his way up to NICU to check in on a six-week-old who was doing his level best to spoil everyone's Christmas.

'You look tired,' Louise said.

'Very,' Rory admitted. 'I'm just off to break some bad news to a family.'

'What time do you finish?' Louise asked.

'Six.'

'Do you want to come for a rubbish dinner at Mum's?' Louise asked.

'God, no.' Rory smiled.

'Honestly, if Anton and you *both* come then Mum will assume I'm just bringing all the strays and foreigners who are lonely...' she pointed her thumb in Anton's direction '...rather than grilling me about him.' She knew Rory's family lived miles away. 'You don't want to be on your own on Christmas night.'

'I won't be on my own,' Rory said. 'Thanks for offering, though. I'm going to Gina's to help her celebrate her first sober Christmas in who knows how long.'

'Gina?' Louise checked. 'Is she the one you're—?'

'She's always been the one,' Rory said. 'It's nearly killed me to watch her self-destruct.' He stood there on the edge of breaking down as Anton's hand came on his shoulder. 'Nothing's ever happened between us,' Rory explained. 'And nothing can.'

'Why?' Louise asked.

'Because she's in treatment and you're not supposed to have a relationship for at least a year.'

'Does she know how you feel?' Louise asked.

'No, because I don't want to confuse her. She's trying to sort her stuff out and I don't want to add to it.'

'She's so lucky to have you,' Louise said, 'even if she doesn't know that she has.' Louise let out a breath. 'Who's going to speak to the parents with you?'

'Just me,' Rory said. 'They're all busy with Henry.'

'I know the parents,' Louise said to Rory. 'You're not doing that on your own. Is there any hope?'

'A smudge,' Rory said, and they headed back to NICU and Anton stood and waited as Louise and Rory went in to see the parents.

Anton loved her love.

How she gave it away and then, when surely there should be nothing left, she still gave more.

How she walked so pale out of a horrible room and cuddled her ex as Anton stood there, the least jealous guy in the world. He was simply glad that Rory had Louise to lean on as Anton remembered that horrible Christmas when he'd been the one breaking bad news.

He would be grateful to Rory for ever for being there for Louise last year.

As they walked out into the grey Christmas afternoon and to Anton's car, Louise spoke.

'Rory's right not to tell Gina how he feels,' Louise said.

'Do you think?'

'I do.' Louise nodded. 'I think you do need a whole year to recover from anything big. Not close to a year, you need every single day of it, you need to go through each milestone, each anniversary and do them differently, and as of today I have.'

It had been a hard year, though the previous one had been harder—estranged from family and friends and losing herself in the process. But now here she was, a little bit older, a whole lot wiser, and certainly Louise was herself.

Yes, she was grateful for those difficult years.

It had brought her here after all.

CHAPTER TWENTY

'OOH…' LOUISE REACHED for her phone as it bleeped. 'We do need to stop on our way to the hotel for condoms because it would seem that I just ovulated.'

'You get an alert when you ovulate?' Anton shook his head in disbelief.

'Well, I put in all my cycles and temperatures and things and it calculates it. It's great…'

'You're going to be one of those old ladies who talks about her bowels, aren't you?'

'God, yes.' Louise laughed at the thought. 'I'll probably have an app for it.'

The thing was, Anton wanted to be the old man to see it.

'Where's a bloody chemist when you need one?' Louise grumbled, going through her phone as Anton drove on and came to the biggest, yet ultimately the easiest decision of his life.

'We could stop at a pub,' Louise suggested. 'Nip in to the loos and raid the machines.'

'We're not stopping, Louise. You need to get to your mum's.'

Louise sulked all the way back to the hotel and even more so when they came out of the elevator and she swiped her entry card to their room. 'I've got the hotel room, a hot Italian and no bloody condoms. Where's the justice, I ask you...'

And then the door opened and she simply stopped speaking. For a moment Louise thought she had the wrong room because it was in darkness save for the twinkling fairly-lights reflecting off the tinsel. She had never seen a room more overly decorated, Louise thought. There was green, silver, red and gold tinsel, there were lights hanging everywhere. It was gaudy, it was loud and so, so beautiful.

'You did this?'

'I don't want you ever to think of a hotel room on Christmas Day and be sad again. I want this to be your memory.'

'How?'

'I rang them,' Anton said. 'They were worried it looked over the top, but I reassured them you can *never* have too much tinsel.'

'It's the nicest thing you could have done.'

'Yet,' Anton said, for he intended many nice things for Louise.

They started to kiss, a lovely long kiss that led them to bed. A kiss that had them peeling off their clothes and Louise stared up at the twinkling lights as slowly he removed her underwear, kissing her everywhere.

'Anton...' She was all hot and could barely breathe as he removed her bra and kissed her breasts. Louise unwrapped her presents with haste; Anton took his time.

'Anton...' she pleaded, touching herself in frustration as he slid down her panties, desperate for the soft warmth of his mouth.

'Your turn next,' Louise said, as, panties off, he kissed

up her thigh. Right now she just wanted to concentrate on the lovely feel of his mouth there, except his mouth now teased her stomach and then went back to her breasts, swirling them with his tongue and then working back up to her mouth.

His erection was there, nudging her entrance, teasing her with small thrusts, and her hands balled in frustration.

'We don't have any—'

'Do you want to try for a baby?' Anton said, throwing caution to a delectable wind that had chased him for, oh, quite a while now.

'Our baby?' Louise checked.

'I would hope so.' Anton smiled.

'You're sure?'

'Very,' Anton said. 'But are you?'

He didn't need to ask twice, but the ever-changing Louise changed again, right there in his arms.

'I'm very sure, but it isn't just a baby I want now. I want to have a baby with you,' Louise said.

'You shall,' Anton said, and it brought tears to her eyes because here was the man she loved, who would do all he could to make sure her dream came true.

The feel of him unsheathed driving into her had Louise let out a sob of pleasure. For Anton, it was heady bliss. Sensations sharpened, and he felt the warm grip and then the kiss of her cervix, welcoming him over and over again, till for Anton that was it.

The final swell of him, the passion that shot into her tipped Louise deep into orgasm. Her legs tight around him, she dragged him in deeper and let out a little scream. Then she held him there for her pleasure, just to feel each and every pulse and twitch from them as his breathing made love to her ear.

She looked up at the twinkling lights and never again would she think of Christmas and not remember this.

'What are you doing?' Anton spoke to the pillow as, still inside her, Louise's hand reached across the bed.

'Taking a photo,' Louise said, aiming her camera at the fairy-lights. And capturing the moment, she knew she'd found love, for ever.

CHAPTER TWENTY-ONE

'WILL IT BE a problem, us working together?' Louise asked. They were back at her home, with Louise grabbing everyone's presents from under her tree. 'Honestly, it's something we need to speak about.'

'We'll be fine,' Anton said. 'Louise, the reason I came down harder on you than anyone is because of what happened in Italy that day when it did all go wrong...but you're an amazing midwife, over and over I've seen it. Aside from personally, I love working with you. I know that the patients get the very best care.'

'Thank you,' Louise said. 'Still, if we get sick of each other...' She stopped then and looked at the amazing man beside her. She could never get tired of looking at him, working alongside him, getting to know him.

'I got you two presents,' Louise said.

He opened the first annoying slowly. It was beautifully wrapped and he took his time then smiled at black and white sweets wrapped in Cellophane.

'Humbugs,' Louise said, and popped one in her mouth and then gave him a very nice kiss.

'Peppermint,' Anton replied, having taken it from her mouth.

He opened the other present a little more quickly, given its strange shape, to find a large pepperoni.

'Reminds me of,' Louise teased, 'my first kiss with the pizza man and I'm also ensuring that if we ever do break up then you will never be able to eat pepperoni, or taste mint, without thinking of me. I've just hexed you orally.'

'You *are* a witch!'

'I am!' Louise smiled.

'Then you would know already that I love you.'

'I do.' Louise's eyes were misty with tears as he confirmed his feelings.

'And, if you are a witch, you would know just *how much* I love you and that I would never, ever hurt you.'

'I do know that,' Louise said. 'And if you're my wizard you'll already know that I love you with all my heart.'

'I do.'

'But I'm about to make you suffer.' She smiled at his slight frown. 'We need to get to Mum's.'

Louise's family were as mad as the woman they had produced.

Anton watched as they tore open their presents.

'A cookery book?' Susan blinked. 'Oh, and a lesson. It's a lovely thought, Louise, but I don't need a cookery lesson…'

'It's for charity, Mum.'

'I could teach her a thing or three,' Susan said, 'but I suppose if it's for charity…' She smiled a bright smile. 'Time for dinner. It's so late, you must all be starving.'

They headed to the dining room, which was decorated with so much tinsel that Anton realised where Louise's little problem stemmed from.

At first Anton had no idea what Louise was talking about when she had moaned about her mother's cooking.

It looked as good as Jennifer's, it even smelt as good as Jennifer's, but, oh, my, the taste.

'That,' Anton said, after an incredibly long twenty minutes, putting down his knife and sweating in relief that he'd cleared his plate, 'was amazing, Susan.'

'There's plenty more.' Susan smiled as she collected up the plates.

Anton looked over at Louise's dad, who gave him a thumbs-up.

'Christmas pudding now,' he said. 'Home-made!'

'If you get through this,' Chloe, Louise's younger sister, whispered to him, 'you're in.'

The lights went down and a flaming pudding was brought in and they all duly sang, except for Anton because he didn't know the words.

It looked amazing, dark and rich and smothered in brandy crème, though had he not had a taste of Jennifer's delectable one then Anton would, there and then, have sworn off Christmas pudding for life.

It was a very small price to pay for love, though.

'Family recipe.' Susan winked, as she sat down to eat hers.

'It's wonderful, Mum,' Louise said.

In its own way it was, so much so that Louise decided to share the smile.

'I'm going to take a photo and send it to my friends,' Louise said, as her mother beamed with pride. 'They don't know what they're missing out on!'

Later they crashed on the sofa and watched a film. Anton sat and Louise lay with her head in his lap. Her sisters were going through the Valentine bras she had left over from the shoot. 'There's your namesake,' Louise said, munching on chocolate as Ebenezer Scrooge appeared on screen. Anton smiled. He had never been happier.

He even smiled as Louise's sister wrinkled her nose. 'What's that smell?'

'Mum's making kedgeree for Boxing Day.' Louise yawned.

'What's kedgeree?' Anton asked.

'Rice, eggs, haddock, curry powder.' Louise looked up and met his gaze.

'How about tomorrow we go shopping for a ring?' Anton said.

'Did you just propose?'

'I did.'

'Louise Rossi...' she mused. 'I like it.'

'Good.'

'And I love you.'

'I love you too.'

'But if you're buying my ring in the Boxing Day sales, I expect a really big one, and if we're engaged, then you can tell me what's going on with you and Jennifer.'

'When I get the ring I'll tell you.'

'Mum,' Louise called, 'Dad, we just got engaged.'

There were smiles and congratulations and after a very dry December Anton enjoyed the champagne as he pulled out his phone. 'I'd better ring my family and tell them the news. They're loud,' he warned.

There were lots of *'complimentes!'* and *'salute!'* on speaker phone as glasses were raised. Much merriment later they came to the rapid decision they would go over there for the New Year and see them and, yes, it would seem they were officially engaged.

Louise checked her own phone and there was a picture of Hugh and Emily sharing a gorgeous Christmas dinner, courtesy of Jennifer and Alex. There was a text too, thanking them for the little pink outfit and hat, which they were sure Baby Louise would be wearing very soon.

There was also a text from Rory and it made her smile.

'How's that smudge of hope?' Anton asked, referring to little Henry.

'Still smudging.' Louise smiled as she read Rory's text. 'It's sparkling apple juice his end and I've been given strict instructions that we're not to say anything, ever, to anyone, about what he said today.'

'I am very glad that Gina has Rory with her,' Anton said.

'And me,' Louise said, and then looked up at the man she would love for ever. 'You do know that you're going to be sleeping on the sofa tonight?'

'Am I?'

'My parents would freak otherwise.' She smiled again. 'Did you know that I'm a twenty-nine-year-old virgin?'

'Of course you are,' Anton said, and stroked her hair. He'd sleep in the garden if he had to.

Louise lay there, her family nearby, Anton's hands in her hair, and all felt right with the world.

Just so completely right.

'I think that I might already be pregnant,' Louise whispered.

'Don't start.' Anton smiled.

'No, I really think I am. I feel different.'

'Stop it.' Anton laughed.

But, then, Anton thought, knowing Louise, knowing how meant to be they were, she possibly was.

They might just have made their own Christmas baby.

* * * * *

LET'S TALK
Romance

For exclusive extracts, competitions
and special offers, find us online:

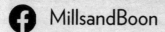 MillsandBoon

 @MillsandBoon

@MillsandBoonUK

@MillsandBoonUK

Get in touch on 01413 063 232